Norma Lloyd-Nesling was born in Wales. Initially, she trained as an English teacher gaining a B.A. (Hons) in literature followed by a Master's degree and Ph.D. from Cardiff University. She now works as a freelance education consultant, visiting university lecturer and is author of a number of academic articles on under-achievement in schools. Her first book *'Season of the Long Grass'* was published in 2007. After living in Berlin and England she returned to Wales. Married, she has one daughter and is currently writing her third book.
She is a Fellow of the College of Preceptors.

To Bob

THE REGIS CONNECTION

Best Wishes

[signature]

Norma Lloyd-Nesling

THE REGIS CONNECTION

AUSTIN & MACAULEY

A CIP catalogue record for this title is
available from the British Library.

ISBN 978 1 905609 90 1

www.austinmacauley.com

First Published (2009)
Austin & Macauley Publishers Ltd.
25 Canada Square
Canary Wharf
London
E14 5LB
Printed & Bound in Great Britain

DEDICATION

For my husband Victor and my daughter Tracey
for their constant love, support and encouragement

ACKNOWLEDGEMENTS

I would like to thank Austin & Macauley for publishing The Regis Connection.

My gratitude goes to all those who shared their memories with me during my time in Berlin. Long gone, their experiences are now part of history. Thanks also to Marianne Denk-Helmold for her memories of the day the Berlin Wall fell.

I would also like to thank my husband, Victor, for relating his military experiences in Berlin when the Wall was first erected, dividing the city and its people. Thanks also to my daughter, Tracey, for her constant encouragement and willingness to read my manuscript.

PROLOGUE

West Berlin 1989

The old man gazed across at the woman in the shabby, ankle-length brown coat. She caught a stray strand of wispy, grey hair and pushed it under her frayed, woollen headscarf. Silent sobs wracked her frail body as tears flowed down the deep crevices in her cheeks. Sadly, she smiled, blew him a kiss and slowly walked away.

For a few minutes he strained his scrawny neck, watching her until she disappeared from sight. Apoplectic with rage he raised his fists at the Grenzpolizei standing on the Wall.

"Schweinhunds!" he screamed in a rage. "Schweinhunds!"

One of the Grepos swung his rifle off his shoulder and aimed it at him. The boy at the old man's side placed a restraining hand on his arm. Angrily, he shook it off, stepped off the slimy, wet boards and shook his fist again. Shoulders sagging he allowed himself to be led down the slippery, wooden steps.

High on a parapet a young woman stood in her wedding dress. The chill breeze teased the delicate, frothy fabric curling it round her ankles. A sudden gust caught her veil covering her face. Two guards stood, rifles at the ready, watching the small crowds that had gathered each side of the barrier. On the west side animated guests in their colourful wedding finery. On the other drab, grey-faced and worn, the life sucked out of them.

Pride lit up the thin, middle-aged woman's face as she saw her daughter clinging to the arm of her new husband. She longed to be near her, to put her arms around her. She stretched out her arms as though to embrace the girl. Silent tears of despair streamed down the channels in her lined face.

"Mutti! Mutti!" the girl cried. "For papa's grave."

Before her mother could protest she threw her bouquet over the Wall. It landed at the feet of one of the Grepos. The woman froze, a hand covering her mouth, eyes darting from side to side with fear.

An expectant hush, silent as death, fell over the wedding party. Rigid and still, a tableau of raw fear, as the guards raised their rifles in a knee-jerk reaction. A young Grepo shuffled uneasily, prodded at the bouquet, before pushing it towards the woman with the muzzle of his gun. Uncertainly, she stared at the flowers afraid to move until he gestured for her to pick them up. Giving her a barely perceptible nod he resumed his splayed stance near the barrier.

Four hundred metres away an army officer in a black Mercedes shifted in his seat. Freckles of light, reflected from the ring on his index finger, danced on the dashboard. Impatiently, he drummed a staccato on the steering wheel. Even the roomy car felt cramped after hours of sitting in the same position. Wincing, he stretched his long frame as far as he could to alleviate the ache in his legs and back.

Screwing up his eyes against the glare of white, late autumn light he peered through the windscreen. Loose groups of people jostled for position on the wooden platform. A blonde, thickset woman waved forlornly at a teenage boy huddled inside a black, padded anorak. Hands thrust deep in his overcoat pockets a gaunt man stood watching the Grepos, eyes full of hate, lips moving angrily with soundless curses.

The concrete mass of the Berliner Mauer loomed ominously in the near distance. Multi-coloured graffiti covered it as far as the eye could see. On the west side large patches of the Wall had been roughly painted. Bright blue, lurid pink and neon green interspersed with slogans and poetic quotations. The officer swept the Wall with his high-powered binoculars, stopping momentarily when a piece of graffiti caught his eye.

'*Every wall will fall some time,*' it declared.

'Not this monster. This could stand for a hundred years or more,' he thought ruefully.

Carefully, he surveyed the concrete blocks of the 'Stützwandelement UL 12.11' and the barbed wire beyond.

As usual, all along the Wall the Mauerspechten *'woodpeckers'* chipped away with their ice picks. Others chiselled out large chunks that fell in dusty heaps at their feet. Some muttered vehemently as they jabbed at the concrete occasionally giving it a hefty kick. Others worked silently, faces set hard with determination, patiently eroding it piece by piece.

He had been watching the activities in the area for hours. For a short time a pale, watery sun had hovered briefly overhead then gradually disappeared behind a blanket of metallic, grey cloud. Now his eyes hurt from staring through the windscreen into the harsh light.

Uneasily, he watched the constant movement of bodies passing beneath the towering structure, most intent on their own business. Still, something nagged at the corner of his mind. In the last hour he had discerned a change in the atmosphere; a feeling of contained anticipation that sharpened his senses.

Slowly, he swept the area a second time swiftly swinging the glasses back to where a group of people stood facing the Wall. In an instant he was alert, focussing intently at a point somewhere beyond the huddle of bodies. Tensely, he waited, then he saw it again.

At shoulder level a large, gaping hole had been knocked right through. A woman was leaning forward peering into the Eastern Sector. On the other side two startled, green-clad Grepos gazed right back at her as she shouted abuse at them.

"What the hell.....? Take a look at this," he said handing over the binoculars to his fellow officer. "Just there to the left of that guy carrying the briefcase."

"Nothing out of the ordinary that I can see Major." The lieutenant shrugged wearily. "We've been here for hours. How about some coffee? I know a great little place on the Ku'damm. Best apple strudel I've ever tasted."

Ignoring the remark he panned the area again for any signs of unusual activity. Forehead puckered into a frown he paused concentrating on a particular spot.

"Look again where that small group is gathering," he insisted.

Adjusting the sights the lieutenant studied the cluster of people jostling each other out of the way.

"It can't be! There's a bloody great hole right in the middle!"

He put down the binoculars and stared at his superior officer in disbelief.

"I don't believe it! The Grepos are just standing there doing nothing!"

"They must have been hacking away for hours. What I can't fathom is, if they know it's there why haven't they attempted to block it up again? Radio Checkpoint Charlie! Find out if anything unusual is going on down there. I'll get hold of Brigade Headquarters. There's definitely something going on here. I don't know what the hell it is, but I can feel it in my gut!"

After a hurried conversation he nodded to his junior officer to move on. Loose groups of Berliners wandered aimlessly near the Wall as though waiting for something to happen. Glittering needles of rain fell gently, sending them into a muttering huddle against the shadow of the Wall. Umbrellas bloomed like flowering cacti in a desert as drizzle increased to a fine, soaking rain.

Still they stood, occasionally darting from one group to the other. Snatched conversations, nodding heads, arms gesticulating wildly to emphasise a point.

"Let's do a little recce along the Wall, but first we'll stop off at Brandenburg Gate. Have a word with the duty officer. Find out if the patrols have noticed anything unusual then we'll head out towards Glienicke Bridge."

Twilight descended in a misty veil as they left the bustle of the city behind. Trailing fingers of thin fog crept across the road temporarily obliterating their visibility. Skirting the Wall they drove towards the south-western suburbs of the city. At intervals sullen-faced Grepos followed their journey from looming watch towers.

"Drive down near the Havel," the major ordered. "Park up where we can have a good view of Phaueninsel Island and the bridge. That's Potsdam over there beyond the East bank"

"I'm aware of that sir," his companion replied testily nudging the car towards an open area on the river bank. "Anyway, what's so special that it brings *you* out here?"

"Memories son; twenty-five years of memories," he mused sinking back into his seat.

It was in the university that he had first seen the tall, blond man with the thin, white scar on his cheek. The proud way he held his head; blue eyes flashing like brilliant sapphires. There was something about him; something vaguely familiar that nudged at the edge of his memory. Like the forgotten lyric of a song it popped up then slipped away before he could grasp it. He experienced a curious sense of déjà vu, even though he had never seen him before.

Through all the daring escapes perpetrated by this legendary man he had no inkling of his true identity. Not until that night on the River Havel when hell had broken out all round him. Even now he relived the helplessness, the anger. He didn't know then why he had felt such an inexplicable sense of loss watching the Stasi car disappear into the darkness. All these years he had wondered about the man who must have perished alone in a Soviet prison.

December 1963 – so long ago. Over twenty five years, but still it haunted his dreams prodding him relentlessly into wakefulness. Closing his eyes he drifted back to a freezing, winter's night. Lying on the spongy ground concealed by thick, fir trees. Branches hanging white with beads of frost that gleamed dimly in the gloom. Overhead, a canopy of black, unbroken cloud threatening snow.

Smells of wet vegetation filling his nostrils as he lay prone on the damp grass. Waiting, watching, listening to the gentle movement of the river as it lapped against the shore. Taut muscles aching with cold, naked fear. Raw anticipation as he waited in the wet undergrowth watching the dark shape floating silently towards them, inching closer and closer. Adrenaline flooding his chest; heart thumping like a drill hammer.

Panic as harsh searchlights flooded the surface of the water. Machine gun fire chattering, sending up plumes of spray; churning up the water round the small, rowing boat. A hail of bullets ploughing into it from all directions. Anguished screams as they made contact with the dim shape floating behind the craft then total silence.

Breath rasping in his throat he waited until he saw a murky shape hit the bank. Muffled orders; mud sucking at boots. Dark figures rushing to the river bank to haul the body out of the freezing water.

Suddenly, the silence was shattered by another burst of bullets near the island. Lights: lights everywhere illuminating the man frantically swimming in the black water. Disbelief as he realised that the swimmer was heading away from him towards the Soviet Sector bank. Triumphant, guttural shouts carrying across the river as hands grabbed at a body and dragged it ashore. Vicious kicks, feeble scuffling as they hauled the man up the bank grunting and cursing. Shock racing through him when he saw that face uncovered. A face he would never forget.

PART ONE

CHAPTER ONE

Germany 1940-1941

The grey-haired, slovenly-looking woman shook her fist, her deeply-lined face contorted with hatred and anger.

"Jew lover!" she screamed.

Her tightly-buttoned, grubby, grey coat stretched to bursting point over her obscenely fat stomach.

A truck lurched to a halt as Peter and Eleanor pushed open the solid, wooden door and ran up the stairs to their third floor apartment. Eleanor slammed the door shut behind them and collapsed onto the sofa, chest heaving from the exertion of running up the steep flight of stairs. Covering her face with her hands she cried,

"Who was that awful woman?"

"She's a sign of the times we live in now Eleanor," Peter replied. "Old man Rosenberg fell in the street yesterday. People were stepping over him as if he were just a piece of garbage."

"They're crazy!" exclaimed Eleanor.

"No, not crazy," Peter cut in angrily, "just mesmerised by Hitler and his promises."

"That's because there's plenty of work and no shortage of food on their tables."

"How can you be so naïve Eleanor. He's a madman! The Jews, gypsies, the mentally infirm: none of them have a place in Hitler's Aryan dream!"

Wearily, he leaned back knuckling his eyes against the glare of a weak, early autumn sun pouring through the window. They felt gritty as though someone had thrown sand in his face.

"What was that?"

Eleanor cowered against the bulk of her husband's body. Heavy footsteps clattered outside pausing at the door of the apartment. With bated breath she listened until they had passed by and ascended to the floor above.

"Don't worry, it's only Mr. Hartmann from upstairs."

"I can't help it. You must stop speaking out against the Nazis. What will become of us if you're arrested?"

"*Nothing* will happen to me. I'm conducting important research for the Reich," Peter replied reassuringly.

Blonde and sturdily built Eleanor was an attractive woman with luminous, blue eyes that lit up her face. Now they flashed with anger as she thought of her Jewish friends who lived in constant fear of being taken away to a concentration camp.

"What about the Bergmanns downstairs? The SS came and bundled them onto a truck in the middle of the night. Nobody seems to know where they took them. I'm terrified Peter."

She glanced at the tiny infant lying peacefully in his cot, blonde and blue-eyed like both his parents.

Peter thrust aside the newspaper he was reading and turned to face Eleanor who still lay huddled up on the sofa.

"It's time to prepare dinner. Julia and Paul will be here soon and you're still not ready for them," he chided her gently.

Taking her hand he pulled her up towards him. Tall, square-jawed, startling blue eyes, blond hair cropped short, he looked the typical Aryan. Light from the oil lamp shone on the fine, golden hairs that covered his lower arms. Eleanor looked up at him her eyes gleaming with unshed tears. She drew his hand to her face and kissed it.

"Promise me you'll be more careful in future."

Peter laughed, picked her up and swung her round and round the tiny room.

"Stop," she giggled, "you'll wake the baby!"

Planting a loud kiss on her lips he set her down on the floor, steadying her in his muscular arms until her head stopped spinning. The steely look in his eyes told her that her pleading was useless.

Peter was the youngest professor in the university. Science was his life, but he was also a philosopher; a hopeless dreamer who loved music and poetry.

"I can't sit back and watch what the Nazis are doing Eleanor."

"You and your principles! They'll get us into trouble one of these days!"

Eleanor busied herself chopping white cabbage for the sauerkraut and setting little roll mops on plain, white plates. She was a third generation German American as fluent in German as she was in English. At Christmas her grandmother still took pride in cooking a traditional German dinner. Even so this life was so different from her life in New York where she had been teaching Art History at the university.

She had been researching some material for her students on Renaissance painters. Running her finger along the line of books between Botticelli and Fra Lippo Lippi her hand came to rest on the large volume she was seeking.

"That's much too heavy for you," said a deep voice from behind her.

Before she had a chance to pull out the book a hand came up and removed it from the shelf. Startled, she turned and found herself looking up into the tanned face of a young man with the bluest eyes she had ever seen.

Her meanderings were interrupted by the grating clang of the bell-pull outside the apartment. Wiping her hands on her apron she hurried to the door and swung it wide.

"Julia, it's so good to see you!"

She hugged her sister then reached up to kiss her brother-in-law.

Taller than Eleanor, with chestnut hair and athletic build, Julia was completely unlike her sister except for her eyes; the same vibrant blue as her sibling. Without asking she knew that her sister's visit to Geneva had been fruitless. Julia shook her head as if she had read Eleanor's thoughts.

"I'm so sorry Julia," she whispered leading her to the old, over-stuffed sofa beneath the window. "What did Professor Steiner say?"

"The same as every other doctor I've seen. There's absolutely nothing they can do. I'll never have children of my own."

Tears clouded her eyes as she watched Paul bending over the baby's cot to grasp his tiny fingers.

"This last pregnancy has really left me feeling weak and tired... so very tired," Julia murmured.

"Steiner made it quite clear that another pregnancy could cost Julia her life," Paul interjected, "and that's something I'm not willing to risk again."

Eleanor felt a stab of anguish knowing that Julia's baby would have been almost two weeks old if he had lived; the same age as her own. Her chest tightened remembering her sister's anguished wailing when she had telephoned from Switzerland the night her baby died. Not even Paul could persuade her that the child was dead. Choked with grief he had to prise the tiny infant out of her arms.

After two miscarriages Julia had conceived again when Eleanor had discovered she too was pregnant. Fit and healthy she had sailed through the nine months. Peter had never seen her look so beautiful or so tranquil. But Julia had suffered constant ill-health throughout her pregnancy.

She looked so frail and wan against the plump, white pillows, blue eyes sunk into dark-grey shadows. Finally, Paul had taken her to Switzerland where she could benefit from the relaxing mountain air close to Professor Steiner's clinic. After a painful, traumatic birth the child had lived for just an hour.

Smells of cooking meat sent Eleanor scurrying to the kitchen to check on the progress of the Wienerschnitzel. Julia busied herself with the canteen of silver cutlery that had been a wedding present from their parents. She felt a sharp stab of homesickness as she pictured her parents swinging gently on the porch that sprawled along the entire front of the white, blue-shuttered house in Chatham on Cape Cod.

They settled themselves round the table and joined hands.

"Wouldn't it be nice if mom and dad came over. We could all celebrate Thanksgiving together," Eleanor said wistfully.

Julia shot an uneasy glance at her husband who appeared engrossed in his meal. Feeling her eyes on him he sliced through a piece of meat then carefully placed his knife against his plate. Without preamble he looked up and announced,

"We're going back to the States."

"Going back, but you can't!" Eleanor said with a hint of panic in her voice. "What about your post in the embassy?"

"I've been offered the option of leaving now or staying on until next spring," Paul replied. "Things are getting pretty messy out here since war broke out with Britain. I've decided to go before the new Chargé d' Affaires takes over in the Berlin Embassy."

"Well, there's nothing to worry about then, is there? If things were that bad they'd close the embassy altogether and ship everybody home," Eleanor said dismissively.

"Maybe, but truth be known, some Americans are getting very twitchy, not just in Berlin. I've heard that a whole batch of Canadians is going over to England to join up."

"The Americans are joining in the war against Germany?" Eleanor asked in shocked tones.

"No, but some think that we should be supporting our allies. On the other hand a hell of a lot feel that it's not their war. They don't want any part of it. Their mindset is that with thousands of miles of ocean between them they're safe; completely cocooned. Even if the Nazis win the war in Europe, they don't believe it'll be a threat to the United States. They're too far away to worry about German bombs. Most think their homeland is impregnable."

"The United States won't stand by and see its traditional allies stamped into submission by Hitler," Peter cut in. "Sooner or later they'll have to make a stand. That could make it very difficult for Americans living in Germany."

Paul nodded grimly,

"Apparently, the U.S ambassador to London has been stirring it up urging Americans living in Britain to pack up and go back Stateside. It's backfired though 'cause a whole bunch of them have set up an American squadron of the British Home Guard headed by General Hayes."

"Yes, but the majority of them *will* be going back to the States," Julia said eyeing Eleanor uncertainly.

"But what will happen to us; to the baby?" Eleanor cut in.

"We've been discussing that. Peter thinks you should take Johann home just in case the situation takes a turn for the worse."

"This is my home now," she snapped, "here with Peter and our son. No, it's out of the question. I can't leave without Peter!"

"Well, if you *don't* you'll be putting yourself and Johann at risk," Paul declared fiercely.

"It isn't just about what we want anymore Eleanor," Peter murmured gently. "It's what's best for our son."

"Even though you're relatively safe at the moment the situation is becoming more fragile by the day," Julia interjected. "Still, you must do what you think is best. And *you*, you should exercise some restraint! Your rantings could place you all in danger."

She glared at Peter as he retreated to the kitchen to fetch another bottle of wine.

"Churchill has been urging Roosevelt to provide armaments," Paul continued, "but he still has to convince the bulk of the American people. The British need help and the President is determined to give them whatever they need to fight the war."

Peter re-appeared carrying a tray laden with a bottle of Schnapps and four glasses with long, dark-green slender stems. He set them down on the ornately-carved, occasional table.

Eleanor watched as sparkling Riesling filled the glasses then settled into the hollow stems.

"A toast!" Peter exclaimed in his deep baritone. "To art, to music and to sanity."

Tossing the wine back in one gulp he replenished the women's glasses then poured a glass of Schnapps for himself and Paul. Unsteadily, he rose to his feet, clicked his heels and gave a mock, Nazi salute.

"And to hell with the Nazis and the 'Little Painter!'" he slurred.

"Peter!" Eleanor gasped in a horrified voice. "You mustn't say these things!"

"We're amongst family Eleanor."

"Damn it man, she's right! Walls have ears in Germany these days," Paul cut in. He moved to the window to draw the heavy, wine-coloured, damask drapes. "These are dangerous times. They've already arrested hundreds of Germans for their political views, many like you for refusing to join the Nazi Party."

Peter sat down heavily and leaned back in the armchair his knuckles pressed against his temples. For a few moments he sat quietly with his eyes closed succumbing to the effects of the alcohol. With a deep sigh he clamped his hands on his knees and slowly rose. Unsteadily, he moved to his wife's side and drew her to the baby's cot.

"Look at him Eleanor, look at him!" he demanded. "You must go home for his sake. You're not German. If war breaks out with the States think what might happen to you if you stay here."

"I'm convinced that Churchill's speech to the British Parliament after Dunkirk will stir up support in the States," Paul interjected. "I happened to be in London at the time and heard it on the wireless. It was very moving. The old bulldog has vowed that the British will never surrender. They'll fight to the bitter end."

Eleanor muttered defiantly,

"It's all supposition and rumour. I'll stay here with Peter."

"You wouldn't say that if you could see the way London's been bombed," Julia shot back. "We were there in September in the Blitz. The sky was black with planes dropping hundreds of tons of incendiary bombs. Huge flames were shooting up into the sky. Everywhere buildings glowing red through a pall of thick smoke and dust that obliterated everything. Searchlights criss-crossing the sky trying to pick out the planes for the gunners. It was almost unreal."

Julia stopped and looked at Eleanor who was standing with her hand her mouth eyes wide with disbelief.

"It's the truth Eleanor. Flames were shooting dozens of feet into the air. It was the nearest thing to Hell I've ever seen. People were running wild-eyed screaming as they searched the rubble for survivors. Mothers searching frantically for children; terrified children screaming for parents. I saw an old man scrabbling in the debris with his bare hands, crying out for his wife."

Eleanor dropped onto the sofa a look of total incredulity on her face.

"Let's leave it for tonight," Paul said wearily as he headed for the door.

"Goodnight," Peter thrust out his hand, "thanks for trying."

Julia gave him a beseeching look as she hugged her sister.

"Goodnight Eleanor. Let me know if you change your mind, but don't leave it *too* late. We're leaving in ten days time."

CHAPTER TWO

Ever since the Kristallnacht pogrom Peter had felt afraid of what was happening in Germany.

"You can't even begin to imagine what it was like Eleanor," he said.

Images swirled through his head as he remembered that terrible night. The crack and crunch of glass as Gauleiters smashed in shop windows. The SA and SS, disguised in civilian clothes, armed with axes, sledgehammers and picks throwing beds, books and tables out into the street.

"I was spending a few days in Munich with Otto. When we heard the commotion we ran out into the street. The SS ordered us back inside, but we watched from an alleyway. It was a living nightmare. Benjamin, a Jewish friend of ours... he was a concert pianist.... had been dragged from the apartment next door. He was standing on the pavement staring up at two soldiers hanging on to a piano right up on the top floor. He was begging them not to drop it. Laughing like maniacs they shoved and pushed until they had it balanced on the window sill. For a few seconds it hung suspended over the ledge then it hurtled to the ground. Beni fell to his knees clutching a piece of shattered, polished wood to his chest as though it were a child. After they smashed his piano they smashed his hands."

Peter could still hear his screams as the bones in his hands were crushed by the heavy blow of an axe, two bloody fingers hanging limply by a string of sinew. The acrid smell of human flesh burning as people were caught up in the flames. Children screaming as they were herded into the street shivering with cold and fear.

"I've never seen such brutality," Peter murmured. "They looted homes, shops, burned synagogues; the hatred was so palpable I could feel it. Some Jews were almost beaten to death if they tried to protest. Neighbours, who had lived peaceably alongside them for years, were screaming insults at them. In minutes the crowd had turned into a vicious, hysterical mob baying for blood."

Peter looked into the near distance his mind full of the terrible scenes he had witnessed. Images that would haunt him for the rest of his life.

"Thousands of male Jews were imprisoned after Kristallnacht," he spat vehemently. "Last week 1 heard about the treatment of some prisoners in Sachsenhaussen concentration camp. It was sickening! Hangings, brutal beatings; it was horrific."

"I don't believe it! It can't be true!"

A friend of mine, one of the professors of anatomy in the medical school, told me about it. He had been ordered to Sachsenhausen to advise the camp doctors. From the car he saw the guards viciously kicking some prisoners curled up on the ground. He couldn't believe what he was seeing. They were smashing their bodies to a pulp with the butts of their guns. Their skulls caved in like pumpkins spilling brains, eyes and entrails all over the place. There was blood everywhere. Believe me he's seen some gruesome things in his time, but he couldn't stomach it. When he finally got to the commandant's office he vomited all over the floor. Before he left he was warned what to expect if he told anybody what he had seen. But he was so distressed he told me and Otto."

"Stop it! Stop it! I can't bear to hear any more!" Eleanor cried.

"It's the truth Eleanor! Now they're arresting whole families of Jews who disappear without trace. Most people are tight-lipped, but I've heard rumours. All they care about is that they have full bellies and good jobs. They can't or won't believe what they hear."

"You look so tired and drawn," Eleanor interrupted trying to change the subject.

"I'm worried about you and Johann living here in Berlin. Why won't you listen to me?" he shouted. "You must leave now before it's too late!"

"Let's not talk about it now. Close your eyes and rest for a moment while I prepare dinner."

Eleanor fussed with the table carefully lining up the cutlery in the precise way she did everything. She liked things to look nice. Looking round the spacious apartment she sighed with contentment. It gave her a sense of pride and satisfaction that she had created a comfortable home for Peter and her son.

A fire glowed red in the grate casting a warm glow over the highly-polished, mahogany furniture. Slender candles, reflected in the mirror over the mantelpiece, flickered as she passed to and fro from the kitchen. Ornate gas lamps shed light over leather-bound volumes in the carved, wooden bookcase.

Music sheets lay in an untidy pile on the carpet next to Peter's violin, the rich wood gleaming in the firelight. Eleanor loved to watch him play, the instrument tucked under his chin on a red, silk handkerchief. Leaning slightly forward, eyes closed, swaying to the strains of Paganini.

Sometimes he played Brahms to soothe the baby to sleep. She smiled at the thought of his exuberance when he played Beethoven's '*Chorus of the Dervishes*' with his university friends. Laughing like excited boys they toasted each other with Schnapps, incurring her anger when she came charging into the living room at the sound of breaking glass.

The sound of a car screeching to a halt in the street below startled her. She scurried to the window, pulled back the drapes and peered through a slit in the net curtains. Soldiers, armed with rifles, were spilling from the back of a truck, their boots clattering on the cobbles. An SS officer barked orders at them as they marched towards the block of apartments opposite.

"Schnell! Schnell"

"Ja Sturmbannfürer!"

The red glow of a cigarette flared at the side of the truck, the face behind it momentarily illuminated. Gaunt and pale, like a cadaver, his gold-rimmed glasses gleamed in the harsh light from the street-lamp. Cautiously, he emerged from the shadows, A tall, thin figure in a black, leather coat, sporting the *'Death's Head'* emblem of the Gestapo. He spoke quietly to the SS officer standing on the pavement then stepped back out of sight. Turning to a young Wehrmacht lieutenant the SS officer spat out an order.

"Oberleutnant! Send your men in. Get the Rosenburgs out now!"

The officer sprang to attention clicking his heels.

"Ja Sturmbannführer!" he answered nervously.

"Break down the door if you have to," the SS officer snarled through his teeth. "Get your backs behind it!" he screamed as the men shouldered the heavy doors.

With a loud splintering of wood the soldiers half fell through the doors into the foyer in a crescendo of noise and jostling bodies.

"What are you waiting for, you fools?"

They ran clanking up the iron stairs to the second floor, rifles banging metallically on the balustrade. A door opened a chink revealing the upper half of an old woman's wrinkled face. Eyes wide with fear she quickly closed the door, and her mind, to the soldiers breaking into the adjoining apartment.

Seventy year old Jacob Rosenberg sat bolt upright on the rickety old chair. Suddenly, the door fell into the room landing with a loud thud amidst a little cloud of dust. Instinctively, he clutched his daughter's hand in a futile, protective gesture. His son, Abram, stood behind them.

"What do you want? We've done nothing wrong!" he exclaimed defiantly.

Scharführer Schmidt raised his rifle butt in the air and brought it crashing down on the younger man's skull. For a moment he stood there, wobbling slightly, before his legs buckled. Like a disjointed puppet he crashed to the floor without a whimper. The sergant kicked him viciously in the groin. Raising his gun he brought it down with such ferocity that they heard the skull crack. But Abram hadn't felt a thing. Mercifully, he was already dead.

"Jew pig!" Schmidt spat giving the corpse another kick in the head then he turned to Jacob.

For a split second the soldiers stopped and stared at the frail, old man. A young, blond recruit, hair sticking up in a short crew-cut, stood uncertainly in the gaping doorway.

Hans looked questioningly at the heavy-jowled Scharführer. Jacob was wailing, tearing at his clothes; staring at his son lying in a crumpled, bloody heap. Roughly, Schmidt pulled Jacob off the chair and pushed his fist into his bloodied face.

"Stop your wailing old Jew, he's dead," he said with more glee than compassion.

Lifting his hand he slapped the old man sideways, from cheek to cheek. He grinned viciously as blood spurted from the old man's nose down the front of his torn shirt. With a knee-jerk reaction Hans put a restraining hand on the sergeant's arm. Apoplectic with rage he pushed him off eyes bulging, dark veins throbbing in his neck. Thick, white spittle slavered at the corners of his mouth.

"Take him," he snarled at Hans, "and don't ever touch me again!"

Gently, Hans led the old man out of the apartment downstairs to the lobby where the Gestapo officer was waiting.

"Where are the others?" the Oberleutnant asked.

"The son is dead, but the woman is still up there with Scharführer Schmidt."

Hans opened his mouth to say something, thought better of it then helped Jacob into the back of the truck. Oberleutnant Kurt Bercholtz looked at him keenly, nodded imperceptibly, and ran up the stairs two at a time.

The sergeant was pressing Ruth down on the narrow cot behind the curtain that served as a bedroom, one hand underneath her flimsy skirt exploring her warm flesh. With the other he unbuttoned his trousers exposing his fat, sagging stomach and genitals. Ruth screamed recoiling in terror as his bloated face covered hers. She could smell beer and stale cabbage on his breath mingled with the stench of rotten gums. He grinned revealing blackened teeth. His face was so close she could see the depth of the pock-marks on his chin. She tried to push him away clawing at his face.

"Jew bitch!" he hissed as she drew blood. "You'll pay for that!"

He clenched his fist and punched her in the mouth shattering one of her front teeth just as Oberleutnant Bercholtz threw back the curtain.

"Achtung!

Bercholtz' eyes blazed with cold fury as Schmidt sprang to attention. Hurriedly, he pushed his now flaccid manhood out of sight, his sausage-like fingers fidgeting clumsily with his trouser buttons.

"Oberleutnant, she kicked me in the crotch. I was just teaching the bitch a lesson. You know how it is? " he leered attempting a placatory, knowing smile.

Bercholtz felt the gall rising in his chest. Leering, Schmidt stood, legs wide apart, in front of the cowering young woman behind him. Before he could stop himself his hand came up and struck the sneering sergeant a stinging blow with his leather gloves.

"No, I *don't* know how it is Schmidt," he retorted over his shoulder as he marched back down the stairs.

Unknown to each other Hans and Kurt had sealed their fates.

"Peter, in here!" Eleanor called urgently from the kitchen. "There's something going on across the road."

Peter stared over her head then gripped her shoulder until she winced with pain.

"Gestapo!" he spat vehemently. "They're probably after old man Rosenberg's son."

They watched as Jacob was bundled into the truck. The SS officer paced to and fro impatiently, occasionally glancing up at the third floor windows. Suddenly, Bercholtz appeared, got into the staff car and slammed the door. Seconds later Scharführer Schmidt emerged pushing Ruth in front of him with the muzzle of his rifle.

"Get in!" he growled shoving her violently up into the back of the truck.

Ruth gasped as the butt of the rifle slammed against her buttocks forcing her forward onto her knees. Oblivious to the grazes, and the metal ridges on the truck floor biting into her flesh, she scrabbled towards her father. Throwing his arms around her he cried,

"Abram, my only son, Abram!"

Grinning malevolently Schmidt thrust his florid face into the gloom of the vehicle and leered at Ruth. Quickly, he slammed the tailgate into place before jumping into the passenger seat of the truck. Bodies wracked with sobs father and daughter clung to each other as they sped through the darkness to the oblivion they sensed awaited them.

Peter stared after the truck until it disappeared. Eleanor knew what he was thinking before he spoke.

"Now do you understand. God knows where they've taken them. I heard that Abram was smitten with a German girl; that he smiled at her on the street. Just an innocent smile, no more than that. But it's forbidden for Jews to feel attracted to Germans so he *and* his family must be punished."

"But how did the Gestapo know?"

"Probably the neighbours. You can't trust them anymore. Some of them are reporting Jews to the Gestapo for any little misdemeanour. They think this will help to protect them. Everybody is afraid of the Gestapo, even Germans."

Peter hung his head, eyes clouded with misery, as he thought of Ruth. Her dark intelligent eyes, the keen interest she had shown in his music. The way her face had puckered into a smile when he had secretly given her one of his books to read.

"I'd give my life for my country, but I'm ashamed when I see what's happening. The way our youth is being brainwashed into believing that what Hitler is doing is right for Germany. It can never be right!" he muttered vehemently

Gathering Eleanor up in his arms he held her close, stroking her hair to calm her trembling body. She looked up into his face her eyes wild with fear and disbelief. For months she had blocked out what she had seen and heard on the streets when she went out shopping. She had noticed the way some of her neighbours glared at her with undisguised contempt. How the women, gossiping in subdued voices, turned their backs when she smiled at them on her way to collect the morning bread. But she had shut it out just as she shut out the newspaper wrapped around dog faeces that had been thrust into their letter box.

"It's just silly children," she told Peter, "getting their own back, because you remonstrated with them about their behaviour on the street."

But she knew in her heart that it was Peter's behaviour that was stirring up hatred towards them. He had such uncompromising ideals. In truth, it was what she loved about him most, his compassion for other human beings. She remembered how he had given his last dollar to a ragged, old hobo as they strolled through Central Park in New York just days before he had brought her to Germany.

Panic rose in her chest clasping its fevered hands like a vice around her throat. Her comfortable life was disintegrating. Like the strands of an old sweater plucked and pulled until it fell in a tangle at her feet. A heap of disconnected threads that held her life and her dreams.

Eleanor sighed and straightened her dress. Resolutely, she marched to the kitchen to prepare the evening meal. Anger replaced fear as she pricked the meat watching the red juices ooze and sizzle in the pan simmering on the enamel stove. Cheeks rosy with the heat from the oven she flicked back a wayward strand of blonde hair, jabbed at the vegetables, briskly stirred the sauce.

Muttering to herself she went into the bedroom to check on Johann. He was fast asleep, his little brow creased into an infant frown. Every few seconds his eyelids fluttered as he gave a crooked smile.

"Wind," Eleanor thought as she lovingly stroked his cheek, then she remembered what Peter had said the week before about taking him to America.

"Not now," she whispered to herself, "there's plenty of time to think about that later."

Closing the door behind her she crept out of the room, motioning to Peter to take his place at the table while she fetched the meat.

He carved it into thin slices, carefully forking them onto a salver while Eleanor scooped vegetables onto their plates. For a few moments they sat in silence watching the steam rise and curl from the hot food. Peter searched Eleanor's face intently, noticing the little worry lines around her eyes.

"Forget about everything tonight. Let's just enjoy our meal," he murmured raising his wine glass. Firelight lit up the wine turning it the colour of a red-setting sun. "Try to forget what we saw if only for this evening."

"But Peter…?"

"No, not tonight Eleanor," he cut in, "but tomorrow we'll talk again about America."

Eleanor opened her mouth to speak, but she could see it would be no use. Peter's face was set; as set in stone as the carved faces on Mount Rushmore.

Eleanor lay awake in their huge, sleigh bed trying to push out the confusion of images that crowded her mind. Peter had fallen asleep almost as soon as his head touched the pillow. More from the effects of strong wine and Schnapps than natural sleep. He lay on his back, his eyelids flickering, lips speaking silent words. It was something he always did when he was troubled. At the side of the bed the baby snuffled letting out an occasional whimper as he too dreamed his dreams. Eleanor felt a sudden, overpowering surge of love.

"So tiny, so vulnerable," she thought. "I couldn't live if anything happened to you."

Tears filled her eyes as she reached out to stroke his silky cheeks. With a deep sigh she turned to the comfort of Peter's warm body.

Wrapped in the security of his muscular arms the night's events seemed unreal. A dream where the sleeper believes he is awake, but subconsciously knows he is only dreaming his wakefulness. The line between dream and reality merely a thread that links and separates two dimensions.

Slowly, Eleanor drifted into a fitful sleep. She was in the cobbled street below, familiar yet unfamiliar. Not really their street, but one that metamorphosised as she moved along its length looking for their entrance. Every time she pushed open the heavy, carved door to step inside she was faced with a black, cavernous hole. Nightmarish screams and lunatic laughter rose up from the swirling darkness. She recoiled in horror as a sinister, lisping voice urged her to enter while bodiless, white, scrawny fingers clawed at the air.

Suddenly, she was running with the baby in her arms. Soldiers ran after her their jackboots clattering on the cobbles. In the corner of her dream a black-uniformed Gestapo officer screamed after them. Eyes as red as the devil, pointed teeth gleaming in the darkness. Beside him a faceless man in a long, black coat reached out to her. His arms grew longer and longer grasping at her like the tentacles of an octopus.

She ran, faster and faster, but the quicker she ran the more her legs seemed glued to the cobbles. As the man caught up with her his face became a skull. Eyes vacant black holes, teeth set in a hideous, grinning 'Death's Head'. Clinging to her son she screamed, louder and louder, until she thought her lungs would burst. Kicking and screaming she felt strong hands hold her down pressing her painfully onto the cobbles.

"Eleanor! Eleanor! Wake Up!"

Her eyes shot open trying to focus as bright sunlight forced its way through her eyelids. Peter was looking down at her with a pained, worried expression. Looking round at the familiar room, the pictures on the wall, the great Ottoman at the foot of the bed, she sighed with relief.

"It was just a dream," she breathed "or was it?"

Panicking, she sat bolt upright, rigid with fear, trying to adjust to a waking state. At the side of the bed Johann cried lustily for his feed.

"No, I'm still dreaming," she argued shaking her head vigorously.

"It's all right liebling, it's all right," Peter murmured gently. "You've just had a nasty nightmare, that's all. I'll feed the baby while you drink some strong coffee. You look as if you need some."

Icy cold rivulets of perspiration ran down her back soaking her nightdress. She couldn't stop shaking. Gratefully, she sipped the steaming coffee warming her hands on the cup. Terror still clogged her throat like a sour, indigestible apple. She couldn't obliterate the hellish images of her dream.

She finished her coffee, slowly dressed and went into the living room grabbing a woollen shawl to cover her shivering body.

"I'll make breakfast," she told Peter as she saw him pottering in the kitchen. "I need something to do. You go and watch Johann."

"I haven't got any lectures this afternoon. We could go for a stroll in the Tiergarten, Maybe stop for coffee on the Unter den Linden and sit for a while in the fresh air."

"I don't know Peter. I feel so tired."

"No arguments, it'll do you good," Peter stated as he moved into the living room to attend to the baby who was grizzling to be fed.

Eleanor stretched her arms above her head rotating her neck to alleviate the tension in her shoulders. Tiredness enveloped her whole body. Wearily, she rubbed the dull ache at the base of her skull. Throwing open the kitchen window she breathed deeply on the cold air until the fuzziness in her brain began to evaporate.

From the street the usual daily sounds reached her ears. Clicking footsteps, greetings shouted from windows, muffled laughter as people stopped to exchange gossip. Boisterous children on their way to kindergarten, the tinkling of a bicycle bell. In the distance the muted sound of tram wheels and morning traffic. It all looked and sounded so normal.

Sunlight filtered through the stained-glass picture set into the window pane casting multi-coloured patterns over the tablecloth. She leaned out of the window her gaze sweeping the length of the street below.

"Guten morgen," she called down to a tall, elegant figure as she walked along the pavement in front of their building. But Frau Hoffman seemed not to hear as she moved purposefully along the street. "Isn't it a beautiful day?" she continued spotting Herr Fleiss looking up at her.

Swiftly, he looked away, mounted his bicycle and pedalled off bumping precariously along the uneven cobbles.

Eleanor shrugged and turned back into the kitchen. She poured coffee into big breakfast cups and set them on the table.

"Don't you think it's a bit strange Peter?" They must have heard me calling."

"It's nothing. They were probably too engrossed in their own thoughts to notice you," he replied.

Peter grabbed his briefcase and headed for the door, a worried frown creasing his usually smiling face.

Launching himself down the stairs, two at a time, he shouted over his shoulder,

"I'll be back around midday."

Over the stairwell he called a greeting to someone on the floor below. Quickly, a door slammed as he came careering round the bend in the stairs. When he emerged into the bright, watery sunlight he bumped into a stocky figure coming in.

"Excuse me, Frau Klocke I…"

Before Peter could finish his mumbled apology the woman barged past him, scurried to her first floor apartment and slammed the door.

From the kitchen Eleanor saw a curtain slide across in the apartment opposite. A puff of cigarette smoke hid the face of the figure staring straight at her through the window. Momentarily, she felt a thrill of fear race down her spine as the smoke cleared and she stared into the eyes of the Gestapo man she had seen the night before. With a barely perceptible nod of recognition he gave her a toothy, malevolent grin then slowly drew the curtain across. Eleanor could still see his outline behind the flimsy nets standing stock still, watching and waiting.

Terrified, she pressed herself against the wall too rigid with fear to move until Johann's gurgling brought her to her senses. She lunged into the living room, grabbed the baby and sank down behind the sofa. Shaking uncontrollably she rocked him in her arms as much to comfort herself as the child. Her heart thumped violently as though it would burst from her chest. A sour taste invaded her mouth, cold sweat ran down her back, beaded her forehead, dripped onto her nose. Taking deep breaths she forced herself to calm down.

"Idiot! It's just a man at the window!" she chided herself, but deep down she knew he was no ordinary man. "Stop hiding like a fugitive. Get up you silly woman. He was probably watching someone else. Why would he want to watch you?"

Gradually, the feelings of panic subsided, but she still felt weak like an invalid who was getting out of bed after a long illness. Her legs felt like rubber as she stood up clutching the baby to her bosom. She crept into the kitchen pressing her body against the wall at the side of the window.

Closing her eyes she tried to blot out the evil face she had seen. Tentatively, she edged her head around until she could see the building opposite. Nothing but a pair of innocuous, lace curtains flapping merrily in the breeze from the open window. She sighed with relief,

"Your imagination is running away with you again Eleanor Brandt!"

For the rest of the morning she busied herself preparing an early lunch in readiness for their afternoon walk. By the time Peter came home from the university she had resolved not to mention the man in the window.

After lunch they caught a tram to the top end of Strasse Unter den Linden. They strolled down the great boulevard, resplendent with ancient lime trees. Into the Mitte, past smart cafés, people jostling and gossiping as they walked. Animated groups, muffled against the chill autumn air, were sitting outside laughing and talking. Businessmen enjoying a Schnapps; young women gazing provocatively into the eyes of their lovers. A few staff from the university immersed in serious conversation.

A short, squat man stood up waving his arms about.

"Old Kruger's at it again," Peter laughed as the man started to storm off. "He's probably lost the argument."

Quaffing beer, his companions completely ignored his outburst. Putting the world to rights or debating a theoretical treatise was a daily pastime.

"Sit down Kruger!" one of them muttered looking warily at the other tables.

Careless talk was dangerous for radical thinkers. The university no longer encouraged free speech and creative thought. She remembered the fury in Peter's eyes when he described the scene of destruction in the Opernplatz.

"It was a sacrilege Eleanor. Thousands of books burned. All that creativity destroyed."

"But why burn books?" Eleanor asked.

"They were considered a threat, not in keeping with Nazi ideology."

"Couldn't somebody stop them?"

"Nobody could or would stop them. The university authorities were too afraid. Jewish intellectuals were rounded up…..deported or killed. Political opponents, even Germans, mysteriously disappeared. I was so enraged I shouted at them, but Otto and Claus pulled me down into the crowd before the SA saw me.

I can still see the pages curling and blackening in the flames. The smell of smoke in my nostrils and that propagandist Goebbels posturing under the protection of the SA. Thousands of pages; millions of words destroyed."

A voice, calling from the small group huddled over their drinks at one of the fashionable pavement cafés, cut into Eleanor's thoughts.

"Peter, over here. Come and join us!"

"It's Otto and Marie from the university. Come on, let's sit for a while."

Everybody shuffled their chairs to make room for them, laughing and talking about their day.

They ordered coffee, fat doughnuts and a beer. Otto leaned over conspiratorially and whispered to Peter.

"Tonight at Claus' apartment…"

He stopped as the waiter arrived with their order. Eleanor dipped her finger in the jam doughnut and let the baby suck at it until he dropped off to sleep.

"What time Otto?" queried Peter when the waiter had disappeared out of earshot.

"Wait 'til after dark. Around seven but be careful not…"

Otto laughed loudly, seeming to enjoy a joke, as two men glanced at them. They pushed past to sit at a table just inside the entrance.

Later, warmed by the hot drink, they set off towards the Tiergarten near Brandenburg Tor. Ahead of them Eleanor could see the imposing structure of the Gate topped with the Quadriga, a winged goddess driving a chariot drawn by four horses.

"To think that she was once Eirene, Goddess of Peace," Peter whispered guardedly in barely-accented English. "Now it's a symbol of Nazism," he spat out indicating the red and white flags emblazoned with a black swastika.

"Be careful, someone might hear you!" Eleanor exclaimed looking round furtively.

"What harm is there in speaking English to my American wife?"

"You'll draw attention to yourself," Eleanor warned in German.

"Ja! Ja! Rules and regulations. Whatever happened to free speech?"

"At least lower your voice!"

"You should have seen the avenue last week. On my way home from the university I saw Hitler strutting onto his platform to watch the parade. My blood chilled to ice in my veins watching the fanatical adulation on the faces of the crowd. The SS marching like arrogant 'gods'. Hundreds of jackboots echoing above the hysterical cheering. Swastikas everywhere… on flags… banners… lamp posts. Flaming torches lighting up the darkness in a sea of red, white and black. It was magnificent, evil, frightening. People were mesmerised, almost like mass hypnosis. When the Führer held up his hand silence fell in an instant. A breathless anticipation rippled through the crowd as they waited for him to speak. Their faces were glowing with adoration; almost reverence."

"Reverence?"

"Yes, reverence Eleanor. The air was electric. Within minutes the crowd, whipped into a frenzy, cheered and saluted their 'saviour'." Peter spat out the words. "It made my blood run cold. More than a thousand people, arms outstretched, chanting, 'Seig Heil! Seig Heil! Seig Heil!' They've been brainwashed Eleanor, brought up to it in the Hitler Youth."

"Forget it Peter, let's just enjoy the afternoon. Incidentally, what was Otto whispering about?"

"Nothing much, just a meeting of some of the faculty; a kind of debating group really. We thought it would be nice to meet somewhere comfortable for a beer and some Schnapps. Perhaps it will be in our apartment next time."

"Well, make sure you give me plenty of warning if you want refreshments. Don't spring it on me last minute like you usually do," Eleanor retorted as they entered the Tiergarten and headed for the zoological gardens.

Peter sat nursing the baby in his favourite armchair, rocking gently to and fro as he sang an old, German folk song. The boy gurgled, his chubby legs kicking free from the shawl. Eleanor was in the kitchen washing up the last of the dinner dishes when she heard the familiar screech of brakes on cobbles. She stopped, frozen to the spot, a plate suspended halfway to the shelf. Peter stopped singing and rushed to the window with the baby in his arms.

"It's the Gestapo again! I wonder what poor soul they'll arrest this time?"

"Come away from the window!" Eleanor snapped.

She pulled at his sleeve guiding him to the sofa, but before he could sit down they heard the splintering of wood. Loud, guttural shouts as heavy footsteps clattered up the metal stairs.

The footsteps stopped on the floor below them. An authoritative voice barking orders: doors opening and closing along the corridor. The sound of hammering on wood then voices raised in protest.

"They've come for the Goldmanns," Eleanor whispered.

Sounds of chairs overturning, cries from the family as they were herded downstairs and thrown into the back of the truck. Doors slammed, the engine stuttered and died then roared into life and trundled away into the darkness.

In the street below an SS officer rhythmically tapped a riding whip against his shiny, black jackboot. Eyes glinting like polished marble, lips set hard, slicing his face like a slash in a crude painting. Casually, he gazed up at the dim lights on the third floor. He felt the familiar sparkle and surge of blood in his veins as he anticipated the game he would play with his victims.

Cruelty gave him more pleasure than the sexual encounters he had experienced. The ripples of heady feeling lasted longer than the frenzied pumping that led to a brief moment of physical gratification. Like last night he thought savouring the memory. Brought about after beating the woman into submission, her wrists tied so tightly to the iron bedstead the rope almost burned through the flesh.

He smiled sadistically as he remembered how he had cut through the ropes, thrown the woman to the ground and kicked her until she was senseless. They were usually prostitutes he picked up in the street, but sometimes he raped a good Jewish girl into submission just to show them who was master. Those were the times Sturmbannfürer Kappler loved best.

Out of the shadows emerged a Gestapo agent, his face illuminated like a hideous, waxworks dummy in a fairground Chamber of Horrors every time he inhaled on his cigarette. As he looked up towards them his glasses glistened in the red glow before his face was covered once again by darkness.

"It's him, the one I saw this morning in the window across the street," Eleanor whispered. "The same man who was here when they took the Rosenburgs."

"Put out the light!" Peter ordered as he went into the living room. "We don't want them to see us."

They crouched down behind the window sill straining to look through the gap under the lace curtains into the street below.

"It's that bastard Fleischer!" Peter hissed. "I've seen him before down at Gestapo headquarters."

"Gestapo headquarters!" Eleanor exclaimed. "What were you doing there?"

"I changed my jacket last minute before I went out and forgot to transfer my papers. They picked me up on the way back from Otto's and took me down to Prinz Albrecht Strasse. Fleischer was there sitting behind his desk looking like a living corpse. He was friendly enough; even offered me one of his stinking cigarettes. They had to let me go in the end, after they'd contacted the university authorities to verify my identity. I still had to go in next day to show my papers."

"There's more to this than you're telling me, isn't there. You never go out without your papers. Everybody knows how dangerous that is."

Peter shrugged off her concerns with his usual dismissive attitude.

"It was nothing," he said putting his arm round her shoulders reassuringly. "You worry too much."

Shuddering involuntarily Eleanor pushed him away.

"Why don't I believe him?" she muttered to herself as she returned to the kitchen leaving Peter still crouched under the window.

"They've gone, the schweinhunds!" Peter exclaimed bitterly as he came into the kitchen. "The Goldmanns, the Bergmanns, the Rosenbergs. I found out yesterday that Anna Maurer and her brother Walter were arrested by the Gestapo."

"Walter Maurer, but isn't he one of your colleagues at the university?"

"Yes, but they've accused him of being involved with some sort of secret underground organisation helping the Jews escape from Berlin."

"How do you know about such an organisation? My God, please tell me you're not involved as well?"

Peter averted his eyes, walked over to the window and gazed into the street.

"Eleanor, you must try to understand. We can't stand by and watch these people being taken from their homes to God knows where. To be tortured, to be murdered! Otto…"

"Otto, I should have known! So that's what your little discussion group is all about. That's what you were arranging this afternoon in the restaurant wasn't it? How could you be so stupid?"

"It's not stupid to be concerned about other human beings," Peter murmured, a hurt expression on his face.

Eleanor, immediately regretting her outburst, flung her arms around his neck.

"I know schatz. After all it's what I've always loved most about you. It's just that I'm so worried about what will happen if the Gestapo arrest you again."

Peter didn't respond, just stroked her hair for a few moments then held her away from him.

"It's time Eleanor. We must get Johann out of Berlin and you must go with him."

She looked at him beseechingly, but knew it was no use arguing.

"I've spoken to Paul and Julia. They've agreed to take you and the baby to London, via Geneva, then back to America. Fortunately, Julia hasn't told anyone at the embassy that she lost her baby. It was too painful for her. She was five months pregnant when she left Berlin on her last trip to Switzerland and they've only been back a few days. They've had no contact with anybody in the embassy for weeks."

"You've already worked this all out, haven't you?" Eleanor muttered bitterly.

"Paul has been going round the embassy handing out cigars, telling them about his new 'son'."

"And you didn't tell me about it!"

"I tried to when they were here for dinner, but you wouldn't listen!" Peter remonstrated angrily.

"How will they believe such a story?" Eleanor interjected. "They'll wonder why he kept the baby's birth a secret."

"We've already thought of that. Paul told them that the baby was very weak when he was born – that it was touch and go for a few days so they didn't tell anybody in the embassy in case the worst happened. They haven't been near their embassy bolt-hole. For the past few days they've been back in their rented house in Glienicke. Julia wanted a little time to herself before she met anybody from the embassy."

"But what if someone finds out… the Gestapo?"

"The baby would have been the same age as Johann if he'd lived; only days between them. Don't you see Eleanor, it's perfect! Paul will claim that Johann was born in Professor Steiner's private clinic in Switzerland. I've arranged for new papers for him in Paul's name."

"But how?" Eleanor asked dumbfounded.

"How isn't important. When they get back to the States they'll claim dual nationality for their 'son'.

"He's a German national, only half American by blood."

"He'll have a new name on Paul's passport."

"But it won't be Johann?"

"No," Peter said quietly, "they'll call him John Paul. We've gone over every detail. Don't forget Paul has diplomatic immunity and you have an American passport."

"I must talk to Julia."

"Tomorrow morning we'll take the bus to Glienicke. The house is close to the woods not far from the river. You'll stay there with Julia. Later in the day she and Paul will take Johann to the American embassy. They're already arranging a party to wet the new baby's head. You'll go with them to the party then return to Glienicke and leave together two days later."

"But Peter…!"

"No 'buts' Eleanor, it has to be done. You must go *now* while you still can. The situation is changing daily between Germany and America. We can't wait until everything blows up in our faces."

Back in the apartment Eleanor spent the rest of the day packing warm clothes. For the baby, a heavy woollen shawl bound with blue satin, an extra blanket and enough milk for the journey.

"It's as well he didn't thrive on my milk," she thought as he grizzled to be fed. His head moved from side to side searching for the rubber teat until his little mouth found it.

"At least he's used to the bottle," she thought ruefully.

Hungrily, he slurped the milk occasionally stopping for breath; his eyelids fluttering when the flow stopped. Eleanor removed the teat until he cried for more.

"You're a greedy little boy Johann Brandt," she smiled gently.

Tears coursed down her cheeks dropping on to the baby's face. She was afraid of what might happen to Peter after they'd gone.

That night they went over the plans, again and again, until she cried out,

"Stop it! I can't take any more!"

"You *must* not make any mistakes when you get to the border. Don't forget the baby is your '*nephew*' and Julia is his '*mother*'. Try not to show your resentment or the border guards will pick up on it."

Peter's voice was querulous with nervous anxiety and emotion.

"You must let Julia nurse him as you go through the checkpoint, even if he is crying, you *must!* Are you listening to me Eleanor?"

"I'll do everything you tell me," Eleanor replied her voice filled with resignation. "He'll be Julia's son, but only until we reach the United States, even if Julia and Paul are registered as his parents."

Tenderly, he gathered her close pressing his cheek against hers.

"This is hard for you, but it's hard for me too. We must do what's best for Johann. I don't want my son to be brought up in Hitler's Germany."

The following morning they travelled the few miles to Glienicke.

"We'll get off here," Peter said, "and take the shortcut."

"How far is it?"

"Just the other side of the woods."

Quickly, they made their way through the gloom avoiding muddy pools created by recent rain. Darkness descended as they entered deep into the woods. Overhead, silent birds rustled in overhanging branches. The melancholy moan of the wind sung softly through the trees, their branches swaying down to brush the tops of their heads. To Eleanor they seemed like tentacles reaching out to snatch Johann from her.

Cold droplets of water dripped down onto her face into her eyes; down her neck soaking the collar of her coat. Brown, mulched leaves clung to her shoes and stockings. The snap of a twig underfoot brought her to a halting stop, her breath coming in short, painful gasps.

"What was that?"

"Nothing, just some small animal scavenging for food," Peter replied as the bushes nearby rustled.

Eleanor breathed a sigh of relief as she spotted a squirrel scurrying across the ground. It froze, looked straight at them then quickly darted towards a nearby tree where it disappeared from sight.

"Stop worrying. Everybody uses this wood as a shortcut from the bus-stop otherwise they'd have to walk right round it. Look, there's the house, right there on the corner."

They crossed the narrow, gravel road and entered the garden through a set of ornamental, wrought iron gates. Julia came out of the garage underneath the house hauling a large tea chest.

"I'm packing up the last of our things. Mostly books and bits and pieces of china I bought out here," she puffed.

"Here, let me help you," Peter offered lifting the heavy trunk onto his shoulder.

"We must be careful what we say. Frau Hirtzell, the owner, is inspecting the basement apartment after the last tenant left. She's a good old stick but a bit nosey. If she sees you she's bound to ask who you are. I've told her that you're visiting me before I go back to the States. Fortunately, the people who own the house next door only use it as a summer house. They own a big hotel in Heidelburg so they don't come here very often."

Julia looked from Peter to Eleanor.

"Everything is ready for our departure. Paul's gone to the embassy to attend to some last minute business. We'll take Johann and join him later this afternoon for the party. Here, give him to me," she said gently taking the baby from her sister.

Eleanor stiffened as Johann started to grizzle and squirm in her sister's arms.

"He has to get used to Julia," Peter intervened, "otherwise he'll cry every time she picks him up. We don't want the border patrol to become suspicious, do we?"

Eleanor's eyes were dark pools of misery as she watched Julia gently rocking him, murmuring endearments into his blond fuzz of hair. At that moment she hated Peter. She wanted to beat him with her fists, claw at his face and eyes, draw blood. Break his heart into a thousand pieces, crushing him as he was crushing her soul. Peter reached out to her as a convulsive sob caught in her throat.

"I know schatz, I know."

For a few minutes he held her close then said brusquely,

"It's time for me to go now. Write to me from Geneva."

He bent down, kissed his son then walked briskly out of the house not even glancing over his shoulder. When he reached the gate he looked back, his face lit with a boyish smile, but his anguished eyes were dark and liquid with unshed tears.

Just before five-thirty in the afternoon Julia struggled into the taxi and settled down with the baby on her lap.

"Pariser Platz – American Embassy," Eleanor instructed the driver.

In total silence they stared ahead, each engrossed in their own thoughts, until they reached the city centre. Trams, packed with tired workers, hummed along their human cargo clinging to the handrails or hanging from the steps. Pavements milled with people wrapped up against the damp, autumn air.

As they sped down Unter den Linden the roof of the embassy loomed into view at the right of Brandenburg Gate. At the entrance the security guard stopped them and looked into the car. Recognising Julia he bent down to the open window as she proffered her security clearance.

"Good afternoon ma'am and congratulations," he beamed. "He sure does look a handsome little guy."

Instinctively, Eleanor was about to respond when she felt Julia's hand on her arm.

"Thank you Corporal," she smiled as he waved them in.

Paul was chatting animatedly to a group of embassy staff. The typical new father boasting about his son.

"And here's the boy now!" he exclaimed leaving the group to join Eleanor and Julia.

"His name's been added to my passport," he muttered in a subdued voice. "We're all set for Thursday. Come on, let's do the rounds with the baby."

Smiling broadly he took him from Julia and announced proudly,

"Let me introduce you to my son, John Paul."

CHAPTER THREE

Black clouds loomed in a heavy grey sky, threatening more rain, as Paul drove over Glienicke Bridge towards Potsdam. Eventually, they left the urban city sprawl behind. Once they reached the open road they headed towards Magdeburg where they planned to stay overnight.

"Tomorrow morning we'll catch a train to Heidelberg. It's important that we look like a normal group visiting friends on our way to Switzerland," Paul warned. "From there we'll hit the road again and cross the border into Switzerland near Schaffhausen."

"There seem to be a lot of military trucks heading the same way," Julia observed casually.

"Bloody hell, there's a roadblock ahead!" Paul exclaimed craning his neck to look round the truck in front of them. "There's something funny going on. I don't like this one bit. I'm going to turn off and detour around it before they spot us."

He swung the wheel sharply to the right onto a narrow side road that led across farm land and woods.

"It'll be all right. I've used this road before. We should exit back onto the main drag about five kilometres ahead."

Streaks of lightning illuminated the dark sky heralding distant, rumbling thunder. Rain splattered the windscreen, slowly at first, then faster and faster, louder and louder. Hammering at the car like an angry mob beating with their fists. It streamed down the windows eradicating the view from the rear of the car. The windscreen wipers swished rhythmically sending water gushing out over the sides of the vehicle. Branches of trees, lashed by a moaning wind, swept towards the sodden ground.

"I can barely make out the road. It's even worse now," Paul muttered as he switched the headlamps full-on revealing a glistening curtain of cascading rain. Dipping the lights he peered through the dense rain that obliterated the road ahead.

"Maybe we should stop until it clears up a bit?" Julia shouted over the clamour.

"No, we have to keep going otherwise we won't get to Magdeberg before dark. We're less likely to look suspicious if we catch the train during the daytime," Paul yelled over his shoulder.

Lightning forked across the sky momentarily illuminating the interior of the vehicle. Their faces looked stark and ghostly in the bleak light. Suddenly, an explosion of thunder rocked the car in a crescendo of loud bangs. Startled, the baby jumped from sleep and started to wail.

"Hush now little one," Julia soothed rocking him gently.

Fighting the shawl wrapped tightly around him he bawled, holding his breath until they thought he would never breathe again.

"Give him to me!" Eleanor ordered.

"But Peter said…"

"I know what Peter said, but if he won't stop crying I have no choice," Eleanor shot back as she gathered the baby up in her arms.

His little body shuddered as he snuggled against his mother. The sobs gradually subsided to an intermittent whimper until he fell asleep.

They jerked and bumped over the uneven road and potholes now filled with muddy water. Every time the car hit a deep hole Paul struggled to keep a grip on the steering wheel to prevent it veering into the flooded ditch at the side of the road. Still he drove on. His face was taut with the strain of controlling the vehicle in such hazardous conditions.

"We've lost a bit of time, but we'll be okay as long as we keep going, even at this speed," he said optimistically.

Eleanor rubbed at the window and peered out into the murky gloom. It had stopped raining, but there was a moist, grey haze in the air that hung low in the woods all round them.

"Another couple of hours and it will be dark," she muttered feeling a stab of anxiety in her chest.

"Don't worry, everything will be fine," Paul assured her as he caught sight of her face in the driving mirror.

They travelled on in silence nervously glancing behind them in case they were being followed. Ahead, tendrils of thick mist trailed across the road impeding their progress. Suddenly, Paul slowed down to a crawl as they rounded a sloping, zigzag bend leading on to a straight stretch of road.

"What the hell's going on?" he muttered between clenched teeth as he clamped his foot on the brake. Quickly, he let the car slip backwards out of sight into a rutted, muddy track that led deep into the darkness of the dripping forest. Dense foliage overhead, along with an outcrop of jutting rock hanging over the road, afforded some camouflage.

About two hundred metres ahead a cluster of military vehicles, slewed haphazardly across the road, prevented anything from getting through. Soldiers, armed with machine guns, huddled either side of a makeshift barrier. An officer marched over to check the occupants of a car pulled onto the grass verge. Paul chewed on his bottom lip.

"They must be looking for *someone*. It's not usual to have a checkpoint this far out from the city on a little used road like this."

"They're looking for us!" Eleanor exclaimed in a panic stricken tone.

"They can't be. Nobody knows about us leaving Berlin today. How could they?" Paul asked.

"I don't know but…" Eleanor stopped short bringing her hand up to her mouth.

"Oh my God, it's him!"

Julia and Paul followed her gaze as she pointed down the road towards a figure in a black, ankle-length, leather coat. His collar was pulled up, partially concealing his face, but she had recognised him in a heartbeat.

"Fleischer, Fleischer the Gestapo agent! A few months ago Peter was arrested and taken down to Prinz Albrecht Strasse. He asked him a lot of questions then let him go. I saw him in the street when they came for the Goldmanns. A few days ago I caught him watching the apartment from the building opposite. I'm convinced he wanted me to see him."

"Arrested, but why?" Julia looked horrified.

"He went out without his papers on him a few months ago."

Paul was staring ahead a set, grim look on his face.

"We've only got two options. We go ahead and try to brazen it out at the checkpoint or we turn round and backtrack. We could find somewhere isolated, sleep in the car overnight and try again tomorrow. With any luck they'll think we've travelled in a different direction and move on."

"They'll do everything they can to stop us taking Johann out of Germany. He may be half American by blood, but he's German born with a German father," Eleanor cried stating the obvious. "If we're caught they'll charge us with attempting to abduct a German national. We can't risk it. Fleischer will recognise me."

"Eleanor's right," Paul sighed. "She could get past the guards, but not Fleischer. Someone may have tipped him off, but I can't see how. Only the four of us knew."

"I found out a few days ago that Peter is mixed up in something subversive. Some kind of underground organisation helping Jews escape."

"The Gestapo have probably been watching him for months. No wonder he was so anxious to get you both out of Berlin. He must have known the risk he was taking. Well, we'll *have* to turn back now and try another route!" Paul growled angrily.

Quietly, he nudged the car back onto the road nosing in the opposite direction. He felt the tyres slipping and sliding on the wet ground. Suddenly, it lurched sideways as the rear, left-hand wheel dropped into a water-filled rut. Paul cursed willing the vehicle to move, but it wouldn't budge.

"Come on, come on!" he urged pumping the accelerator.

The engine screamed as wheels fought to grip the sodden earth. From the checkpoint muffled orders barked in guttural German; the thud of feet as soldiers charged up the road. Miraculously, the wheels caught in a flurry of churning mud and undergrowth. Paul struggled to keep control as they shot forward and careered back along the road.

"Hang on, this could be a bumpy ride!"

"Halt! Halt!"

The chatter of machine gun fire peppered the air echoing all around them. Behind them slamming doors, the clunk of gears hurriedly engaged, engines screaming in protest as vehicles hurtled after them.

Paul yelled over his shoulder,

"Keep your heads down. Get down on the floor."

Terrified, Eleanor and Julia crouched down shielding the baby between them. Lurching from side to side they sped down the road. Frantically, Paul drove ahead at breakneck speed his eyes constantly flicking towards the driving mirror.

"I think we're losing them!" he shouted over his shoulder. "There's no way they can keep up with this beauty. Okay, you can get up now."

Breathing a heavy sigh of relief the women settled themselves in the rear. The baby, wakened by the bumpy movement, let out a wail.

"He'll have to be fed soon or he won't settle down. How can I heat his milk?"

If only she had been able to breast-feed him like other mothers, but her milk had been inadequate.

"Have you got anything at all?" Julia queried.

"Only what's left of his last bottle and that's only just tepid."

"Well, you'll have to try him with it."

Johann moved his head from side to side as Eleanor attempted to push the teat into his mouth.

"Thank God," she murmured as he started to suck.

For thirty minutes they drove back down the road expecting at any moment to hear the sound of vehicles behind them.

"What are we going to do?" Julia asked anxiously.

"They won't have given up, you can bet your life on that!" Paul exclaimed. "It's more likely they've radioed ahead and set up more road blocks. We can't go back, but we can't go on much further either."

"There was a farm a couple of miles down the road. Perhaps they'd put us up for the night, especially when they see Johann. We could say there's a glitch with the car," Eleanor interjected.

"We can't take that chance. If you're right about Fleischer they'll have patrols out searching for us already."

Suddenly, the crack of gunfire echoed somewhere behind them accompanied by the muffled roar of an engine. Startled, Paul pushed his foot hard on the accelerator almost willing the car to move faster. Both women peered through the rear window straining their eyes for any hint of movement. Rain lashed from a black sky that had closed over the tops of the trees like a canopy of pitch.

"They must be right behind us!" Paul bellowed over the shriek of the engine. "I can see a light."

Julia's head snapped around. She could just make out the single beam of a headlamp.

"It's a motorcycle coming up very fast!" she cried.

They kept going as the vehicle gained ground until it was alongside them. The rider flashed his lights signalling for them to pull in, but Paul kept going. The motorcycle roared past skidding to a stop about thirty metres in front of them. The driver dismounted waving his arms for them to stop.

"We'll have to stop," Paul muttered in a resigned voice.

The car slewed to a halt almost careering into the ditch. They sat staring ahead while the rider dismounted and came round to the driver's side. All they could see was his featureless, white face masked by goggles, the lower half covered by the collar of his grey greatcoat. Paul rolled down the window as the figure lifted his goggles and bent down to look inside the car.

"Peter!" he gasped.

"Eleanor, are you all right?"

Peter peered anxiously at the baby who was now sleeping peacefully.

"Yes, but how…what are you doing here?"

"There's no time for explanations now. Paul, follow me!"

Peter gunned the motorcycle and pulled away. Occasionally, he glanced quickly over his shoulder to see if they were still following behind.

"Don't worry buddy we're right behind you," Paul muttered struggling to keep the car out of the muddy ruts created by trucks and farm vehicles.

Ahead of them Peter bumped down the uneven road slewing from side to side. Suddenly, he gestured for them to slow down.

"You'll be diverting onto a narrow track through the woods about five hundred metres down the road on your left. Drive *in* the ruts as best you can, especially when you turn off. There are so many tracks with any luck they'll think you've gone straight on. Keep driving until you see the track fan out four ways. Take the right fork until you're deeper in the woods and wait there for me. I'm going on ahead for a half kilometre or so."

"But…," Eleanor's words were drowned in the roar of the engine as he accelerated away from them.

Peter waved his hand as he passed the turn-off. He gestured for them to pull off the road then gunned ahead slithering from side to side as wheels hit mud.

"It's so murky I can barely see the track," Paul complained as he forged further into the forest. "I'll have to keep the headlamps off until we're in a bit deeper in case they're seen from the road."

The swish of the windscreen wipers momentarily gave them a glimpse of their surroundings. Dark, forbidding trees, heavy with rain, loomed over them. Set in motion by a moaning wind they discharged their burden over the car where it flowed in fast rivulets down the windscreen obliterating visibility.

"This place gives me the creeps," Julia shuddered pulling her coat tightly around her shoulders.

"Hell and damnation!" Paul exclaimed as they dropped into a pot-hole.

Pressing his foot on the accelerator he urged the vehicle forward, but it refused to budge.

"The back wheels are sliding on the mud," he yelled over the cacophony of hammering rain and wind. "I'll have to put something under them to get a grip."

Hurriedly, he dragged some broken branches, pushed them in front of the back wheels and into the pot-hole.

"Julia, get behind the wheel and drive forward very slowly. Gently does it, gently now. Don't push your foot down!" he shouted as the wheels spun and failed to grip. "Eleanor, you'll have to get out and help."

Grunting with the effort they managed to push the car forward a few centimetres before it dropped back into the hole again.

"Keep pushing!" Paul panted.

Feet slipping and sliding in the mud he pressed his back against the boot. Suddenly, the car lurched forward as tyres clutched the branches. Arms and legs flailing wildly he fell backwards into the mud. Overcoat soaked, heavy with filthy water, he pulled himself upright and staggered to the front of the car.

"There doesn't seem to be any damage. Julia, get in the back," he ordered squeezing into the driver's seat.

"Are *you* all right?" Eleanor asked anxiously.

"Except for a soaking wet backside I'm fine," he grinned pointing down the track at a four-way fork in the clearing.

Three kilometres further up the road Peter thought,

"They must be there by now."

He pulled into the side of the road and waited. After ten minutes he heard the muted sound of an engine grinding its way towards him.

"Danke Gott!" he breathed.

The first truck came into sight, the beam of its headlamps penetrating the blackness.

"Halt! Halt!"

Waving his arms about Peter stood in the middle of the road bathed in the glare from his motorcycle headlight.

The convoy of three trucks and a military car lurched to a halt. A black-clad figure stepped from the car into the driving rain. Suddenly, he toppled to one side dropping awkwardly into a deep pot-hole filled with filthy water. Enraged at his loss of dignity he screamed at the soldiers who rushed to his side to pick him up.

"Incompetent schweinhunds!" he bellowed striking the nearest soldier with the back of his leather-gloved hand.

Brushing himself down Fleischer strode towards Peter.

"Well?"

"As I came round the bend I caught sight of them ahead. I was driving so fast I skidded. My motorcycle hit a rock flinging me over the handlebars onto the road. By the time I'd picked myself up and gathered my senses they had disappeared over the crest of that slope ahead. I travelled along the rode for a few kilometres, but nothing. Vanished, just like that!"

"They cannot vanish into thin air! They must be hiding somewhere!"

"Mein Gott! She'll pay for this, the bitch!" Peter spat vehemently. "She will *not* take my son away from me."

"I can promise you that Herr Brandt," Fleischer murmured coldly as he inhaled slowly on his cigarette. "Search the area!"

he roared. "Find them and when you do bring them to Gestapo headquarters!"

"I'll search with them Herr Fleischer. I intend to find my son."

"As you wish Brandt... driver!"

The driver scurried to the car and leapt behind the wheel. Hurriedly, another soldier sprang to attention and rushed to open the rear door for Fleischer to get in.

"Back to Berlin!" he barked.

Peter watched as the car careered away into the blackness of the night.

Soldiers started to fan out in all directions, collars turned up against the weather.

"We'll never find the bastards now. I'd rather be in a bar with a stein of beer in one hand and a woman's soft breast in the other," complained a fat corporal. Wiping the lashing rain from his face he trudged through the sodden grass. "My feet are cold."

"Be quiet you fool! We don't want that gormless sergeant telling tales to Fleischer. Anyway you're too fat to be cold and too ugly to get a woman," laughed his companion harshly as they disappeared into the undergrowth.

Peter followed behind occasionally catching them up. At intervals he lagged behind waiting in the murky light before hurrying to catch up with them again. After ten minutes he was satisfied that they were far enough ahead of him. Drifting away he cursed loudly as he pretended to trip over a stone. Periodically, he stamped at the wet ground to let them know he was still behind them.

Eventually, an eerie quiet fell over the forest. Peter held his breath at the sudden sound of a twig snapping underfoot. Dropping to the ground he waited for a shout and the sound of running feet. Something wet and cold slithered over his hand. Rooted to the spot he listened as it rustled into a dry, rain-protected hole under a nearby tree.

"A snake!" he thought recoiling in horror.

He had always been terrified of snakes ever since he was a small boy. Shuddering, he remembered Abelhardt, his boyhood friend, laughingly putting a small snake on his head. It had slithered inside his collar and worked its way down to his waist. Terrified, his mother had come running from the house when she heard him screaming.

Cold sweat broke out on his forehead, dripped down his face. His heart thudded in his ears, beating faster and faster until he thought his chest would explode. He didn't dare move until he was sure he was still alone. Slowly, he counted to twenty, stood up and leaned against a tree taking in deep breaths to slow his heartbeat.

"Get a grip you fool," he chided himself. "Now is not the time to be concerned with childish fears."

Quietly, he moved forward until he was in sight of the road. It was deserted. He decided they must have gone round in a semi-circle back to the trucks and moved further along. When he jumped over the rain-filled ditch onto the road he saw the tail lights of the last truck bouncing along in the distance.

Hurriedly, he scanned the area looking for his cycle. He was relieved to find that it was still lying on the ground partially concealed by bushes and water-logged vegetation. Grunting with the effort he yanked the bike upright. He pulled on his helmet and goggles, gunned the engine and roared off in the opposite direction.

Paul stamped his feet on the car floor trying to keep his circulation going.

"Where the hell is he?" he muttered. "It's been over an hour and a half."

"It must be the Gestapo!" cried Eleanor. "Fleischer's got him! I know it!" she moaned.

Paul didn't answer. The same thought had been going through his head. He was puzzled as to why Peter had gone off in the first place.

"We'll wait another half hour. If he hasn't turned up by then we'll have to find somewhere to hole up for the night."

The sisters huddled together to keep warm, the baby snuggled up contentedly between them. Nobody spoke for the next fifteen minutes, lost in their own thoughts and fears. Suddenly, Eleanor sat up straight in her seat.

"What was that?" she asked fearfully.

"What was what? I can't hear anything," Julia said staring into the gloom outside.

"I could have sworn I heard an engine. I'm sure I did."

"Nah, you're imaging it," Paul rejoined.

He cocked his head to one side listening intently.

"Hey, wait a minute. You're right it *is* an engine!"

Suddenly, a motorcycle surged out of the trees behind them squealing to a stop.

"About time pal," laughed Paul getting out of the car. "Where the hell have you been?"

"Let's get out of here as fast as possible. We can talk later," Peter shot back.

As he rode past he smiled at Eleanor and blew her a kiss.

"Come on, they'll be waiting for us."

The rutted farm road tapered into little more than a stone-strewn path the deeper they drove into the woods. Fortunately, the car was solidly built, but Paul still had difficulty manoeuvring over the rough terrain. Occasionally, he winced when they hit a small boulder impacted in the sodden earth. Hands clamped on the steering wheel he swung hard around the obstacle.

In the back seat the sisters were flung upwards their heads hitting the cushioned roof. Eleanor clung tightly to the sleeping infant every time they dropped back heavily into their seats.

"You all right back there?"

"Yes, we're fine, but much more of this and Johann will be awake screaming his head off," Julia yelled above the noise of the engine.

Impeded by fallen debris from immense trees they inched forward. Rain hammered down on the roof of the car drowning Julia's shouts.

"I can't see a thing!" Paul yelled. "I'll have to take a chance and switch on the headlights."

They trailed his fading tail light as Peter appeared and disappeared in the gloom. Sudden patches of visibility revealed him waving them forward, like a commander at the head of a battle. Suddenly, Paul slammed on his brakes almost colliding with the back of the motorcycle.

"It's going to be rough going up that rise," Peter shouted pointing at a steep gradient barely visible between the over-hanging foliage, "but then we'll be safe!"

Engine screaming in protest, spinning wheels failing to grip they juddered ahead a few metres at a time. Sporadically, the car pitched forward as they hit patches of solid stone. A final, mighty lurch and they wobbled over the crest of the hill into a small clearing.

Lights behind the curtained windows of a large log cabin glowed dimly in the darkness. At their approach a door opened spilling light onto a dark, wet veranda that ran along the front of the building. Peter dismounted, ran up the steps and grasped both hands of the featureless figure outlined in the doorway.

Turning quickly he strode to the car, and took the baby from Eleanor. Stiffly, she climbed out stamping her feet to get the circulation moving. Julia followed wincing with pain as her leg buckled under her. She rubbed at it while she hobbled painfully towards the cabin and stepped inside.

CHAPTER FOUR

"This is Frau Helga Jung and her husband Manfred - loyal friends."

"Friends?"

"Otto is Helga's nephew."

"But I don't understand..."

"You will liebling, you will. Now you must eat and get some rest."

"Welcome," beamed Helga.

Blonde, rosy-cheeked, smooth skin devoid of any traces of make-up, she moved with an easy grace that belied the weight of her ample figure. Bright, blue eyes lit up her face creating a cluster of crinkling lines around her nose and eyes. It was difficult to tell her age as it often is with well-covered women, especially those who favoured a chignon. She could have been forty or fifty-five.

"You must be tired and hungry," she continued, "after so many hours on the road. Come, Frau Brandt give me the baby's formula and I'll make it up."

"Thank you," Eleanor replied wearily, "but please call me Eleanor."

"You can feed him first then you can eat yourself."

Minutes later Helga reappeared with the baby's bottle then busied herself with setting out a meal. The men huddled together in the far corner, conversing in low voices as they sipped beer from earthenware steins. The women stretched their legs in front of a roaring fire set in a rough stone chimney that reached the ceiling. Eleanor gently rocked the baby as he noisily sucked at his milk.

"Our meal is ready," Helga announced.

She ushered them to a large table covered with an expensive-looking, embroidered cloth laden with plain, wholesome food. Hot soup, sauerkraut, black bread, steaming potatoes and generous portions of Wienerschnitzel.

"Wunderbar!" Peter sighed dropping into a chair.

Manfred poured wine into glasses engraved with a gold crest and gold rims, incongruous in the rustic atmosphere. Filled with sparkling Riesling they caught the gleam of firelight. Hurricane lamps, hanging from rough beams, swayed slightly as a sudden draught from ill-fitting windows moaned through the gaps.

"It's beautiful," Eleanor murmured fingering the tablecloth; such delicate embroidery."

"This, the glasses and a few other trinkets were all we could bring with us when we left Berlin," Helga smiled ruefully. "The rest of our possessions were confiscated by the Gestapo."

"But why? You're German!"

"Yes and so is Manfred, but his maternal grandfather was half Jewish. As far as the Gestapo is concerned he has tainted blood. We had a good life in Berlin, a nice house near the river in Kladow. In summer we used to take our little boat, row down river to our favourite spot to picnic under an enormous weeping willow." A faraway look clouded her blue eyes. "I can still see it so vividly. Bright sunshine reflecting on the water, the sound of insects buzzing in the undergrowth, silver fish darting in the cool waters." She sighed, "Ach, those days are gone."

"How do you know Peter?"

"Manfred taught in the mathematics department at the universität. The Nazis wanted him to get involved with their weapons' design, but he refused. They hounded him night and day threatening him, accusing him of being a traitor. When his lineage was discovered they sacked him; threw us out of our house on trumped-up charges. An enemy of the Third Reich!" she sneered. "Peter remonstrated with the university authorities, but they were too afraid to stand up against the Gestapo. Besides, little by little, they were taking over the university and installing Nazi sympathisers. He was with Peter and Otto in the Opernplatz the night they burned the books."

"Enough!" Manfred said jovially rising to pour more wine. "Let's enjoy our meal and talk about the old days, ja, then we will talk of more important matters."

Ash spewed onto the hearth as Manfred threw an armful of logs onto the fire. For a few minutes the glow died before they sputtered and crackled in the grate igniting into tongues of orange flame. Shadows danced on the walls in the subdued light. Warmth licked their faces lulling their bodies into a delightful torpor. Manfred smiled at the women through the haze of a half-smoked cigar, puffing at it contentedly for a few moments before leaning back in a shabby, over-stuffed chair.

"You'll be safe here. For six months we've been hiding from the Gestapo. We have very little, as you can see," Manfred swept his arm round the room, "but we're happy, at least as happy as we can be in Hitler's Germany. Going back to Berlin is not an option for us, or for you. We had a plan to get out of the country and take you with us, but now it would be extremely risky."

Gradually, Peter and Manfred unfolded the means of their escape. It would be impossible to get over the Swiss border by road. Blockades would be set up at every conceivable access point swarming with soldiers and Gestapo checking for their escape.

"I can't believe they're going to so much trouble to find a baby," Eleanor remarked.

Manfred looked across at Peter who hung his head.

"They want Johann to get at me. When I came to the checkpoint I told Fleischer I was looking for you, trying to prevent you leaving the country with Johann. I thought it would put them off the scent for a while if they knew I was searching for you, but Fleischer knows."

"Knows what? I don't understand Peter."

Avoiding her gaze he said quietly,

"Various factions have been opposed to Hitler's regime since he took power, but they've been mostly unorganised. Some groups just petered out altogether, but there's a growing concern amongst some Germans particularly since Kristallnacht."

Peter looked at her intently watching for her reaction.

"Thousands of mentally-impaired people, including Germans, have been murdered. Euthanasia Hitler calls it, but it's mass murder of innocents who are too vulnerable to defend themselves. Ordinary Germans believe the lies he spews out. Some because they have full bellies; others are afraid so they shut their minds to it."

Peter hesitated looking to Manfred for support.

"There's an underground movement that assists people in getting out of Germany. Jews, Catholics who have openly criticised Hitler, even Germans like me whose lives are at risk," Manfred said.

"Are you telling me that you're a member of this group?" Eleanor cried turning to Peter.

"Not just a member Eleanor, one of its key members." He paused, "Our leader is a man known only as *Regis*."

Speechless, Eleanor slumped heavily on the sofa unable to take in what she had heard.

"You're tired," Peter continued. "You'll feel better after a good night's sleep."

She let him guide her into a tiny, low-ceilinged room; too low for him to stand upright. Johann was wrapped up warm, asleep in a roughly-made crib beside the bed, making faint whimpering noises as he dreamed his infant dreams. A double bed filled almost the entire space with just enough room for a small, wooden washstand. On top a bar of cheap soap and a blue and white jug, filled with water, standing in a large bowl. Fresh white towels, embroidered at both ends with the same crest Eleanor had seen on the wine glasses, were set out neatly on the bed.

"Another remnant of her life in Berlin," she thought ruefully splashing her face with cold water.

Peter laughed when she pulled on the voluminous nightgown thoughtfully provided by Helga. Making a face she quickly jumped into the soft bed. Gratefully, she let her head sink into the big, feather pillows patting the empty space beside her. Peter climbed in and took her in his arms pressing her body against his. She could feel the heat in his loins, his strong hands caressing her body as they whispered together in the dark.

"There's something else I have to tell you," he murmured against her hair, "but you must promise that you will never speak of it to anyone, not even Paul and Julia. My cousin's life would be at stake."

"Your cousin?"

"Prinz Friedrich Von Landenenberg

"Are you telling me you're royalty?" Julia asked incredulously. She leaned forward amazement written on her face.

"We're related to one of the deposed royal houses. I'm merely a count. There are many deposed nobility in Germany who would like to see the monarchy restored. They believe it would bring stability to our country and rid us of the Nazis."

"I can't believe it!"

"My real name is Peter Albert Christian von Landenenberg," Peter slurred as exhaustion overcame him.

"What?" Eleanor exclaimed sitting bolt upright, but there was no response.

Exasperated, she gazed down at his supine body as gentle snores filled the room.

Johann's wailing penetrated Eleanor's consciousness in that dreamlike state between sleep and full wakefulness. She squinted against the weak, watery sunlight flooding into the room. Disoriented by the unfamiliar surroundings, she panicked when she leaned over and found the crib empty. Throwing back the covers she was about to get out of bed when the door opened. Peter came in holding a cup of steaming coffee. Through the open door she could see Helga cradling Johann, coaxing him to take his bottle.

"Stay there and drink this before you get up," Peter ordered. "Helga is enjoying nursing Johann."

Purposefully, he turned and walked from the room before she could respond.

Eleanor finished the last dregs of her coffee, anxious to relieve Helga of duties she was obviously enjoying.

"Take him," Helga said, "I have breakfast ready for you."

"Where are the others?"

"Julia is outside in the shed. We've rigged up a makeshift shower. It's just a bucket of water. If you pull the string it will pour over you; just enough for a good, overall wash and rinse. Not much hot water I'm afraid, but another kettle full should take off the chill. The men are discussing the plans they made last night," she continued inclining her head towards the veranda where the men were sitting on the steps sipping coffee from large mugs.

Manfred was talking animatedly as he scratched a rough map in the dirt with a stick.

"Obviously Switzerland is the logical means for us, but leaving Germany via the normal roads is not an option. The Gestapo will have alerted every border patrol and probably brought some of them in closer. It's impossible! The only way is through the Swiss Alps. We have to hide up here for a few more weeks. By then it will be December. Conditions in the mountains will be far too treacherous for the women. We could only get so far up." He shrugged his shoulders. "*If* we could reach one of the gummi huts we could stay there until the snows melt in the spring. Not even the Gestapo would venture that far up the mountains in winter."

"It's a possibility, but we'd need adequate provisions to see us through the winter months," Paul interjected, "and a good guide."

"Provisions are not a problem. A team of men, working in relays, could get enough up there. Besides, the huts are usually stocked with some tinned food and basic necessities for stranded climbers. Obviously, there's plenty of wood for fuel.

The main problem is getting to the Alps without being detected. They know we'll try to get over the border through the mountains if the roads are blockaded. A man on his own would have a chance, but women and a baby..."

"There *is* another way," Peter broke in quietly. "We could get them out by sea."

"By sea?" Manfred laughed. "That's impossible!"

"Think about it. It's the last place they would think of, isn't it?"

"Yes, because the idea is ridiculous. We would have to get into France, Belgium or the Netherlands, all of them crawling with Germans. What do you suggest – Hamburg?" Manfred laughed.

"Not Hamburg – Warnemünde."

"Warnemünde! Are you insane? The Heinkel aircraft factory is there. There's some secret research going on in Peenemünde as well. There'll be SS and Gestapo all over the place."

"But it's still a seaside resort. Lots of families go there, even in winter, walking their dogs on the beach. Some people even sail during the holiday period."

"No, I agree with Manfred. It's madness!" Paul cried incredulously.

"Just listen for a few minutes. You and Julia are Americans. Currently, there are no restrictions on your movements. The Nazis don't know yet that you're involved in trying to get Johann out of Germany."

"But they know we're together."

"All they know is that Eleanor is with a group of people trying to leave the country; that you also left Berlin heading for Switzerland before returning to the United States. We can get you back to the city into the American embassy. Spread the story that Julia was still too weak to travel across country – that it was a mistake. You'll stay in the embassy with the baby until we contact you. Eleanor will stay here with Manfred and Helga.

I'll return to our apartment furious that she's disappeared with Johann"

"Fleischer will be suspicious. He already knows you're involved with something subversive."

"At the moment he has no concrete proof of my involvement with the organisation. It's all supposition. Don't forget he thinks I'm a distraught father in search of his son. I'll cooperate with him as much as I can to put him off the scent."

"Then what?"

"You'll stay in the embassy until just before Christmas then travel to Warnemünde under the pretext that the sea air will help Julia to recuperate."

"It'll be crawling with Nazis from Berlin taking their families there for the holidays. What if we're recognised?" Paul snorted.

"An American on leave – you'll mingle amongst them and participate in the celebrations."

"It's crazy!" Paul snapped. "I can't put Julia at risk like that!"

"When most of the holiday-makers leave you'll stay on for a few more days taking the air. That's when we make our move."

"But what about Eleanor and us?" Manfred interjected.

"It's easier for you to get to the coast alone. Eleanor and Helga will travel together. They're not looking for two lonely women, a widow and her sister, in search of company over the holidays. They're both blonde, blue-eyed and could easily be mistaken for sisters. Eleanor speaks fluent German so that's not a problem."

"I still say it's too dangerous!" Paul cut in.

"Think about it. The Gestapo will be searching the roads to Switzerland. Why would they search the coast?"

"I suppose you have a point," Manfred murmured.

"Naturally, they'll stay in a different hotel; something more modest, befitting two working women from a small town. Manfred, you'll have to hide out in one of the outlying villages with one of our group until we can transport you to Warnemünde."

"You'll never get them across the English Channel," Paul retorted.

"We won't be going over the channel. We'll be heading for Sweden."

"Sweden – we'll have to go up the coast and into the Baltic! There'll be German ships swarming all over the place!"

"Besides, we'd never get a boat to take us," Manfred cut in.

"Remember Nils."

Manfred glanced quickly at Peter, a glimmer of comprehension flashing across his face.

"I understand now, my friend. Extremely dangerous, but it might work."

"Understand what?" cried Eleanor who had just appeared on the veranda.

"Leave the details to us," Peter replied. "Just be ready when it's time for you to leave here."

"But the baby. I must be with Johann."

"No schatz, it's not possible. Johann must go with Julia to the embassy. How can she turn up without him? He's supposed to be her child, remember?"

"But…"

"There's no other choice. They must get ready to leave immediately," Peter said firmly.

She nodded, eyes bright with tears.

CHAPTER FIVE

Eleanor held Johann to her stroking his head while he snuffled against her breast. Reluctantly, she handed the squirming infant over to Julia who was already sitting in the rear of the car.

"Don't worry my dear, I'll look after him as though he were my own child. I love him too you know."

Julia didn't look back at the abject figure staring after them. Gradually, the car dropped down the slope into the forest below then disappeared from sight.

For hours they bumped along rough country roads until they were able to access the autobahn into Berlin, at any moment expecting to be stopped and questioned.

"We'll go straight to the embassy. It'll be safer there than going back to the house in Glienicke," Paul said as they traversed the Unter den Linden.

It was thronged with people enjoying a brief spell of sunshine. Just as they were about to exit the avenue he glimpsed a flash of black moving through the crowds to the edge of the pavement.

"My God, it's him, Fleischer! No, don't turn around; just look straight ahead. We don't want to look suspicious."

Paul breathed a sigh of relief as they drove up to the gates of the embassy. A soldier, with a bristling crew cut, stepped forward leaning towards the window.

"Your identification sir?"

"Of course," Paul pulled out his pass.

"Thank you Mr. Conrad, sir," he said as he waved them through the gates.

At the corner of the building opposite a solitary figure, in a black, leather coat, stared after them a look of pure hatred in his eyes.

"Paul, you son of a gun!" a voice called as a tall, rangy man emerged from the building. "What on earth are you doing here? I thought you'd left for Switzerland?"

"We had, but we've had to come back. Julia's had a few problems since John Paul was born. The travelling was too much for her. Besides he was fractious most of the time. We couldn't get him to settle. He grizzled most of the way."

Julia, face waxen, smiled wanly at Emmett Johnson, a senior diplomat who had been at the embassy when they first arrived in Berlin. He and his wife, Kate, had become good friends over the years.

"It was too soon to take on a long journey by road," he remarked solicitously. "Take it from me son she needs time to get over it. Kate was just the same after our first girl, but the three boys just came, one after the other, and she simply thrived on it."

"With any luck we'll be able to stay in the embassy for a couple of months. As you know I had the option of staying on until next spring before going back Stateside."

"Well, they haven't got a replacement for you yet. I'll square it with the 'man upstairs'. Don't worry, it'll be all sorted by the time the new Chargé d' Affaires arrives in post."

"Thanks Emmett."

"Now young lady, let's get you inside. You look as if you need some hot coffee. It'll put some colour back into your cheeks."

The men talking animatedly on the veranda could have been two friends discussing their favourite sport. Intermittently, shoulders shrugged, hands turned palms up silently questioning the other, perplexity turning to smiles of understanding. Their voices rose and fell sometimes rising to a crescendo of disagreement.

"It's the only way Manfred," Peter insisted. "Nils can be trusted. He despises the Nazis after the way his young brother, Olaf, was treated when they invaded Norway. According to eye witnesses he was beaten then dragged like a dog through the streets for speaking out against the Reich. Nils hasn't heard a word from him since. Several of his Norwegian friends have tried to find out and get word to him, but the boy seems to have disappeared from the face of the earth."

"I still think it's too risky. We'll be blown out of the water if we're spotted. The whole area is under heavy surveillance, because of the Heinkel factory. There's been a lot of testing going on there lately; experimental aircraft and other things," Manfred argued.

"That's why they're unlikely to be looking there. Another yacht won't attract too much attention. Even some Nazi officers have boats there. People sail close in to the shore in winter when the weather is fine. The problem is we'll have to wait for a good day: sunny with a stiff breeze, enough to get them out on the water."

"But what about us; what about the baby in those conditions?" Paul queried.

"Do you think I'm not aware of the danger to my son?" Peter growled. "You're an experienced yachtsman. You've been on the sea in all weathers. All you have to do is sail up the coast until darkness falls."

"Easier said than done buddy."

"Eleanor and Helga will be taken out to sea by a member of the organisation," Peter continued ignoring the remark. "Manfred, you'll be picked up somewhere along the coast near Rostock. Getting to Stockholm by sea isn't an option. If there's a very severe winter it may be frozen over that far north. Nils will be ready to pick you up in his fishing boat to take you across the Baltic to Malmö in Sweden. Our people are already there. They'll take you safely across land to Stockholm where you'll stay until the spring. You and Helga will be given refuge there. As Americans Paul and Julia will be able to move freely until they're ready to leave. Subsequently, they will be flown out from Stockholm to London."

"What happens when Paul and Julia are missed?"

"Once Nils gets you on board Paul will scuttle the boat. After an initial search they'll assume you ran into trouble and the boat went down. Eventually, some of the wreckage will be washed up along shore. The Nazis won't waste much time worrying about American lives."

"You seem to have got it all worked out."

"I had to have an alternative plan to get them out, just in case. This is your opportunity to get out too. To live without hiding, miles from anywhere, in constant fear of discovery. You must think of Helga. Sooner or later the Nazis would track you down here. You know that. Come, let's talk with the women and make our preparations."

The man in the black, leather top coat stood silently watching the happy couple wheeling their baby down to the gates and out into the street. His gaze followed them as they entered the Unter den Linden and strolled towards the Tiergarten. A small dog, released from its lead, ran up and yapped at his legs. It jumped up excitedly trying to lick his hand, drawing attention to him. Viciously, he kicked the animal sending it howling back to its owner.

"What is it? What's wrong?"

Fleischer stared wordlessly, the look in his eyes filling the elderly woman with fear as she scooped up her pet. Bowing her head she shuffled past the sneering Gestapo officer holding the whimpering dog tightly in her arms. She did not look back until she reached the corner then hurriedly disappeared from sight as Fleischer ran towards the main thoroughfare.

The Tiergarten was full of strollers with babies in prams, elderly couples walking arm in arm, young people hand in hand. Children chased each other, dodging in and out of walkers, mothers chattering and laughing at their antics.

"Such a beautiful day," Julia commented forlornly. "Everything seems so unreal, as if it were all a dream. Poor Eleanor. It will be all right won't it Paul?"

"Peter will get word to us as soon as he has everything in place."

"But how will we get out of Berlin now?"

"We'll get out. Don't worry, Peter has a very detailed plan. For the time being we're safe in the embassy. Nobody suspects anything other than that Johann is our son; that we returned because you were too sick to travel."

The sleeping baby stirred, let out a whimper then opened his eyes screwing them up against the harsh, white autumn sunlight.

"It'll be time for his feed soon. Let's stop and have a hot drink while I give him his bottle."

Lulled by the unseasonable warmth, the normality of people chatting at adjoining tables, they settled down with their coffees and warm apple strudel. Hands behind his head, Paul leaned back tipping his chair off its front legs to rest against the wall. The baby noisily slurped his milk making sudden cries as he lost the teat and found it again. Through half-closed eyes Paul followed the progress of two little boys running round and round the trunk of a big tree. Startled, he sat bolt upright almost losing his balance until the chair found firm ground.

"It can't be..." he murmured.

"What did you say? What is it? What's wrong?" Julia demanded catching sight of his ashen face.

"Over by that tree. It's him again, Fleischer!"

"Oh, my God, he must be following us!"

"He could be out for a stroll just like everyone else. Still, I must admit it seems to be more than a coincidence. Just stay calm and don't show that we've seen him. We'll walk right past him laughing, showing how much we're enjoying the day."

Paul struggled with the pram as he pushed it past tables and chairs, mingling with the throng of walkers.

"Don't look at him: smile, just keep talking to the baby."

Paul said something to Julia and they broke into laughter. A happy, contented couple enjoying their child. As they drew level with the tree Fleischer emerged and walked slowly ahead of them then stopped. He turned as they passed him smiling down at the gurgling infant. It took all Julia's strength not to scream as he lowered his face to the pram to get a better look at him."

"Guten tag. You have a beautiful baby Frau.....?"

"Conrad," Paul interjected.

"Ah, you are Americans?"

"Yes, attached to the American embassy."

Fleischer stood upright, giving a little bow as he clicked his heels together sharply.

"Enjoy the rest of your day Frau Conrad."

Abruptly, he turned on his heel, smiling his malevolent smile, and marched back the way they had come towards the entrance.

Julia clung to Paul's arm, her body trembling with fear, overcome by a sudden surge of bile into her throat.

"He knows Paul, that's why he's following us! What are we going to do?"

"Nothing. We're Americans. He can't touch us or there would be an outcry in the States. Besides, I've got diplomatic immunity. It'll be okay. We'll just sit tight until we get word from Peter to move."

"Let's get back to the embassy. I feel safer there."

Julia choked back her fear as they tried to appear nonchalant; their casual pace belying the fear plucking at their hearts. Only the metallic clang of the gates shutting out the world behind them brought a sense of relief.

CHAPTER SIX

A curl of wood smoke rose from the chimney, dissipating into the air. To a casual observer the rustic cottage lent an aura of peace and tranquillity in a troubled world. Strong winds had howled through the forest during the night sending the trees into a frenzy of thrashing movement. Dawn had delivered a calm, bright morning that lifted the spirit. Sunshine shone on the clearing; surrounding trees dripped sparkling tears of rain from branches that fell on the grass like carelessly scattered diamonds. From inside the cabin the sound of muted voices carried on the breeze. The smell of freshly brewed coffee filled the room as the women busied themselves preparing breakfast.

"We must leave the cottage the day after tomorrow if we are to get the women to my uncle's to set up a plausible background for them. One of my uncle's farm workers will take them to Warnemünde a few days before Christmas. He will remain in the area in a safe house until they've left the country. False papers have been prepared for them."

"I'm still not sure about this Peter. It's not so bad for Eleanor. She's still an American regardless of her marriage to you. She can produce her passport and papers if she's caught, but Helga….."

"It's just as dangerous for Eleanor. If she's found out they'll want to know the whereabouts of Johann. She may be an American, but she'll stand accused of trying to smuggle out a German born child. No Manfred, this is the only way," Peter said firmly.

"Are we to leave everything!" Helga cried. "My beautiful table linen, my glasses; they are family heirlooms! I risked my life to get them out of Berlin!"

"I'll take what I can and hide it at my uncle's place, but only your most treasured possessions. Everything else must be destroyed along with the cottage."

"I brought very little with me, but I must keep this," Eleanor insisted caressing the white, embroidered baby shawl that she had carried Johann in when they left the hospital after his birth.

Peter took it from her gently prising her clutching fingers from around the shawl.

"I'm sorry liebling, but you can't take it with you. If you're stopped and searched how will you explain it? I'll take it with me back to Berlin and store it safely in the apartment as if you had left it behind when you fled with the baby. Nobody will question that. One day you'll wrap little Johann in it again, I promise."

"Come Eleanor, let's pack our things," Helga murmured.

Over the following two days Peter hammered home the details of his plan. The women learned as much as they could about the area where they were supposed to live, memorised their new names and family backgrounds; familiarised themselves with their fabricated working lives.

"Eleanor, your papers claim you are a graduate assistant working to fund your studies. You're doing research for a doctorate in Renaissance art at the university in Magdeburg. The Gestapo is not likely to investigate unless someone becomes suspicious of your new identity. The gallery belongs to one of our organisation. Only one other woman works there and she's also one of us. That shouldn't pose any problems for you, given your expertise in art and the time you spent helping with restoration work when you were a student."

"What about Helga?" Manfred asked.

"Helga, you worked as a companion and personal assistant to a retired university professor, helping to collate and record artefacts collected on his many expeditions before the war. He knew he was dying and made you promise to finish the last chapter of his book if he died, using his notes. You remained in the house after his death to fulfil that obligation. His house is situated in a rather remote spot so it's unlikely that his assistants would have been seen. Even his food supplies were delivered by van. He didn't like interruptions and rarely had visitors except for my uncle who is dealing with his estate."

"But surely, they will be able to trace his name through university records."

"It's all been arranged with my uncle whose archaeologist friend died a couple of months ago."

"So, you're using his real name?"

"Yes. He had no family. He was a sick man, very temperamental, so difficult to work for that his assistants came and left on a regular basis. Some had had enough after a few days, packed up and left."

"*Das is gut* Helga." Manfred nodded. You have enough experience from your days working in the museum archives to carry it off."

"Manfred, I'm afraid it will be more difficult for you. You'll have to be moved by our people, under cover of darkness," Peter observed grimly.

"You're right, of course. I will not be able to take on another identity. My photograph is on Gestapo files, because of my Jewish grandfather. That has been so since I refused to work with them on their secret military projects in Peenemünde. They have been searching for me ever since. I would have no chance in the open."

"The women must be ready to leave at midnight. We'll stay until morning to obliterate any traces of our existence here."

The women, looking strained and pale, sat just inside the door of the cottage waiting. At a quarter to twelve the sound of a vehicle straining up the steep slope to the cottage alerted them.

"He's coming!" Peter muttered urgently. "Put out the lights. Stay inside until I come to get you."

He disappeared through the door, bolted across the clearing and merged with the undergrowth. A few minutes later a dark-coloured van came ploughing through the trees. As it emerged into the clearing Peter clicked his torch rapidly on and off three times, the signal for recognition. Lit up from the beam of light gold letters, painted on the door, discreetly declared.

"*Walter Knecker – Undertaker.*"

"Am I glad to see you!" Peter said as he shook hands with Walter, a thick-set man in his early fifties, dressed in a rumpled, black suit.

"Are they ready? We must leave immediately!"

The door of the cottage opened spewing light into the clearing. Manfred, silhouetted in the doorway, was ushering the women out onto the veranda. Quickly, they descended the steps and walked towards the vehicle. Eleanor let out a choked cry as she drew near the van.

"But it's an undertaker's van like the ones they use to take bodies to the hospital mortuary."

"Get in!" Peter ordered curtly.

The women squeezed into the single passenger seat hauling their small suitcases with them. A flash of white in the back caught Eleanor's eye. She turned around gasping with horror at the mound covered by a taut, white sheet lying in the rear of the vehicle. The interior of the van spun round and round as nausea gripped her. Leaning out of the door she retched violently.

"Get a grip on yourself Eleanor. This is no time to be squeamish! Walter is risking his life to get you away from here."

"It will be all right," Helga soothed as Peter slammed the door shut.

Walter eased the van slowly forward and over the slope. The cadaver in the back slid forward as the slope steepened, its head protruding into the space between the seats, brushing Eleanor's shoulder. She covered her mouth with her hands stifling the scream that rose in her throat.

They drove for hours over rough terrain, bumping and jerking over stones and through water-filled ruts. The closeness of their huddled bodies in the restricted space was their only source of heat.

"We can't let the heat build up too much," Walter told them, "or our friend in the back will start to stink."

"It's already stinking," Helga muttered screwing up her nose in disgust. "I don't think I can stand it much longer."

"Well, it's not going to get any better for a while yet." Walter replied. "Once we hit the main road you'll have to go underneath the body. It could be even worse there."

"Underneath!" Eleanor shuddered. "What do you mean underneath?"

"There's a false bottom under the van. It will be very cramped, just thirty-five centimetres high. You'll have to lie flat on your backs, maybe for an hour or so, but you will be safe there."

At the end of the narrow country road Walter slewed the van to a stop and told them to get out.

He went round to the back of the van, dislodged the chrome bumper and pointed to a yawning, rectangular space just under the metal platform holding the corpse.

"Get in!" he ordered. "We haven't much time. It will be light in a couple of hours."

Both women recoiled at the sight of the swathed body in front of them. Drawing a huge gulp of air into her lungs Helga clambered in. There was just enough room for her to turn onto her back. She pushed her feet against the metal floor levering herself backwards until she felt her head touch the frame of the passenger area. Eleanor pushed in beside her, but the space taken up by the well-built Helga left little room for movement either side. She clawed frantically at the floor.

"It's no good. I can't get right inside."

"Try to turn over on to your back."

"I can't, it's impossible!"

"All right, slide out. You'll have to go in face up. Put your head and shoulders in as far as you can and I'll try and push you back."

Eleanor knelt down, leaned backwards and thrust her head and shoulders into the yawning, black space. Every muscle screamed in protest. She felt as though her back would break with the strain. Walter put his hand underneath the small of her back, lifted her slightly and edged her, centimetre by centimetre, into the van. When she thought she could stand no more he gave a mighty shove. Her legs left the ground as her buttocks moved onto the metal. Using her hands she pushed herself fully inside the vehicle.

Both women lay motionless, staring into the blackness, not wanting to acknowledge the nightmare above them. With just centimetres above and around them movement was impossible.

"I'm going to close up now. There are plenty of air holes in the panels at the sides. They've been designed to let in air from the grid in the roof. You must be brave for a bit longer."

Walter slammed the metal cover back into place and expertly screwed on the bumper.

Inside the compartment it was totally black and seemingly airless. Helga started to tremble, her legs banging against the metal floor. She clutched at Eleanor.

"We're being buried alive!" she screamed. "Let me out! Let me out!"

"It's all right, we have plenty of air," Eleanor soothed surprised at her own calmness. "It won't be for long."

With a stifled choke Helga muttered,

"I'm sorry. It's just that I've always had a fear of confined spaces. I'll be fine... fine."

"I know how you feel. I've always been a little afraid of the dark. My parents had to leave the landing light on and the bedroom door open or I couldn't get to sleep. Even now I can't sleep with the door closed."

They both fell silent battling their inner demons as they contemplated the journey ahead.

Above them the engine stuttered, died then burst into life. The van rolled forward very slowly, eventually gathering speed. As they trundled through the night every bump in the road was accentuated, because of their cramped position. Sweat standing out on their foreheads they gasped in horror every time the van negotiated a bend in the road and they heard the corpse sliding around. The sickly smell of putrefying flesh filled their nostrils. Eleanor gagged as bile forced its way into her throat. It trickled down from the corners of her mouth, but she was powerless to stop it. Her arms were piniomed to her sides, stiff and lifeless.

"Helga, we must move as much as we can. Try to move your head from side to side; wiggle your fingers and toes, just to keep some life in them. Try to think of something pleasant; something clean like fresh snow, spring flowers or the smell of the sea."

A few minutes later the vehicle came to a juddering halt. Above them a guttural voice ordered Walter to get out of the van.

"Where are you going in the middle of the night? Who are you with?" the soldier demanded as he leaned forward and stared through the window.

"There is no-one with me; well, not exactly."

"What do you mean? What's in the back. Open up!"

"But I am…!" Walter whined pointing feebly at the lettering on the door.

A burly sergeant lumbered towards them cursing as he stepped into a patch of mud. He shook it from his boot shouting,

"Shut up, do as I say. Open the doors, now!"

Walter walked slowly to the back of the van and fumbled with the lock, the two soldiers close at his heels. He hesitated for a few seconds.

"Get out of my way!" the sergeant screamed.

Ferociously, he shoved Walter to one side, grabbed the handle and swung open the door recoiling as the awful stink hit him full force. He took one look at the white, bloodless foot sticking out from beneath the shroud and vomited all over his boots.

"I tried to tell you Sergeant. I'm an undertaker. This poor man was found dead in an alley at the side of a bier kellar amongst all the food slops and garbage; beaten to a pulp poor soul. They stole his money, even his boots. He must have been there for quite a while, because his body was covered with maggots. I'm taking the body to the hospital mortuary for a post mortem.

"Close the door!"

The sergeant retched violently again then covered his mouth with a large, red handkerchief. "Get it out of here!"

Walter jumped into the driver's seat and slowly eased the van back on to the road.

"That'll teach you, you Nazi bastard!" he laughed his face creasing into a wide grin.

Half an hour later the van jerked to a stop throwing the women violently towards the front of the van. A sharp cry of pain as bone met metal with a sickening thud. The sound of screws being released; the clank of metal followed by curses as the front panel fell noisily to the ground. Walter peered inside.

"Are you all right?" he queried anxiously.

Silence for a few moments then a weak voice answered,

"Yes, we're all right."

"Come on, you can get out now."

Eleanor tried to move forward, but her arms and legs were stiff at her side. Suddenly, she shouted,

"Oh, my God! Helga isn't breathing!"

Walter caught hold of her ankles and pulled with all his might until her legs appeared. Gently he eased her out until he was able to lower her to the ground. She just lay there staring wide-eyed, taking in great gulps of air. Walter's face was wet with perspiration: it dripped on to his neck soaking his coat collar. His heart thumped in his chest like a devil on a bass drum. Hurriedly, he reached inside the vehicle as far as he could and pulled Helga from the waist turning her sideways to ease her from the van. She gave a little moan as her hair caught on the edge of the door.

"Danke Gott! She is alive!"

Eleanor hung onto the outside edge of the van floor and eased herself into a sitting position.

"I'm all right," she murmured rubbing at her sore body, "just see to Helga."

Walter quickly bent over Helga and massaged her arms and legs. When she finally opened her eyes he gave a low grunt of satisfaction before sinking to the ground, exhausted by his exertions.

"She'll need to rest for a while, but not too long. We can't afford to stay here. We must get on to the main highway if we are to reach the estate before dawn."

CHAPTER SEVEN

As the first glimmer of light threw its tentacles over the firmament, they pulled onto a rough road that led through dense woods. Gradually, the road surface became smoother as they gently undulated up a hill towards a pair of massive, wrought-iron gates bearing a coat of arms emblazoned with gold. Walter revved the engine and waited. From a little stone cottage, set back from the side of the gates, an old man appeared bleary-eyed from lack of sleep.

"Can't a body get any rest?" he complained.

"Open the gates Ludwig. Quickly!" Walter urged.

Ludwig leaned his full weight on the right-hand gate. Grumbling and muttering to himself he pushed it backwards until it was wide open gesturing for them to come inside. Walter waved to the old man and headed up the long drive.

Either side, mature lawns stretched out like an emerald carpet dotted here and there with shrubs still in their autumn colours. Along both sides of the drive, dying remains of flower borders struggling to maintain a hold on life; withered brown heads hanging to the ground. In the distance tall, Sequoia trees, lindens and a mighty oak shielded the approach to the house. Just visible through the foliage, set back near the perimeter, a high, grey-stone wall topped with concrete. Shards of jagged glass stuck up from the concrete like giant porcupine quills threatening to rip into soft flesh.

As they left the camouflage of trees the impressive house came into view set on a gentle elevation about four hundred metres away.

"Wow!" Eleanor exclaimed. "So this is Uncle Friedrich's pad."

"Pad?" queried Helga.

"House, home…"

"Ja, it is very impressive," Helga agreed.

From that distance it was reminiscent of English Georgian style, but as they drew nearer Italian and French architectural influences could be seen. Built from stone and brick, windows sweeping from ceiling to floor with long, wooden shutters barely visible on the inside. The drive swung round in an arc in front of the house then looped back to meet the driveway. Wide, marble steps, narrow at the top, gradually widening at the foot, flanked by intricately-carved balustrades pitted with age. At the top a massive, oak door carved with deer and other wild animals, chased by men on prancing horses wielding swords. Over the door, under crossed parchment scrolls, a gilded crown. Underneath, a fluttering banner with the words,

'In Honour We Live. With Honour We Die.'

A lake, shimmering silver in the early morning light, surrounded the building on three sides.

As they approached a light came on in an upstairs window. Seconds later golden light flooded the steps as the wide door was flung open. A rotund figure carrying a storm lantern scurried down the steps to greet them.

"Please come! Come!" he muttered urgently.

Hurriedly, they ascended the steps through the doorway into a magnificent reception hall. Rich tapestries hung from the walls between gilded mirrors and deer heads mounted on wood. Below the mirrors refectory tables holding fine porcelain vases and pastoral figurines.

They followed the little man clattering across the marble tile floor to one of the many rooms that led off from the hall. He pushed open the heavy double doors, bowed slightly, clicked his heels together and departed without another word.

A tall, grey-haired, military looking man, wearing a wine-coloured, velvet smoking jacket, beckoned them inside. He ushered them to huge leather chairs set around a blazing log fire. Smiling, he stepped forward and grasped Walter's hand.

"Welcome my dear friend. It's good to see you safe and sound."

"This is my cousin, his highness Prince Friedrich von Landenenberg," Walter indicated.

"*Your* cousin!" Eleanor exclaimed turning to the prince. "But I thought you were Peter's uncle."

"Yes, my dear. We are all of the same blood. Please, you must call me Uncle Friedrich. My wife, Princess Marie Juliana," he continued as an elegant woman entered the room from a narrow side door.

Eleanor sat down heavily in the enormous wing-backed chair her brows knitted in perplexity.

"So, you are Peter's wife?" she said turning to Eleanor with a swish of silk skirt.

"Yes, but I don't understand...!"

"We will talk later." She pulled a bell cord hanging near the fireplace. "First you must have something hot to drink and some breakfast."

Walter threw another piece of wood onto the fire. It caught the dying logs, stuttered and burst into life sending flames shooting up the chimney. Comfortably settled with another cup of coffee Eleanor luxuriated in the warmth. Friedrich sat down facing her, casually crossing his long legs.

"So you see Eleanor we, and others like us, are fighting the madman from within our ranks. We're all part of an organisation to overthrow Hitler before he destroys Europe. We tried to stop him before the war broke out, but he's too strong. He's given the German people prosperity, jobs, full stomachs; that's all they can see. He has too many of his kind around him, protecting him. But we must keep on trying."

"What part has Peter played in all this?"

"He was involved before he even met you, but our organisation is still highly covert. Nobody has ever broken ranks. That's why we did not come to your wedding. We didn't want to show any connection between us and Peter. However, the Gestapo have become suspicious of him. He's been very forthright in his criticisms of the way the Jews and others have been treated. They've been watching him for months. That's why he's so anxious for you and the baby to leave Germany."

"Why didn't he tell me? Why couldn't he trust me?"

Stunned, Eleanor sat motionless staring into the fire. She thought she knew Peter; knew his very soul. Images of their life together danced before her eyes in the flickering flames. How they had discussed their previous lives, vowing never to keep secrets from each other. Now, he had betrayed that trust her soul felt empty, bereft. Steel clamped round her heart like a vice. This was the second time he had deceived her. In that moment she hated him for not loving her enough to trust her.

Friedrich studied her carefully. Peter was adamant that she could be trusted, but could he now trust this woman; a woman who felt betrayed by the man she idolised. Disloyalty harboured such strong emotions.

"Eleanor, the more you knew the greater the danger. He was only trying to protect you."

"I know nothing!" she spat vehemently. "I don't *know* this other Peter."

"He's the same man you married, my dear; an idealist, a seeker of truth and justice. That will never change."

"How *dare* you speak to me about truth!" Eleanor's voice was shrill with hurt. "I married a university teacher, now I find out he is an aristocratic resistance fighter. No wonder he rarely spoke about his family. He said they were all dead."

"They are, my dear. His mother, his father and his young sister: killed in a motoring accident in Leipzig on their way to church. An accident that was designed to happen, but nobody could prove it. Fortunately, both Peter and his elder brother, Wilhelm, were in Switzerland with their grandmother at the time."

"Yes, I know he has a brother in the navy, on the U-boats. Peter told me his military service was deferred, because of his research at the university. That's why he isn't in the army."

"That also is true. He hates Hitler, my dear, not his country. Do you think he wouldn't spill his blood for Germany? Do you love him Eleanor?"

"Of course I do. That's why it hurts so much."

"Then you must understand that his deceit lies in love, not betrayal."

Eleanor looked hard into Friedrich's blue eyes; Peter's eyes, Johann's eyes, for any trace of duplicity. She saw only the intensity of his trust and belief in his nephew. A warmth encompassed her soul. At that moment she felt as close to Peter as though he were sitting next to her.

"It hasn't sunk in yet, but I think I understand now."

"Peter will be here in a couple of days then you can talk." He smiled at the women. "Now, you must rest after your harrowing journey. When you are refreshed I'll show you the house and gardens."

Later that afternoon they strolled through the magnificent grounds. Rather eclectic in style. A formal French garden with precisely clipped trees, tiny hedges, intersected by pink, gravel paths, stretched away from the stone, Italianate terrace. Behind the house herbs grew in profusion near a paved area containing grey-stone, age-mottled flower pots. Beyond, a small rose garden interspersed with evergreen shrubs. A riot of flowering plants, at various stages of decay, bordered a large expanse of lawn that reached outwards to the lake.

Inside the enormous conservatory, set at the side of the building, tropical plants were being tended by an ancient gardener.

"It's beautiful!" Helga exclaimed appreciatively.

"Ah, but you should have seen it in its heyday," remarked Friedrich. "Such wonderful garden parties before the war. Now, it's falling into decay. All the strong, able men are away fighting in the war."

He fell silent, lost in his memories. As they walked back to the house a figure came down the steps and hurried towards them.

Friedrich spoke quietly to his estate manager, Bruno, who had inherited the job after his father died. His family had worked for the Landenenburgs for over a hundred years. Friedrich knew he could trust him with his life. The ruddy-cheeked, stocky little man could have been a living model for a Toby jug: plump, smiling and jovial, but his eyes conveyed a shrewdness that generated respect in employer and employees alike.

"We have created plausible backgrounds for my niece and her companion. All that remains is to get them safely to Warnemünde when the time is right."

"You can rely on me your highness."

"I have never doubted that," Friedrich replied grasping both Bruno's hands in his. "Like your father and grandfather you've been a most loyal friend."

"It's important that they are not seen here. They'll be safe if they stay within the confines of the house and gardens where only our people are permitted. Most of the estate workers are trustworthy, but that doesn't include thwarting the Gestapo."

"I agree, it will be difficult for the next few weeks until we get them to the coast. You'll have the details as soon as my nephew contacts me."

Bruno marched briskly down the drive, waved and disappeared through an ornamental gate that led from the formal garden to the lake.

CHAPTER EIGHT

Hundreds of kilometres away Manfred and Peter were carrying out their plans. From the shed, at the side of the cottage, Peter wheeled out his motorcycle loaded with the panniers holding Helga's few precious possessions. Carefully, he placed a small, rolled-up grey blanket over the top of one and a waterproof groundsheet over the other.

"They've searched me once already at both checkpoints," Peter said, "so they probably won't bother to look again. The same guards will be back on duty by the time we get there."

"But they'll expect you to be travelling alone."

"I've already thought about that which is why we are going on the motorbike. A mile or so before we reach the blockade I'll drop you off in the woods then double back through the trees after the check."

"That's crazy, why not just bypass the checkpoint?"

"Simple, I want it to look as if I've been searching for Eleanor the whole time; that I am returning to Berlin angry and frustrated at not finding her. That way they'll be less suspicious. Don't forget, I have to stay in the apartment for as long as possible. I have no doubt that Fleischer will be watching me even more closely now."

"I understand, but it's very risky."

"It will be dangerous whatever we do. Once you're delivered to the safe house, outside Berlin, you'll stay there until our people move you nearer Warnemünde. You'll remain hidden until it's time for you to leave the country."

Later that afternoon both men systematically placed dried grass and twigs on the floor of the cottage; on the cushions of the rustic furniture, underneath the rough curtains and on the floor under the mattresses.

"We can't afford to use petrol to start the blaze. Fleischer would spot that in an instant. Make sure that anything personal has been removed or destroyed. We don't want any evidence to point our way. The fire must look as natural as possible as if it started by accident. I'll scatter a few cigarette ends a little way from the cottage and leave a few beer bottles lying around as though somebody has been using the cottage as a hang out."

"A couple of lovers perhaps?" Manfred laughed grabbing a bottle of brandy.

He took a big gulp and offered it to Peter who shook his head.

"I must keep a clear head and so must you," he rebuked.

Manfred stopped with the bottle halfway to his mouth, took another swig then poured the rest over the sofa.

"They probably won't be fooled for long so the further away we get the better. We must start the blaze now. It will be less noticeable during the day. Only smoke will be seen from below. We'll have to hide in the woods for a few hours until dark then we'll make our move."

Peter moved around the cottage touching the grass with a lighted taper, waiting until the flames jumped into life, then ran outside to join Manfred. For a few minutes they stood and watched the flames shoot up the curtains devouring them in seconds. The fire spread rapidly across the floor, from one pile of grass to another, burning everything in its path gradually licking up the dry log walls

Satisfied the flames had taken a strong hold Peter jumped on his motorcycle. Gunning the engine he gestured for Manfred to jump on the pillion seat. Manfred's feet had barely left the ground before the motorcycle roared out of the clearing into the camouflage of the trees.

They rattled and jolted down the steep path until they reached the forest floor where the road widened slightly then forked in three directions.

"Over there!" Manfred cried, indicating the right hand path.

For almost an hour they lurched over rough terrain until they reached a dense patch of seemingly impenetrable undergrowth. Peter screeched to a halt sending earth spewing from the wheels. Manfred jumped off and pulled the bushes back as he moved deeper inside the tangle of undergrowth.

"Follow me!" he ordered urgently.

Peter slowly edged forward until he came level with an enormous oak. Manfred flapped his arms to indicate that he should stop and pointed upwards.

"Up there! I often used this tree as a lookout when we first came to the cottage. The branches are big enough to hide comfortably and you can see the road from here. We'll be all right here until dusk."

Manfred retraced his steps closing the gap in the undergrowth behind them. After camouflaging the bike they climbed the oak and settled in to wait.

Through his binoculars Peter saw billowing smoke rising from the forest. Below, an army staff car slewed to a halt closely followed by a couple of trucks.

"Damn it! There's more of them than I thought!"

Tailgates crashed down. Soldiers spilled from the rear of the trucks and stood to attention. Soundless words barked orders sending men scurrying into the trees out of sight. In the back of the staff car Peter detected a sudden movement and the merest glint of light on glass.

"Fleischer!" he muttered. "It didn't take him long! We'll stay here until they come down and move on towards the checkpoint. By that time it will be dark and we can ride on the road as long as we stay well behind them. I'll have to drive without lights until we hit the other side of the blockade."

For the next hour they watched and waited. Dusk fell rapidly turning the grey, metallic sky into a black pall that seemed to hang low over the trees. Little pin-point lights bobbed erratically; suddenly appearing and disappearing as soldiers negotiated the tortuous incline. Tail lights glowed as the last man scrambled aboard the trucks. In a blur of headlights they rumbled away closely followed by the staff car.

In the rear Fleischer clenched his fists. A pulse throbbed near his temple.

"You've thwarted me again Brandt. This time you will suffer for it," he vowed his eyes glassy with rage.

Peter was already at the bottom pulling the motorcycle out of the undergrowth. They parted the bushes ready to roll the motor cycle out onto the path. Sharp thorns scraped painfully at their hands, whipped back slashing at their faces.

"Hang on!" Peter shouted.

The motorcycle shot forward almost tipping Manfred off the pillion.

They waited twenty minutes concealed just inside the forest perimeter. When he was sure the convoy was well ahead of them Peter bounced onto the road. The cycle skidded into a water-filled rut threatening to throw them off. It took all his strength to keep them upright. The bike trembled then suddenly shot forward into the blackness of the night. Peter prayed that the moon would stay hidden behind the low-hung clouds. Kilometres ahead, in the dark interior of the staff car, Fleischer was issuing instructions to the SS officer sitting next to him.

"Strange, very strange." Fleischer bared his teeth in a rictus smile. "Why would this be lying embedded in the mud outside the cottage?" He twirled the ripped, rubber teat between his thumb and forefinger. "Brandt chasing after his wife and son, her sister coming back to Germany with a new baby... very odd. When we get back to Berlin contact Günter Knef in Switzerland. Find out all you can about Frau Conrad's sojourn there even if he has to break into the clinic to steal her records."

"Ja, Herr Fleischer."

"Schnell! Schnell! We want to get back to the city tonight, dummkopf! Drive to Brandt's apartment immediately we arrive back in Berlin."

Fleischer's smile was pure evil.

Before they hit the blockade Peter left the road to drop Manfred just inside the woods near a large outcrop of rock. Above and behind it an enormous fir that had been struck by lightning, its charred branches jutting high above the roadside.

"Stay here until I come back for you. Don't come out even if you hear a motorbike. Just wait until you see a torch flash on and off rapidly three times. Do you remember how we used to imitate a screech owl when we were kids? That's the sound I'll make. When I hear you answering me with the same call I'll pick you up."

Without another word he was gone.

Discontented, guttural shouts and the metallic clink of boots on stone reached Peter's ears before he approached the checkpoint. As he swung round a bend onto the straight two soldiers sprang into the road.

"Halt! Halt!"

Rifles levelled at him they stepped aside as a burly sergeant came forward. The same man who had challenged Walter.

"Where are you going?"

"Berlin."

"For what reason?"

Peter's stomach churned with apprehension. Icy rivulets of perspiration ran into his eyes. A rush of adrenaline surged through his chest. His hands felt hot and clammy inside his leather gloves.

"It's where I live. I have to get back tonight. Look I've been through here before. My name is Brandt – Peter Brandt. I've been searching for my wife. She's run away with my son."

"I wish my wife would run away," the sergeant smirked, "and take her old hag of a mother with her."

"She thinks she can take him back to America, the bitch!"

"I haven't seen your identification. I've only just got here."

"Another sergeant was on duty. He was complaining he was sick."

"That was old Willy. Too much beer and Schnapps in his guts. I've been sent here as his replacement. Show me your papers."

Peter opened his greatcoat, pulled out a wad of papers and thrust them at the sergeant, a note of impatience in his voice.

The sergeant affected a bored air as he circled the motorbike, eyeing the panniers that held Johann's shawl and Helga's bits and pieces. Peter held his breath. It would be all over if the shawl was discovered. As the sergeant lifted one of the straps Peter blurted,

"Look, I need to get to Berlin as quickly as possible to see Herr Fleischer of the Gestapo. You know he's looking for her too - had patrols out for days."

Fear and indecision flitted across the man's face at the mention of Fleischer. For a few seconds he hesitated before calling to a soldier operating the barrier,

"Let him through!"

Little puffs of white vapour ballooned in front of his face as Peter expelled air from his lungs. Cautiously, he moved forward using all his willpower not to gun the engine and roar forward. Muscles trembling with pent-up tension he approached the barrier. The bored-looking soldier suddenly sprang to attention.

"Heil Hitler!"

Nausea welling up from his stomach threatened to engulf Peter as he extended his arm to acknowledge the salute.

"Heil Hitler!"

Before his tail light had disappeared into the darkness the sergeant was already in the makeshift patrol box talking animatedly into the telephone.

After driving a few kilometres Peter left the road and entered the woods. Progress was slower than he had anticipated. The recent, heavy rains had left pools of water congealed with soft mud as the water dried up. Visibility was minimal.

Battling against overhanging branches he slithered precariously over slime-covered ground, negotiating the looming outlines of trees in the murky gloom. Suddenly, he hit something solid. The back wheel reared into the air throwing him onto the handlebars. Toppling sideways he landed on a protruding rock with a jarring thud.

Winded, his breath coming in short, sharp gasps, he lay face down on the soggy ground. Momentarily, he panicked because he couldn't breathe out, only inhale. Struggling to regain his composure he eased himself upright. The feeling would soon pass if he remained still and calm.

After a few minutes his breathing returned to normal. Slowly, he moved his arms and legs.

"Nothing broken Danke Gott!"

Getting to his knees he winced as pain caught at his ribcage. He pressed his hand over it to ease the discomfort. With the help of an overhanging branch he slowly pulled himself to his feet. His stomach felt as though he had been kicked by a horse, but otherwise he was all right. Furious that he had lost time he righted the motorbike and hauled himself onto the saddle. Nausea washed over him again. He leaned against a tree trunk until it subsided. His hands shook uncontrollably as waves of pain washed over him.

"Pull yourself together man!" he rebuked.

Every jolt and skid activated the dull ache into searing pain as he fought to keep the motorcycle on course. When he thought he could bear it no longer the familiar landmarks he had been looking for appeared through the slight mist that was rising from the forest floor. He came to a halt listening intently in the darkness. No guttural voices of soldiers or labouring engines; nothing but the slight moaning of the wind as it ruffled the trees

He pulled out his torch and clicked it on and off three times. Cupping his hands to his mouth he let out a muted shriek. There was no answering call. His bowels moved uncomfortably as he waited in the darkness. Suddenly, he heard it; a faint call somewhere to his right. He flashed the torch again in the direction of the sound and waited motionless.

Seconds later the bushes rustled. Suddenly, Manfred appeared at the side of the outcrop of rock.

"Jump on!" Peter ordered, "We haven't got a minute to lose. I must drop you off and get back to Berlin before Fleischer. Otto has already arranged everything. Our people will hide you in the Grünewald for a couple of days until it's safe to move you nearer the coast."

"The Grünewald!" exclaimed Manfred. "That's sheer lunacy! I'm bound to be spotted! The forest is being used to store ammunition supplies. There'll be soldiers roaming about all over the place."

"You'll be hidden underground. It won't be very pleasant, but it's the last place the Gestapo will look. First Otto will take you to Jenz' farm before daybreak. You'll hide out there until tomorrow night."

Dawn broke shimmering white over the city. Peter shut off the engine and dismounted a street away from the apartment block. He bumped the motorbike over the cobbles, careful to stay in still dark shadows, until he reached the rear of the houses. A narrow lane led to a small courtyard behind his apartment. Confident it was still too dark for him to be seen clearly he positioned the vehicle against a wall, unstrapped the panniers and slung them over his shoulder. He bent over and touched his hand to the engine cover giving a grunt of satisfaction. It had lost its heat quickly in the cold morning air.

Quickly, he adjusted the panniers and carried them up the steep, wrought-iron staircase to his door. Cautiously, he turned the lock, stepped to one side as the door swung open, waited a few seconds then peered inside. Musing over the panniers he wondered what he could do with the contents. Was it only a week ago that he and Eleanor sat talking quietly over dinner while Johann gurgled in his crib? His heart wrenched when he thought about how happy their lives had been until the war. Now he felt he would never hold them safe in his arms again.

Evidence of their absence was everywhere. In the film of dust covering the dining table and mantelpiece. The untidy pile of clothes on the big armchair; the clutter of unwashed dishes in the sink; the empty crib in the bedroom with its blue, embroidered blanket. Suddenly, Peter felt bereft as though he were grieving for a lost loved one. He sank onto a chair burying his head in his arms. Shuddering, silent sobs shook his entire frame.

"I will not lose them! I cannot lose them!"

Now he knew he dare not see Eleanor, not even in the sanctuary of his uncle's home. Shoulders slumped he contemplated his life stretching out before him. If he had no hope of ever seeing them again his life would be meaningless.

"I will not let that happen," he murmured as he surrendered to a fitful sleep.

Light pierced his closed eyes accompanied by a persistent pounding. A voice barked from somewhere at a distance. Peter shot up from the chair rubbing his eyes.

"Open up," a rasping voice shouted, "or we'll break down the door!"

Rushing into the bedroom Peter pulled back the covers, rumpled the sheets, fisted the pillow into a hollow. Hurriedly, he stripped off his clothes, flung them onto the floor and pulled on a pair of pyjama bottoms. Wrapping his dressing gown around him he hobbled barefoot to the door just as the voice ordered,

"Put your shoulders to it and break it down!"

"What is it? I'm coming! I'm coming!" Peter shouted in an angry tone.

Pulling open the heavy door he was confronted by three soldiers, rifles raised ready to smash the door in. The SS officer he had seen with Fleischer was leaning against the balustrade with a mirthless smile on his lips.

"Why didn't you answer the door immediately?" he demanded.

"I was asleep, exhausted after travelling most of the night. You can check where I was with Herr Fleischer – looking for my wife and son."

"Who do you think sent us here Brandt?" the officer replied standing aside for a black-clad figure who appeared from his vantage point at the side of the door.

"Herr Fleischer, it's good to see you," Peter said extending his hand.

Fleischer ignored the gesture. Instead he pushed past Peter and walked into the apartment.

"Where were you during the night?"

"You know where I've been ever since my wife ran off; looking for her and my son."

"Where have you been staying?"

"Staying? I haven't been staying anywhere. I've been on the road constantly trying to track them down. I've only been coming back here late at night after travelling for hours. You can check with your guards at the blockade. They stopped me early yesterday evening."

Fleischer's eyes bored into him with malevolent intent, but Peter didn't avert his eyes. His gaze remained steady but his voice registered anger.

"Am I not free to go about my business? I am a German citizen. Am I to be questioned in my own home?"

Fleischer gestured to the panniers partially concealed in a corner of the room.

"What do you have in them?"

"There's nothing in them Herr Fleischer."

"Then you won't mind if we take a look."

Peter sneered angrily, "See for yourself!"

He walked across, picked up the panniers and thrust them into Fleischer's hands.

Fleischer didn't bother to open them. Their weight and flexibility showed they were empty. Turning on his heel he marched through the door, his look telling Peter that, sooner or later, he would be back.

Peter closed the door as the last soldier went down the stairs to the next landing. He smiled to himself as he looked at Helga's gold-crested wine goblets in the glass-fronted cabinet. In the bedroom he opened the chest of drawers. Inside were Helga's embroidered tablecloth and Johann's shawl. He picked it up, held it to his face and breathed deeply. His heart contracted as the infant smell of his son filled his nostrils.

"That bastard Fleischer will never get his hands on you, my son," he vowed.

In the street below Fleischer sat in the black car staring up at the window. Intermittently, the tip of his cigarette glowed as he drew smoke into his lungs. He knew Brandt was lying and he intended to make him suffer. One slip, just one tiny mistake, and he would be ready. He luxuriated in the thought of Peter begging for mercy as the Gestapo thugs beat him to a pulp, but for now he would wait and watch.

"Back to headquarters!" he commanded. He turned to the SS officer baring his teeth in a lethal smile." Believe me, I haven't finished with Brandt yet."

CHAPTER NINE

The temptation to see Eleanor plagued Peter, but he forced himself to stay away from his uncle's. Occasionally, he walked in the Tiergarten with Paul and Julia grateful for the contact with his son. Each time he was reluctant to leave him behind amongst the crowd of promenading couples with their children. He hated playing the dutiful brother-in-law envious of their child.

He led as normal a life as possible. Every morning he went to the university, worked at his research, and straight home again. On the odd occasion he stopped off to have a beer or a Schnapps with Otto and his friends. It wasn't difficult to affect a gloomy air as they exchanged information in hushed voices.

"Manfred is in the Grünewald," Otto reported. One of the foresters is hiding him in a dug-out under his work hut until we can get him out to the coast."

"Can he be trusted?" Peter asked.

"The Nazis were responsible for the death of his grandfather, a protestant pastor who spoke out about Hitler's 'euthanasia' policy. Like so many others his murder couldn't be prove, but there's no doubt they had blood on their hands. Hermann was in university at the time. Suddenly, his grades started to deteriorate even though he knew his work merited higher marks. He wasn't thrown out, but his position became untenable. Now he has a job in the forestry department."

"Have you got a safe house?"

"Yes, on an old farm south of Rostock."

"When will you make your move?"

"Next Monday, at midnight. They're transporting wood from the forest to the coast. It will be taken by road then transferred to a goods train. Manfred will be going with it. He'll be hidden amongst the logs. They'll be stacked in such a way that he won't be visible nor will they be able to remove the cargo for search purposes. They wouldn't dare. Its movement has been ordered by the Führer himself. It couldn't have worked out better."

"Good, once he has been moved we can work on our plan for Eleanor and Helga. They must be in Warnemünde a few days before Christmas."

Manfred shivered on the coarse blanket in the damp dug-out under the floor of the work hut. His limbs ached unbearably in the cramped conditions. The smell of earth, urine and human faeces, in a covered bucket in the corner, filled his nostrils. For the first couple of days he had retched constantly. Gradually, he became used to the smell relieved only when Hermann came late at night to empty it. The hole, just six feet square, had earth walls shored up with rough logs. There was no distinction between day and night, just permanent blackness.

Muffled voices, heavy footsteps on the wooden floor above him. A labourer, using it for his coffee break, lit the stove. Manfred thought he would suffocate from the smoke seeping into the hideout. He tried to stifle his coughing by burying his head into the blanket, pressing his face into the earth floor.

A faint chink of light penetrated the gloom. Hermann's storm lantern swaying near the wood-burning stove that sat on top of the entrance to the dug-out. Suddenly, he heard his voice shouting at the labourer.

"You had a break an hour ago. Get back to your work!"

The worker clumped out throwing back a muted insult as he slammed the rickety door behind him.

Hermann hurriedly shifted the stove a few centimetres to let fresh air into the earthen cell, crouching in front of it to conceal the gap.

"Are you all right?" he called urgently.

"I think so," Manfred replied weakly. He coughed trying to clear his lungs of smoke. "It's lucky you came back when you did otherwise I would have died in here."

"Don't worry, it won't be for much longer. I'll come tonight to empty the waste then you'll have some clean air."

"Have you heard any more from Peter?"

"Your nephew, Otto, passed it down the grapevine. We go at midnight this coming Monday."

Manfred slumped against the wall of his prison grateful to be still alive, even more thankful that his ordeal in the forest was coming to an end.

Only Hermann's nocturnal visits and the distant noises of workers in the forest marked the passage of time. He couldn't read in case a light was spotted. For hours he mentally stripped down the engine of his old car and reassembled it again. Sometimes he argued a point with soundless words. He played chess visualising the layout; the moves he and his opponent would make until they reached 'checkmate'.

As the hours and days passed Manfred kept one thought in his head. Helga. Soon he would be with Helga.

"We move tonight!" Hermann whispered urgently when he came to the hut to collect some tools. Hurriedly adding, "Be ready!" as the sound of approaching voices grew louder.

After what seemed an eternity of endless night locked in darkness Manfred heard the stove being moved; scraping against the stone as it was pushed aside. Little flurries of dirt and wood shavings fell onto his face as he looked towards the sound. Not moving a muscle, not daring to breathe, he waited until he heard Hermann's voice whispering in the blackness.

"Time to go."

Legs like jelly Manfred struggled to his feet clutching at the air. Waves of weakness washed over him. For a few seconds he steadied himself against the earthen wall. Dim light flooded the hole. Strong hands reached in waiting to clasp his own. With a mighty heave Hermann hauled him up onto the hut floor where he lay gasping in the cool night air. Manfred massaged his aching limbs relishing the sensation of free, unrestricted movement.

"Can you walk?"

"Yes," he replied taking a few tentative steps.

He staggered across the clearing where a truck loomed dark against the trees, its engine ticking over. Hurriedly, Hermann pushed a few of the heavy logs to one side then instructed Manfred to climb inside to the centre of the load.

"Catch!" he called quietly, throwing a canister of water and a bundle wrapped in cloth after him. "There's enough cheese and bread to keep you going until tomorrow night."

"I'll never forget this Hermann," Manfred said his voice choked with emotion. "You have risked your life for me."

"We are all part of the same brotherhood. I know you would do the same for me."

Hermann jumped in the driver's seat, gently accelerated and pulled away towards the rough road that led out of the forest onto the main highway.

They trundled through the night stopping occasionally for Hermann to dart into the trees at the edge of the roadside to relieve himself. No such luxury for Manfred. He urinated through the small gap in the logs underneath him, the sound muffled by the engine.

Just before dawn the truck came to a halt. Hermann stood with his back to the truck pretending to urinate against a nearby tree.

"This is where you are being picked up. Karl is one of us. He will take you to the safe house just outside Rostock."

Seconds later the logs were thrust aside, one by one, until the hole was large enough for Manfred to squeeze out into the open.

"Quickly!" a voice said sharply.

Grasping hands propelled Manfred towards a vehicle camouflaged by dense foliage.

"In the back!" the voice ordered. "Behind the baskets!"

Manfred scrambled towards the back of the baker's van into an aperture between baskets full of freshly made bread. A panel was drawn across in front of it. He could hear baskets being shifted and pushed against his hiding place. He winced as his back jolted against a rivet on the metal wall of the driver's cab.

"Don't worry, we'll be there in about fifteen minutes or so," whispered Karl, "then we'll transfer you to a meat wagon that will take you to Rostock. We must be extra careful. They've been on the lookout for you for months."

Fifteen minutes later the van lurched to a halt at the end of a winding farm road that led to an abattoir. Manfred jumped out and ran towards a high-sided truck where a grizzled man, in a blood-spattered leather apron, was holding open the back doors. In the gloom of pre-dawn the nightmarish squeal of a reluctant animal being dragged into the slaughter house chilled his spine.

Inside the truck animal carcasses hung from hooks. He pushed his way through them slipping on a little pool of blood that had started to congeal on the floor. The smell of dead flesh caught in his nostrils. At the back of the truck more carcasses were stacked against the metal wall.

"Climb in behind them and we'll pile them up in front. It stinks a bit, but we should get to Rostock without much trouble. Most of the meat is going to hotels on the coast, but some of it is to feed the workers in the Heinkel factory and the military installation in Peenemünde. Consignments of meat are sent there regularly so the truck is a familiar sight," Karl explained as he pushed the last carcass into place.

"How long will it take to get to Rostock?"

"A few hours at least."

Karl slammed the doors shut and left Manfred in stinking darkness.

The truck had been rattling its way along the highway for hours. In the darkness of the interior Manfred thought about Helga and his joy at seeing her again. He prayed, as he always did in times of despair, his lips moving silently. What they were doing was extremely risky, suicidal he believed, but it was their only chance to grasp at happiness and freedom. With his mind on Helga he fell into a restless sleep. He was awakened by Karl's voice, urgent and insistent.

"Manfred!"

He stirred, rubbing at his cramped limbs. Karl pushed aside the bloody meat. Suddenly, Manfred, overcome by nausea, clamped his hand over his mouth. He struggled towards the open doors taking great gasps of fresh air into his lungs. An overpowering smell of animal dung, mixed with strong farmyard smells, hit him when he dropped from the truck to the ground. His stomach lurched into his mouth. Turning, he vomited onto a rotting compost heap. Woozily, he wiped his mouth and grinned weakly. Karl grabbed his arm to steady him.

"I'll be all right. It's just being cooped up with all that bloody meat."

"Come in," interrupted a cheerful voice from the kitchen doorway of the farmhouse. "A good meal, something hot to drink and you'll be fine."

The bare flagstones in the kitchen were softened by a bright floral tablecloth and cushions on the wooden chairs. Overhead, copper saucepans gleamed as they caught the light from the flickering flames of the fire.

Frau Sandler chattered incessantly while she loaded Manfred's plate with food and filled his mug with steaming coffee. Gratefully, he warmed his hands on the mug feeling a comfortable glow suffusing his whole body. For now he was safe, but what the next weeks held for him and Helga he dare not imagine. Hope burned like a bright candle in his soul, flickering and dying. Bursting into life again as faith uplifted his spirit sending it soaring towards the divine being.

CHAPTER TEN

Helga was sitting in the window seat of the library gazing sightlessly at the almost leafless trees on the far side of the lawn. Lush green grass had faded into its winter hue. Only the manicured shrubs, set in the ornamental garden, preserved any vestige of the greenness reminiscent of summer. She watched two crows settle onto the lawn pecking at the grass. Startled by the sound of an approaching vehicle they hip-hopped over the gravel drive before flying into the safety of a nearby tree.

Eleanor was standing on a wheeled step ladder, reaching for a leather bound volume of poetry, when Friedrich entered the room. She turned temporarily losing her balance as she heard the click of the door quietly closing behind her. Weight had fallen from her face accentuating her usually well-covered cheekbones. The slightly drawn look benefited rather than detracted from her looks, adding a distinctiveness that healthy plumpness had denied her.

"Good morning," Friedrich smiled. "I have some good news for you."

"You've heard from Peter!" Eleanor cried climbing down from the ladder.

"Yes, my dear. All is well. Peter has been living a relatively normal life not to create suspicion. He has even been able to see little Johann sometimes in the Tiergarten."

"Johann... my baby," she choked, her eyes cloudy with pain, but she held back her tears.

"What about Manfred?" Helga interjected.

"Manfred is well. He's hiding away in a safe house near Rostock."

Helga let out a sigh of relief.

"Tomorrow you must pack your things and be ready to travel to the house of my archaeologist friend," Friedrich continued. "Your 'sister' has travelled from Magdeburg to help you. A week before Christmas I will take you into the city station where you will get on a train to the coast."

"A train, but that's too dangerous!" cried Eleanor.

"Bruno will spread a rumour in the nearby village that the book you have been working on has been completed. You're going to the coast with your 'sister' for the holiday celebrations."

"But we'll be recognised!" Eleanor blurted. "They'll be watching out for us."

"It *is* a risk, but they're not looking for two German sisters. They're searching for an American with a baby and a German woman not connected to each other. Why would they suspect that you would be travelling together? They're looking for you for two totally separate reasons. In any case Berlin is the last place they would expect you to turn up. Fortunately, you were fluent in German before you came to live here. You don't even have the trace of an accent. Marie Juliana will help you to change your appearance to match the photograph in your papers."

Helga slumped back down onto the window seat. Eleanor stood motionless for a few moments. Engrossed in their own thoughts neither woman spoke as Friedrich scrutinised them intently. He wondered whether two very frightened women would be able to carry it off. Fear, anguish, desperation flitted across their faces at the thought of what they were knew they had to do. Anger fired their determination.

"Tell us what we have to do," Helga declared resolutely.

She looked at Eleanor who nodded her agreement.

"Don't worry Friedrich. We'll do what have to do."

"Good, now let's go to the drawing room. Marie Juliana is waiting for you."

Pale, wintry sun shone into the drawing room illuminating the crystal glass decanter on the highly-polished mahogany cabinet. Marie Juliana, dressed in a fine, rust, woollen suit sat in a wing-backed chair, her long legs elegantly crossed at the ankles. Her diamond ring threw off little bursts of light as she gestured for them to sit down. Beams of watery sunlight penetrated the Georgian-style windows reflecting on the gold picture frames. Dust motes swam like miniature, heavenly bodies in perpetual motion giving the room a slightly surreal air.

When they had settled themselves comfortably with some hot chocolate Marie Juliana outlined her idea.

"We need to change your appearance to match your identity papers. There's not much to be done. Helga, shall we start with you, my dear?"

"Yes, Princess Marie…"

"Please, you know I prefer you to call me Juliana. Only Friedrich calls me Marie Juliana. He just loves the sound of it tripping off his tongue," she laughed affectionately.

She rose from her chair indicating to Helga to stand up.

"Turn around please. Now, I think we should cut your hair shorter; get rid of the chignon and adopt a more modern style. Perhaps some make-up; a little mascara, some light lipstick, no rouge, your cheeks are rosy enough," she laughed patting Helga's face. "A smart suit, dark, I think. It will make you look slimmer and taller, and a hat. Nothing too expensive otherwise it would arouse suspicion. Just tasteful enough for a woman who has been working for an eminent professor. You'll need to carry a good book on archaeology and a guide to museums in the Rostock area."

"But I never wear make-up. I'll feel so self-conscious."

"Nonsense, you'll get used to it."

"Now, it's your turn Eleanor," she smiled.

Sighing gently, she realised how very fond she had become of her nephew's wife during the short time she had been staying on the estate. Both she and Friedrich had longed for children, but it was not to be. Startled, she acknowledged that she was beginning to think of Eleanor as the daughter she had never had.

"We could part your hair, comb it to one side and let it hang shoulder-length. A pair of spectacles with plain glass, an inexpensive floral skirt, cardigan and flat shoes. No make-up. You are the shy, studious younger sister struggling to fund her post-graduate university studies. Perhaps an artist's pad and a water-colour case to paint some seascapes when you are on holiday. Obviously, we'll pack a small suitcase each with any clothes necessary to cover the few days in Warnemünde."

Satisfied, she motioned for them to follow her upstairs to try out her ideas.

Helga surveyed herself in the cheval mirror, twirled this way and that giving a little gasp of surprise at the strange reflection staring back at her.

"I look so… so young!" she exclaimed.

She looked at least ten years younger with the new hairstyle, smart charcoal-grey suit, ivory-coloured blouse and black court shoes. The slight touch of lipstick and mascara gave her a more sophisticated look; generated an air of self-confidence that surprised her. She looked and felt like a different person. Giggling nervously, she twirled in front of the mirror looking appealingly at Friedrich for his approval.

"My word, you are a beauty Helga!" he exclaimed bringing a rush of excessive colour to her cheeks and neck. "Except for a slightly fuller face you are the image of the photograph on your new papers."

"Here, put this in your handbag," Marie Juliana intervened handing Helga a museum guide.

Eleanor suddenly appeared from the dressing room next door. The transformation was remarkable. Not only did she look younger, but more vulnerable and unsure of herself. She peered owlishly through the plain glass of her spectacles.

"Typical graduate student," Marie Juliana commented. "The glasses give you that slightly pre-occupied look. Someone who is immersed in academia and has no time for trivialities."

Friedrich took hold of his wife's arm and smiled down at her.

"You have done your job well, my dear, very well indeed."

CHAPTER ELEVEN

Otto looked around cautiously as he entered the small café. As usual it was crowded with people. Bankers, university professors, lawyers and those wanting to be seen in the right place at the right time. Peter was sitting in a corner with a clear view of the entrance.

"Otto, over here!" he called in a loud voice, deliberately attracting some attention from other familiar diners.

It was important for them to behave as normally as possible during the run up to Christmas.

"You're late again! I was just about to order lunch without you."

A colleague sitting at a nearby table laughed as Otto passed him.

"Late again Otto. You're impossible!" he laughed.

Peter jumped up, slapped Otto on the shoulder motioning for him to sit down. After they had drunk half of their steins of beer they placed their lunch orders with the waiter, sat back and idly surveyed the room. Nothing unusual caught their eyes. People were eating, drinking, laughing at some joke or other. Everything looked perfectly normal.

Near the window a stocky man in a grey overcoat sat reading a newspaper, totally oblivious to the activity going on around him. Occasionally, he raised his thick, shaggy eyebrows and fixed on a particular item of news. Sporadically, he turned a page folding it down in a very precise manner.

"I haven't seen him here before," remarked Otto smiling at Peter as though they were sharing an amusing thought.

"You're right, we'd better be careful. Guten tag Günter." He returned a wave from a tall, rangy man who had just entered.

Günter smiled, nodding his head in acknowledgment to Peter. Glancing around the room he walked over and sat down at the same table as the man with the newspaper. They greeted each other affably. Seeming like old friends they chatted amiably together over coffee.

The waiter appeared with a large tray stacked with luncheon orders.

"Bitte," he growled, hurriedly depositing plates of cured meat, sauerkraut and black bread in front of them followed by another small stein of beer.

"Danke," Otto replied.

The waiter moved to the next table to deal with an indignant looking woman complaining in a loud voice about how long she had waited to be served.

"I've seen Günter in here dozens of times, but I've never seen his friend. Still, I can't help feeling I've seen him before." Peter's brow puckered. "I know I've seen him and recently, but where?"

Peter pronged a piece of meat, shoved it into his mouth and took a swig of his beer. At the same time watching the man between the rim and the cover of the stein.

"Manfred has reached the safe house on the coast," Otto murmured.

"Good! I also have good news. Eleanor and Helga are in Professor Arzt' house in the country just outside Magdeburg. They'll be travelling to the coast by train, via Berlin, a few days before Christmas. They've been well briefed. All we can do now is wait and pray."

"What about Paul and Julia? Are they ready to move?"

"Yes, they're going down to Warnemünde at least a week before on the pretext that the sea air will do Julia some good. It's just as well they're not staying in the same hotel. That would be very hard for Eleanor. I worry about how she'll react if they bump into her with the baby."

"She's tougher than you think Peter. Walter Knecker told me how calm she was when they travelled in the undertaker's van from the cottage. She was more composed than Helga. She'll do what she has to do for Johann's sake."

"I hope you're right," Peter muttered, his face creased with concern.

CHAPTER TWELVE

Two women stood close together on the edge of the crowd at Magdeburg Hauptbahnhof. The elegantly dressed woman, in a dark suit, patted the arm of the frumpish, younger woman who blinked owlishly at passing travellers walking up and down the platform. Heads bent in whispered conversation their body language indicated that they were either very good friends or close relatives. The younger woman clutched an artist's folio case as though she were afraid that it would be snatched from her grasp at any moment.

As the train approached the station steam and smoke belched from the huge engine. Doors swung open along its length. People, impatient to get out, spilled from the carriages barely waiting for the train to groan to a halt.

When the last passenger had disembarked, the milling throng pushed their way into the train hurriedly searching for vacant seats.

"In here!" Helga cried as she pushed open the door to an empty compartment.

Gratefully, she sank down heaving a sigh of relief as Eleanor pulled the door closed behind her.

"I must take off these shoes. They're killing me."

A look of pure bliss washed over her face when she kicked them off rubbing at her cramped toes. Eleanor took off her spectacles, massaged the red marks either side of her nose then placed them in her lap.

"No, you must leave them on otherwise you may be recognised."

Reluctantly, Eleanor put them back on just as an elderly, ruddy-faced man pushed his way inside.

"Guten tag," he smiled affecting a shallow bow, stepped over their feet and slumped into the far corner.

With a mighty groan the train shuddered into life, its wheels screeching against the rails as it chugged out of the station. Eleanor looked across at Helga who had closed her eyes feigning sleep. It would stop their fellow passenger attempting to engage her in conversation.

She retrieved a book from her small suitcase, studiously avoiding the gaze of the man in the corner who seemed intent on starting up a conversation. Was she imagining it or was he staring at her as she pretended to read her book? She felt the hair on the back of her neck prickle and rise. A trickle of cold perspiration travelled down her back meeting the waistband of her skirt. She felt as though a steel band had encircled her chest squeezing the heart out of her. Hysteria rose like bile in her throat as she struggled not to give way to the feeling of panic that engulfed her. For forty-five minutes she kept her eyes firmly directed at her book.

The screech of wheels and a series of chugging coughs penetrated her thoughts. They were slowing down; approaching a station.

"Excuse me fraulein."

Their travelling companion had risen from his seat and was staring down at her feet. Hastily, she withdrew them smiling nervously at the man who was now grinning like a Toby jug at her discomfort. He pushed past them into the corridor. Within seconds he passed the window, nodded at them and strode off down the platform. Breathing a sigh of relief Eleanor slumped into the corner of the carriage completely exhausted from her fear.

"I'm glad he's gone," Helga muttered looking after the man. She looked at Eleanor's pasty complexion. "Are you all right?"

"Yes, yes, I'm fine."

I have to get a grip she thought otherwise I'll never make it to the coast.

For the rest of the journey Eleanor concentrated on her book. She dared not think what might have happened if the ruddy-faced man had been suspicious of them. She stiffened, her heart beating in her chest like the wings of a captive bird. They were approaching the station in Berlin.

"We have to wait thirty minutes for the train to the coast," Helga said, looking around warily at other passengers thronging the platform.

Some were standing around with bored expressions. An army officer paced back and forth impatiently looking at his watch. Porters trundled past dragging trolleys stacked with suitcases. Trains arrived and departed, at regular intervals, precisely on time. A small child clung to her mother's coat looking imploringly at her as she explained her reason for sending the child away.

"Papa and I have decided it is best for you to stay on Aunt Frieda's farm for a while. You'll love it in the country. She'll teach you to milk the cows and ride a pony."

"Real cows mutti?"

Eleanor looked away her chest tight with a sharp, maternal pang.

"Let's have a coffee while we wait; try to look as unconcerned as possible," Helga said linking arms with Eleanor.

She propelled her towards the café where a beetle-browed, stocky man sat in a grey overcoat.

"Excuse me," Eleanor apologised as she squeezed past him to a vacant table.

Briefly, he looked up at her before returning to his newspaper. There was nothing in his look to alarm Eleanor, but she experienced an inexplicable sense of foreboding especially when he strode by their compartment after boarding the train.

A freezing white mist obliterated the coastal town as they approached Warnemünde. Buildings loomed like huge ships in a fog-covered sea. They trudged towards the hotel, thin ice crackling underfoot. Thankfully, thick topcoats provided by Marie Juliana helped protect them from the cold.

"It's perishing," Eleanor complained.

"We're on the Baltic coast. It can get very cold here in winter," Helga replied.

A young lad rushed to help them with their suitcases as they entered the small foyer of the hotel. Guests were standing around sipping aperitifs waiting to go into the brightly-lit dining room. Black-clad waiters, in long white aprons, fussed with last minute touches to the tables.

After checking in they followed the boy to the room they would share. It was well-worn, but clean and comfortable. Dark, highly polished furniture, high twin beds with matching embroidered bed covers and a chest of drawers. On the dressing table a large pink-patterned jug with a bowl for washing.

"We must only unpack our essentials," Helga instructed. "We must be ready to go at a moment's notice."

Hurriedly, they splashed cold water on their faces and headed downstairs to the tantalising smells of roasted meat.

The dining room was dressed in seasonal decorations. Huge logs crackled in the grate occasionally spitting out glowing, red sparks. At the side of the stone hearth a Christmas tree sparkled in the light from the fire. Colourful baubles, painted with swastikas, hung from its branches. A photograph of the Führer replaced the tradition angel. Around the walls garlands of fir tied with red ribbons. Above the mantelpiece, dominating the room, another picture of the Führer flanked by two huge flags emblazoned with swastikas.

Eleanor shuddered involuntarily as a waiter showed them to their table. He handed each of them a menu and scurried off to serve other guests.

"The Christmas tree…"

Helga leaned over and whispered to Eleanor,

"Forget about it. Try to look as though you're enjoying yourself." She laughed gaily for the benefit of the other guests. "We're supposed to be here to enjoy the festive season."

For the rest of the meal they chatted animatedly. Two sisters bent on having a good time before escaping to their bedroom exhausted by tension.

They awoke next morning to a flurry of snowflakes hitting the window pane. The fog had lifted revealing a white sky that hung overhead like cotton wool. Beneath the window excited children were chattering, joyful to see the fat crystals falling from the heavens.

"That's all we need, snow!" Eleanor muttered vehemently. "Nobody is going to go out on the water in these conditions"

"I'm sure some arrogant, Nazi idiot will want to defy the elements," Helga retorted. "Let's go down to breakfast. Perhaps a little stroll from where we can view the harbour, get our bearings. It's only a light snowfall but wrap up warm."

"Yes, we need to familiarise ourselves with our surroundings. Later we can walk through the town. Perhaps have some hot chocolate. Just look as normal as possible."

In the lounge of their luxurious hotel Paul gazed through the window at snowflakes dancing in the wind, beating faintly against the glass before drifting slowly to the ground. Johann gurgled, eyelids drooping as Julia rocked him gently in his pram. Christmas Eve had always been a special day for Paul. Even as a child it held more excitement than Christmas Day. A greater feeling of anticipation about what the following day would bring. Now, his anticipation was tinged with fear and apprehension. His heart contracted watching his wife with the baby he had grown to love. Soon he would have to hand him over to Eleanor and leave his wife bereft.

A waiter wandered from table to table announcing discreetly,

"Spiced wine will be served shortly sir, compliments of the manager."

"Thank you…"

"May I attend to the table sir?"

After placing some used coffee cups onto a tray he bent forward to wipe the table. Casually he whispered,

"You go the day after tomorrow. Tonight, at the party, look for the man with the jewelled deer head on his stein. When he asks if you like it say it is unusual; fit for a king."

Startled, Paul stared after him while he circled the room occasionally stopping to take an order. For a few moments he sat motionless trying to gather his composure and tune in to what he had just heard.

"What is it Paul? Are you all right? You've gone quite pale."

"The waiter," he murmured. "Come on, let's get out of here so we can talk."

In their suite he told Julia about the information imparted by the waiter and the man he had described.

"We must be very careful in our approach tonight. A mistake could be fatal."

"I'll pack our things…"

"We're supposed to be here until New Year," Paul cut in. "The maid would find it odd if we packed our suitcases now. Besides we can only take one small bag, just the necessities. Just be sure to have warm clothing at hand, especially a head-covering and a warm shawl for the baby. It will be extremely cold at sea."

Shuddering at the thought, Julia busied herself with arranging clothes in the wardrobe so they would be at hand for their journey. A long, heavy coat and boots for herself and a thick, woollen shawl for the baby. At least they wouldn't look suspicious given the severity of the weather. Finally, she placed a canvas bag, decorated with reindeer, ready for Johann's baby food and diapers.

"Let's go back down now and mingle with the guests. A glass of mulled wine will lift our spirits,"

Paul smiled as he opened the door, but his eyes revealed the anxiety he felt. For a few seconds Julia held him close breathing in the smell of soap and shampoo from his freshly-washed hair. Lightly, she kissed him on the cheek and headed for the stairs.

Eleanor and Helga walked along the seafront taking in their surroundings; noting little points of interest that would serve them well when it was time for them to leave. They walked quickly now above the boiling waters, shielding their eyes against the spume blown over the sea wall by a cold, biting wind that penetrated their thick topcoats. Flurries of snow, which were settling fast, flew into their faces and mouths preventing prolonged conversation. They huddled together battling the wind that threatened to blow them sideways into the sea.

"It's so cold, let's go for a hot drink before we freeze to death," Eleanor shouted over the whine of the wind. "Besides, watching eyes will begin to wonder why we're being so reckless."

Tittering and laughing, like two defiant school girls disobeying their parents' safety precautions, they made their way back. An elderly man in a fisherman's woollen hat and jacket grinned toothlessly at them. Suddenly, he lurched towards them walking sideways as he felt the full force of the singing wind. Struggling to maintain his balance he shouted an apology almost bumping against Helga who put out an arm to steady him. Pulling his collar up tighter around his ears he leaned forward as if to thank her.

"Keep on walking!" he said urgently. "You leave with Nils the day after tomorrow. I will be in touch. Walk here tomorrow after breakfast."

He continued along the quayside staring out to sea for a few seconds with pale, watery eyes. Satisfied that they had not been seen he trailed them as they headed back towards the town.

After dinner Paul and Julia sat round the roaring log fire laughing and joking with other guests. Some were accompanying a group of children singing carols in the foyer of the hotel. Others were lost in thought remembering fathers, brothers and sons in bleak bunkers and trenches. Outside the haunting sound of a boy soprano singing '*Stille Nacht*' echoed through the room. A choir, dressed in white surplices and red cassocks, slowly walked in and stood beside the Christmas tree. A frail looking, white-haired woman grasped her husband's hand. She dabbed at her eyes, a silent, convulsive sob caught in her throat.

"Rolf…" she whispered.

"I know liebling, I know," he murmured patting her arm to comfort her.

Suddenly, the peace was shattered as an SS officer marched in stamping snow off his boots. He stood legs apart, hands on hips, a cruel smile playing on his arrogant face. Recognition dawned as he spotted a large, red-haired, jovial man with heavy jowls sitting in a corner by the fire.

"Rudi!"

"Horst! What are you doing here? I thought you were in Berlin for the festivities?"

"I was, but now I am here."

Offering no other explanation he took a drink from a scurrying waiter and leaned his elbow on the mantel. With a sweeping glance he surveyed the room, studying the faces of the guests, until his eyes rested on Paul and Julia.

"Americans!" muttered Rudi vehemently, a look of distaste on his face. "They're as bad as the British!"

Jowls shaking he struggled to his feet, stomach bulging, face ruddy from the warmth of the fire and an excess of Schnapps.

"A toast my friend," Horst laughed. "We will beat the British into submission. They are no match for brave Germans. One day we'll rule the world, ja? The Führer!"

For a split second nobody moved then the whole room was on its feet, heels clicking, arms outstretched in the Nazi salute.

"Heil Hitler!"

"Heil Hitler!" chorused Rudi holding his stein aloft.

Mesmerised, Paul watched as Rudi lifted the deer-crested stein to his lips and drank deeply.

"It's him! I'm sure of it," he whispered, barely able to contain his excitement and fear as the two men slapped each other on the back.

For the next hour they laughed and sang with the other guests. The SS officer, more than a little drunk, had slumped into a chair next to Rudi.

"Be careful Paul," Julia murmured as he pushed back his chair. Moving towards the fireplace he deliberately stopped at a few tables to exchange banter with merry-makers. When he was close enough he stared at the stein. Rudi stood up and loudly proclaimed another toast.

"You like my stein American?"

"Yes, it's very unusual, especially the eyes," Paul remarked.

Rudi gave him a penetrating glance and said loudly,

"Of course it's unusual, the eyes are real rubies," he declared sweeping the stein round the room, slopping beer over the floor.

"It's beautiful; fit for a king," Paul laughed.

Rudi looked at the SS officer. His eyes were closed, his mouth hung open, lips loose and flabby. Spittle ran down from one side of his mouth onto his chin. For a fleeting moment a look of utter contempt crossed Rudi's face then he looked at Paul.

"Fit for a king and more fit for a German!" he spat pushing past Paul to the other side of the room.

Gradually, the revellers wearily trudged upstairs to their rooms calling last minute festive greetings. Paul and Julia followed Rudi who was trailing a woman supporting her slightly tipsy husband by the arm. As they came up behind him he missed his footing on the stairs and sprawled face down. The drunken man jeered loudly as Paul helped Rudi to his feet.

"Your room, in one hour. Leave the door unlocked," he whispered.

Struggling to his feet he climbed clumsily up the stairs, growling and complaining at the man in front.

An hour later the bedroom door opened quietly. Rudi stepped swiftly inside. Paul and Julia had been sitting in the darkened room sipping the drinks they had brought up with them. Hurriedly, he closed the door holding a finger to his lips.

"Only the waiters are still downstairs," he said. "Everyone else has gone to bed including that drunken pig, Horst. Still, we must be very careful."

"I've been told we are to leave the day after tomorrow," Paul ventured, "but that's as much as I know."

"Fortunately, the snow has stopped. The weather is breaking otherwise there would be no chance of putting a boat out. If it stays fine I have no doubt the more experienced sailors will go out on the water for a couple of hours. You competed in a lot of sailing events when you were at university?"

"Before the war I sailed off Nantucket and Rhode Islands during vacations. I competed in a lot of off-shore racing in the U.S. and Britain."

"Good! Tomorrow at dinner I'll challenge you to a race. One of our people will hire you a boat. It's not unusual. I often sail close to shore in winter. You'll be reluctant, but I'll insist hinting that you are a soft American afraid to put to sea. Frau Conrad will come aboard with the baby to see you off until the others are out on the water. She must hide below deck. There will be very few people around. Most of them will stay in the comfort of their hotels to enjoy the organised activities."

"But if anyone is watching us they'll know I'm still on board," Julia cut in.

"A decoy, wearing your clothes, will be seen leaving the berth with a baby wrapped up against the cold. Nils has been bringing down a cargo of iron ore from Luleå in Sweden. By the time it's dark he'll be waiting up the coast to take you on board. I cannot stress too much how dangerous this operation will be. Everything depends on you holding your nerve."

"We'll be ready," Paul said looking at Julia who nodded in agreement, "but what about the others."

"Manfred will be picked up under cover of darkness a few miles up the coast. Your sister-in-law and Helga will walk alongside the berths admiring the craft. We will already be on deck having some Schnapps with a party of people. Julia will invite them aboard for a glass of wine. When the party leaves they'll stay on board below. Make a big show of waving to those on the quayside as you sail out. We'll have waterproof clothing on board ready for you."

"I don't know how to thank you," Paul said grasping Rudi's hand.

"No need. He is Peter's son," Rudi replied looking down at the sleeping infant. "Now good luck and may God be with you."

Back at their hotel Eleanor and Helga tried to appear nonchalant as they nibbled little spicy cakes and sipped hot coffee. Furtively, they whispered about their encounter with the old seaman.

"We must go soon and walk along the quayside until he approaches us. Thank goodness the snow stopped last night. The clouds are breaking up at last," Helga commented, looking through the big picture window at the ponderous sky.

"You're taking advantage of the fine weather I see," said the concierge as they left the hotel, "but you'll be back in time for luncheon, yes?"

"Of course, we're looking forward to it."

Helga shot him a disarming smile that sent the colour rushing to his face.

"Such a handsome woman," he sighed closing the door behind them.

Helga looked about seeming to admire the ocean as waves crashed against the sea wall near the lighthouse. As they turned to walk back a small, unsteady figure appeared in the distance ambling towards them, a dog at his heels. When he drew closer he threw the stick at some point in their path. The dog hurtled forward yapping excitedly, his tail wagging furiously as he tried to pick up the stick. The old seaman caught him by the collar and bent to pick it up just as the women were about to pass.

They pretended to play with the animal laughing and patting it until it rolled over onto its back waiting to be tickled. The old man chastised his dog for bothering the women then whispered,

"Walk on the quay tomorrow around lunch time. Frau Conrad will invite you on board for food and drinks. When the guests start to leave hang back. They will not all leave together. It's unlikely they'll be watching when you slip out of sight below deck. Kommen sie hier!" he called to the dog then walked on towards the lighthouse.

Alarmed at the prospect of what would happen the following day the women dragged slowly back to the hotel. Greeting them with a wide smile Herr Gebauer ushered them into the little lounge for pre-luncheon drinks. For the rest of the day they threw themselves into the festive atmosphere joining in with other guests as much as possible.

Weak shafts of sunlight pierced the crack in the heavy drapes lining the windows. Julia stirred wearily, squinting against the light as Paul threw back the curtains. *Der Zweite Weihnachtstag*, St. Stephen's Day, had dawned with a burst of wintry, white sunshine tingeing every surface with silver light. He gazed out at a pale, blue sky dotted with a few ponderous, white clouds edged with silvery grey. In the distance seagulls keened over the metallic-grey waves. A low wind, barely stronger than a breeze, moaned across the rooftops. He opened the window, stretched his arms high above his head and breathed deeply.

"What a beautiful day!" he exclaimed.

"Close the window! Do you want us to get pneumonia?" Julia chastised grabbing her dressing gown from the big ottoman at the foot of the bed.

"Well, at least it's not snowing. There are a lot of people out already."

Groups of people were walking along the beach promenade. Children scampered alongside or ran ahead excited to be outside in the clear, crisp air. Figures carrying life-jackets, oars and other paraphernalia were already heading for the yacht harbour.

The dining room was almost empty while they waited to be seated. A robust figure, sitting near the window, stood up and smiled when they entered.

"Guten tag Frau Conrad," Rudi said inclining his head slightly before turning to Paul.

"It's a wonderful day, is it not?"

"Indeed it is Herr Zimmermann," Paul replied.

"I'm taking out my boat, *Serilda,* today. Just a couple of hours close to shore. Do you sail Herr Conrad?"

"I've done a bit of competitive sailing over the years."

"Ach, so you will sail today?"

"It's rather cold for sailing don't you think?"

"Nonsense, Germans sail in all weathers not like the soft Americans," Rudi laughed derisively.

Seemingly stung by the insult Paul glared up indignantly at Rudi, his eyes glinting with anger.

"I'll sail with you, no problem. I've been out in worse weather than this I can assure you!"

"But darling…" Julia protested, "I thought we were going to spend the day together?"

"Better still, a race Herr Conrad. Reinhardt…" He called to a man at an adjoining table. "Will you hire out *Lorelei* to the American?"

"Ja Rudi, but only if you promise to beat him."

"It's settled then, my *Serilda* against the *Lorelei*. The prize will be our dinner tonight. Perhaps Frau Conrad can join us for an early lunch on board before we sail."

"Please be careful," the hotel manager muttered as they made their way back to their room to don their outer clothes, "Herr Zimmermann is a very experienced sailor, but sometimes a little reckless."

"So am I Herr Grubermann, so am I," Paul replied.

Dressed in warm clothing and stout shoes they descended the stairs. Little Johann was tucked into his pram wrapped in a heavy, woollen blanket. Julia had draped her shoulders in a colourful, red scarf patterned with tiny Christmas trees and reindeer.

The yachts in the harbour were alive with eager sailors and their luncheon guests eating hot sausages, quaffing Schnapps and sparkling wine. As they approached the *Serilda* Rudi jumped onto the quayside to greet them.

"Come aboard," he invited gesturing towards the *Lorelei* which was moored next to *Serilda*."

"She's beautiful!" Paul exclaimed with genuine admiration.

"Ja, she is fast too," Reinhardt said proudly.

"Not as fast as *Serilda*," Rudi cut in.

"We will soon see," Reinhardt retorted with a touch of acrimony. "The American may be a better sailor than you after all."

The three men clinked their glasses downing the Schnapps in one swallow.

Julia took the baby below out of the cold then rejoined the men on deck. In the distance two women were idling along admiring the boats. When they drew near the older woman called,

"Guten tag! You have a good day for sailing!"

"I'm not going out. I'll be going back to the hotel later. Say, why don't you come aboard for a drink. I could do with the company," Julia laughed indicating the men who had wandered over to the *Serilda*. They appeared completely engrossed in discussing the technical qualities of their respective craft. "As you can see I've been deserted."

She waved to a group of women on the boat moored alongside calling for them to join her on *Lorelei*.

Clambering aboard they laughed and joked about the intensity of the conversation coming from adjoining yachts. Within minutes they were exchanging gossip about their families, all thoughts of war temporarily banished from their minds.

The blonde sisters, animated and flushed with excitement, sipped their glasses of wine. To a casual observer they appeared slightly intoxicated, but they were careful not to drink too much. They would need their wits about them. When the yacht was ready to sail the guests dispersed, amongst a clamour of noisy goodbyes, to go their own ways.

Helga and Eleanor had surreptitiously hidden away below decks before the last guests left. Julia also disappeared below calling to the others that she would pick up the baby and follow them. Ten minutes later a lone figure could be seen scurrying alongside the berths with her baby hugged against her chest. One of the disappearing crowd waved back at her. She raised a hand in acknowledgement just as they turned towards the town. Quickly, the figure walked towards the promenade where the waves were crashing against the piles of rocks that formed a sea wall.

Eventually, the first boats left the harbour, under motor power, negotiating the channel leading to Rostock before heading for the open sea. The wind was perfect for sailing, not too strong, but sufficient for easy manoeuvrability once the engines were cut. Above, the sky was a clear, cold, cerulean blue. Rudi waved to Paul as he expertly turned his craft into the wind signalling he was about to start the race. For two hours they ploughed backwards and forwards keeping close to the shore. They were running neck and neck. Rudi, his face even more ruddy from the cold, threw his head back and jeered at Paul. He nosed the *Serilda* ahead and pointed her towards the horizon.

"Who are those fools?" sneered an army officer as Paul veered after Rudi. "It will be getting dark soon. They should be sailing back to the harbour now."

"It's Rudi Zimmermann trying to win his dinner. I shouldn't worry about him. He's an expert sailor; knows these waters like the back of his hand," his companion laughed turning his boat towards the shore.

On the beach a lone, grey-coated figure levelled his binoculars at the yachts receding in the distance. His small, pig-like eyes under the heavy, black eyebrows glinted malevolently in his jowly face. On the *Serilda* he could just make out the single outline of a man on the otherwise deserted deck.

The challenge by Rudi Zimmermann was the talk of Warnemünde. The sailing fraternity was out in force to watch him humiliate the American. Still, there was something odd about the way they had suddenly turned out to sea. Was it recklessness, generated by the desire for victory, or was it something else? He had been observing them ever since his arrival from Magdeburg where he had been rounding up Jews for transportation to concentration camps. For a few moments he stood pondering the circumstances before turning swiftly towards the yachting harbour. He would watch and wait.

A cloak of darkness had descended over Warnemünde when the man in the grey coat returned to his hotel. Overhead, bright twinkling stars shone in a canopy of midnight-blue velvet. Clouds of white steam burst from his mouth and nostrils. He walked faster slapping his arms against his sides to keep warm. He shouldn't have stood waiting for so long in the cold. Now the frosty, rarefied air hurt his tobacco-damaged lungs as he breathed faster from the unusual effort of his pace.

The niggling doubt Eberhard Neumann had felt had been confirmed. The other sailors had waited for hours until Rudi Zimmermann had returned safely, but there was no sign of the American. Talk of a search party had been abandoned. If they had strayed too far out it would be too dangerous, because of the presence of German and British naval ships in the area. He must contact Berlin immediately. Herr Fleischer would not be pleased with the news that the American had disappeared, but first he must speak with Frau Conrad.

The brightly-lit lounge of the hotel was a clamour of voices all debating the disappearance of the boat. Herr Grubermann was relating how he had warned the American not to accept Rudi Zimmermann's challenge when Neumann walked in.

"I am Herr Neumann. Where is Frau Conrad?" he demanded.

Looking slightly startled Grubermann stuttered,

"I assume she is in her room."

"Well, take me to it. We'll soon see if she's there," Neumann spat vehemently.

"But sir!"

"You dare argue with an officer of the Gestapo? Get out of my way or Herr Fleischer will want to know why you have impeded one of his officers."

Grubermann visibly paled then stepped aside as Neumann roughly pushed past. Reluctantly, he followed him upstairs.

The Gestapo agent knocked loudly on the door, but there was only silence from inside. He pounded the door with his fist, to no avail.

"Open it!" he ordered the manager who had appeared beside him with a large bunch of keys.

"Perhaps she is asleep?" ventured the manager.

"Open it I said!"

Grubermann fussed with the keys until he found the right one then inserted it into the lock. Hesitantly, he pushed open the door.

"She's not here Herr Neumann."

"I can see that!"

"She can't have gone far, her clothes are still here."

Neumann's eyes swept the room taking in the open suitcase in a corner, the evening gown crumpled across the top of a chair. He rummaged amongst the clothes and shoes in the wardrobe, prodded the few cosmetics still on the dressing table. He examined the baby's cot that was made up with white sheets, but no blanket. There was something not quite right here.

"Strange, very strange. She has a baby, but there are no baby clothes here or any of the necessities she needs for her child. Why is that, I wonder?"

Grubermann shrugged his shoulders murmuring in a frightened voice,

"I have no idea Herr Neumann. The last time I saw her she was going to the harbour with Herr Conrad and the baby. They seemed like such a nice family."

Neumann pushed him aside without replying. He rushed downstairs to reception where he commandeered a telephone.

"Gestapo headquarters, Berlin," he barked at the operator, "and be quick about it!"

CHAPTER THIRTEEN

Out on the black, undulating sea Paul looked up at the sky. He fought to keep the yacht on course as waves crashed across the hull. Spray shot metres into the air cascading back onto the deck. Dusk had quickly turned into pitch-black night. The stars had all but disappeared covered by a blanket of low cloud. The wind was howling now, whipping the sea into a frenzy. Frantically, he hauled in the sails and switched to power. Struggling to keep control of the yacht he tried to turn her into the wind as a wave hit them to starboard. It had started to snow again. Little flurries that whipped across his face, filling his mouth. A sudden, loud bang brought a squeal of terror from Helga.

"What was that?" she shouted to Paul.

"It's okay! Just a wave hitting us head on!"

Terrified, Helga clung to a cupboard door as the boat rocked and dipped like a fairground ride.

"It won't be long now," Paul bellowed above the crash of the sea. "Rudi's navigational bearings show that Nils should be within two nautical miles."

"Thank God for that!" Helga shouted over the noise of the engine and the blustering wind. "I've never been a very good sailor."

Eleanor held Johann tightly to her chest, terrified that she would drop him every time the yacht climbed a wave and lurched back into the sea. At last she had her son back in her arms.

"I won't lose him again," she cried.

"Don't worry, we'll be safe soon," Julia comforted.

She tried not to look at her sister. An unbearable, almost physical pain consumed her. He was as much her son as Eleanor's. Jealousy stabbed at her chest; a hot, throbbing ache.

She had to remind herself that she had never been his mother, only his protector.

Paul knew that if they failed to reach Nils soon they were in serious trouble. They were likely to wander into one of the German U-boats that patrolled the Baltic or, worse, succumb to the elements. He didn't dare use any navigational lights in case they were spotted. Even his sailing skills wouldn't stand up to the kind of weather he knew was looming. Manfred had been right. It *was* madness, sheer madness!

Screwing up his eyes he peered into the darkness ahead. The biting wind whipped at his face making his eyes and nose stream. He dragged his hand across his face feeling the rough, icy particles that were beginning to form on the cuffs of his heavy jacket. Every new wave that buffeted the boat felt stronger, threatening to tear the wheel from his hands. It was impossible to hear anything above the roaring of the foaming waters and the moaning wind.

"God damn it, where are you Nils?" he shouted as a gust sent the yacht keeling to port. His muscles strained as he struggled to keep her upright against the grasping tentacles of wind. Miraculously, he managed to keep her steady until she regained her equilibrium. His heart was pounding in his chest. He shivered violently; beads of cold sweat trickled down his back, but still he kept her steady. All he could see was a black curtain filled with dancing snowflakes.

Suddenly, Paul spotted a dim light. It flickered then disappeared as flurries of snow obliterated his vision. Was it a light or was it his imagination playing tricks on him? It was now appearing and disappearing at regular intervals. Was it Nils or was it a German ship? At any moment he expected the harsh beam of a spotlight to sweep the waters around him.

He kept on sailing in the direction of the light knowing that at any moment he might be rammed by another vessel who couldn't see him without his navigational lights: closer and closer until a hull loomed like a wall in front of him. He swept the bows and stern with his night glasses until he could just make out some letters. It was the *Christina!*

"Thank God!" he muttered.

Paul shone his torch at the bridge clicking out the signal they had arranged. Dimly, a thin beam came back confirming the signal.

Nils had stopped the *Christina's* engines and was lying dead in the water as they came alongside. Still, it was a dangerous operation trying to get aboard in winds and driving snow. Paul lunged at the rope a sailor had thrown over the side to secure the *Lorelei*. Above, a rope ladder unfurled over the hull in readiness for them to board. He shouted down the hatch.

"Come on, it's time to move. Eleanor, stay below until last. I'll take Johann on board with me."

Momentarily, Helga ducked back inside as the full force of the wind and sleet hit her in the face. She looked fearfully at the rope ladder swaying backwards and forwards, slapping against the hull. The roiling sea threw the *Lorelei* against the *Christina* with such force that Paul lost his balance and hit the deck. Struggling to his feet he shouted over the wind,

"Come on! We haven't got any time to lose."

Grabbing Helga he pulled her roughly towards the side while he stretched overboard lunging for the swaying ladder that a seaman on deck was trying to hold steady.

"I can't! I'll drown!" she cried hysterically.

"We might all drown, but it's the only chance we have. Now, stop blubbering and get on the ladder," he yelled.

Helga grasped at the rope and began to climb with Paul pushing from behind. Halfway up, the ladder swung dangerously propelling her against the hull with a loud, metallic thump.

"Go on! Keep going!" Paul shouted. You're almost there!"

She froze as the ladder began to sway even more dangerously. Suddenly, another face appeared high above them. A seaman dropped over the *Christina*'s side, gingerly lowered himself on to the ladder. Slowly, he descended towards her until he was close enough to reach out.

"Give me your hand! Don't look down!" he ordered pulling her up behind him. Strong arms grasped her and hauled her over the side. She collapsed in a heap on the wet deck. Another seaman threw a blanket over her shoulders and hurriedly eased her to her feet.

"Let's get you below."

"Thank you! Thank you!" Helga wept as she was led below deck.

A gust of wind threw Julia against the hull with a jarring thud as she started up the ladder. Weaker than the other two women she stopped to catch her breath. The wet rope slipped from her fingers. She fell backwards and started to slide down towards the foaming water. Frantically, Paul threw himself at her pinning her to the hull with his weight. Panting from the effort he pushed her upwards towards the waiting sailors.

"Eleanor, give me the baby!" he ordered.

She shrank back hugging Johann to her, a look of total horror on her face.

"No, he's coming with me!"

"You'll never get on board carrying him as well! Give him to me!"

Roughly, Paul grabbed the baby and pushed Eleanor towards the ladder. She started to climb turning to glance at Johann. Paul signalled to the man on board *Christina* who reached out and hauled Eleanor on deck.

Satisfied that the women were safely aboard Paul discarded his waterproofs. Wrapping the baby tightly in the jacket he tied it with the sleeves. He sat on the wet deck, bundled the baby in a piece of sail, swathed it around his shoulders and tied the ends under his chin. Next he pulled the bottom ends of the sail tightly together so that it formed a sling on his back. He looked over his shoulder to check that Johann had enough air. He was fast asleep oblivious to the drama taking place around him.

Making the sling was the easy bit. Now he had to get the baby on board. If he was thrown against the hull the child would be crushed to death.

With his heart in his mouth he put a foot on the ladder. With the next step it started to sway violently. On board the seaman had been watching with alarm. He motioned for Paul to get back on deck. Swaying dangerously the sailor clambered down the ladder and dropped onto the yacht's deck.

"Start climbing! I'll come behind you to act as ballast!" he shouted over the howl of the wind.

Slowly, Paul hauled himself up with the sailor pushing from behind. His wet hands were so cold he could barely keep hold on the rope. Waves threatened to snatch them away plunging them into the churning waters below. A faint cry came from the bundle on his back startling him.

"Hold on little buddy, we're nearly there!" he yelled.

Gasping from the exertion he climbed steadily, afraid to look up. Then he felt hands dragging him on board. He fell face down on the deck gasping for breath.

"Tell the captain they're all aboard," a voice said urgently.

Within seconds the dim figure of a man on the bridge was issuing orders. Suddenly, the ship's engines throbbed and juddered into life as the ice-breaker got underway and ploughed into the waves.

"We're heading for the Baltic port of Oxelösund south of Stockholm," Nils told them as they sat wrapped in blankets cupping their hands around large mugs of hot coffee.

"I thought we'd be going up through the Gulf of Bothnia to Luleå near the Norwegian border? Isn't that where most ships pick up iron ore?" Paul queried.

"In the summer, but Luleå is more difficult to access during the winter months even with an ice-breaker like *Christina*. It's much further north. Often frozen over at this time of year so we use Oxelösund to ship iron ore to Germany. From there you can go to Stockholm where you'll be safe. I've just off-loaded a consignment in Hamburg.

"What about the U-boats?"

"I make this voyage regularly. They're used to seeing *Christina* sailing up and down the Baltic. German troops and weapons are being transported via the railways in Sweden, as part of the transit agreement with Germany, but it's still a neutral country. There's no advantage in Hitler launching an attack on Sweden. Now I must get back to my duties."

"Thank you," Eleanor whispered looking down at Johann asleep in the little wooden box the ship's carpenter had thoughtfully provided.

Nils nodded and returned to the bridge where his second officer was sweeping the horizon with his night glasses.

On a spit of coastal land, between Rostock and Rügen, a figure dressed in seaman's jacket, knee-length boots and woollen hat clambered aboard a fishing boat. Hurriedly, he hid below deck grateful for the warmth.

"Come on, let's get going," a voice shouted above the noise of crashing waves, "and keep the lights out. If we're seen…"

The wind snatched the voice away in a cacophony of noise.

The boat bobbed crazily for a few minutes until it reached deeper water, its engine sputtering and coughing like a wheezy old man. Slowly, they inched forward picking up speed as they headed out to the open sea.

Manfred slapped his hands vigorously on his arms to stave off the cold; wiggled his toes inside the waterproof boots. For over an hour he had been hiding in the rocks lashed by wind and snow. The cabin was unheated, but he welcomed the meagre shelter it provided.

"We'll rendezvous with the *Christina* in two hours," the grizzled captain shouted through the hatch.

He slammed the door shut before Manfred could respond.

Minutes later a surly seaman, in oilskins, thrust a mug of coffee at him. He pulled out the cork of a bottle of Schnapps and held it up.

"I'll need a clear head, especially in this weather," Manfred said refusing the offer.

For what seemed like hours they pitched and tossed through the swelling seas while his companion consumed large quantities of Schnapps. Manfred studied the man. There was something about him that he didn't like. Perhaps it was the sneering curl of his lips or the tendency to avoid direct contact with his eyes. Every time Manfred looked at him he turned away busying himself with a piece of rope or examining charts. Why wasn't he outside with the others? Manfred felt a tiny jab of fear in his chest. He couldn't pinpoint the reason, but he didn't trust the man.

Suddenly, the captain lunged down struggling to close the hatch door against the force of the wind.

"It's getting pretty bad out there. The wind has increased and it's snowing much worse now. The transfer will be more difficult…"

The captain stopped, head cocked to one side, his eyes staring into space. Putting his foot on the step he stuck his head through the hatch door.

"Quiet!" he ordered. "Cut the engine!"

For a few seconds nothing could be heard except the whining of the wind and snow beating against the cabin's windows. Then Manfred heard it, the low grumble of a ship's engine; big, powerful engines that churned the sea into a white froth.

"It's a German cruiser!" the skipper shouted. "We're right in its path!"

"Turn to starboard!" he yelled at the seaman in the wheelhouse.

If they were lucky they could disappear before they were spotted, but they had already been seen.

"Achtung! Achtung! Come alongside, I repeat come alongside!"

A malevolent glint of hatred gleamed in the eyes of the seaman standing with the charts in his hands.

"Jew pig!" he snarled at Manfred.

The captain turned towards him, his eyes registering disbelief. The man pushed him aside, grabbed a storm lantern and climbed out on deck. He signalled to the cruiser, swinging the storm lantern backwards and forwards.

"What's going on?" the skipper demanded coming up behind him.

"You're helping a Jew escape! Come out Jew! We're waiting for you!"

Manfred's terrified face appeared in the hatch doorway. Suddenly, the captain lunged for the seaman, screaming at him as he tried to wrestle him to the deck.

"Bastard, Nazi bastard!"

The harsh gleam of a searchlight pierced the darkness lighting up the surreal scene; a tableau of men locked together, almost like two lovers. A shot rang out from the ship echoing over the water. For a few seconds the captain stood up straight, his hands still round the agent's throat. He clung to him, blood trickling from his mouth onto the seaman's upturned face. Suddenly, his back arched and he slid down onto the deck. His body convulsed, twitched one last time then he was still; his eyes wide with the horror of betrayal.

Manfred struggled as the crewman heaved him out of the cabin into the glare of the light. Dragging him to the side of the vessel he fought to tie him up. Manfred struck out at him grazing his jaw, but the man tightened his grip. He struggled, lashing out with his feet, but the agent held him in a vice-like grip. Suddenly, Manfred brought his knee up and thrust it hard into the agent's groin. Giving a short gasp of pain he clutched at his genitals with one hand, but the other still held him in its grip. Incoherent with rage he bent Manfred over the side of the boat, his hands round his throat. As he brought his fist back to deliver a blow Manfred grabbed him by the arms. He tried to struggle upright as the sea crashed over the gunwale.

The next wave lifted the boat up into the air. For a split second it hovered suspended on the crest, turned in towards the German ship and dropped, the bow ploughing into the ocean. A second wave hit her broadside. She keeled over throwing both men into the boiling cauldron of white-tipped, black sea. The cruiser ploughed into the fishing boat scattering wood and metal over the water. What was left of her danced on the surface as though some demon from below spun it in his hands. Creaking and groaning in its death throes the wreckage sank beneath the waves.

The agent screamed as the force of the sea threw him against the hull of the cruiser. He thrashed his arms desperately trying to swim away from the ship as it slid past, but every time he moved a few strokes away he was hurled back against unforgiving metal. When the searchlight picked him out his battered, dead body was still beating the hull like a mute drum in the night.

In a frenzy of terror Manfred struggled to swim away as the cruiser passed. He lifted his arms, tried to wave, but felt himself being dragged towards the stern. The noise of the propellers drowned his faint cries as the water churned white and furious. All he felt was a thud as the looming blades hit him. He reached out to grab at something white in the water; something white and bloodied. A leg - whose leg? He clung to it laughing hysterically. There was no pain, only freezing water foaming with his blood as his other leg floated away from him. The murderous propellers caught him again churning his torso like a mincer; turning the sea red with his blood. His last image before the blackness of eternal oblivion was Helga.

The cruiser's searchlight arced over the waves in a futile attempt to detect survivors. An officer barked an order to the men waiting to lower a ladder over the side.

"Return to your posts," he said lowering his night glasses. "There is no way they are still alive."

In Rostock a man in a grey coat smiled with satisfaction as a radio operator translated a message from the cruiser.

"Boat sunk - no survivors - I repeat, no survivors."

On board the *Christina* Helga shivered in the warmth of the wardroom. Unaccountably, a feeling of utter despair washed over her. She knew she would never see Manfred again.

CHAPTER FOURTEEN

In Berlin Peter lay in the bed he usually shared with Eleanor. News of Manfred had reached Rudi in Warnemünde and relayed to Berlin. A knife of anguish sliced through his chest.

"One day," he vowed, "I'll avenge your death."

But for now he felt immense relief that his family had arrived safely in Oxelosünd. From there they had been taken across the icy countryside to a house in Stockholm where they would remain for the winter. It would be a long time before he saw his wife and son again. For now he would go to the university as usual; try to live as normal a life as possible. Tomorrow night he would travel to the country to see his uncle and set their plans in motion.

Friedrich despised Hitler, the posturing Goebells and his other thuggish aids. For years he watched as the Party grew to fearsome proportions, whipped into a frenzy against any group that did not fit with Hitler's dream of pure-blooded, perfect Germans. Opposition groups like the Edelweisspiraten, the Meuten organisation in Leipzig had sprung up, but they had no real lasting effect on the spread of Nazism. Hitler had become an unstoppable force.

Even some misguided, aristocratic families had helped to raise funds for the Nazi Party before the war. But for the most part they only pandered to the Nazis. *Regis* involved some powerful families, some of whom vainly hoped for the restoration of the monarchy. Only four people knew the identity of its leader – codename *Regis*: Peter, Rudi, Bruno and Princess Marie Juliana.

Friedrich worked covertly while seeming to sympathise with the Nazi party. He had cultivated 'friendships' with important Nazi officials to gain their trust. Even Hitler himself had attended parties on his estate. In reality, he detested the coarse little Austrian.

Friedrich stepped into the impressive hall while Peter stripped off his sodden top coat. He had travelled through the night, in freezing rain; stopping only to take a swig of Schnapps from a flask or relieve himself against a tree at the side of the road.

"Peter, it's so good to see you my boy."

"I have so much to tell you…"

"Not now. You're soaking wet. First you must change into dry clothes then we can talk, ja?"

Peter entered the library wearing a pair of his uncle's slacks and a warm sweater. Marie Juliana rose from her chair and hugged him to her. She stood back looking him up and down.

"You are getting so thin!" she cried. "You're not eating properly!"

"I've been so worried these past few weeks. Eleanor was so adamant about staying in Berlin even after the air raids started last August. They haven't done much damage, but they have become more frequent over the last few months."

"Sit here by me and tell us all that has happened."

She busied herself pouring coffee from an elegant, silver pot. After passing a cup to Peter and Friedrich she settled back and waited patiently for Peter to speak.

"First the good news is that Eleanor and Johann are safely in Sweden with Paul and Julia; also Helga. The sad news is that Manfred did not make it to Nils' ship.

Marie Juliana gasped in horror when he related the circumstances of Manfred's violent death.

"Rudi heard it from a drunken, talkative relative of one of the sailors on board the cruiser."

"Poor Helga."

"Otto is devastated. Although Manfred was only his uncle by marriage he was like a father to him. You know his own father, a devout Catholic, died in a demonstration defending his beliefs; speaking out against the persecution of religious groups."

"It's too horrible to contemplate," Marie Juliana shuddered.

"There's no more we can do now except wait. In the spring we'll try to get them out of Sweden to London and, eventually, to America," Peter added. "I must get back to Berlin tonight before I'm missed. The Gestapo have been secretly watching me for months, but they're much more obvious about it now."

Shortly after breakfast Bruno arrived. For the rest of the morning the men huddled in close conversation behind the closed doors of Friedrich's study.

"Every day fresh stories of Hitler's brutality reach my ears. Murder disguised as euthanasia," Bruno muttered. "Is it true that they gassed mental patients in the jail at Brandenburg?"

"It is true," Friedrich replied. My contacts in the Catholic church tell me that some of the cardinals have been voicing their concerns for many months over the Euthanasia Decree. Cardinal Hlond sent details of what is happening to the Pope at the beginning of the year and Cardinal Bertram has protested to the Reich Chancellery."

"I heard in the university that a professor, I dare not name him, has been trying to persuade eminent heads of psychiatry to protest, but they've remained silent." Peter scowled. "The killings are gathering momentum. It's not only Jewish mental patients, Germans too."

"Our organisation has few members, but we must keep on doing as much as we can," Friedrich responded.

"The majority of German people support the Führer, but there are some small pockets of resistance. In the army, the Protestant and Catholic churches, the universities and amongst ordinary working-class Germans. If we could enlist…"

Friedrich placed a restraining hand on Peter's arm as the door opened quietly.

"We've talked enough. Now it is time for luncheon. You will join us Bruno?"

"Thank you, but I have to attend to some urgent business."

He looked knowingly at Friedrich who nodded in agreement.

Peter arrived back in the apartment around midnight. He switched off the motor cycle's engine and walked it round the back of the building as he had done previously. For a few seconds he stood, immobile in the darkened courtyard, watching and listening for the slightest sound. There was nothing. When he closed the door behind him he did not see the black-clad figure walk from the lane outside and stare up at the darkened windows, his evil eyes glinting behind gold-rimmed glasses.

"So, you've been on your travels again Brandt, but we'll soon find out where you have been."

Turning sharply he marched down the lane into an adjoining street where a staff car waited for him.

"Prinz Albrecht Strasse!" he snapped at the weary drive who was slumped at the wheel.

Hurriedly, he clambered out and opened the back passenger door for Fleischer.

"Be quick about it you dolt, and if you ever fall asleep on duty again you'll be back on the front lines!"

The rumble of wheels on cobbles penetrated Peter's consciousness as he lay in that dreamlike state between sleep and full wakefulness. Screeching tyres, slamming doors, marching feet accompanied by barking orders. The clank of jackboots against metal stairs echoed throughout the building then stopped outside the door of the apartment. A fist hammered on the solid, oak door.

"Open up!

Peter sat bolt upright in the bed momentarily confused by the noise and shouting.

"Open up Brandt!"

He stumbled out of bed and hastily threw on his robe.

"I'm *coming!* Can't a man sleep in his own home!" he shouted angrily.

As he opened the door it was pushed towards him with such force that he stumbled backwards.

"What's going on? What do you want?"

"You Brandt, that's who we want," said the SS officer who sauntered into the hallway slapping a riding whip against his leg. "You are to come with us."

"Where? Why should I come with you?"

A stab of fear caught in Peter's chest. What if they had arrested Eleanor? But no, she was in Sweden wasn't she? Otto had confirmed her safe arrival he reassured himself.

"Get dressed, now!" the officer barked. "We're taking you on a little visit to Prinz Albrecht Strasse to see Herr Fleischer."

He pushed Peter roughly towards the bedroom door and watched as he hurriedly dressed. A soldier nudged him towards the stairs with the muzzle of his gun.

"I must remind you that I am a respected professor at the university," Peter protested indignantly.

"You can protest to Herr Fleischer when you get to Gestapo headquarters," the officer sneered pushing past Peter down the stairs.

Fleischer greeted Peter with a cold smile that somehow enhanced the evil lurking behind his eyes. He directed him towards a chair facing his desk. Languidly, he sat back as though he were about to chat with an old friend. His eyes gleamed behind the metal-framed spectacles. He leaned towards Peter, elbows on the desk, hands together as though in prayer.

"Where were you yesterday Herr Brandt? You were not at the university."

"No, I was out in the country looking for information about my wife and child."

"Are you sure about that Herr Brandt?"

"Of course I'm sure. I've been worried…"

"I think you're lying," Fleischer cut in mildly.

"I am *not* lying," Peter emphasised trying to hide the mounting fear in his chest.

Suddenly, Fleischer thrust his body towards Peter,

"You *are* lying!"

He crashed his fist down on the desk spilling the ink in the silver pot. Peter watched it as it spread soaking the edges of some papers. Fleischer angrily pushed them to one side. A nerve quivered in his temple. The veins in his neck bulged. He screamed in impotent rage,

"You are lying Jew lover! Your wife and son are in Sweden!"

Peter felt the bile, born of fear, recede in his throat. A strange calm descended over him. They could do whatever they wanted to now; they were safe. Smiling benignly, he looked straight into Fleischer's eyes. He was still smiling when the Gestapo officer struck him a fierce blow across the face with the back of his hand. The jagged skull mounted on Fleischer's ring broke the thin skin on Peter's cheekbone leaving an angry, bleeding gash. Blood ran down his face into his mouth, trickled down his chin staining the collar of his shirt.

"I will ask you one more time. Where were you yesterday?"

"I told you Herr Fleischer, looking for my family."

Behind Peter the door opened quietly. A bald, fleshy-faced man, muscles running to fat, sauntered into the room. A second man, black, sunken eyes staring from his cadaverous face, followed him and closed the door.

Roughly, the fat man pulled Peter to his feet and dragged him along the corridor down a flight of stairs into a small room. A bed with a dirty mattress lined one wall with a covered bucket set in the corner; no tap or sink. No windows, just a bare bulbless socket that hung from the ceiling under which a straight wooden chair had been positioned.

The stench hit Peter's nostrils as he stumbled inside. The dirty, green walls glistened with dripping condensation that trickled silently to the floor. Damp smells mingled with stale urine, faeces and sweat brought his hand up over his nose and mouth.

"Make yourself comfortable," the fat man sneered sweeping his arm across the room.

Slamming the metal door shut he laughed uproariously as he clumped along the corridor followed by the living corpse, silent and watchful.

Peter didn't know how long he had been in the dark cell. As his eyes became accustomed to the gloom he could just make out a chink of light at the side of the metal, sliding plate in the door. How long had it been? Two hours, three or more? He had no way of telling after they had stripped him of his watch. It was just the beginning of their games. Lock him in a windowless room, without light, to gradually wear him down.

He lay back on the damp mattress and collected his thoughts. How much did they already know? They knew that Eleanor had escaped to Sweden, but did they really know any more? Nothing pointed to his involvement and no-one but Bruno knew he was related to Friedrich, not even members of the organisation.

He and Wilhelm had taken their maternal grandmother's married name when they had gone to stay with her in Switzerland after their parents' death. Though German born she had met her second husband, Josef Brandt, during a walking holiday. She never returned to Germany. Peter and Wilhelm spent long periods of their childhood in Switzerland happily walking the mountains near her chalet or fishing in the lakes in the Bernese Oberland.

Six months after their parents' death their grandmother had contacted Friedrich begging him to secure the boys' future. She knew she was very sick and that, sooner or later, they would have to return to Germany.

The German national registration system meant that comprehensive records were kept on all its citizens. Bruno had been working compiling information as part of his cover in the organisation. He was instrumental in destroying all records relating to the boys, inserting new information and obtaining false papers for them before they returned to attend boarding school in Bavaria. A fund had been set up in his grandmother's name stating that she wanted the boys educated in her homeland. Peter and Wilhelm Von Landenenburg no longer existed.

At intervals the fat man came to check on him calling outside the door; taunting him, reminding him that they were still there. Soon they would be back and it would begin. Peter knew only too well what would happen. Too many of his contemporaries had perished within these walls. Nobody knew where they went, only that they were never seen again.

Suddenly, the panel slid back. Two black eyes peered through the hole before the panel was swiftly closed with a loud clang. He sat up at the metallic sound of bolts being drawn back, the groan of rusty hinges. Now it would begin.

From somewhere high on the wall a harsh, white light snapped on. Peter covered his eyes against the glare as a piercing brightness illuminated the room. The fat man grabbed Peter and thrust him into the chair under the hanging wire. Silently, the man with the hollow, sunken eyes walked across and stood in front of him. Expressionless, he gazed at the prisoner as though examining an insect. When he finally spoke it was with a slight lisp that seemed to enhance his sinister features; like the sound of a hissing snake.

"Have you anything to tell us Herr Brandt," he lisped politely.

"I've told you everything. There is nothing more to tell."

"Very well. Corporal Krause…"

He nodded at the fat man. Grinning maliciously he punched Peter in the stomach knocking the wind out of him. As he lurched forward, clutching his stomach, Krause delivered a vicious blow to his face, then another under his chin, snapping his head back. The chair toppled to the ground throwing Peter onto its hard surface.

"I have nothing to tell you," Peter mumbled through his blood-filled mouth, "nothing!"

"You'll have something to tell by the time I've finished with you scheisenhausen!"

Krause continued to punch and kick until he was breathless from the effort. Brauer, the hollow-eyed man, watched impassively nodded again then left the room with the fat Untersharführer close on his heels.

"We'll be back Herr Brandt," he hissed.

Peter crawled to the bed and hauled himself onto the mattress. Blood oozed from his lips onto his shirt. He pressed his handkerchief to his face in an attempt to stem the blood pumping from his nose. Taking deep breaths he waited for his head to clear. Eventually, he was able to stand up and limp across the room. A wave of nausea washed over him and he vomited all over the cell floor. Engulfed by dizziness he staggered back to the bed, head full of cotton wool, and dropped onto the stinking mattress.

Twice more they dragged him from the bed. Brauer looking on while Krause punched and kicked him until he was covered in raw bruises. Finally, they came no more. He drew up his legs, curled painfully into the foetal position and sank into an exhausted sleep.

Early next morning he awoke in total darkness to guttural, barking commands. The heavy door swung open to reveal Fleischer silhouetted against the light in the corridor, the cadaverous SS officer behind him. Peter tried to sit up, but the pain in his head forced him back.

"So, you have had time to think Herr Brandt," Fleischer began. "Perhaps this morning you'll have something to tell us then you will be free to go."

"I can't tell you what I don't know," Peter groaned.

"Very well," Fleischer replied, his voice barely more than a whisper.

Turning towards the door he signalled to Krause who was waiting down the corridor. He appeared carrying a brazier full of glowing coals. Carefully, he placed it near the chair in the centre of the room. Fleischer exchanged a brief glance with the burly corporal. Turning briskly he marched out closing the door behind him.

Krause leaned against the wall, lit a cigarette and blew out a stream of foul-smelling smoke. Grinning, he stirred the coals with a long, slender poker then thrust it deep into the fire. Brauer wrapped his leather-gloved hand in a towel, retrieved the poker and held it close to Peter's face. He could feel the heat flushing his skin as Brauer moved it slowly backwards and forwards. Without warning he brought the tip of his glowing cigarette down onto Peter's hand then quickly removed it. Peter let out a sharp cry and bit hard on his already swollen lips.

"That was painful, wasn't it Brandt?" the SS officer lisped.

Peter did not respond. He stared straight ahead as though concentrating on something on the far wall. Again Brauer touched him with the glowing tip. This time he was ready and barely flinched.

"So, you want to be a hero Brandt?"

The SS officer nodded to the Untersharführer. Gleefully, he pressed his cigarette onto Peter's arm keeping it there until the skin sizzled red raw. Searing pain ravaged his body as Krause pressed it down on his arms, time and time again. Bending over he rolled up Peter's trousers and pressed the cigarette on the soft flesh of his inner thigh. Without warning he kicked out delivering a vicious blow to his kneecap.

Waves of pain washed over Peter as he slumped to one side. He felt himself falling; falling into swirling blackness and blessed unconsciousness. Brauer threw a bucket of ice- cold water over his head.

"I want you to feel the pain Brandt," he snarled.

Krause threw him onto the bed and smashed his fist into his mouth breaking one of his teeth. Through the blood and bits of ripped flesh Peter whispered,

"Nothing, I know nothing."

Again Brauer brandished the glowing, red-hot poker, this time near Peter's right eye.

"It would be very painful if you accidentally lost your eye."

Peter recoiled in horror as Brauer jabbed the poker at him diverting it to the side of his head at the last moment. Suddenly, the door swung open and Fleischer swaggered inside.

"Are you ready to tell us what you know Brandt?" he asked quietly.

"I have nothing to tell. I cannot tell you what I don't know."

"Give me names Brandt then you can go free."

"This will make the bastard talk," Brauer snarled, leaning over Peter with the sizzling poker.

"Brauer, enough!" Fleischer commanded. "You are free to go Herr Brandt."

Brauer looked at Fleisher angrily as he dragged Peter from the chair and pushed him towards the door.

"Clean him up before you throw him out," Fleisher said walking briskly from the room, eyes gleaming with frustration.

He could barely contain the fury welling in his chest. Brandt had a part in his wife's escape to Sweden and was part of an organisation. Of that he was sure, but he had to be careful. This was no Jew, but a respected German professor well-known in the academic world. But he was also known for speaking out against the Nazis and had refused to join the Party. His neighbour, Herr Fleiss, had reported on his nocturnal wanderings and his friends from the university who visited the apartment late at night. Fleischer guessed that Brandt would not reveal anything about his interrogation as this would attract attention to the organisation. One way or another he would have to get rid of him and his traitorous friends.

A watery sun hung in a white sky ponderous with scudding grey clouds. The street was curiously empty as the car approached Peter's building. He brought his hand up to shade his eyes wincing when he touched the bruises that had already turned purplish-black. As the car lurched to a stop an SS officer reached over, opened the door, and pushed Peter roughly out onto the wet cobbles. The curtains in the second floor apartment twitched. Herr Fleiss stared malevolently down at the man limping towards the front door. Fleischer would reward him well for informing on the Jew lover.

For the rest of the day Peter lay on his bed. His bruised body ached from the beating he had suffered at Gestapo headquarters. Gingerly, he touched the cigarette burns. Crusty scabs were already forming on his arms and legs. Every time he moved spots of blood from broken scabs dripped onto the sheets. He curled up into the foetal position to ease the dull ache in the pit of his stomach and drifted into sleep.

He awoke to the sound of footsteps descending from the upstairs apartment. Voices in muted conversation drifted from the floor below. A small group had gathered on the landing talking in hushed tones. Peter leaned over the balustrade. Herr Fleiss stared at his battered face with a mixture of contempt and satisfaction. Two of the women scuttled downstairs swiftly slamming doors behind them. Frau Klocke backed into her apartment eyes brimming with tears.

Painfully, he dragged back to the living room. He forced himself to drink some coffee through his swollen lips. Dipping a piece of bread until it was soggy he eased it between his lips. Now was not the time to lose his strength. Peter had to warn Otto and Claus, but he dare not contact them through the organisation. For that he would have to go to the safe house where he knew he would be followed. No, he would have to sit tight until he could go to the university when the staff returned after the Christmas break. Questions would be asked, but a fall from his motorcycle would cause such injuries. That would be his excuse. Brauer had been careful not to burn him where it could be seen, except for his hand. A bandage would solve that problem. Gingerly, he touched his face. This was just the beginning. Soon the Gestapo would be back.

CHAPTER FIFTEEN

Peter whistled softly to himself as he walked to the tram that would take him to the university. Work would ease the pain of not seeing his family. Besides, it was work he loved doing. A project he had begun long before the war, but the Nazis had commandeered his research for their own ends. At first he had protested vehemently determined not to cooperate with them.

"There's no such thing as academic freedom anymore Peter," his old mentor had told him. "Best to keep working. You can still work in your own way."

A knowing look passed between them.

"It would be a good cover for the organisation," Peter mused. "At least I'm close to Otto and Claus."

"Ja, think how easy it is for you to communicate messages."

Reluctantly, he had yielded to the posturing Nazis who came periodically to examine his research.

The door into the corridor opened and closed quietly. Light footsteps approached his desk.

"Peter…"

He looked up at Otto who was staring at him with a look of total incomprehension on his face.

"What on earth has happened to you?" Otto continued finally recovering his voice.

"Just fell off my motorcycle, that's all," Peter said ruefully. "You know me, going too fast on wet cobblestones, as usual. It was bound to happen sooner or later."

A junior lecturer in Peter's faculty sniggered as he wrote on a blackboard at the far end of the room. They had both seen him sucking up to the Nazis on their visits. He was always hanging about pretending not to listen to conversations.

"I've been struggling with this equation for weeks, but now I think I've solved the problem."

Otto leaned in closer as if examining the paper on the desk.

"After work this evening, in the café where we usually meet."

"Yes Peter, I think you've cracked it this time, but I must get back to my students before they blow up the laboratory."

Otto was watching Claus quaff a large stein of beer with one hand while he stuffed his mouth full of brockfürst with the other.

"Look everybody, he's finally fallen off his motorcycle," Otto laughed. Peter gazed ruefully at his peers who thronged the adjoining tables.

"You look as if you've been beaten up by a heavyweight boxer," yelled one of the crowd,

"Ja, ja," Peter grimaced trying to grin with his split lip. "Somebody must have left a pool of oil on the cobbles."

Playfully, the man on the next table clapped him on the back. Wincing with pain he lowered himself carefully into a hard, wooden chair.

When they had finally been served with more drinks Otto leaned over.

"What the hell's been going on? How did this happen?"

"You didn't fall off your motorcycle, did you Peter?" Claus muttered.

"It was the Gestapo," whispered Peter. "They suspect I'm part of some kind of organisation."

"How much do they know?"

"I don't know, but they think you two are also involved. Someone has been giving them information about my movements and your visits to the apartment. It's only a matter of time before they haul you in as well."

"What are we going to do?"

"We can't do anything at the moment, just carry on as normal, but be prepared."

"What about our plans to get the Levine family out of Berlin. It's scheduled for the end of this week."

"It will have to go ahead. It's sheer luck that they haven't been found already."

"But Peter...,"

"There are five children in that underground tunnel. It's due to be filled in with earth next week. What choice do we have? If they stay there they may be buried alive. If the Gestapo get to them they'll be sent to a concentration camp to be tortured. No, I can't live with that on my conscience. We must go ahead!"

The two men looked at each other.

"Agreed," they nodded.

In a dark corner at the far end of the room a thickset man, in a grey overcoat, sipped his beer. Partially hidden by a large table lamp, he scrutinised them over the top of his newspaper.

The cobbled street was dark and slick with rain. Peter walked quickly down its length staying in the shadows of the buildings that loomed above him. Buildings full of eyes and ears to report strange movements in the night. Thankfully, a blanket of heavy clouds had hidden the moon enveloping the back streets in a blanket of clinging blackness. Light mist, accompanied by fine rain, drizzled down his neck from the brim of his hat soaking his shoulders. Leaving the cobbled alley behind he moved closer to the river bank. His feet squelched in the soft ground underfoot saturating the bottoms of his trousers. Cold droplets of water descended from overhanging trees bursting into a shower as he pushed them aside. Heart thumping he ploughed through the undergrowth towards where the Levines waited in the old sewage tunnel. Peter started as he heard a movement in front of him then relaxed. It was Claus.

"Otto is already at the tunnel," Claus said urgently. "We must hurry."

A few more paces brought them to a clump of tangled bushes. Claus pulled them aside. Reaching down he pulled up the turf using a lever to raise the rough piece of wood underneath. Peter shuddered to think that the family had been underground for four weeks.

Claus dropped into the hole after Peter carefully drawing the wood and turf over their heads. On hands and knees they crawled about fifty metres emerging out into a small earthen area shored up with concrete blocks. A gaping hole on the back wall indicated where the pipe had linked with the rest of the tunnel that ran underneath the river.

Huddled in the stinking space five children, ranging in age from two to thirteen, lay on filthy mattresses stained with urine. Hungry, luminous eyes stared from pale, pinched faces. The only warmth was provided by a rusty old burner that also served to heat tins of food. Candles in wine bottles illuminated the area with a dull glow that cast eerie shadows around the walls. The Levines each nursed one of the younger children while the eldest boy stared defiantly at the intruders.

"It's all right Aaron; they are our friends," his father said soothingly. "They're going to help us get out of this stinking hole."

"Get the children into warm clothing and put these on," Otto instructed pushing a pile of worn topcoats at him. "Be ready to leave within thirty minutes. There's no time to lose. Claus will stay with you. Get them to the mouth of the tunnel as quickly as possible."

Peter and Otto crawled back along the tunnel. They eased the wooden cover up just enough to take in the surrounding area. After scrambling out they moved quickly up the riverbank. A few hundred metres away they stopped, listening for any sound of movement.

"There it is!" Otto whispered indicating the shadow of a small boat bobbing on the water. "Come on!"

Peter jumped aboard swiftly freeing the rope fastened to an overhanging tree. He pushed the boat from the bank until the current took it. Silently, it floated effortlessly downstream towards the tunnel. Grabbing the oars Peter and Otto rowed into the bank.

"Otto, you wait here while I go and fetch them. Ten minutes should be enough time," Peter whispered before disappearing in the undergrowth.

As Peter approached the tunnel Claus scrambled out onto the wet grass.

"Quickly," he said urgently.

Thrusting his arm inside he hauled out Naomi Levine and her youngest child.

Within five minutes they were all above ground and heading for the river bank. Otto held the rope taut as the family clambered aboard.

"Stay out of sight," he ordered.

Hurriedly, they scrambled under the flimsy, black, canvas canopy. Peter and Claus jumped aboard pushing with all their might until they floated away from the bank. Gradually, they picked up speed and drifted downstream with the current.

Starting the outboard motor was not an option. It was quiet along this stretch of the river. Any noise would be carried over the water in the stillness of the night. They would have to rely on the current and the oars. It was such a dangerous operation, but it was the only way to get them out. At least this way they would have a chance of survival.

Peter's stomach churned when he thought of what might happen to them if they fell into the hands of the Nazis. Shuddering, he tightened his grip on the tiller, keeping under the dark shadows of the trees well away from the middle of the river. For now mist, rain and darkness embraced them like a comforting blanket. In a few hours dawn's unwelcome light would expose them like dead fish on the water.

Slight, misty drizzle had turned to heavy needles of rain that bounced on the surface of the river. The tarpaulin covering the family was full of water, almost touching their heads. Isaac Levine pushed at it sending it gushing into the boat.

For an hour they drifted silently with the flow. Occasionally, they dipped the oars to control the direction of the craft. Black shapes of boats, moored along the river bank, loomed in the darkness. Periodically, the harsh screech of an owl from nearby trees. The muted splash of small rodents slipping into the water startled them into fearful watchfulness.

"So far so good," murmured Claus peering through the darkness at the houses set back from the bank.

"Keep your voice down. The slightest sound is magnified over water," Otto reprimanded.

He knew the waterways in Berlin like the back of his hand. For years he and his wife Gisela had spent every weekend navigating the river in their boat, even in winter.

Under the awning the terrified children clung to heir parents. Only the two youngest had fallen into an uneasy sleep.

"Hermann is waiting a few hundred metres further on to take them into the woods. They'll stay in the dug-out where he hid Manfred for two nights then they'll be transported with the next shipment of logs," Peter whispered. "The Führer has ordered the movement of a massive consignment of timber to the coast. Nils is on his way up the Baltic coast. He'll take them out on the *Christina* to Sweden, but this is the last time we can use him for a while. Somehow, the Gestapo found out about Manfred, but what they didn't know was who was picking him up. The fishing boat didn't get as far as the *Christina*."

Ahead a low bridge loomed out of the mist. Otto pointed the prow towards the centre to avoid the stone supports and give them clear passage.

"It won't be long now Isaac…"

Otto's voice trailed off as he spotted a minute movement on the bridge.

He steered the boat between the parapets hoping to hide in the darkness. Frantically, the men back-paddled desperately trying to slow the boat down, but the current was too strong. It swept them out the other side.

Suddenly, the glare of a searchlight swept over the river illuminating the darkness around them.

"Halt! Halt!"

"Keep going! Keep going!" Peter shouted over the din.

A single shot rang out over their heads followed by the chatter of machine gun fire.

Otto pulled his scarf up to his woollen hat so that only his eyes could be seen.

"Stay under the tarpaulin," he shouted at the shadowy figures huddling underneath.

Too late! Harsh, white light flooded the boat revealing its terrified, pitiful cargo. The children were screaming now; clinging to their parents.

"Halt! Halt!"

Peter turned just as the bullets hit Otto. His back arched as he struggled to keep hold of the oar. Mouth wide in a silent scream he slumped over tilting the craft to one side. Blood trickled from the side of his mouth as he tried to maintain a hold on the side of the boat.

"Otto!"

Silently, he stared at Peter, his body twitching convulsively, eyes glassy with approaching death. Peter lunged towards him; grasped his arms. For a heartbeat his body teetered in a macabre pose. Peter grabbed at him as he fell overboard. A hail of gunfire sprayed the boat churning up the water, flooding the little boat.

"Hold on!" he yelled above the cacophony of gunfire.

Desperately, he clung to Otto's wet, dead hand. Horrified, he felt it slipping, slowly slipping from his grasp.

"Otto!"

But Otto had already disappeared into the deep, black depths.

Another burst of gunfire shattered the still air around them sweeping the boat. Peter and Claus futilely tried to paddle their way out of range. Suddenly, a chilling wail from under the rough canopy filled the air. Peter turned, the nightmarish scene indelibly printed on his memory for the rest of his life. Three of the children lay sprawled next to their mother. The little girl, a garish, bloody hole in her forehead, lay on her back eyes wide, blood dripping onto her lifeless face. Pathetically scrawny legs, splattered with blood, stuck out from beneath her coat.

Curled into the foetal position, her brothers looked as though they were sleeping peacefully either side of their mother. Arms thrown carelessly over her thin body Naomi nursed her baby. Only the blood seeping through their clothes belied the surreal tableau lit by the penetrating beam of light.

Blinded by the brightness Isaac was standing now, facing the bridge, his eldest son at his feet clinging to his legs. He screamed towards the light tearing at his clothes. A fresh hail of bullets swept the boat drowning his convulsive sobs.

Aaron stood up to pull his father back down under the canopy. For an instant the boy stood stiff and rigid, his hand outstretched to his father. Suddenly, he crumpled like a rag doll, dead before his head hit the wooden seat. Isaac's screams died in his throat as bullets tore into his body; the force sending him overboard into the swirling, black water.

Bullets rained from the bridge even though they had almost drifted out of range. Peter and Claus threw themselves into the water and swam for the bank. Suddenly, Claus' upper body reared up as a hail of bullets caught him in the back and head. He fell backwards into the river. Feebly, he thrashed the water, his life ebbing away with the current. He floated downstream until his body snagged on a partially submerged tree. When the Gestapo picked him up he was lying face up in the water, teeth bared in a grotesque, silent protest.

Peter dived underwater swimming with all his strength. Floating tentacles of reeds caught at his legs threatening to entangle him; to pull him down into the murky depths. His lungs were bursting. He thought his head would explode, but he kept going letting the undercurrent, which was swifter at this point, propel him forward.

He broached the water like a breeching whale, his breath rasping painfully in his throat. Coughing and spluttering he dog-paddled while he scanned up river. There was no movement on the river, no dark shapes following him, but they would not give up. Fleischer would not be satisfied until they found him dead or alive.

Slowly, he brought his breathing under control. He didn't know how far the current had carried him. It was quiet now. No gunfire, no guttural voices barking orders, only the soft lap of water against the river bank. He had to get out of the water to find shelter and some dry clothes.

Hermann must have heard the commotion and driven away before he was detected. Swimming to the bank he reached for the branch of an overhanging tree. Straining, muscles protesting, he hauled himself out of the water and collapsed exhausted onto the wet grass.

For a few minutes he lay there, face down. Memories of the horrific slaughter he had witnessed flashed in front of his eyes like scenes in a speeded up film. His old fear returned as something crept across his back prompting him to sit up. He had to get away from there. They would already be searching the river.

Dogs barking in the distance confirmed his fears. Soon they would pick up his scent. Moving silently towards the dense undergrowth he pushed his way through. Rain-soaked branches dripped onto his head and shoulders. It was dark, very dark. Mulched vegetation stuck to his trousers. Mist hung low concealing trees that suddenly loomed into his vision. Thicker close to the ground it swirled round his ankles. Shivering violently, impeded by the weight of his water-logged clothes, he stumbled on.

"It can't be far to the road now. I must keep going! I must keep going!"

Suddenly, he heard a new noise, the snap of a twig underfoot. The slightest of sounds, but to Peter it echoed like thunder in his ears. Holding his breath he stopped stock still. Rooted to the spot he listened intently for another sound.

They must have surrounded me, baited me like an animal ready for the kill he thought. In the darkness his eyes moved rapidly from side to side.

"It won't be easy you bastards! Come and get me and I'll take a few of you with me," he muttered.

Suddenly, a hand clamped over his mouth. An arm came round his neck preventing any movement. He struggled furiously, desperately trying to turn his body so that he could get a grip on his assailant, but he had lost his strength in his battle with the river.

"Calm down!" a voice whispered urgently. "It's me, Hermann."

Peter felt a wave of relief and nausea wash over him. Hermann took his hand away and reached out to steady him.

"Let's get going!" he ordered. "The quicker we get away from here the better."

He dragged Peter upright and propelled him towards an opening in the trees. A car, its engine idling, waited in the lane just beyond the woods. Hermann pushed Peter inside, rammed his foot on the accelerator and roared away.

Peter slumped in the rear shivering from head to toe. Hermann thrust a flask at him.

"Drink some of this," he said, "it will warm you up."

Gratefully, Peter took a big swig from the flask coughing violently as the liquor hit his throat. He was still cold, but he felt much stronger now.

Hermann looked over his shoulder from the passenger seat taking in Peter's haggard appearance.

"We saw what happened. The bastards mowed them down like animals. They didn't stand a chance," he spat. "We were close by the rendezvous when you and Claus went in the river. I followed you along the bank."

"Thank God," Peter breathed. "The dogs were out. They would have picked up my scent in no time at all."

The car left the lane and crunched up a gravel drive surrounded on both sides by tall fir trees. At the far end a squat, run-down house sat amongst tangles of shrubbery. Another vehicle emerged from behind the house as they pulled up.

"Get in the van," Hermann urged. "Good luck, my friend!"

Within seconds the car was crunching back down the gravel drive.

A figure lunged out of the baker's van. Hurriedly, he helped Peter into the vehicle.

"Here, put these on," he urged, gesturing towards a pile of dry clothes on the back seat. I usually make my deliveries at six near to your apartment. It's being watched, but we have arranged for a little diversion."

Before dawn cast fingers of pale, pink light over the horizon they negotiated the cobbled streets surrounding Peter's building. The driver stopped near an alley and turned to Peter.

"Make your way to the apartment. Don't forget they're looking for someone, but they don't know it's you. When the commotion starts that will be your chance."

Peter grasped the driver's hand,

"Thank you. I don't know your name."

"It's better that way. My family, you understand."

Slowly, the van moved round the corner into the next street.

Peter ducked into the alley following his old familiar route, unaware that Fleischer had seen him after his previous excursion. The sound of boots on cobbles brought him up sharp. Staying in the shadows he pressed himself against the wall listening for the footsteps as they came closer and closer. Breath ragged he fought back the panic rising in his chest. Cold sweat ran into his eyes and down his back. They were patrolling the lanes around the apartment waiting to see if he had been away and would come back. Suddenly, a voice shouted,

"Halt! Halt!"

A vehicle screeched to a stop followed by a loud thud. Guttural voices shouted angrily, running feet then muted laughter. Peter edged to the end of the wall and peered round. The driver of the baker's van was standing in the middle of a pile of bread and flour scattered all over the cobbles. Waving his arms he gesticulated wildly at a group of laughing soldiers.

"My bread, it's ruined!" he wailed. "Some of this is for the barracks and Gestapo headquarters. You'll pay for this!"

At the mention of the Gestapo soldiers hurried into the road and started picking up the bread.

"Achtung!"

Clouds of white dust covered his jackboots as an officer stamped into the mêlée. Furiously, he spun on his heel.

"Quickly, you fools," he ordered. "Clear up this mess and get him out of here!"

Peter waited until the guard near the front door of the apartment strode towards the others. Swiftly, he lunged into the courtyard and up the fire escape easing himself through the window.

Light poured in through the open curtains. Someone was hammering on the door. A voice barked,

"Open up!"

Quickly, Peter donned his robe and opened the door. Fleischer pushed past the SS officer into the hall.

"Where were you last night Brandt?"

"Where was I? Here of course."

"Don't toy with me Brandt. You were not here last night."

"Where else would I be? You didn't come to the apartment, did you?" Peter queried chancing his luck.

Fleischer was bluffing. They would not have come so soon after he had been detained. He wasn't a Jew or a gypsy. Even the Gestapo had to have solid evidence to arrest a German, especially an academic carrying out important research for the Führer.

"Search the apartment!" the SS officer ordered.

"Some Jews were caught last night trying to escape from Berlin," Fleischer began. "We know they had help. The bodies of two of your colleagues, your friends, were fished from the river. A third man escaped. I think that man was you Brandt!" he snarled.

"I can assure you I was…"

Peter stared at the SS officer standing in the doorway of the bedroom. His eyes gleamed triumphantly as he sneered,

"Perhaps you can explain this Herr Brandt?" he smirked. With his riding crop he picked up a sodden shoe covered with grass and bits of reeds. "These are your shoes, are they not?"

Peter's shoulders sagged. He slumped onto the sofa wracking his brain for an explanation. What a fool he was not to remember his shoes were wet.

Fleischer nodded to a soldier. Roughly, he hoisted Peter off the sofa and pushed him towards the door with the muzzle of his gun.

"It was raining yesterday," Peter protested as they bundled him down the iron staircase. "I went for a walk by the lake. Do you think I'm stupid? I would have got rid of them if I had been the man you wanted."

He grimaced as they herded him into the back of the car. Slamming the door they shot off in the direction of Prinz Albrecht Strasse.

"Yes Peter Brandt," he thought bitterly, "you *are* a stupid man."

Fleischer threw the shoes onto the floor in front of his desk, a look of blatant satisfaction on his face.

"Do you deny these are your shoes Brandt?"

"No, but I deny I was near the river last night. I was in my apartment."

"Then how are your shoes in such a mess?"

"I told you I went for a walk near the lake yesterday after I left the university."

"You went for a walk, but it was down on the river bank, wasn't it?"

Brauer, who had quietly entered the room, brought his hand back and slapped Peter hard opening up the unhealed split in his lip. Lifting his hand again he gave Peter an evil grin.

"Not yet Brauer," Fleischer purred in a silky voice pushing his face close to Peter's. "Come Brandt, tell the truth. I am not

Brauer. I don't like to hit people, especially men of your intellect."

Peter didn't respond. What was the point? He stared ahead, his eyes fixed on the far wall, blood trickling from his swollen lips. Fleischer walked out leaving the door open. Outside Krause, the fat corporal, lounged against the wall waiting impatiently for Brauer to give a signal.

"Achtung!" Brauer snarled bringing the thuggish corporal to attention. "Take him downstairs!"

Roughly, Krause hauled Peter from the chair and pushed him towards the door. He dragged him down the corridor into a cell-like room similar to where they had put him last time. The same dirty green walls, naked bulb under a straight-backed chair, foul-smelling bucket. Dominating one wall a metal bath filled with dirty water.

Krause flung him into the chair under the harsh light. Brauer sauntered in drawing on a foul-smelling cigarette.

"Take off his shirt!" he ordered, his cadaverous face pure evil.

Stripped to the waist Peter waited sweat pouring down his back. A yellow crust had formed over the burns on his hands and leg, but most of them were superficial. This time he knew it would be worse.

Brauer loomed over him and pressed his cigarette on one of the sores. Peter clamped his jaws together stifling the cry that rose in his throat. Systematically, Brauer pressed the glowing tip on each sore until Peter cried out with pain.

Grinning with satisfaction Brauer circled the chair jabbing the cigarette at Peter. On each shoulder, his ribs, the fleshy part of his stomach. His whole body felt as though it were burning. Peter tried to get up from the chair, but Krause pushed him back punching him hard in the face. His lips looked like raw meat, bruised and mashed, oozing blood down his chest.

"Well Brandt, now tell me where you were last night."

His pain temporarily forgotten Peter screamed at Brauer,

"There *is* nothing more! You are doing this because I refused to join the Nazi Party!"

"We are well aware of your sentiments, but don't think your position in the university will protect you for much longer."

Krause was fidgeting with something above Peter's head. Looking up he saw that he was unravelling the electric wire so that it almost reached the floor. His fat, sausage-like fingers removed the bulb then unscrewed the socket to reveal the bare wires. Horrified, Peter turned to Brauer as realisation dawned on him. Before he could utter a word Krause pinned his arms to his sides and tied them with a leather strap. Gleefully, he waggled the wire in front of Peter's face then touched him lightly on the wrist. Peter recoiled as the shock travelled up his arm.

Twice more Krause touched him lightly with the wires. The third time he pressed it down hard. Again and again he held the live wire to his body. From a distance Peter heard piercing screams then he realised they were his own: louder and louder until his head slumped forward onto his chest.

Every time he lost consciousness Krause slapped him across the face until he was aware of his surroundings. Dragging Peter towards the metal bath he thrust his head through the scum floating on top into icy-cold water. Krause held it there until Peter thought his lungs would burst. So I will drown after all he thought ironically.

Filthy water filled his mouth, clouded his eyes. He couldn't hold his breath any longer. Suddenly, Krause pulled his head back. Spluttering and gasping Peter drew in great gulps of fetid air. Again Krause thrust his head under the water until he felt himself drifting, drifting into blackness; detached from his surroundings and pain as though it were happening to someone else.

Images of Eleanor and Johann floated inside his head. Walking in the Tiergarten; Eleanor in her wedding dress; singing Johann to sleep. Naomi Levine's pale, anguished face:

175

lifeless eyes, tangled limbs, rivers of blood. A macabre, bloody tableau of a Renaissance painting. He slid to the floor, his legs buckling under him. From a distance a voice snarled,

"Get up Brandt!"

He was falling, falling into a deep, black pit.

The room was spinning, spinning round and round. Two faces leered over him grinning satanically, bared teeth like wolves after their prey. Gradually, the dizziness stopped and the mists cleared. Peter looked up at Krause who was standing over him fists clenched. Viciously, the corporal kicked him in the groin. He doubled up in agony drawing his legs up under his chin. Roughly, he dragged him across the cell and threw him into the bathtub.

Peter lay there unable to move, his head thrown back, long legs dangling over the end. As Krause leered over him Peter saw he was holding the live wires in front of him. Recoiling in horror he struggled to get out of the bath. If he touched him it was certain death.

"That's enough Krause," Fleischer ordered from the doorway, "at least for now."

Krause whirled round at the sound of Fleischer's voice. Losing his balance he slipped in a pool of water on the greasy floor. Mustering all his strength Peter lunged out of the bath throwing himself against the opposite wall where the floor was dry. Off balance Krause wobbled near the bath, still holding the live wires. His screams filled the cell echoing down the corridors as he tumbled into the dirty water. Futilely, he clawed at the edge of the bath, eyes bulging, his body convulsing in an horrific dance of death. One final twitch and he was still. Brauer was standing completely still in the far corner, a look of total disbelief on his corpse-like features.

Fleischer stared at the gruesome scene.

"You fool!" he screamed at Brauer who was staring vacantly at Krause.

Recovering his composure he lisped,

"That arsehole Krause electrocuted himself," he said flatly.

"I can see that! Get out!" Fleischer raged. "There will have to be an investigation over this. You will have a lot of explaining to do."

Brauer came to attention, clicked his heels and stamped out of the cell.

Consumed with hatred Fleischer stared at Peter lying in a crumpled heap against the wall. He knew the Jew lover was lying, but he didn't have enough proof. He wanted him dead like his traitorous friends, but there were other ways of dealing with him. His research had been slow; questions were being asked. Now was the time to implement his contingency plans.

"It is time Brandt; time for you to serve the Fatherland," he murmured.

CHAPTER SIXTEEN

Nobody knew what had happened to the bodies of Claus and Otto except Gisela. Early, the morning after the shootings, pounding fists startled her from sleep. Frightened neighbours watched from behind lace curtains in their smart houses beside the river in Kladow.

"What do you want?" Where are you taking me?"

"You are to be taken to the mortuary," Kappler, the SS officer informed her.

"The mortuary!"

A thrill of fear shot through her chest. Otto had been out all night. He had stayed in the city overnight after celebrating a colleague's retirement.

"Has something happened to my husband?"

"No more questions," Kappler snapped. "You will know soon enough."

Gisela slumped in her seat, her heart fluttering like the wings of a captive bird.

"No, it wasn't true. Otto couldn't be dead!"

Taking deep breaths she willed herself to calm down.

"There's some mistake. I'm certain of it," she assured herself.

Gisela shivered with apprehension when she saw the still shape on the gurney; the tag tied to the bloodless foot.

"This *is* your husband?" queried the Gestapo official as the attendant drew back the sheet.

Otto's white face, the skin stretched tightly over his cheekbones, lay in horrific pose. His teeth were drawn back like those of an animal; an animal full of hate for its predators. Bullet holes riddled his body; those visible in his chest already blackening at the edges. Gisela gasped and would have slumped to the ground if the SS officer hadn't supported her slight frame. Slowly, she nodded and turned away from the body pushing Kappler's hand from her arm. She gave him a look of such cold hatred that he flinched; a sensation he rarely experienced.

Four weeks later Gisela received another visit in the middle of the night. Too frightened to answer the door she cowered in her bed as the SS hammered it into splinters.

"What do you want?" she demanded.

"You are a good-looking woman Frau Wagner; blonde and blue-eyed. The type of woman who can breed fine, German children in the Lebensborn. You are to come with us on the orders of the Führer. Consider yourself fortunate that you haven't been shot for treason like your Jew loving husband."

Gisela recoiled in horror as the SS officer approached her and flung back the bedclothes. Involuntarily, her hand moved to her stomach in a protective gesture.

"We know all about the Jew lover's brat, but he will be the first of many," he sneered. "Your other children will have fine, German SS officers for their fathers."

He turned to his subordinate.

"Take her!"

"No, I won't go. Don't touch me!"

Gisela screamed and kicked as they bundled her down the stairs into the back of a car waiting to take her to the nursery near Munich.

Gisela had heard rumours about the Lebensborn; how they took away children and gave them to Nazi families to raise. Even fair-haired, Polish children had been snatched from their parents and transported to the Fatherland to be adopted by Germans. What chance would she have to keep her child? A child of pure, German blood with all the physical Aryan qualities Himmler admired.

Gisela was surprised at the care and comfort she was given at the Lebensborn. Clean nurseries, comfortable rooms and good, nutritious food. Food to build Hitler's super, Aryan race that would one day rule the world. Cold hatred clenched her heart like a vice when she thought about what might become of her unborn child.

There were around thirty expectant mothers in the home, mostly young and unmarried. They were happy that they were being looked after by the nurses and doctors. Most of them had been mated with tall, blond, blue-eyed SS officers.

"I've given birth to five magnificent sons for the Führer," a buxom blonde boasted. "I will be well rewarded for my efforts for the Fatherland."

Some of the officers were married men with families. In their twisted mentality it was considered an honour to father as many illegitimate children as possible to populate areas with the super race.

Gisela was only weeks away from confinement. The doctors were pleased with her. She was young and healthy; a wonderful specimen. That's what they were, specimens, the women and their children. An experiment in eugenics for the obsessed Himmler.

She kept to herself during communal activities, sitting alone in a quiet corner. On the third morning a rosy-cheeked blonde, who had been surreptitiously watching her, came over and sat next to her.

"Ilse," she introduced herself. "I've been here for five months. My baby is due soon."

"How can you stand it?" Gisela asked.

"Oh, it's not so bad. They look after us and the food is good, better than I had before I came here."

"But don't you care about what will happen to your baby? I've heard rumours…"

"Keep your voice down! Don't worry, you'll be fine. The baby will be looked after. This is my third. The other two have been adopted by good German families."

"Your third, but…"

"The first was by Marius, my boyfriend, but he's in the army. I don't know where he is now. The second was by an SS officer…" Her voice trailed to a whisper, her eyes clouded with pain, "and this one…"

She laughed aloud and patted her stomach. I don't even know the father's name except that he is in the SS. What about you?"

"Otto, my husband is dead. I didn't want to come here. The SS forced me to come."

"Well, you'll just have to make the best of it. Not all of us are happy with the arrangement, but we have no choice. Let's go and eat. If you don't they'll force you. Their only concern is that you have a healthy baby; that is the most important thing for them."

"I hate them!" Gisela spat the words.

"Don't be a fool!"

Looking round furtively Ilse propelled Gisela towards the dining room.

Later that afternoon Ilse took Gisela to the nursery to see the new born babies. Some mothers were feeding their children. Others stared vacantly at the walls while their offspring gurgled in their cribs. A young girl, who didn't look more than sixteen, was crying hysterically as she rocked her baby. A nurse approached her and tried to take the child, but the girl refused. Roughly, the nurse prised her arms away while another snatched the baby from the whimpering girl. Suddenly, she let out a keening cry and jumped out of the bed. Nightgown flapping around her legs she ran screaming into the corridor. Gisela never saw her again.

Women huddled together whispering, casting sly glances at Gisela. When she passed by conversation stopped mid sentence. Not even Ilse would tell her what had happened to the poor girl, or the baby, except that the child had a club foot. Scraps of information from overheard, hushed conversations filled her with horror and anxiety. Gisela knew she had to get out of the Lebensborn home, but she had no-one to turn to; nobody she could trust. Otto was dead. Her mother lived over two hundred kilometres away. There was no way she could contact her. It was hopeless.

As the baby's birth drew closer she was filled with despair. Sitting in a corner on her own she picked at her food refusing to socialise with the others. She just sat staring vacantly with her hands over her stomach.

"They won't take my baby," she vowed, "I will die first."

Every day the pregnant women walked in the gardens. Part of the programme for healthy living, to ensure the welfare of the unborn child. Without protest Gisela donned her coat and dragged outside with the others.

It had rained heavily overnight, but now a fine drizzle filled the air, little more than a mist of rain that fell straight down from a murky, grey sky. Everything looked so forlorn and depressing; it suited Gisela's mood. She walked alone along the wet path. Tall pine trees skirted the perimeter of the gardens inside high stone walls. Moisture dripped from branches that overhung the path adding to the puddles, saturating the grass verges. She thought about Otto; how proud he had been when she told him about the baby. Stifling a sob she looked away as one of the nurses called from across the lawn.

"Come along, we must go back indoors now. We don't want to catch cold do we?"

Gisela dragged her feet, unwilling to go back into what had become her prison. If she stayed out, got wet enough, perhaps she would get pneumonia and die before the baby was born. That was preferable to what awaited her in this infernal place.

"Hurry now!" the nurse called from the shelter of the big double doors. Reluctantly, Gisela walked slowly back along the path. Branches creaked as a low wind moaned through the trees like an anguished voice calling out to her.

"Gisela! Gisela!"

She stopped and looked around, but the garden was empty except for the nurse still hovering in the doorway. For a split second she thought it was Otto, but he was dead. Her imagination was playing tricks on her, because she had been thinking about him as she always did when she walked in the garden. Momentarily, she faltered then quickened her pace towards the building. She hesitated, listening for the sound. There it was again. She heard her name being called, but now the voice was more urgent.

"Gisela! Don't stop, just keep on walking. Don't look this way. It's me, Peter."

Branches moved barely perceptibly as he moved through the undergrowth keeping pace with Gisela. Her heart leapt with a joy she hadn't felt since she had been brought to the Lebensborn. Covering her face she pretended to cough.

"Peter! Is that really you? I thought you had been arrested by the Gestapo?"

"I was but they let me go. There's no time to explain. You must go back inside or they'll get suspicious. I'll come again. Just be sure to walk in the garden every day along this same path. I'm making plans to get you to a safe place."

His voice died away amongst the swaying branches and rain now hammering the path, soaking her clothes. A nurse ran out, grabbed her arm and pushed her towards the building.

"You *wilful* girl. Think about your child!"

Gisela *was* thinking about her baby. Hope sparked in her breast lightening her footsteps as she ran towards the door.

For the next two weeks Gisela took the same path, but there was no sign of Peter. She felt heavy and cumbersome when she walked. Seemingly absorbed in her own thoughts, her eyes traced the line of trees for any movement or sound coming from the undergrowth. But Peter did not come. Towards the end of the second week her waters broke on the daily walk around the garden.

"Why hasn't he come?" she thought despairingly as she was led indoors by a clucking nurse.

When her contractions started coming closer together they ushered her to the delivery room. Spotlessly clean white, sanitised walls: nurses in crisp, starched uniforms smiling at her reassuringly. It was unreal, like the terrifying images she experienced during her restless nights after Otto was shot. But this was no dream just a waking nightmare.

"He'll come back! He'll come back!" she cried through her pain, not realising she was speaking aloud.

"Who'll come back?" the young, blonde nurse asked.

"Her husband was shot by the Gestapo trying to help Jews escape from Berlin," interjected the thin, bespectacled doctor who had just entered the room. "She is fully dilated now. I can see the head. Push down when you have the next pain," he instructed.

Gisela smiled with joy when her baby was delivered. The doctor slapped the infant on the bottom. Her eyes brimmed with tears as a lusty cry filled the room.

"He is a fine specimen," the older nurse declared putting the baby in Gisela's arms.

"Yes, you have a beautiful son," the doctor smiled kindly.

Patting her arm reassuringly he walked briskly out of the room. He hated these moments; moments of pure joy. Soon elation would turn to despair and hopelessness for this girl, but Himmler would have another fine Aryan.

Gisela gazed at her son, so tiny and vulnerable, little dimples in his cheeks just like his father. Otto's son. Her heart contracted with fear when she thought about him being taken away from her. Hot tears fell onto the baby's face as she cradled him, rocking backwards and forwards in a frenzy of desolation. The nurse, who had been busy clearing up, came over to her.

"No, you can't take him!" Gisela screamed at the nurse

"There's no need to worry. He must be washed for the doctor to examine him to make sure he's healthy." The baby let out a strong wail. "Not much to worry about with this one. Rest now and we'll bring him to you very soon. He'll need to be fed on your pure milk," she added prising the baby from Gisela's arms.

Gisela thought her heart would break when the nurse carried the baby away. Thirty minutes later she brought him back for his feed. Noisily, he sucked at her breast, translucent eyelids fluttering with contentment.

"Your name will be Martin," she whispered. "Martin Otto Wagner. I swear before God that nobody will take you from me."

As soon as she was able Gisela wrapped up the baby and took him for a stroll in the garden with the other new mothers. Every day she walked the path where she had heard Peter's voice. She had almost given up hope when, two weeks after the baby's birth, she heard a whisper coming from the bushes.

"Gisela, it's me, Peter!"

"Peter, thank God! I thought something had happened; that you weren't coming back."

"I came a few days later, but I couldn't see you anywhere. I overheard one of the women talking about your son."

Barely able to control her anxiety Gisela whispered,

"They'll take him Peter. Most mothers only have their babies for a few months while they are breast-feeding. After that they're taken away and given to a German family to raise. I'll never see him again."

"That's not going to happen Gisela. You'll be out of here within the week. I promise."

"But it's impossible. We are watched all the time, even here in the garden."

"You'll be passed a note by a contact who delivers vegetables here. Once you have read it destroy it immediately. Eat it if you have to, but get rid of it. Be sure to wrap yourself and the baby up as warmly as possible. Be ready to go at short notice."

Gisela started to say something, but Peter had gone. She was filled with relief: at the same time terrified that something would go wrong. What if they were caught? They would be shot or sent to a concentration camp. She dared not speculate.

"Pull yourself together," she chastised. "'It's your only chance to keep little Martin with you."

On the steps the nurse blew a shrill note on her whistle signalling for the women to move back inside. Gisela walked swiftly to catch up with the others as they drifted towards the doors. Alert to prying eyes she knew she must be on her guard at all times. No signs of agitation or anxiety to raise suspicions. All she could do now was wait.

Days later Gisela bumped into a delivery man on her way to the dining hall. He wobbled slightly tipping some of the contents of the crate he was carrying.

"Excuse me, mein frau," he apologised chasing the cabbage that had rolled towards Gisela. She bent to pick it up and handed it to him. "Danke."

As he took it he slipped a piece of paper into her hand then swiftly disappeared down the corridor.

Palms wet, hands shaking with the anticipation of being caught, Gisela tucked the note into her blouse and hurried in for lunch.

In high spirits Ilse chatted jovially throughout the meal. It was all Gisela could do to concentrate as she tried to swallow her food. Whatever happened she mustn't let anyone, not even Ilse, know about the plans.

Gisela stood up scraping her chair noisily on the linoleum floor. She was too anxious to sit eating with the others.

"What's your hurry?" commented Ilse. "You haven't eaten your stewed apples yet."

"My stomach feels sour. I think I'm going to be sick," she groaned heading for the lavatory.

Hurriedly, she pushed open the door of the cubicle and pulled out the note.

"Tomorrow – 15.00 hours – we'll create a diversion - wait on the path at the far end of the garden. Wrap up warm."

She re-read the instructions, tore the paper into tiny pieces and dropped it into the lavatory bowl. Startled, she heard the outer door creaking open. A voice shouted,

"Gisela, are you all right?"

It was Ilse checking on her. Dear Ilse, she had become such a good friend. She wished she didn't have to deceive her.

Gisela pretended to retch, spat loudly into the pan and pulled the chain. She watched until every last bit of paper flushed out of sight.

"Yes, I thought I was going to be sick in the dining room. I'm fine now; just a bit of bile, that's all."

Back in their room Ilse talked incessantly about her plans after her baby was born. Gisela wasn't listening. She was pondering on the instructions for the next day.

"What on earth is the matter with you Gisela. I don't think you heard a word I said, did you?"

"I'm sorry, I feel a bit feverish and shivery, that's all. I think I may be coming down with a cold. I'll wrap up warm this afternoon when we go outside, just in case."

At least that will give me an excuse for wearing extra clothing," she thought as the nurse appeared with the baby.

"Don't say anything," she whispered to Ilse. "They won't let me near Martin if they think I have a cold."

Gisela tossed and turned all that night. Dreaming first of walking through green fields full of spring flowers with Martin gurgling in her arms. From somewhere beyond the verdant grass, a smiling figure walked towards her. Otto! Arms outstretched she ran towards him. Suddenly, his face melted away, like wax from a candle, until it became a grinning skull that replicated itself until there were hundreds of them. Bony talons reached out and snatched the baby from her. Throwing him into the air; kicking him like a football from one to the other.

She awoke sweating with fear. Cold rivulets of perspiration crawled down her back soaking her nightdress. Gisela crept out of bed and peered through the window. Scudding across the sky dark, heavy clouds tinged silver by a white, wintry sun creeping over the horizon. Fingers of pale, silvery-grey light spread slowly across the sky. A gleaming hoar frost had transformed the garden into a magical fairyland.

Cold morning sunlight slanted through the trees illuminating strings of droplets frozen as they dripped towards the ground. Branches hung their heads heavy with icicle swords. Small stones scattering the earthen edges of the path shimmered, sparkling like diamonds set in jet. Threads of frost filigreed the path creating delicate, intricate patterns of icy lace. Gisela shivered. Even her thick, flannel nightdress failed to protect her against the chill

"Such beauty," she sighed, "beauty that conceals the evil within these walls."

The morning seemed interminably long to Gisela. Curbing her frustration she chatted with the other women on the usual topics. Progress of their babies or pregnancies; baby names although they knew that any name they chose would be ignored.

At last it was time for their afternoon stroll. Only very severe weather stopped them walking outside. A bit of frost was nothing. Cold, fresh air was considered vital for good health and strong children. At last it was time.

"Wrap up warm, all of you," instructed the nurse. "It's quite cold today. You must put on a coat in this weather," she snapped at one of the girls. "No huddling in groups gossiping. Be sure to keep moving, that way you'll stay warm."

Gisela thanked God for the unexpected frost. Now they would all have to pad themselves with extra clothing diverting attention away from her.

Gisela donned thick woollen slacks, a heavy coat and fleece-lined boots she had used for skiing before the war. Finally, she wrapped herself in a heavy scarf topped by a knitted cap with side flaps to pull down over her ears.

Martin slept snugly inside a padded, one-piece suit with a fur-trimmed hood. Even this was insufficient to ward off the extreme cold. A woollen blanket provided extra warmth. She packed spare diapers around her waist strapping more to her legs. Satisfied that the baby would sleep after his feed she ventured out into the garden.

Some women were already out shivering in the cold. Bursts of white vapour punctuated their conversation as they briskly walked under the frozen trees. Gisela strode purposefully towards the end of the garden slowing down as she came close to the oak tree. Suddenly, an alarm shrilled from inside the home. Thick, acrid smoke poured from the open door as a nurse stumbled out coughing and spluttering.

"Fire! Fire! Form a group and stay away from the building. That is an order!"

Pandemonium as nurses and orderlies poured through the open doors. Confused by the turn of events the women clung to their babies huddling in a disorderly mass in front of Gisela.

"The building has been completely evacuated!" shouted one of the orderlies.

In the near distance the sound of a fire engine. Within minutes it swung through the entrance and lurched to a halt. Fireman spilled onto the gravel drive connecting hoses to fire hydrants, rushing towards the building with axes at the ready. A fireman disappeared inside as two police cars and an ambulance screeched to a halt. Black, noxious smoke, thicker now, belched from the doorway. It drifted down the garden almost obliterating the figures of the women.

Shocked, they stared at the drama unfolding before them. Behind them Gisela stepped backwards, edging closer and closer to the oak tree, until she was standing directly underneath it. Peter's face appeared amongst a tangle of undergrowth.

"Now!" he whispered.

He grabbed Gisela's arm and pulled her behind the bushes. For a few seconds they waited, but nobody had noticed amongst the confusion.

"Keep low and skirt the wall," Peter ordered. "There's a gate a few yards away."

Gisela almost fell spread-eagled in the frozen mud as she caught her foot in a tree root. Peter grabbed the baby and made for a high, wooden gate concealed by young trees that had sprouted in front of it. He dislodged a notch, peered out then turned the rusty iron ring. It creaked, the sound seeming unnaturally loud to Gisela whose heart was hammering like a piston engine.

As Peter stepped out he signalled to a man near the corner of the side street. The man turned up his collar and nonchalantly lit a cigarette. Puffs of smoke mingled with his frozen breath. An ambulance drove slowly round the corner easing quietly to a stop outside the gate. Quickly, Peter bundled Gisela and the baby into the back.

"You'll be taken to my uncle's estate in the country for a few weeks. From there you'll be smuggled into Switzerland by one of our organisation. Goodbye Gisela."

"Thank you Peter…"

Too late, he had closed the doors. Wheels screeching, they sped away past the main gate of the home as though they were taking casualties to the nearby hospital. Peter gave one last look at the retreating ambulance and disappeared from sight.

PART TWO

CHAPTER SEVENTEEN

Switzerland and Germany 1941

Gisela gazed out over the majestic Swiss Alps so beautiful in summer. Now winter was setting in she felt suffocated by their proximity. After spending a month with Peter's uncle she had been taken over the border to the Bernese Oberland. Thinner, hair dyed chestnut brown, wire-framed spectacles worn on the end of her nose, she looked completely different from the Gisela in the Lebensborn.

False papers had been obtained in the name of Erika Koch, the widow of an accountant from Zurich. Her neighbours had heard about her situation. Koch had been tragically killed in a skiing accident on one of the black runs. His body had never been recovered after an avalanche swept him away. Together, with her infant son, Martin, she had set up home in the mountains to be near where her husband had died.

Her chalet, on the edge of Mürren, afforded her the anonymity she craved; but it was lonely, so very lonely. Sometimes she took the funicular down into Lauterbrünnen stopping for coffee and apfelstrüdel in one of the restaurants. Fortunately, it was a German speaking area so there were no language barriers. The locals, curious about a woman and baby living alone in the alps, spoke kindly to her whenever she walked into the village. Eventually, she got to know the villagers, but she never entertained them: never accepted their invitations for fear of detection by Germans who still took skiing holidays in the area.

Only Gerda, the daily housekeeper, alleviated the boredom. Chores finished they settled down with strong, black coffee dipping sweet buns into the steaming liquid. Gerda told her all the local gossip. When she talked about the war Gisela feigned mild interest. She did not want to arouse suspicions. There were those who harboured admiration for the Führer. Peter had saved her life; given her son a chance of life. Like Otto, she would play her part in helping *Regis* and the organisation whenever she was needed.

Overhead, the moon shone in a crystal, clear sky illuminating the majestic peaks of the Jungfrau Joch. Stars embedded in the velvet, midnight-blue canopy, shone as they had shone for a million years; stars that looked bright and big enough to touch. Already the weather was changing again. A wind moaned softly through the pine trees blowing heavy, dark clouds towards the mountain until the moon was obliterated. It was black outside now; black and empty.

The first, fat snowflakes fell past the window to be devoured by the snow-covered slopes. Gradually, it increased until the window looked like a snowy-white, lace curtain against the backdrop of the alps. Chinks of light from nearby chalets spilled liquid gold over the snow. Sounds of boisterous laughter, carried on the wind from passing villagers, enhanced her loneliness. Sighing, she gathered up her son in her arms. He was what gave her the strength to live, to look forward into an uncertain future.

A fierce yellow sun shone in a canopy of brilliant blue, lifting Peter's spirits as he strolled along the Unter den Linden. Eleanor had wintered in Sweden waiting to be shipped over to the United States, but it had become more and more dangerous to sail the Atlantic, because of attacks by U-boats. When she finally left, Helga opted to stay in Sweden, fearing she may be interned if she travelled to the United States. Besides, Eleanor and the others had American passports so they were able to fly from Sweden to London. Eventually, they landed safely in Boston in April 1941.

It was summer now. Peter imagined her, tanned and healthy, sitting on the beach in Cape Cod. He smiled at the thought of Johann playing in the sand, hair bleached white blond. He missed them so much, but they were safe now with Eleanor's parents. At least he had that to comfort him.

He walked to a table at a nearby restaurant and ordered coffee. Casually, he opened his newspaper appearing engrossed in its contents, but he was watching the man who had stopped in the café next door. The same man who had been following him since Fleischer released him from Gestapo headquarters. A stocky man in a grey suit, a Panama pulled down over his eyes. Fleischer had left him alone, but he knew he was being watched day and night. Sometimes it was a different man. Occasionally, a tall, blonde, elegant woman trailed behind him pretending to window shop.

Questions were being asked about the progress of his research. He had been ordered to hand over work he had already completed for scrutiny by the Gestapo. Soon Fleischer would act to remove Peter from the university. He would force him into the Wehrmacht regardless of the importance of his research to the Third Reich. Peter was prepared to give his life for his country, but he didn't want to fight for an ideology he detested. It was only a matter of time before Fleischer made his move.

During the summer vacation Peter travelled to his uncle's estate. Using his motorcycle was not an option. His apartment was under surveillance night and day. He must walk to the station and try to board a train without being seen. He was in luck. Today the stocky, overweight man was following him.

Peter ambled along, carrying a large shopping bag, as though out for a morning stroll. Occasionally, he stopped to look in a shop window, gauging the distance between himself and the agent. Gradually, he increased his pace walking faster and faster. He glanced behind. The agent was running now, panting with the effort of keeping up with Peter's long strides.

At the next corner he loped the length of the block then darted into an alley. For a full two minutes he watched the entrance until he saw the agent stumble his way past.

"With any luck the bastard will have a heart attack," Peter grinned.

Satisfied that he had lost the agent, Peter set off in the opposite direction.

On reaching the Bannhofstrasse he darted into the lavatory. Quickly, he applied some glue to his chin and upper lip. Next he patted on a false beard and moustache. It was difficult to put in place without a mirror, but he had no choice. He stripped off his jacket and trousers to reveal a smart, dark business suit. Delving into the bag he pulled out a black Homburg and a black medical case. Finally, he donned a pair of gold-framed spectacles. Taking a deep breath he tentatively opened the cubicle door. There was no-one in sight. He took stock of his appearance in the mirror over the hand basin.

"Excellent," he murmured giving his moustache a little tweak. "You're a credit to your profession Dr. Stahlecker."

Satisfied with his disguise he stepped out onto the platform to mingle with the crowd. Everywhere, watchful eyes scanned passengers: in the cafeteria, the ticket office, boarding trains. His heart skipped a beat as he purchased his ticket. It was impossible for him to go directly to his uncle's house in the Brandenburg. First he would have to travel towards Munich before returning north. It would be a long, tortuous journey to get to the estate.

After two stops he changed trains, changed again after another four stops, dodging in and out of cafés and crowded platforms. Finally, he boarded the train for Munich. Finding an empty compartment he slumped onto the seat nearest the window. Outside an SS officer marched purposefully down the platform where a tall, thin man waited. After a brief conversation they boarded the train.

"Gestapo," Peter muttered. "I'd know the vicious pigs anywhere."

Doors slammed, wheels screeched against metal as the train lumbered away from the platform. They would be checking passengers all along the train. He would have to brazen it out.

The door in the next compartment slammed shut. Unsteady footsteps approached as the train lurched down the track.

"Identification!" the agent snapped from the doorway.

Peter hurriedly delved into his case and produced his papers. He forced himself to remain calm, but his heart was hammering in his chest. He felt the blood rush to his head staining his cheeks. Laughing, he pulled out a handkerchief and dabbed at his face.

"Phew, it's hot in here!" he exclaimed.

"You are a medical doctor?" the agent said examining the papers.

"Yes, I'm on my way to a conference in Munich."

Staring hard at Peter the agent handed back his papers. For a second he hesitated at the door, a steely glimmer in his eyes. Without another word he clicked his heels and marched out. Peter could hear compartment doors opening and closing all along the corridor. Sooner or later he knew they would be back. He had to get off the train.

Too late, the train was slowing down. Passengers were hauling luggage down the corridor to the exit doors blocking his escape. They must be approaching a station. Now they would come back for him. He was trapped like an animal in an abattoir.

With a squeal of brakes the train sidled into the platform. Cautiously, Peter stepped into the corridor. A crowd had gathered at the external door waiting to get out. Suddenly, a commotion towards the rear caught his attention. The SS officer was shouting orders at a group of soldiers who had appeared from the guards' van. They lunged onto the train emerging a few minutes later with a swarthy middle-aged man. Protesting loudly, they hauled him out of the station into a waiting car.

Peter stepped onto the platform just as the Gestapo agent walked past.

"You are leaving the train?" he queried.

"Just stretching my legs."

"Enjoy your conference Herr Doctor."

Turning abruptly he marched into the ticket office to make a telephone call. Through the window his eyes followed Peter as he re-boarded the train. Abruptly, he slammed down the receiver and bolted onto the platform. The front carriage was already chugging away from the station. Cursing, he yanked open a door and threw himself inside the second carriage. Brushing aside offers of help he lurched down the carriage pushing aside passengers smoking in the corridor.

At the rear of the train Peter closed the lavatory door quietly behind him, stepping quickly back into the recess near the external door. Cautiously, he lowered the window and peered out. Six carriages ahead the engine was steaming round a curve in the track. Most passengers had their window blinds only partially closed against the glare of the sun. If he tried to get out on the curve he would be seen by people in the carriages at the front.

Off the bend the train chugged onto the straight quickly gathering speed. Peter eased open the external door and waited. About twenty yards ahead a grassy bank sloped away into some dense undergrowth. Gingerly, he stepped out onto the metal foot panel. Leaning precariously to one side he struggled to force the door shut. An open door would be seen and reported. Mustering all his strength he jumped, trying to clear the shale at the side of the track. Thick, coarse grass cushioned his fall as he landed on the steep slope. Unable to stop he rolled downhill stopping with a bone-jarring thud against a tree trunk.

For a few moments he lay spread-eagled on the grass his breath coming in short, ragged gasps. Watching the puff of steam recede into the distance he smiled imagining the Gestapo agent frantically searching the train. There wasn't another station for over thirty kilometres. By then he would be heading back to the Brandenburg.

Wincing, he dragged himself upright steadying himself against the tree. A sharp pain shot through his ankle, but he had no trouble putting his weight on it.

"Nothing broken, just a bit bruised," he muttered tentatively pressing his ribs.

In the distance smoke curled from a cluster of houses. Whistling merrily he walked gingerly across the fields. He knew the village well. From there he would be able to contact Friedrich.

Tendrils of pale, golden light crept across the sky heralding a bright orange sun peeping over the horizon. Along a narrow farm road a flatbed truck trundled along loaded with milk churns. Peter scratched under his cap at the scruffy, dark wig covering his blond hair. Stripped of his beard, black moustache, elegant clothes replaced with rough farm clothes, there was little resemblance to the smart doctor on his way to Munich..

Questioned by colleagues about his vacation plans he had hinted about going on a walking holiday in the Austrian Alps. For now Friedrich would hide him. He had urged him to get out of Germany, but their work was not finished. In September he would return to Berlin.

Peter walked jauntily down the corridor towards his room in the university.

"Guten morgen Dresner," he said affably to the professor walking towards him.

Dresner grunted, averted his eyes and marched briskly towards a group huddled in close conversation. Whispering, they turned away when Peter approached them and hurried to their various departments. As Peter turned the knob on his door he heard movement from inside. A voice barking orders, hurried footsteps, drawers opening and closing.

"What are you doing in my lab?" Peter demanded.

A soldier, arms full of boxes stuffed with papers, pushed past him.

"We are confiscating your papers on the orders of the Führer," snapped a voice from behind the large desk.

It was Fleischer. Sunlight reflected on his glasses, glinted on his gold tooth. It accentuated the hollows of his face, adding to his devilish appearance.

"It is unfortunate Brandt, but it seems your research has been terminated due to lack of progress. There are many other projects that are doing far better than yours. We will, of course, find you a more suitable occupation."

"I bet you will," Peter sneered.

"The Wehrmacht needs you now Brandt, at the Russlandfeldzug. Take him!" Fleischer snarled.

The Russian Front. Peter's shoulders sagged as a soldier edged him forward with his rifle. This time there was no way out.

"I'm not a coward Fleischer. 'I'll fight for my country, but only for my country."

Head held high he stared into the black eyes of the Gestapo agent without flinching, clicked his heels and marched out.

CHAPTER EIGHTEEN

United States – Cape Cod – July 1941

Eleanor had been back in the United States since April. For the first few weeks she had received letters, via Helga in Sweden, assuring her that Peter was safe in Berlin. The messages had suddenly stopped in late May. She had heard nothing since.

Johann was growing into a sturdy little boy with the same blond hair and blue eyes as his father. Something had happened, she was sure of it. She was desperate for information, but she was thousands of miles away, completely helpless.

She watched Johann scrabbling in the sand, his hair shining almost white in the sun. She didn't want to leave him, but she had to try and find out what had happened to Peter.

"Are you out of your mind Eleanor!" Julia shouted in frustration when she heard her plans. "You can't go back to Germany, you fool!"

"I won't be going back to Germany. I'm going to find Gisela. Helga wrote that she's living quietly in the Swiss Alps. Switzerland is neutral. Nobody can touch me there."

"There are spies everywhere, even in Switzerland. The Germans still go there to ski in the winter. The whole idea is madness. Do you hear me? Madness!"

"Perhaps, but I'll be closer to the organisation there. It will be easier to trace Peter."

"If they knew where he was they would have found him by now."

"My mind is made up. I'll be leaving for Bern next week."

"And what about Johann? Have you thought about him; about who'll look after him when you're gone?"

"You *will* look after him, won't you?" Eleanor looked pleadingly at her sister.

Julia sighed loudly and sank onto the sofa. She knew Eleanor only too well. Once her mind was made up she was like a stone wall. Nothing would change her mind, not even her mother, even though she cried and pleaded with her to see sense. She even accused her of being irresponsible, of disregarding Johann's well-being.

"Come now mother, I have every confidence that he'll be loved and looked after by all of you. Paul loves him too. He's been like a father to him, but Peter is his father. If there's any chance of finding him, however slim, I must take that chance."

Eleanor fastened her seat belt, drawing air deep into her lungs to steady her nerves. Claustrophobia hit her like a hammer as soon as the stewardess closed the cabin doors. Her heart fluttered as the plane shot down the runway. Rigid with fear she squeezed her hands together until her knuckles were white, willing herself to stay calm. It was only her second flight, but already she hated flying. Nothing could convince her that a plane could stay in the air for hours on end without crashing to the ground.

She couldn't quite believe she was on her way to Switzerland. Julia and Paul had friends there who had promised to put her up for a few days. When they were trying to escape over the border into Switzerland Peter had given her the name of a contact living in Bern. A trusted member of the organisation who acted as a conduit for anti-Nazis trying to get out of Germany, but it was over a year ago. Perhaps he was no longer living there.

She pushed the thought out of her mind along with her terror of flying. She was too agitated to eat much, but the stewardess persuaded her to have a gin and tonic to calm her nerves. Sleepy from the alcohol, she closed her eyes and thought about Peter. His face swam before her, fading in and out, while she listened to the drone of the engines.

Eventually, she fell into a fitful sleep. Peter was standing on top of a hill looking down at her, beckoning for her to go to him. She ran and ran, but as she drew close to him the hill retreated as though an invisible hand was pushing it away. She called to him,

"Peter! Peter!"

Arms still outstretched to her he floated towards the hill and disappeared over the misty horizon.

"Are you all right?" queried the stewardess, placing a hand on her shoulder.

Eleanor started when she realised she was still on a plane thousands of feet above the ground.

"Yes, I'm fine thank you. I was dreaming. It must have been the gin and tonic," she laughed shakily.

"Well, you'd better fasten your safety belt. We'll be making our final approach very shortly."

CHAPTER NINETEEN

Switzerland 1941

After a bumpy landing Eleanor emerged into bright sunshine. Carrying hand luggage, passengers were walking the short distance to the arrivals hall. People were sipping coffee, reading newspapers, checking timetables; it all looked so normal. She surveyed the crowd of people waiting for passengers to file through the gate. Some were holding up pieces of cardboard with passengers' names written on them. Suddenly, a man on her left pushed to the front of the group and held up a card with a familiar name on it. Not her name, but one given by Paul when he had telephoned his friend.

"It's not wise to have your real name called out," he had said, "just in case."

When she acknowledged him the man ran to the end of the line and took her bag. He extended a hand.

"Blake Preston. It's great to see you Eleanor," he said with a strong Californian accent. "Jenny, that's my wife, is preparing a meal for you. I expect you're exhausted and hungry. Airline food isn't up to much."

He prattled on while he negotiated the traffic leaving the airport. A few miles from the city he veered off onto a smaller, quieter road.

"Do we have far to go?"

"No, the other side of Thun on the edge of Interlaken. It's lovely there this time of the year."

Tall pines and rocky outcrops dotted steep, green mountains. Crystal clear waterfalls cascaded down to the valley floor. Tucked into the foot of the mountains red-roofed chalets, their façades decorated with colourful murals. Logs stacked in neat piles covered the sides. A faint sound of cow bells, tinkling in the distance, caught her attention.

"It's breathtaking," Eleanor murmured.

Between the roadside trees water glinted in the distance. Eleanor gasped as the lake came into view. Shimmering aqua-blue beneath a backdrop of snow covered alps. Sunlight bathed the surface, glancing off the wake of white-sailed boats surging through the water. A crowded lake steamer glided on the mirror-like surface, so beautiful it was unreal.

Blake pulled up a gravel drive in front of a large, impressive house.

"We're here," he called as a petite brunette ran to the garden gate to greet them.

"Welcome to Switzerland, my dear," Jenny enthused leading Eleanor into the chalet. "It's so good to see someone from back home. I'll show you to your room so you can freshen up before dinner."

Eleanor came downstairs to the sound of laughter and clinking glasses. Blake and Jenny were sitting outside. A table had been laid for dinner.

"It's been so hot this week we've been eating out here most evenings," Blake said waving her to a chair.

When she had arrived the shutters had been closed to keep out the heat. Now she saw French doors flung wide open to reveal a large veranda overlooking the lake.

Early evening light glistened on the snow-covered Alps looming in front of them, giving them an ethereal appearance.

"It's even more beautiful than I imagined. So quiet and peaceful."

"We're between the lakes here, Thun and Brienz. There's lots to see and a number of trips you can take on the steamers."

"That's a wonderful idea, but I must go back to Bern. I'd like to rest up for a day or two first though."

"I'm on leave for a week so I can drive you there," Jenny volunteered."

"There's a shop I have to go to; an antique store. A man there may be able to help me find out what's happened to Peter."

"Not a problem. I know the town well. Shouldn't be hard to find if you have the address."

Two days later the women drove into Bern. The shop was located in a back street well away from the main shopping area.

"It's down here somewhere," Jenny confirmed turning into a narrow, cobbled street little wider than an alley.

"There!" Eleanor exclaimed pointing to a grubby window, barely noticeable until they were upon it.

An ancient accordion took pride of place on a dusty table in the window along with a grandfather clock set against one side wall. A free-standing, glass display case crammed full of watches, cuckoo clocks, old carving tools and miscellaneous bits and pieces covered the back wall.

"Looks more like a junk shop to me!" cried Jenny pulling up the handbrake. "Come on, let's go in and take a look."

A bell tinkled when they pushed open the door, its glass panel filthy with years of grime. Startled, Eleanor took a step backwards halting Jenny's progress as an enormous stuffed, black bear loomed into her peripheral vision. The gloomy room had an air of stagnation about it as though time had been suspended. Dust motes danced and swirled in beams of sunlight that penetrated the dirty window.

A quiet cough brought them up short. A little, dark-haired man appeared from a curtained doorway behind the counter. Yellowish skin, dark, purplish pouches under his knowing black eyes.

"Guten tag," he greeted them. "May I help you?"

"Thank you," Eleanor replied warily, "we're just browsing."

"Is there anything in particular that you are wanting?" he queried.

"I'm particularly interested in old wood carvings of birds. My husband is a keen collector. I promised to take something back to the States for him."

"Ah, I have just the thing," he smiled.

Turning to the window display he extracted a carving of an eagle clinging to a branch.

"It's beautiful, but not quite what I want. Perhaps a different bird, maybe a chuff." Eleanor hesitated. "An alpine chuff evokes memories in the heart."

Eleanor watched the man for any sign of recognition of the password given her by Peter, but there wasn't a glimmer of response.

Taking a chance she lied,

"I remember seeing some beautiful carvings when we were here in 1939."

"Of course, that was in Herr Kappel's day. There were a number of such carvings, but it was an antique shop then, now…" He spread his arms and looked ruefully round the shop. "Now, I sell everything, even junk."

Eleanor had started to perspire heavily under her thin blouse. It was pouring down her back soaking the waistband of her cotton skirt. She was desperate now, desperate to find out what had happened to Kappel. Before she could say anything the junk dealer continued,

"Herr Kappel retired last year and bought a house in Merligen on Lake Thun."

Eleanor's heart sank. Now she would never find him. After purchasing a small wood carving she stopped to admire an ornate clock. Impatiently, Jenny grabbed her arm and gently nudged her outside.

"What a stroke of luck!" she exclaimed. "Merligen is only a short distance from our house. You can see it on the other side of the lake. Come on, let's go back and have lunch on the veranda. I can show you how close we are."

Eleanor gazed across the brilliant, aquamarine water at clusters of chalets dotted along the edge of the lake on the far side. Kappel was there somewhere further up in the next village. As a steamer chugged towards a wooden pier a crew member threw a thick rope over the side. Another man lowered the gang plank while the first man jumped onto the pier and secured the rope. Seconds later a motley crowd poured down the gang plank scurrying like ants towards the village.

"They're so close I could almost touch them," she thought lowering the binoculars Jenny had produced.

Protected by a large, bright, yellow parasol she sipped a glass of cold, white wine watching the light reflecting on the lake. A faint, warm breeze rippled the surface of the water. Lower down the bank a group of youths were diving off a makeshift board whooping with delight. So much pure light, so much colour and beauty. It was almost painful to absorb.

Suddenly, the steamer let out a blast on its hooter warning would be passengers that it was about to leave. Three little figures scurried towards the boat waving their arms. They jumped aboard just as the gang plank was about to be raised. The steamer reversed its engines, turned its bows inwards and slowly chugged across the lake.

"Tomorrow," she murmured, "tomorrow I will find Kappel."

CHAPTER TWENTY

Early the next morning Eleanor and Jenny walked the short distance to the pier. They dangled their legs over the side watching the steamer chug its way up the lake. Once aboard they went over their plan to find Kappel. After all Merligen was just a small village like most of those along the lake.

After disembarking they walked briskly away from the pier into the village. Some people were fetching bread from the bakery; the early risers were already shopping for groceries. A man walked leisurely through the main street urging on a few cows with the aid of a stick. The bells around their necks tinkled prettily in the clear, morning air.

Eleanor couldn't imagine anything interrupting the peace and tranquillity of this serene place. The horrors of war seemed so distant, even though it was just a border away. The old junk shop dealer had told them that Kappel had set up a small wood-carving business supplying gift shops in Interlaken and surrounding villages. It shouldn't be too difficult to find him. They wandered through the village until they came upon a large chalet with an adjoining workshop. Through the stable door came sounds of someone singing an old, German folk song. Suddenly, the singing stopped and they heard another, older voice.

"That's very good, my boy, very good."

"Thank you Herr Kappel," the boy replied.

Eleanor's heart fluttered with anticipation. At last they had found him.

"Guten Morgen," she called leaning through the open half of the stable door. "Herr Kappel?"

"Ja, I am Kappel," replied an elderly man with snow white hair and eye brows.

He looked like pictures she had seen of Pinocchio's father.

On a wooden work bench lay finished and partially completed carvings. Wood chips and small tools lay in disarray over its entire surface. A rosy-cheeked boy of around thirteen was sitting at the bench diligently carving what looked like the lid of a musical box.

"May I help you?" Kappel queried, indicating the beautiful display of carvings on a shelf at the side of the workshop. "You are American? Perhaps you would like to see me work?"

"Yes, I would like that very much," Eleanor replied.

"Please to sit."

He waved them to a couple of three-legged stools set against the work area. Picking up an unfinished carving he worked in silence for a few minutes.

Fascinated, the women watched as the figure miraculously started to take shape before their eyes.

Eleanor's mouth was so dry she could hardly speak. She was glad to be sitting down, otherwise her wobbly legs would have given out under her. Clasping her hands tightly, to stop them trembling, she spoke haltingly,

"An alpine chuff evokes memories in the heart."

The old man didn't flinch. He continued carving without looking up. Eleanor waited as the seconds ticked away. Again she murmured,

"The alpine chuff evokes memories in the heart."

Just when she thought he would not respond he turned to her.

"The heart has many memories," he said quietly.

"But the chuff and the beautiful edelweiss live in my heart forever."

Finally, the old man raised his head and spoke to the boy,

"Tobias, go into the house. Make some coffee and bring me a pastry," he called after him.

"Now my dear," he said swivelling in his chair, "how can I be of service?"

Suddenly, Eleanor felt overwhelmed with emotion. Tears filled her eyes as she tremulously told Kappel why she had come to Switzerland.

"Peter, my husband, told me that if ever I was in trouble and needed help I could come to you. You remember Peter, Peter Brandt?"

"How could I forget? Five years ago he saved my life. I was suspected of helping my sister and her Downs Syndrome child flee from the Nazis. If it wasn't for him they would have both died, but he smuggled them over the border into Switzerland. Now she looks after me. Sadly, little Hildegard died two years ago. Peter and his uncle hid me away for weeks until they could get me out. Now I try to help the organisation here in Switzerland."

Eleanor related how they had left Berlin for Sweden and eventually returned to the United States.

"In the first few months I had news from Helga, but recently it's dried up. I've heard nothing since last September. Something must have happened otherwise Peter would have got news to Helga somehow or other."

"It's not as easy now as it was early on in the war. Gestapo and SS pigs are everywhere, but knowing Peter he would have found *some* way of getting a message out. It's best not to linger here. Come back next Thursday on the pretext of buying a carving. By then I may have some news. Be careful Eleanor. Switzerland is neutral, but there are spies everywhere."

The women called back jovially to the old man.

"Goodbye Herr Kappel. I hope you'll have finished the piece I like soon. I'd like to buy it before I go back to the States."

Eleanor almost danced back to the pier. Jenny had to restrain her for fear of arousing the curiosity of the villagers. Steaming back across the lake she could hardly contain her excitement. Her heart felt lighter than it had been for months.

"There's nothing you can do now except wait," Jenny said, "so we might as well go into Interlaken tomorrow. A bit of sight-seeing will do you good… take your mind of things."

Eleanor sighed, "You're right, of course," but she had no enthusiasm for the idea.

Eleanor squinted when she pulled back the shutters. Bright sunlight burst into the room shimmering on the crystal dressing table set, reflecting on the brass bed rail. Quivering golden light mottled the dark oak, polished furniture. Dust motes swirled in a crazy dance as she shook the embroidered bed cover. Throwing the windows wide open she stepped out onto the tiny balcony. Still and flat as a mirror the glistening, blue-green lake stretched away into the distance under an azure sky. Intermittently, soft plopping sounds carried across the water as fish nosed the surface. Fluffy white clouds hung like cotton wool over snow-covered peaks. Brilliant, green grass spilled down the mountains right to the water's edge.

Across the lake, on the low slopes, a tiny figure trudged up a mountain path with a load on his back, a small herd of goats in his wake. The faint tinkling of bells carried across the water as they bent to nibble at the grass.

People were already gathering on the piers waiting for the steamers to take them to work in Interlaken and the hotels in the villages dotted along the banks. Beguiled by the serenity her spirits soared. Breathing deeply on the fresh, clear air she determined that she would enjoy the rest of the week.

The two women strolling along the gritted path towards the pier looked like any other tourists out for a day trip. A light breeze ruffled their hair as they clattered up the gang plank among the crowd of embarking passengers. Engines throbbing, the steamer reversed, swung round and settled onto its course. Children darted in and out of legs. Two boisterous, young men supported their cycles against the metal sides of the boat. Occasionally, they laughed uproariously, giving each other playful shoves. An elderly, bearded man sat on a large box containing life-jackets completely engrossed in his newspaper. A middle-aged man in lederhosen and walking boots nodded at a black-clad, old woman in traditional, white lace cap. Two nuns giggled girlishly as the steamer lurched slightly in the wake of a boat crossing its path.

As they nosed into the pier in Interlaken West Eleanor screwed up her nose in distaste.

"What a pong! What is it?"

"Just the horses," Jenny laughed.

Through a gap in the crowd Eleanor spotted them waiting to take tourists around the town. Quaint, brightly-painted, open carriages garlanded with flowers. Horses snuffled in nosebags, ears sticking out from white, lace caps pulled over their heads. A big, golden chestnut twitched its plaited tail tied with shiny, red ribbon. Red and white Swiss flags flew from the upper windows of shops. Smaller ones had been stuck into window boxes filled with red trailing geraniums.

People idled along the pavements window shopping; gazing at cuckoo clocks, lace tablecloths, wood carvings, music boxes and pen knives. An atmosphere of muted excitement and anticipation filled the air.

"Shall we have a cup of coffee first?" Jenny queried. "We can sit outside."

She pointed to a veranda that stretched across the front of a small hotel on the main street. Small tables, laid with yellow cloths, were already filling up. They sat in a shady corner away from the entrance and looked at the drinks' menu. A black-clad waiter in a spotless, white apron, napkin folded over his arm, quietly appeared at their side.

"Bitte?" he queried.

"Zwei kaffee bitte," Jenny replied.

Neither of them spoke until the waiter returned with their refreshments a few minutes later.

"This is a great place for people watching," Jenny laughed. "I always come here when I'm on my own, because it's so lively. It's a good spot for the parade."

"The parade.......?"

"First of August is Swiss National Day. Everybody comes in from the surrounding villages. There's marching bands, beer wagons, locals in national costume. It's absolutely wonderful!"

"Sounds great. I'd love to come."

"Everybody has a day off so Blake will be able to join us. We can have lunch here."

After they had finished their coffee they walked up the main street. Eleanor turned her head to look across the large green, edged with sycamore trees. Giving a sharp intake of breath she stopped entranced. The Jungfrau Joch loomed majestically, its peaks covered with snow glistening in the morning light. It seemed so close she thought she could reach out and touch it.

Slowly, they ambled up the street. Eleanor continually twisted her head to look at the mountain. It was like a magnet pulling her towards it.

"The '*Young Maiden*' affects a lot of people like that. Even now I feel a sense of awe every time I look at her," Jenny remarked.

The crowds started to thin as they neared Interlaken Ost at the top end of town. At the foot of the Harder Külm they bought tickets and boarded the funicular that would take them to top of the mountain.

Eleanor felt a twinge of fear as the train laboured uphill at a very steep angle. They climbed higher and higher until the town below looked like a model village. With a slight bump they came to a halt at the summit. People poured from the carriages, many of them in sturdy walking boots with knapsacks on their backs.

"What are those metal badges on their walking sticks?" Eleanor queried as a couple walked past her heading for the steep path.

"It shows which mountains they've climbed. Some people come out here on walking holidays and climb different ranges every year."

A well-dressed man, in a stylish Panama hat, brushed past them heading for the viewing area. Others were heading for the steep, tortuous path that descended to the valley floor. There wasn't much else to do except admire the view and wait for the funicular to come back up.

Fifteen minutes later they boarded the train for the downward journey. From that angle the drop looked even steeper. In the front car the man in the Panama was admiring the view through the large window.

The following day they took the Wengernalbahn rack railway train to Kleine Scheidegg, at the foot of the Eiger's north face. After stretching their legs they boarded the Jungfraubahn that tunnelled through the Eiger to the top of the Jungfrau. At intervals the train stopped at small platforms. Passengers poured out to gaze across the Eiger Glacier through windows that had been carved in the ice. The higher they went the more difficult it was to breathe. Eleanor felt slightly nauseous by the time they reached the Jungfrau station

"It's the altitude," Jenny informed her. "We'll have a hot chocolate before we go outside."

Eleanor didn't expect what she saw when they eventually walked from the restaurant up a low rise. The stunning Aletsch Glacier stretched out for miles in front of her, covered with a fresh layer of snow. In the near distance Huskies were pulling sledges full of tourists while skiers swept down dangerously, steep slopes. An instructor was urging on novices balancing precariously on skis. A girl lay flat on her back, skis in the air, while her friends jeered at her predicament.

Overhead, the sun shone brilliantly in an azure sky. Below their vantage point large, fluffy white clouds hung in the air so close they seemed within reach.

"It's breath-taking," Eleanor murmured. "I've never seen clouds underneath me before."

"We're over 3,500 metres up, that's why the air is so thin."

A man, sitting on an outcrop of rock just in front of them, surveyed the mountains with a pair of binoculars. Eleanor felt vaguely uneasy.

"Isn't that the same man who bumped into us yesterday on the Harder Külm?" she asked.

Jenny turned towards the direction she was indicating, searching the lingering group of people watching the skiers.

"I can't see…"

"There, there in the Panama hat!"

"Yes, I think it is, but why are you so anxious about it?"

"We saw him yesterday. I'm sure he passed by when we were having coffee outside the hotel. He stopped to ask directions in German."

"Well, this is a German speaking area. You're being paranoid Eleanor. He's probably just a tourist. They all tend to visit the popular attractions, you know. It's more than likely you'll bump into him again before the week is out."

Eleanor wasn't convinced. She felt certain she was being followed. Not even the group of Swiss students, singing folk songs on the return journey, could allay her anxiety. She had allowed herself to become complacent in this awe-inspiring country, but she vowed to be more vigilant for the rest of the week.

Sunrise broke over the alps setting them aglow; suffusing the snow-covered peaks and crags with a soft, pink light. Tentacles of brighter sunlight reached out over the horizon searching for a hold on the day. Gradually, the firmament swallowed the first touches of dawn turning the sky cerulean blue. Bright sunlight burst onto the surface of the lake glancing off undulating ripples of aqua-blue.

August the first 1941. Eleanor sat on the veranda staring over the water. Here, in this beautiful country, it was hard to believe that Europe was still embroiled in a bloody war with Germany. The cruelty, the hate, the unbelievable atrocities, seemed a world away. She couldn't bear to think about what might have happened to Peter in the hands of the Gestapo.

After a late breakfast they drove into Interlaken. Crowds of people thronged the main street searching for a good vantage point for the parade. In the Kürsaal a Viennese quartet played a Strauss waltz. Girls dressed in folk costume handed out chocolates for the children. It was hot, very hot.

The women sought out some shade while Blake queued for beer from one of the stalls set amongst the manicured lawns and brilliantly-coloured flowerbeds. People idled through the grounds laughing, gossiping, scolding excited children. A small, blond-haired boy darted past straight into the path of a man almost knocking the beer from his hand. Eleanor's heart gave a painful lurch. It was him, the man in the Panama. Then he was gone, lost in the crowds surging towards the street.

Dressed in a white cotton dress, embroidered with tiny flowers of blue and yellow, Eleanor sat sipping a glass of ice-cold, white wine. Blake had pre-booked lunch insisting on being seated outside on the raised veranda. They would have an excellent view of the parade without having to move from their seats. She leaned forward as the sounds of a band reached her ears. The crowds on the pavement started to cheer at the sight of the parade coming down the street.

First the marching band appeared followed by a group of mountaineers. Horsemen, in medieval costumes and chain mail, trotted by on their magnificent mounts. Miners, carrying huge pieces of rock studded with rhinestones, bent double with the weight. Hideous-headed alpine monsters lunged into the crowds grabbing people; dragging them into the street, frightening small children. Suddenly a loud cheer as William Tell, carrying a crossbow, came into sight followed by his young son. Washerwomen flapped wet sheets soaking spectators on the pavement. Men clanging enormous bells drowned out the clamour of the crowd. A herd of cows, heads bowed with the weight of heavy bells around their necks, ambled slowly past the hotel.

People, sitting on the wall in front of the hotel, stood up as the parade neared them obliterating the diners' view. A waiter hurried out and ordered them off in a voice edged with irritation.

"It's wonderful!" Eleanor cried.

"There'll be celebrations tonight and fireworks on the green."

As they left the hotel she saw the man in the Panama again watching her from across the street. She stared directly at him. He smiled, gave a barely perceptible nod and disappeared into the crowds thronging the pavement. A thrill of fear coursed through her. This wasn't paranoia. He was definitely watching her.

That evening they watched the celebrations around the lake while they dined on the veranda. Children, roped together in a line, sang as they marched on the path below them carrying lighted, coloured lanterns. All round the lake little pinpoints of light moved as revellers grouped to eat and drink, sounds of their laughter winging over the water. Deep in thought Eleanor toyed with her food.

"What's wrong? I can make something else for you if you want?" Jenny offered.

"I'm convinced I'm being watched. Once I've seen Herr Kappel next Thursday I must leave."

Blake started to protest, but she cut him off,

"I must or you'll both be in danger."

Herr Kappel's stable door was closed when they arrived at the workshop. Cautiously, Eleanor knocked, but there was no response. It was ominously quiet. Slowly pushing the door open they stepped inside closing it behind them. It was so dark they could barely make out the work bench. As they stumbled forward a low groan came from the back of the room. Jenny fumbled for the light switch. Momentarily, the glare from the naked light bulb blinded them. Then they saw the crumpled heap in the corner. Herr Kappel was lying in a pool of blood, his legs drawn up under his chin as though trying to protect himself from blows.

"My God!" Eleanor exclaimed, "What's happened?"

He moved the hand clutching his stomach. Blood oozed out of a large wound permeating his shirt.

"Who did this to you? Jenny, go fetch a doctor!"

"Too late," the old man murmured.

Blood gurgled in his throat; seeped from the corners of his mouth as he tried to speak.

"Gestapo; they are everywhere. You must leave… immediately. Go to Mürren… to Chalet Annaliese. I did not tell them….you will be safe…"

"Herr Kappel! Herr Kappel!"

His eyes were wide open, pleading, lips formed into a final, silent word. Jenny took the old man's hand and felt for a pulse.

"It's no use, he's dead."

Eleanor's hand flew to her mouth, horrified by the broken body of the old man.

"It's my fault. He'd be alive if I hadn't asked him to help me."

Silently, they pushed open the door and peered out. Satisfied that the area was deserted they slipped into the garden. Hurriedly, they headed for the steamer that had just arrived.

Back at the chalet Blake pleaded with Eleanor to call the police, but she refused.

"I must go to Mürren," she insisted.

"All right, but I'll go with you. If you're being followed there's no point trying to get up there in daylight. You can't get an automobile up there. You'll either have to get the cable car from Stechelberg or the funicular from Lauterbrünnen. There's a train from Grütschalp into Mürren. Either way you'll be spotted if they're watching you. The only other way is to use a motorcycle. We can ride part of the way then we'll have to walk across the mountain. It's a long way and it can get cold in the night, even in summer. You'll need warm clothes and walking boots."

She started to protest, but Blake was adamant,

"We'll leave just after midnight tonight, by auto. We'll switch to the motorbike just before we get to Lauterbrünnen. I have a good friend there who won't ask questions."

CHAPTER TWENTY ONE

The house was in complete darkness as though everyone had retired for the night. Eleanor's feet felt hot and sweaty in thick socks and walking boots. She threw the waterproof jackets, Jenny had provided, into the rear of the car and got into the front seat. Not a glimmer of light could be seen from the house, but she knew Jenny was watching them anxiously from behind the shutters. Blake free-wheeled down the drive into the lane with the headlamps switched off. A single street light, about two hundred metres away, cast a faint glow over the nearest chalet lying in darkness behind a hedge of pine trees.

Silently, the car moved forward down the slope onto the main road. For a few seconds they waited, watching for any sign of movement. Anyone trying to lurk in the dead of night would find it difficult unless they were in a vehicle, but there were no cars or any sign of life. Blake turned the engine over willing it to start first time. It stuttered into life settling into a gentle purr. He edged the car onto the road and sped off towards Lauterbrünnen.

About two kilometres outside the village he pulled off the road onto a narrow track that led to a large, dilapidated, wooden hut. Hurriedly, he jumped out, unlocked the door and wheeled out an old motorbike. Carefully, he covered the car with a tarpaulin from the boot then signalled to Eleanor to get on the pillion. She had hardly straddled the motorcycle before they were hurtling across the field and bumping onto the road.

Lauterbrünnen was completely deserted: the funicular had shut down for the night. Except for muffled voices drifting into the street, from one of the hotel bars, it was dark and empty.

Blake pulled onto the old road leading up to Mürren and cut the engine. Nothing except for a faint rustling in the undergrowth at the edge of the road. They waited a full five minutes until they were satisfied they were not being followed then headed up the unmade road.

Dark shapes of trees and rocks threatened to engulf them as they drove along the uneven surface. Blake had hooded the headlight so visibility was dangerously inadequate.

"A moving light would immediately attract attention," he explained.

Eleanor could feel the wheels sliding on loose shale. Fortunately, the moon had disappeared before they left the house protecting them from any watchful eyes. Now the clouds were parting moonlight bathed the clearing ahead with silvery light.

They came out of the shelter of the trees into a wide, grassy clearing that sloped steeply down to the valley below. The Jungfrau Joch, illuminated by silvery moonlight, loomed large in front of them, even more beautiful at night. A slight breeze shifted the clouds sending dark shadows over the mountains, obliterating the moon, leaving them in blackness again. Another fifteen minutes saw them on the outskirts of Mürren. Blake switched off the engine.

"We'll walk from here," he said propping the motorcycle behind a pile of logs.

Stealthily, they walked down the main street to the far end close to an ancient chalet.

"This isn't it. It must be down the other end," Eleanor whispered.

They retraced their steps straining to read the names painted on the chalets.

"There's nothing more down there so it must be outside the village," Blake mused.

Eleanor grabbed his arm as they came close to where the motorcycle was parked.

"Up there!" she whispered urgently.

She pointed to the vague outline of a building clinging to the side of the mountain high above them. Look, there's a path leading up to it!"

Eleanor peered at a rough sign attached to the wire fence that ran either side of the path.

"Chalet... Annaliese! That's it! Look, there's an arrow pointing up there."

The glow of a single lamp shone dimly about two hundred metres above them.

"We'd better push the motocycle up just in case we need to make a fast getaway. We can free-wheel down, if necessary."

Blake hauled the bike up the rough incline, Eleanor pushing from behind, until they came out onto a small patch of lawn surrounded by flowers and shrubs. Close up the chalet was much larger than they had supposed. Two large bedroom windows overlooked a veranda covering three sides. A dog barked from somewhere inside the building, but no movement came from the house. Furtively, they crept to the solid wood door. Blake was about to pull the bell-chain then stopped, his hand suspended in mid air.

"It's the middle of the night. What am I going to say if it's the wrong place?"

"It can't be. There wouldn't be two chalets with the same name in such a small village," Eleanor retorted.

"Well, here goes."

He rang the bell and waited. Nothing happened. Suddenly, a dog barked from inside. Sensing their presence it threw itself against the door in a frustrated frenzy of snarling. Involuntarily, Eleanor took a step backwards almost falling off the veranda down the wooden steps. Suddenly, the dog was quiet, hushed by a stern voice behind the door.

"What do you want at this hour of the night? Go away or I'll call the police. Do you here me?"

"Herr Kappel sent us," Blake informed the bodiless voice.

"I don't know *anyone* called Kappel. Go away!"

Moving to one side Blake motioned to Eleanor. Taking a deep breath she moved towards the door.

"An alpine chuff evokes memories in the heart."

Silence except for the sound of laboured breathing.

Trying to keep her voice steady she repeated,

"An alpine chuff evokes memories in the heart."

Eleanor could feel the hesitation then the voice replied quietly, anxiously.

"The heart has many memories."

"But the chuff and the beautiful edelweiss live in my heart forever."

There was a faint rasping sound then a voice ordering,

"Come closer, in front of the spy-hole, where I can see you more clearly."

Blake moved forward into full view. After a few seconds the voice, sharp this time,

"Now the woman. I want to see her face."

An audible gasp emanated from behind the door, then the sound of wooden bars being lifted, keys in the lock, bolts drawn. Suddenly, the door was thrown open to reveal a slim woman with chestnut-brown hair. A look of shock and incomprehension flitted over her face.

"Eleanor!" she cried.

"Gisela?"

Gisela dragged them inside and quickly re-bolted the door. She led them into a spacious living room decorated in carved, oak furniture. Hastily, she took an armful of logs from the rough basket beside the grate and replenished the dying embers of a fire. Motioning them to a worn, over-stuffed sofa she sank heavily into a deep armchair.

"Eleanor, I can't believe it!" she exclaimed over and over again.

"You're so thin Gisela... your hair... if it wasn't for your voice I wouldn't have recognised you."

"I had to take on a new identity when the organisation brought me here. How... why are you here in Switzerland? I thought you had gone back to America."

"I did go back after a brief stay in Sweden. We were lucky we could get out on our American passports, but Helga had to stay there. You heard about Manfred...?"

"Yes," Gisela said simply, getting up from the chair. "I'll make some coffee then you can tell me the whole story."

"Not for me thanks," Blake declined. "I need to get back home and go about my normal business otherwise it might arouse suspicions. With any luck, by the time they realise you've gone I'll have told as many people as possible that you had to return to the States at short notice, because your mother has been taken ill."

After giving Eleanor a quick hug he was gone.

They watched his shadowy outline through a chink in the shutters until he had melted into the darkness. Sipping steaming, hot coffee Eleanor related all that had happened since her arrival in Switzerland.

"But how did *you* get here?" she queried.

Gisela related her harrowing story of how Peter had helped her escape from the Lebensborn home. How *Regis* had smuggled her out of Germany and set her up in the chalet.

When she had finished she beckoned Eleanor to follow her up the narrow stairs to a bedroom at the back of the house. Quietly, she eased open the door and walked to the cot set against the wall. Eleanor followed and gazed down at the little boy; fine blond hair tousled above chubby pink cheeks.

"This is my son, Otto's son, Martin Otto Wagner," Gisela murmured.

Eleanor felt a stab of pain thinking of Johann thousands of miles away.

They talked until a pale light crept in through a crack in the shutters. Gisela did not know Kappel. She had not known that Blake was involved with the organisation and had had no warning of the night's events. She didn't know how to get in touch with them, only that they would contact her when they thought her safety might be threatened.

They didn't leave the chalet for three days. Eleanor paced the living room willing for something to happen. Most of the time she spent chatting with Gisela, breaking into fits of laughter recalling the happy evenings they had spent together. It seemed a lifetime away; a time they would never recapture.

Tired from lack of sleep Eleanor stretched her aching limbs. As usual her eyes strayed to the snow-covered alps. Each time she was mesmerised by their beauty, drawn into them like a magnet. At times they overpowered her, filling her with an overwhelming sense of claustrophobia. Curious locals, who had seen her with Gisela in the village, had been told she was a cousin on an extended visit.

Tourists passed below the chalet heading for the cable car station to take them up to Berg and the Schilthorn. Suddenly, two of them turned towards the bottom of the path that led to the chalet. Laughing and chatting they scrambled up the path occasionally stopping to turn and admire the view of the alps. When they reached the gate leading to Chalet Annaliese they turned right and followed another path that would take them further up the mountain. Eleanor watched them furtively, unsure of why they had taken this route away from the other walkers. There was nothing up beyond the chalet except a small shed for wintering the goats.

Running upstairs she watched them through a back bedroom window. In fits of laughter they dropped to the ground. The man lifted the woman's hand and kissed it theatrically. Pressing herself against him she giggled and lifted her face to be kissed. After about five minutes the woman opened her knapsack, took out a package and handed her companion a sandwich. He lay back, face turned to the sun, occasionally taking a swig from a bottle of beer.

"Lovers," Eleanor thought with a twinge of envy as she turned away.

In her bedroom she picked up the German book she had been reading and started towards the stairs. Curiosity guided her to the window again, but the man had vanished. Alarmed, she ran downstairs to Gisela who was flicking a duster over the highly-polished dining table. Now she stood completely immobile, head to one side, listening for something.

"I just heard a sound, a tapping noise," she whispered. "I'm sure of it. There, there it is again. It's coming from the kitchen."

For what seemed an eternity they waited. It was more urgent now, a persistent staccato. Stealthily, she moved into the kitchen dropping to the floor behind the door. The tapping stopped, replaced by a low voice whispering the same coded message Eleanor had used.

"It's a contact from the organisation!" she exclaimed opening the door.

A tall, bronzed man of around thirty slipped inside. Hurriedly, he turned to Eleanor who had followed Gisela into the kitchen.

"You must stay here until the weather turns later in the year. The Gestapo have been watching you ever since you arrived in Switzerland. Kappel knew they were following you. He managed to warn us, but they got to him... he was a good man."

"It was my fault," Eleanor said miserably. "If I hadn't gone looking for him..."

"They would have caught up with him sooner or later. He was more active in the organisation than you think."

Eleanor opened her mouth to speak again, but he motioned her to be silent.

"Now listen carefully. I haven't much time," he said looking through the window at the girl still lying on the grass. "You'll need some money to see you through." He pushed some notes into Eleanor's hand. "When the first snows fall be ready to move. We will do our best to get you safely back to the United States. We will not contact you again unless it becomes dangerous for you both to stay here. This is probably the safest place you can be... the Gestapo don't know about it. Our people will be watching the chalet day and night, but you must still be vigilant at all times."

Cautiously, he looked out at the girl. She blew him a kiss, the signal that it was all clear, before he ran back up the slope behind the house. Jumping up she caught his hand and they giggled their way back down onto the road. Eleanor felt helpless knowing that she was unable to continue her search for Peter. All she could do was wait for the snows to come.

Autumn proved to be a quiet time in Mürren after the summer tourists had drifted away. By November the village was preparing itself for the skiers who would soon descend on them. Colourful woollen sweaters, bobble hats, skis and snow goggles filled every shop window. The first light snowfall had transformed the area into a sparkling Christmas card.

Plump flakes dropped past the window as though a giant hand was sprinkling confetti. In the distance the train from Grütschalp chugged its way to the village. The lower reaches of the mountain, and the valley below, were gradually blending with the snow-capped peaks of the alps. Overhead a slate-grey sky, filled with dark, snow-laden clouds, pressed down on the village.

Twilight enhanced the falling snow when light spilled out from the chalets creating a display of dancing snowflakes. Golden puddles appeared and disappeared as doors opened and closed against the cold. Thicker now and faster, fat crystals fell straight to the earth covering it with a dazzling white blanket, beautiful but suffocating. A low wind moaned, ruffling tree tops, driving snow scurrying against logs piled high for the winter.

Snow had fallen heavily all night consuming the village as though someone had indiscriminately thrown a box of icing sugar creating strange and vague shapes. All morning Eleanor paced restlessly, occasionally picking up a book, staring at the words without seeing. Martin sat on the rug playing noisily with some saucepans, banging them loudly with a wooden spoon. Sleep had eluded her; all she could think of was that she would soon be sent back to the States then she would never see Peter again.

"You'll get used to it," Gisela smiled coming in with a mug of hot chocolate.

"I've been thinking," Eleanor said tentatively. "I must go back to Germany; go to Peter's uncle; try to find out what's happened."

"Are you insane! They'll pick you up as soon as you cross the border!"

"Maybe?"

"There's no maybe about it. Who do you think you're dealing with Eleanor, boy scouts?"

"I know very well what they're capable of, but I'll never rest until I find out if Peter is alive or dead."

Two days later they recognised the same bronzed contact labouring up the path hauling cut logs on a sleigh. After placing them on top of the neat pile, stacked high against the side of the chalet, he came onto the veranda stamping snow from his boots. Gisela opened the door, thanking him in a loud voice when she spotted the postman coming up the path. Sound carried in the mountains.

The contact repeated the passwords before she invited him in for coffee. Warming his back in front of the blazing, log fire he sipped the hot liquid. Impatiently, Eleanor waited for him to speak.

"I'm sorry," Matthias said hesitantly, "but we can't find any trace of Peter. His uncle has been trying for months to find out what's happened to him."

"Then I must go back to Germany. I must find him," Eleanor spoke with determination.

Shocked, he coughed violently as the coffee went down the wrong way.

"That's not an option. No, the organisation won't allow it. It's madness! You would be putting lives at risk. I can't believe you're even contemplating such a thing!"

"I'm an American and fluent in German. If you can get me some German papers and a timetable I can find my own way there by train." Eleanor was determined. "I've done it before when Helga and I travelled to Warnemünde. Please."

"We've tried every source and contact, even into Spain: he's vanished."

Eleanor's face was set in stone. Nothing would change her mind.

He sighed,

"Very well, but I doubt that our contacts in Switzerland will even entertain it."

He left promising to return as soon as possible if he had the go ahead.

"Tomorrow we'll arrange for false papers," Matthias told her on his next visit to Chalet Annaliese. It will take a while. Once you get to Zurich we can hide you until we can get you safely to the border. After that you're on your own. It will be early December before we can move you, even colder than today, so you'll need winter clothes, German made clothes."

"I've been here since August so I only have a light, waterproof jacket and some walking boots."

"You mustn't carry or wear anything American or you'll arouse suspicions. We can't risk lives for this, not even for Peter. I doubt that *Regis* would sanction this foolishness. He would understand that decision."

"Yes," Eleanor said quietly, remembering poor Kappel.

CHAPTER TWENTY TWO

Germany 1941

Eleanor, dressed in a heavy wool coat, hat and fur-lined boots tried to look relaxed as the train pulled out of the station. Warily, she looked at her companions. They looked fairly ordinary, all wrapped up against the cold. Gradually, they left the train, at various points, until she was alone rumbling towards the border. After clearing the first checkpoint, on the Swiss side, the train slowly laboured towards the German side braking to a halt with a piercing, metallic screech. The remaining passengers alighted watched by a young trooper who didn't look old enough to shave.

The small group huddled on the platform shoulders hunched, hats pulled low over faces. White vapour escaped above the scarves pulled tightly up around their mouths. A small, rotund man muttered as he stamped his feet to keep warm. Waving his rifle at them a soldier ordered them to produce their papers.

Behind the grimy windows of the guard house an officer sipped coffee from a large tin mug. His eyes swept over the freezing passengers then he turned to speak to someone out of sight. On the platform the guard gave a cursory glance at the papers handed over by the rotund man.

"Danke,"

His familiar tone indicated that the man travelled over the border on a regular basis.

One by one the other passengers handed over their documents until the procedure was completed. Eleanor breathed a sigh of relief when the guard thrust the papers back at her.

"Schnell!" he ordered them back onto the train.

Gratefully, they scrambled aboard. The engine let out a burst of steam and slowly edged forward. Suddenly, loud shouts came from the guard room. A figure ran down towards the front of the train.

"Halt! Halt!" to no avail.

The driver couldn't hear him above the noise of the rumbling wheels.

Suddenly, a volley of shots rang out, more shouting, booted feet clattering on concrete. Without warning the train lurched to a stop, billowing steam shooting into the air. Carriage doors slamming, heavy footsteps marching down the corridor, the clunk of rifles. All along the train doors opening, harsh demands for papers, doors sliding shut.

Eleanor sat rigid with terror as footsteps closed in. Suddenly, the door was pushed violently aside. Two guards demanded her papers and handed them to a man who had come up behind them.

"Vas is loos?" she queried trying not to look at them.

"What is wrong?" sneered a venomous voice.

A man entered the compartment, lifted her chin so she was forced to look at him.

"You, *you* are what is wrong Frau Brandt."

Speechless, Eleanor stared up at the face of the man in the Panama. Now he was wearing a black hat and a black, leather coat. The Gestapo *'Death's Head'* emblem on his lapel mocked her, growing before her eyes into a huge, terrifying skull. Struggling to maintain her composure she stated emphatically,

"My name is not Brandt. My name is Ingeborg Finkel."

"I lost you for a while in Switzerland Frau Brandt. But I knew that, sooner or later, you would try to find that traitor husband of yours."

It was all Eleanor could do not to scream at him; to deny what he was claiming about Peter. Steeling herself she said calmly,

"I told you my name isn't Brandt, it's Finkel."

"I think not. Take her!" he snarled to the guards.

So, this is Gestapo headquarters Eleanor thought as she sat in front of a large desk. Across from her Panama man stood smoking a stinking, black cigarette, a half smirk on his face. Suddenly, the door behind her burst open. Coldly, a voice ordered,

"You do not smoke in my office. Put out that cigarette."

The man hastily looked around for somewhere to put it. Finding nothing he squeezed it between his fingers giving a little grimace of pain as he touched the glowing end. With a slight shrug of his shoulders he retreated into a corner behind her. The other man swept past her and sat in the chair behind the desk.

Eleanor looked up and stared into the cold, black eyes of Fleischer. Her heart hammered painfully, her palms felt clammy. She caught her breath revealing the anxiety she felt. Silently, he scrutinised her intently, sweeping his gaze over her face as though reading her every thought.

Without warning he wrenched open a drawer, took out a photograph and held it up in front of her. It was a picture of her with Peter and Johann sitting outside a restaurant in the Kurfürstendamm. It was the last time they had gone there before they left Berlin.

"So, Frau Brandt or Finkel, whichever you prefer, why have you come back to Germany with false papers?"

She didn't answer. It was no use trying to deny it, but she wasn't going to admit it either.

Fleischer glanced towards the man in the corner. He stood in front of her, legs splayed. Suddenly, he brought his hand back and delivered a stinging blow to her left cheek.

"I'll ask you again Frau Brandt. Why have you come back to Germany?"

Eleanor hung her head on her chest. Her head was spinning from the force of the blow.

"I have nothing to say."

His subordinate delivered another vicious blow splitting her top lip. Blood filled her mouth, dripped onto her chin.

"Answer me!" Fleischer roared.

"To find my husband," she blurted.

"Ah, so you admit, at last, who you really are?"

"What's happened to him?"

"I don't know if anything has happened to him, do you Schiller?"

He looked quizzically at the man who had slapped her across the face. Schiller laughed loudly baying like a hyena.

"Where is he?" Eleanor continued.

"Ah, now that I can help you with," he grinned devilishly. "Take her downstairs!"

Viciously, Schiller grabbed her arm, dragged her from the chair and propelled her towards the door. As he pushed her roughly into the corridor Fleisher called,

"Incidentally, Frau Brandt, your husband may, or may not, be alive. I don't know or care."

"You know where he is," she screamed at Fleischer.

"We know he was involved with an organisation smuggling Jews and other undesirables out of Germany."

Eleanor's legs buckled under her as Schiller dragged her downstairs to one of the interrogation rooms. Roughly, he threw her down on the hard, cold floor in a windowless room. It was very damp. The air smelled fetid like a room full of decaying, unwashed bodies. She crawled towards a long, narrow camp bed set against the dripping wall. Dropping onto the stinking mattress she curled into a ball. Never had she felt so desolate. Images of Peter and Johann swept before her eyes like an accelerated film unreeling. Peter in the living room poring over his books, Johann, his hair catching the sunlight, playing on the beach in Cape Cod. She couldn't get rid of the swirling images. Silently, she screamed inside her head, over and over again. Exhausted, she fell into a nightmarish sleep haunted by Fleischer's cadaverous face.

A hand grabbing her by the hair roused her in the middle of the night. She assumed it was the middle of the night, because the room was completely dark; not a chink of light to be seen. Roughly, the soldier pressed her against the mattress and began to fidget with her clothes. His breath was hot, rank with the smell of beer and stale food. Panic rose in her chest as he tore at her sweater. She tried to push him off, but the full weight of his body was on top of her, his hand covering her mouth. Mustering all her strength she shook her head free and sunk her teeth into his hand.

"Bitch!" he yelped slapping her face from side to side.

Eleanor screamed, a loud, keening scream. Suddenly, a chink of light appeared under the door. Loud footsteps marched down the corridor and stopped outside. The door crashed open letting in harsh light from the naked bulbs outside. Consumed with rage Fleischer stood silhouetted in the doorway, staring into the cell.

"Get out!" he screamed. "I will not allow that kind of behaviour here."

Eleanor sobbed quietly, all the fight knocked out of her. She felt sick, full of revulsion at the sight of the slobbering man who had tried to rape her.

"Frau Brandt," Fleischer said solicitously, "are you all right?" She recoiled as he approached the filthy bed.

Hate gleamed in his eyes belying the soothing tones.

"You will feel much better tomorrow then we can talk again."

Quietly, he closed the door behind him leaving Eleanor staring into pitch blackness.

In that limbo state between sleep and wakefulness Eleanor squirmed restlessly on the damp mattress, its rancid smell filling her nostrils. She tried to open her eyes, but they seemed glued together. Her head throbbed with painful regularity like a ship's engine getting up speed. Forcing her eyes open she panicked in the darkness thinking she had gone blind. Then she spotted a glimmer of light coming from under the door. Mouth dry, heart thumping painfully she struggled to adjust to her surroundings. She felt sick and her face hurt where the guard had caught her with his ring.

Taking deep breaths, to slow her hammering heart, she assessed the situation thinking about what had happened the night before. Why had Fleischer intervened ? Why did he appear so concerned? She eased off the bed steadying herself against the slimy wall. Peering through the gloom she detected a muted, white object in the corner. She sank to her knees and crawled over the damp floor groping with her hands until she touched it. Shuddering with revulsion she relieved herself in the stinking lavatory pan. Gagging from the smell she staggered back to the bed and threw herself face down.

"Pull yourself together! Get a grip!" she muttered sitting up and swinging her legs off the bed.

She paced to and fro trying to clear her head. She wasn't fooled by Fleischer, but she wouldn't let him know that until she was ready. Someone was coming!

Muffled sounds from behind the door, the click of a light switch illuminating the shabby, filthy room. Schiller was standing in the doorway smiling pleasantly.

"Good morning Frau Brandt. I trust you slept well?" he queried affably. "You must freshen up then you can have some breakfast."

Filled with revulsion Eleanor stepped tentatively towards him. She wanted to claw at his ugly face, but she forced herself to stay calm.

Feigning confusion she allowed Schiller to lead her to the washroom.

"Take your time," he smirked waving a hand at the facilities.

Gratefully, she lathered herself with soap. Grabbing a small, wooden nail brush she scrubbed her hands and arms until they were red raw. The harsh soap stung her eyes and set the wound on her face aflame. She couldn't get the thought of the slimy lavatory out of her mind. Satisfied she had cleaned herself as thoroughly as possible she took a deep breath and stepped out into the corridor. Schiller was leaning against the wall, a cigarette dangling from his lips.

"Herr Fleischer would like to see you now," he rasped in his smoker's voice.

He opened the door of the washroom and tossed the cigarette into one of the lavatory pans. Pushing her gently forward he guided her back upstairs.

Fleischer was sitting behind his desk poring over some documents. He stood politely when she entered.

"Please," he said, waving her to the same chair she had sat in the night before. "I'm sure you would like some refreshment," he continued, indicating the tray of coffee and rolls placed on a small table at the side of the desk.

Eleanor was about to refuse then thought better of it. She needed food to stay strong. Accepting the coffee and sweet bread she sat back in her chair waiting for Fleischer to speak. If her situation hadn't been so serious she would have laughed out loud. It was like a comic farce. Fleischer swung from side to side in the swivel chair smiling a hideous, benign smile while she sipped delicately from a china cup. He said nothing until she had finished her second roll.

"You feel much better now?" he looked at her quizzically. "I must apologise for the behaviour of that pig in your room last night. He *has* been punished."

Eleanor stared into her cup. Peter had told her about the Gestapo's methods; how they tried to lull suspects into a false sense of security. Her only hope was to keep up her pretence of ignorance.

"So Frau Brandt, perhaps we can have a little talk now?"

He glanced quickly to the back of the room.

Schiller hadn't said a word since he had brought her in, but she knew he was still behind her. She could hear his faint, laboured breathing. Peter had told her about that too; how Fleischer didn't do his own dirty work.

"I've told you, I know nothing. My husband never discussed anything like that with me, only his work at the university."

"Come now, you must have talked of other things besides work."

"No!"

"Brandt is part of a secret organisation."

"No!"

"What is the name of the organisation?" he snapped, a distinct edge of irritation in his voice.

"I told you I don't know what you're talking about. We had few friends," she lied, "and they only came occasionally for dinner. We kept ourselves to ourselves."

Fleischer walked behind her chair, paced towards the door then came back. He loomed over her then hissed,

"You're lying!"

Schiller moved quickly to her side. He slapped her hard breaking the skin that had started to heal over the cut made by his ring the night before. Involuntarily, she brought her hand up to her face. Pushing it away Schiller hit her again, harder this time, so hard it jolted her teeth. Dizziness washed over her. Her head slumped to one side blood dripping from her swollen lips.

"I don't know! I don't know!" she cried. "I only came back to find Peter. Please tell me where he is and I'll go back to America."

"That isn't possible now," Fleischer grinned, obviously relishing the moment.

"I don't understand…"

"But it's very easy to understand Frau Brandt. Yesterday, the Japanese bombed Pearl Harbour destroying your ships. It's inevitable that within days the United States will also be at war with the Fatherland. You will *never* leave Germany."

Eleanor slumped forward and slid off the chair into a crumpled heap. Nothing had prepared her for the shock of knowing that Americans had been bombed in their homeland.

She didn't remember them dragging her back downstairs and throwing her back on the bed. She knew the interrogation would get worse until she could no longer bear the pain. She thought of ways to end her life, searching the room for something sharp enough to cut her wrists, but there was nothing.

Schiller soon returned with the soldier who had tried to rape her. He leered at her, poking his tongue out lasciviously, while he stripped her naked with his eyes. She understood it was all part of the game to break her spirit. Even the rape attempt was rigged to put Fleischer in a good light so that she would talk, but she had no intention of giving him any information. She had partially told the truth about the organisation; she didn't know its name. Friedrich had refused to tell her for her own safety and the safety of its members.

"You can't reveal what you don't know, my dear," he had told her when she discovered Peter was involved.

Schiller stepped outside and held the door ajar. Grabbing her by the hair they man-handled her down the corridor and pushed her into another room. A dirty bath took up one wall. Under a naked light bulb, hanging on a long flex, a wooden chair had been positioned. Little did she know that this was the same room where the Gestapo had tortured Peter.

"Now, Frau Brandt," Schiller hissed, "shall we try again? What is the name of the organisation? Who is the leader? Where are their headquarters?"

Eleanor stared straight ahead refusing to look in his direction. Angrily, he barked at her again, his words rapid and clipped like staccato gunfire. Spittle ran from the corner of his mouth, glistened on his chin. Over and over again he bombarded her with the same questions until her brain reeled.

Frustrated, he pulled her from the chair and threw her to the ground.

"She needs cooling down Hinkler. Perhaps some cold water will clear her head."

Roughly, Hinkler dug his fingers into the back of her neck, dragged her to the bath and forced her to her knees. Without warning he plunged her head into the bath of icy water. For a few seconds he held her, while she struggled to free herself, than pulled her up coughing and gasping for air. Again and again he plunged her head into the water.

"Enough!" snarled Schiller.

Throwing her back on the chair Schiller placed his hand under her chin forcing her to stay upright.

"Perhaps the cold water has helped you remember more clearly?"

"I... I don't know anything... I don't..."

Again Hinkler dragged her back to the bath and forced her head under the water. This time he kept it under much longer. Eleanor struggled, flailing her arms in a futile attempt to raise her head out of the water. Then everything went black. Her upper body slumped forward into the bath.

"You fool!" Schiller shouted. Bending over her he pressed his fingers against a pulse. "You almost killed her!" Schiller was screaming at Hinkler now, beside himself with rage. She was no good to him dead. He wanted her alive to give him the information Fleischer wanted. "Do you want to be sent to the Russian Front?"

Hinkler blanched, his eyes full of fear and apprehension.

Eleanor stirred on the uneven, damp slabs. She didn't know how long she had been unconscious. Shivering, she curled herself into a ball, her face almost touching Hinkler's boots. Her head had begun to clear, but she knew they were not finished with her yet. For another ten minutes Hinkler intermittently pushed her head under the water, careful this time not to keep her under too long. After each session they hauled her back to the chair for Schiller to fire questions at her. She did not talk, just hung her head as though completely confused.

"So, you refuse to tell us anything?"

"I can't tell you what I don't know."

"You know something," he screamed, frustrated by her refusal to impart information.

Eleanor let out a yelp of pain as Schiller kicked her hard on the ankle bone. She bent over attempting to rub her ankle, but he prevented her.

"A little pain sharpens the brain," he hissed giving her another kick. "All right, all right, I'll tell you," Eleanor cried. She would play them at her their own game for now.

"That's better," Schiller said, calmer now.

"Yes, I have heard there's an organisation, but I don't know what it's called or who runs it. I don't even know if Peter was involved. All I want is to find out what has happened to him."

"Take her back," Schiller ordered. "Tomorrow we'll talk again Frau Brandt and next time you *will* tell me the truth."

Eleanor lay on the dirty bed all that day rehearsing what she would tell them. If she wanted to survive she would have to give them some plausible information; just enough to play for time. Fleischer would keep her alive until he had all the information he wanted then they would kill her. If only there was some way she could contact Friedrich, but she knew it was hopeless. In her last letter Helga had told her he had been seriously ill. Since then all sources of contact had dried up. No, she would have to rely on her own cunning for the time being.

Fleischer was notorious for his brutality. He took sadistic pleasure in the grizzly torture meted out by his minions. But he seemed wary of going too far with her. So America was officially at war with Japan. Outright hostilities had been simmering on the back burner since the Germans had attacked an American destroyer in September 1941. Now with Japanese aggression on American soil hostilities between the United States and Germany would escalate. But for now Fleisher would have to exercise a degree of caution.

That was her only hope in the days that followed. On the third morning Hinkler dragged her back to the torture cell and tied her to the wooden chair. The jowly corporal leered at her as he approached with a lighted cigarette end. He held it close to her face, so close she could feel the heat. Fear shot through her like an electric current. Beads of perspiration sprouted on her forehead; dripped down onto her nose and cheeks. She was nauseous with fear, but she was determined not to show her terror.

Struggling against the ropes she tried to sit erect in the chair as Hinkler loomed over her again. He pressed the glowing cigarette lightly on her throat then quickly removed it. Tears of pain pricked her eyes. Then he came at her again. This time he pressed the glowing end firmly against the back of her hand, again and again, until she let out a gasp of pain.

"A brave woman," a voice said from the doorway. Fleischer sauntered into the room smiling sadistically at Eleanor.

"Now, tell me the name of the leader of the organisation."

"I can't tell you what I don't know," she almost screamed at him.

"Very well, you may proceed corporal."

If she hadn't been tied up his fist slamming into her face would have knocked her off the chair. The second punch landed on her cheekbone. With a faint, whimpering sound her head slumped forward onto her chest.

Grabbing her roughly under the chin Hinkler yanked her head upright. Again and again he punched her until she slumped forward. Blood gushed from her nose into her mouth. It trickled into her cleavage. Breathing hard Hinkler put his hands between her breasts and wiped the blood away, panting with sexual excitement. But Eleanor did not know. Blackness had engulfed her, propelling her into a dark abyss. Her head was spinning; she couldn't breathe properly. Pain washed over her in waves as she struggled to remain conscious.

"Not so pretty now, eh?"

Hinkler laughed obscenely shoving a mirror in front of her face.

Eleanor struggled to open her puffy eyelids and stared into the mirror. Large, bluish bruises had already formed covering her face. She was barely recognisable. Her hands and throat throbbed from the pain of the cigarette burns.

"The names Frau Brandt, the names!" Schiller persisted.

But Eleanor was too weak and battered to respond. She knew she couldn't tolerate any more beatings. Soon she would be dead. Johann's face swam before her eyes drifting with her into oblivion.

From somewhere at the edge of her consciousness she heard Fleischer's snarling voice.

"Brandt is serving the Fatherland somewhere in Russia, *if* he is still alive. You'll never find him now so you might as well give us the information we want."

"I know nothing... nothing... I am an American."

"You are also a German traitor. You have German blood and a German husband. Get her back in the other cell. A spell in a camp may loosen her tongue! When she comes back I'm certain she will be ready to talk."

Furiously, he stormed out of the room. Hinkler dragged Eleanor down the corridor and pushed her inside the cell. Early the next morning she was thrown into the back of a truck and taken to a concentration camp.

CHAPTER TWENTY THREE

Ravensbrück 1941 - 1944

They had been travelling for what seemed like hours. Every bump and jolt created a new wave of pain that washed over her in hot flushes. At first, too dazed to notice, she realised that she was not alone. Two women lay huddled together in the far corner of the truck crumpled up with pain. An old woman sat staring straight ahead muttering to herself, her lips moving soundlessly. At her elbow a middle-aged woman sobbed hysterically as she clung to a young girl. Another sat staring defiantly ahead her eyes gleaming with naked hatred. Eleanor didn't know where they were taking her. All she remembered was hitting the cold, metal floor of the truck.

"Where are they taking us?" Eleanor murmured in English.

"You're British?" the woman beside her asked in heavily accented English.

"American."

"American?

"I'm third generation German American. I was living in Berlin. It's a long story," Eleanor replied in German.

"They're taking us to Ravensbrück. It's a concentration camp for women about ninety kilometres north of Berlin. Those two are Jews, mother and daughter, God help them." She inclined her head to the women at the back of the truck. "The rest of us are political prisoners – enemies of the Third Reich."

"I've heard some rumours about the place," Eleanor ventured.

"Not rumours, not even the truth. It's much worse than you've heard, believe me. There are thousands of women there; gypsies, Russians, Poles, even German dissidents like me.

Women are beaten, starved to death, tortured. If they're lucky they'll be shot."

Horrified, Eleanor slumped forward, her anger replaced by raw fear.

They bumped along the uneven road for another hour until the truck rumbled to a stop. Guttural voices, heavy footsteps as the tail board was dropped. A soldier levelled his rifle at them ordering them to get out.

One by one they struggled to their feet and jumped out of the vehicle. The older of the two Jewish women landed heavily in a heap. For a few seconds she lay on the cold concrete unable to move.

"Up Jew, get up!" a voice ordered.

An SS officer swaggered towards them. The old woman struggled to her feet prodded by the young soldier.

"Line up, over there!"

The officer paced along the line examining each woman.

"You!" he said pointing at the old woman. "Step forward….you are no use to us if you cannot work… and you," he indicated her daughter. "Take them away!"

"We can work, we can work hard!"

"Don't be concerned… we'll give you special treatment old woman," he laughed.

All except Eleanor looked away. They knew what that special treatment would be.

After they had been processed Eleanor and the others were taken to one of the long buildings set in uniform lines. Rows of bunks lined the walls in the harshly-lit room. A single blanket covered each bed, inadequate for the intense cold of a German winter. Apart from the beds the room was empty.

"Those are your beds," the guard growled, indicating the four bunks with bare mattresses right at the back of the room. He pushed them forward with his gun. "In ten minutes you will be allocated your work."

Eleanor touched the red triangle sewn on her sleeve. She had been classified as a political dissident.

The harsh whine of a siren startled Eleanor awake the next morning. Women dressed in skimpy, inadequate clothing rushed outside into the freezing air. Dozens of long, narrow, concrete billets covered the camp as far as she could see. High walls reinforced with barbed wire and electrified fences enclosed the perimeter of the camp. Guards monitored them from watch towers strategically placed along the walls. Shuffling women, weak from hunger, shushed wailing children dragging behind them, afraid to draw attention to themselves. Anonymity meant survival.

Outside, hundreds of women stood shivering in the icy cold. Dirty clothes, unwashed bodies, enormous eyes staring from faces, sagging skin, bones barely covered by flesh. Some didn't have the strength to stand upright on their own unless supported by other prisoners. Clouds of white vapour poured from their mouths like steam engines dissipating in the cold, early morning air. A woman hissed at her elbow,

"Bastards! Filthy Nazi bastards!"

The same SS officer walked slowly along the line of cowering prisoners.

"Shut up you fool or we'll all suffer," whispered a young woman at her side.

Unable to meet his eyes he chucked a shaven-haired woman under the chin with his riding crop forcing her to look at him.

"This one and this one," he spoke softly, "and the little girl," he continued, listening to her racking cough.

"No! Please, spare my child!"

Nodding curtly to the guard he strode away slapping his leg with the whip. The guard nudged the mother and child out of the line and marshalled them away behind the buildings. Eleanor turned to look, but she whispered again,

"Keep staring straight ahead."

Finally, they were dismissed and made their way to the factory where they had been allocated to work. Terrified now Eleanor asked,

"What will happen to them?"

They're sick, no longer of any use to them. They'll be shot."

"Shot? What about the child?"

"The child too. There's all sorts here. Jehovah's Witnesses, gypsies, Czechs, Poles, Austrians. Just be thankful you're not a Jew. By the way my name is Greta," she said in a matter of fact tone.

Inside the factory women toiled over their work, their children alongside them. Ragged, under-nourished, bags of bones with swollen bellies and huge pleading eyes.

That night Eleanor lay in bed listening to barking dogs and the tramping feet of the guards. Silence as they stopped at a hut. Screams as someone was dragged out and taken away. Greta had told her about the horrors of the camp; how children were strangled, shot or drowned. About the brutality of the doctors and nurses; people who were supposed to preserve life but chose to destroy it. Burning shame swamped her thoughts; shame that German blood ran in her veins. Then she thought about Peter, Otto and other Germans who had helped people escape the camps.

Over the months that followed she witnessed brutality beyond her comprehension. Peter had been right all along. The Nazis were insane, bestial and inhuman. Why hadn't she believed him? But worse was to come. A few months after her arrival at the camp rumours began to circulate. The Jews were disappearing in droves. Those who were sick, too weak to work, were transported to 'convalescent' camps until they were fit to resume their duties. They never reached their destination.

Eleanor was the object of special attention for different reasons. She was of pure German blood and could produce Aryan babies. Children who would be groomed to serve the Fatherland. She provided the best genetic material for Himmler's eugenics' experiments.

"It is your duty and an honour to be 'coupled' with an SS officer," she was informed. "This is your contribution to the Third Reich."

Her first child, a blond, blue-eyed boy lived for just three days; too weak to cling on to life.

"So much like Johann," she wept against his face.

Savagely, the nurse snatched the dead child from her and carried it away, holding it dangling from one arm like a rag doll. She knew where she was taking her beautiful boy. He would be thrown in the incinerator, like a diseased animal, along with dozens of other babies who had died. At least her son was dead and would feel no pain. Many were thrown into the fire while they were still alive.

Three miscarriages followed. Eleanor was left in agony by nurses who looked at her with contempt for not delivering a lusty, German son. She lay in her billet wracked with pain, soaked in her own blood. Silently, she thanked God that her babies had died. When she regained her strength she was dragged in front of the camp doctors. They had decided that her usefulness as a vessel for Aryan motherhood was finished. But she was pregnant again; the result of a brutal rape. This time they aborted the foetus in order to use it for their experiments. Immune to Eleanor's screams they aborted it without anaesthetic.

A few days later a beefy nurse took her to one of the 'treatment' rooms. It was very cold.

"Where are you taking me?" she cried in a panic.

"Don't worry, it is just for a little treatment."

White, tiled walls gleamed harshly under the operating lights. Two large sinks took up most of one wall. Against the opposite wall a trolley full of instruments left uncovered. In the middle of the room an operating table with a head rest, and a drain set in the floor. A hoist dangled over the table. It looked like the kind of room where a post mortem would be carried out. The nurse pushed her forward,

"Take off your clothes," she ordered, "everything!"

Eleanor felt no emotion; she was dead inside. She didn't care what they did to her now. Peter was gone, probably dead, but little Johann was safe from the horrors of the Nazis. That was all that mattered to her. Slowly, she stripped off her ragged, dirty garments and waited, motionless, her arms hanging limply at her sides.

"Get on the table!"

Eleanor slumped to the floor, her knees hitting the hard tiles.

"Get up onto the table!"

She struggled to her feet and put her upper body onto the operating table. Too weak to haul herself up the nurse impatiently yanked up her legs. She lay there shivering violently until a masked doctor came into the room. Only his eyes were visible between the surgical mask and the cap tied behind his head. Glassy, hard blue eyes devoid of compassion.

Without preamble he took a syringe, held it up and briefly squirted it. Roughly, he injected the fluid into her arm and left the room. Passively, Eleanor waited for the substance to take effect. She knew what they were doing, testing new drugs on prisoners; experimental drugs.

Finally, they ordered her to dress and a guard took her back to the factory. At least she wasn't digging roads. Every morning a contingent of women dragged themselves, their shovels and picks, to toil for hours in all weathers. Exhausted, weak from hunger, they were barely able to shuffle back to their billets at night.

Eleanor felt sick, her bowels so loose she was unable to prevent herself from soiling her grubby under-garments.

"Ach, you stink like a zoo!" the guard laughed.

"Please, I must clean myself," she implored.

Eventually, the smell was so bad that the other women began to retch.

"She is affecting production. Take her back to her billet to clean up," the factory supervisor instructed the guard.

She took a piece of rag and dragged herself to the sanitary block. Feebly, she lathered her body with a block of harsh, washing soap. It stung her eyes and left her skin feeling raw and itchy. After washing her soiled clothes she returned to her bunk where she collapsed into a deep sleep; so deep that the guards had to prod her awake for roll call the following morning.

For the next few weeks they regularly injected her with various drugs, taking copious notes when her body started to react. Wearily, she climbed onto the operating table and waited for the doctor to inject her. Instead, a nurse placed each of her legs in a hoist and pulled them up into the air. Frightened she cried out, struggling to free herself.

"What are you doing? Stop!"

"That's enough of that! It's just a little experiment!" the nurse snapped looking at the doctor.

He loomed over her, his eyes glinting above the surgical mask. Horrified, she watched the scalpel in his hand moving towards her. Searing, hot pain raced through her lower body then she blacked out. When she regained consciousness she was back in her bunk Greta hovering anxiously over her.

"What did the bastards do to you?" she choked, clenching her fists over and over again.

Still filled with the horror of it Eleanor moved her lips, but no sound emerged. Closing her eyes she drifted back into oblivion.

For months Eleanor suffered brutal, bestial treatment in the name of scientific experimentation. Electric shocks, savage examinations and exposure to dangerous x-rays. Eventually, when she thought she could no longer tolerate the agony it stopped. Their experiments had left the lower part of her body hideously scarred. She knew that she would never again know the joy of holding a new baby in her arms.

Her hate grew like a canker in her chest. Time after time she studied the faces of the doctors and nurses when they stripped off their surgical masks, burning them into her memory so that she would never forget. Hate nourished her, helped her to survive the horror.

In the darkness of the billet she and Greta whispered feverishly in the dead of night. Others had tried and failed, but they still made futile plans to escape from the camp. If only she could get back to Switzerland to Gisela. She had been such a headstrong fool endangering herself and others in the organisation. Now she was paying the price for her stupidity.

In the years that followed Eleanor kept a diary written on scraps of paper filched from waste bins. Every detail, every experiment was recorded. Prising out a large knothole in the floor beneath her bed she hid the notes underneath. Each time replacing it, pressing it into position so that it was hardly noticeable.

Every time the guards kicked open the doors to search the building Eleanor held her breath terrified that they would find her cache. She breathed a sigh of relief when they found what they were looking for and dragged some poor creature into the compound. Silence until shots rang out. Relief when the guards marched away from the hut. Life resumed as though nothing had happened. Survival was the only thought in their minds; survival of the fittest or those who chose to collaborate with the guards.

CHAPTER TWENTY FOUR

Germany 1944 - 1945

Eleanor heard a car screech into the camp and lurch to a halt outside the commandant's quarters. Guttural voices shouting orders, the tramp of jackboots closing in on the hut. Kicking in the door an SS officer swaggered inside looking distastefully at the filthy women in their ragged clothes.

"All of you, outside, schnell!" he ordered. "I have been instructed to take you on a little trip."

A faint smile played on his lips like a child who knows a secret he is dying to tell. Guards prodded the women outside into the compound. It was a sweltering, hot day. The cloying smell of death, mixed with the stink of unwashed bodies, hung heavy in the air.

"Something's up," Greta whispered through the side of her mouth.

A watching guard brought his rifle up and rammed the butt into her stomach.

She dropped to the ground gasping, the wind knocked out of her.

"Leave her!" ordered the SS officer as Eleanor attempted to pick her up. For a few moments she stared straight into his eyes with a look of such contempt that he brought his whip up and struck her across the face.

She would never forget that face; the hollow cheeks, the evil eyes; the same eyes that had watched her in the street below her apartment in Berlin. There wasn't a flicker of recognition. How could he recognise the pitifully thin woman; the sunken eyes, bloodless skin, matted hair? An angry red scar ran from her hairline to her mouth where a guard had smashed his gun into her face knocking out one of her front teeth. But she would never forget Kappler; never forget his devilish face.

It was late summer nineteen forty four. She had been in Ravensbrück almost three years. There were thousands more prisoners in the camp now. The billets were over-crowded, crammed with bodies in unspeakable sanitary conditions. Eleanor hated having to share lavatory and washing facilities with hundreds of other inmates. When it became too crowded men, women and children were rounded up and taken away. Those who were old, sick or infirm were transported to death camps like Auschwitz.

That afternoon Eleanor stood in a long line of prisoners waiting to board trucks to transport them from the camp.

"You are being sent to another camp," Kappler told them. "We have a train waiting for you."

"My God! They're sending us to a death camp!" whispered a woman behind her. "We'll never get there. I've heard rumours… they'll gas us in the freight trucks."

"Shut up! Can't you see you're frightening the children!" Eleanor said over her shoulder.

Guards prodded and shoved them into box cars like animals. Suddenly, Greta shouted as she was steered away from Eleanor to another wagon.

"Eleanor! Eleanor!"

Viciously, a guard slammed the butt of his rifle into her back and herded her into the freight car. Eleanor tried to peer out of the slats, but she was pushed back by the sea of bodies.

"Stay calm," she told herself. "Stay calm."

Children clung to their mothers whimpering in the darkness. Fifty of them were packed together so tightly Eleanor could barely move her limbs. Those who could stand hung onto the sides of the wagon. Too weak to remain standing others slid onto the floor gasping for air in the tangle of legs. Suddenly, the train jolted forward sending those standing sprawling into each other.

"Stay calm," Eleanor told herself. "Stay calm."

Day turned to night as the train trundled along carrying its pitiful, human cargo. The darkness swallowed her up in a suffocating mantle of fetid odours. The smell of raw fear more powerful than unwashed bodies, urine and faeces.

The only fresh air and light came through narrow slats in the side of the cars. Filthy straw covered the floor. In the corner of the wagon two open buckets served as lavatories. Filled with human waste they had spilled over onto the straw covering it with excrement and urine. Prisoners, stripped of their dignity, relieved themselves in the bucket in full view of the others. When their scanty supplies of food and drinking water were exhausted they were left to starve.

A sickly middle-aged man, with a wracking cough, spewed his guts over the floor soaking the straw. Hurriedly, a woman threw some of the dry straw over it in an attempt to stop the smell spreading. It had little effect.

During the second night the sickly man stopped coughing. Semi-conscious he shouted obscenities as he slipped deeper and deeper into a coma. Towards morning they heard a deep gurgle coming from his throat. His body twitched spasmodically for a few seconds then he was dead. Tears streaming down her cheeks his wife bent over, kissed his bluish lips then covered his face with her shawl.

When the train stopped in the next sidings they banged on the wooden sides for a guard.

"My husband," cried the thin, dark-skinned woman. "My husband is dead."

The guard peered through the slat at the body and called to someone out of vision. Sounds of hurrying feet on gravel; someone climbing up to the slats. A pair of eyes scanned the ragged mass, Kappler's eyes.

"He's dead. Leave him there," he snapped.

"But sir….."

Kappler spun on his heel and glared and the young soldier. "You dare to question me?"

"No sir!" he shouted standing to attention.

Horrified, mothers held their children close trying to shield them from the sight of the body lying in a crumpled heap in the corner. Each time the train stopped hands flapped through the slats begging for water, for bread. Wild-eyed with hysteria a woman pushed her way towards the narrow opening shouting,

"Open the door! Let me out!"

Consumed by claustrophobia she clawed at the slats trying to force a way out. A guard slammed his rifle against the car.

"Get back or I'll shoot," he screamed.

The long days were the worst. The heat was unbearable. Stale sweat permeated the box car mingling with the smell of death from the dead man's body. It was so hot they could hardly breathe, that is when they dared to breathe. Some covered their mouths and noses with their hands. Women picked up their skirts and held them over their faces.

Food and water had been exhausted. Just a small amount of fusty liquid remained at the bottom of a rusty, old bucket.

"We must keep this for the children," Eleanor said.

She tried to wet her lips, but her tongue was so dry it rasped against the roof of her mouth.

Suddenly, one of the younger men jumped up, watery eyes red-rimmed. A haze of beard growth, like dandelion fluff, caught the narrow beam of light from the slats.

"What about the rest of us?" he demanded. "We also need water!"

"Be quiet and sit down," ordered a thin, bearded man. He was big-boned, a mountain of a man if he had been well-fed.

"We are entitled!"

"We are *all* entitled. Entitled to food, to live our dreams, but we are *here* in this stinking cattle car. The little ones; they don't know that they have no dreams, no future. Only death awaits them. Let them have what little comfort they can before the end."

A woman nursing an infant, sucking at her dried up breast, whimpered at the image of her dead child.

Admonished, the young man hung his head in shame. Looking at her he whispered,

"I'm sorry, so sorry. It's only because I'm so thirsty."

"We know my boy," soothed the big-boned man, "we know."

The boy dropped onto the straw, his head in his hands, and wept.

Hour after hour the train trundled on its death journey. They didn't know where they were; whether or not they were still in Germany. Time had no meaning; only hunger and misery had meaning. Eleanor, arms wrapped around herself in a protective pose, tried to stay alert. One of the men, filthy with weeping sores, grinned at her revealing his rotten teeth. Avoiding his eyes she stared straight ahead seeing nothing, engrossed in her own thoughts. Sidling across the floor of the wagon he came up against her, pressed his face against hers thrusting his hand inside her flimsy blouse.

"Get away from me!" Eleanor screamed pushing him away.

Fists flailing she punched him over and over again. She caught him a glancing blow bursting a sore; squirting yellow pus onto her hand. Shuddering, she wiped it off with her skirt. From somewhere at her side a hand lunged into view and yanked the man to his feet.

"I'll make this the last time you put your hands on a woman!" snarled a deep voice.

Eleanor heard the crunch of bone as his fist made contact. Howling with pain the filthy man slunk off into a corner clutching his nose.

Shuddering, Eleanor crawled as far away from him as possible.

"Thomas," the big-boned man introduced himself.

"Thank you," Eleanor faltered then did something she had not done in years. She buried her head in her arms and sobbed.

"He won't try to touch you again."

Suddenly, the train screeched to a stop throwing prisoners and buckets against each other. The smell was unbearable now as human waste seeped into the already soaked straw.

They waited, listening to the guards' voices coming from outside; waiting again for the pull of the engine, but nothing happened. All day they lay trapped in the suffocating heat and stink. Eventually, a guard came with a ladle of fresh water and held it up to the slats. Prisoners pressed their faces to the gap trying to catch some water in their mouths. The guard laughed cruelly as the liquid spilled down into the straw.

"Lick it up, pigs!"

Eleanor grabbed the empty water bucket and held it under the slats to catch the meagre trickle of water. One of the prisoners edged towards her, threatening now, licking his lips in anticipation.

"For the children," Eleanor said backing away.

Thomas thrust his body in front of her daring him to come closer.

Suddenly, the women were on him clawing and scratching at his face, kicking, punching. The man screamed over and over again, but they kept on in a frenzy of violence stamping on his face until it was mashed and bloody.

Thomas pulled them off, one by one. Panting, weak with exertion, they retreated into the darkness of the car. Horrified, at the raw hate she had seen in the women's eyes, Eleanor slumped against the wall cradling the bucket in her arms. Thomas dropped down next to her and patted her arm.

"It's all right. You'll be safe with me," he murmured reassuringly.

The train was stationary all day and the next. After the first two days Eleanor lost track of time. Another prisoner died clutching her dead baby to her breast still sucking for milk. Sitting there, head slightly inclined, her child in her arms like a defiled painting of the Madonna and Child.

Periodically, scant quantities of water were poured through the slats followed by pieces of mouldy bread. They ate ravenously, eyes darting from side to side like birds, watchful for grasping hands that would snatch the food away.

By the time the engine wheezed into motion again most of the prisoners were so weak they just lay in the straw waiting to die.

Eleanor had given most of the water she had gathered to the children. The remainder she shared with Thomas, carefully preserving a few drops for the next day.

"They're in God's hands now," he said.

Gently, he lifted a little girl and squeezed a damp cloth into her mouth, but it was no use. Her head and arms hung limply like a rag doll. Tenderly, he lay her back down on the straw and covered her face.

The train was travelling faster now, jumping over points as though the driver was trying to make up time. Suddenly, a massive thud sent them sprawling sideways. Wheels screeched against metal, cars ran into each other sending Eleanor crashing to the floor. Momentarily, the wagon juddered as though the train was running off the track then settled.

They waited for the sound of voices, for movement. Nothing, then pandemonium broke out. Guards ran up and down, outside the train, shouting at prisoners clamouring at the slats. Soldiers thrust their rifles at them forcing them back down. Sounds of running feet, screams, shots fired indiscriminately.

Thomas pressed his face into the gap trying to catch the words being barked at the soldiers further up the train.

"The engine has derailed... something on the line... a log of wood...I can see the front of the train on the curve of the track," he muttered. "Look, we're off the rails!"

Eleanor stood on an upturned bucket and peered out. The train had jack-knifed off the track, but was still upright. Machine gun fire chattered as prisoners tumbled out of the first three cars. Scattering in all directions they feebly tried to avoid the stream of bullets. The body of a man jumping down the bank froze as a hail of bullets caught him. He fell head first tumbling over and over until he hit a boulder. A woman, running with a small boy in her arms, fell forward on top of him clutching her shoulder. Blood oozed from the wound, but she still tried to protect her son. Shushing the crying baby she turned, face up, and looked at the young soldier standing over her. Behind him Kappler screamed,

"Shoot them you idiot!"

For a split second he hesitated, reluctant to shoot. His hands shook. He felt sick. Closing his eyes he raised his gun and took aim. As he did so he deliberately stumbled against a stone. His shot missed the woman and child.

Only a few weeks ago he had been helping his father on the farm, now this. Appalled by what he had witnessed on his first train guard duty he shivered in the heat. The SS officer pushed him aside and aimed his pistol. He shot the woman twice in the back of the head then shot the child. No emotion, no regret, no compassion.

The SS officer prodded the soldier with his pistol.

"You, get down to the front of the train. You'll answer for this when we get back to Berlin!"

Immediately, the soldier snapped to attention and marched briskly towards the front carriages.

Miserably, Eleanor sank to the floor. Now she would be in this stinking hole until she died from thirst and starvation. All along the line of wagons guards were hammering bolts securely into place ensuring there was no way of escape. Thomas sighed heavily and leaned back against the door. He almost lost his footing as it moved slightly. Startled, he gently pushed it. A small crack of light appeared around the edge of the door. He pushed again, this time more forcefully. The door opened a few centimetres revealing the bolt that was hanging by its screws. Eleanor was alert now staring at the light.

"The force of the impact must have loosened it," Thomas said incredulously.

"We must escape!" Eleanor cried pushing her hand out of the gap and tearing at the bolt.

"No, wait, they're still hammering the bolts back into place. The guard may come back!"

He squeezed his fingers through the slats and turned the screws until they were back in place against the door.

It was two days before the train lurched forward metal wheels grinding harshly against the rails. They could hear Kappler screaming orders,

"Back on the train!"

An over-weight guard ran past panting with the effort, his face flushed and beaded with sweat. For a brief moment he stopped, doubling over. Breathing hard he glanced at the box car then stumbled forward when the officer shouted after him.

"Bastard," he mumbled. "I'll have a heart attack at this rate."

"Thank God, he didn't notice," Thomas said blowing air from his lungs. "We must try to think calmly. The train will no doubt stop again in a few hours. It will be dark by then. That will be our chance."

Sitting amongst the filth and bodies Thomas and Eleanor planned their escape knowing that their chances of survival were slim. But it was better then being gassed and thrown into a crematorium. Exhausted, they slept fitfully waiting for the sudden lurch that would let them know the train had stopped.

When Eleanor awoke it was pitch dark outside; no moon shone to light up the night. Straining her eyes she peered outside to assess the landscape. All she could see was a thick forest of trees stretching out of her line of vision. She had no idea where they were; whether they were still in Germany or if they had crossed the border into Poland. Thomas stirred then sat bolt upright rubbing his arms to increase the circulation.

"We haven't stopped yet," Eleanor murmured miserably. "Perhaps we won't stop again before we get wherever they're taking us. What time do you think it is?"

"I have no idea; they took my pocket watch. It was my father's and his father's before him. He gave it to me when I was ordained."

Eleanor stared at him,

"You're a priest?"

"Yes."

A Catholic priest?"

"Yes, but I'm classed as a political dissident. I spoke out too much against the Führer. I'm a man of God. Not a good thing to be in Hitler's Germany. I tried…"

He broke off as the train lumbered to a halt and rushed to the door. There was no activity outside, just the sound of the engine hissing steam.

"They must be waiting for a signal to change," Thomas said urgently. "We must act now or it will be too late."

Gently, he pushed the door slightly, squeezed his hand out and unscrewed the loose nuts. The bolt didn't fall as he thought it would; it just hung there stuck to the wood. He prised open the sliding door and peered out. It was deserted. Swiftly, he lowered Eleanor to the ground then jumped down behind her rapidly screwing the bolt back into place.

"Get under the train!" he whispered.

Quickly, she squeezed between the gaps in the wheels and lay prostrate between the sleepers. Her heart was beating wildly making it difficult for her to breathe. Taking deep breaths she forced herself to calm down. She let out a little cry as the train jerked and started to move slowly forward.

"Thomas…"

The words died on her lips, lost among the rumbling wheels.

"Stay face down and press yourself into the ground as hard as you can," he yelled flinging himself down a few metres in front of her.

Terrified now, she held her breath as the box cars passed over her; labouring at first then gradually gathering momentum. Dark shadows of the metal undercarriage loomed over her, threatening to catch in her clothes and drag her along the track. The line of cars seemed endless like freight trains in America that she had watched when her parents had taken her across country as a child.

It seemed like an eternity before the last wagon passed over them and receded into the distance. They waited until the tail light had completely disappeared before rolling off the rails down the embankment into a newly-furrowed field.

"Come on," Thomas urged. "We must get to the cover of the woods before it starts getting light."

Even though it was only about five hundred metres away it seemed like kilometres to Eleanor. Weak from hunger they half walked, half stumbled the distance, until they fell exhausted into a tangle of undergrowth beneath the shelter of the trees. Panting, they dropped down onto the dry grass, too fatigued even to lift a hand. Eventually, Thomas stirred and pushed himself into a sitting position.

"What do we do now?" Eleanor said with a catch in her voice. "We have no food. We don't even know where we are."

"We'll soon find out," Thomas replied. "It will be light soon Try to get some sleep. You'll need your strength for the days ahead."

CHAPTER TWENTY FIVE

A bright light pierced her eyes as she lay in that sweet state between oblivion and awareness. From somewhere far away the drone of an engine picked at her subconscious. Her eyes shot open as the noise increased in volume. It was coming towards her. She sat up now, alert to every sound.

"Thomas!" she whispered urgently. "Thomas!" but there was no response.

She moved out of the direct beam of sunlight and squinted into the gloom. Despairing, she wailed inwardly not knowing what to do. He had gone in the quiet of the night and left her alone. A rush of adrenaline swamped her chest. Her heart pounded like a sledge hammer. A sour taste rose from somewhere deep in her throat.

Trembling with fear she crawled towards the sound that came from beyond the woods. Lying prostrate she lifted her head and observed a figure on a tractor in an adjacent field. As it came closer she realised it was a young boy around fourteen years old. His mouth was pursed as though whistling, but she couldn't hear anything above the noise of the tractor.

Slowly, she edged forward striving for a clearer view. Suddenly, a hand came from behind her and clasped her mouth. Terrified, she struggled as someone grabbed her, dragged her backwards and pushed her flat on the ground. Her body went limp when she saw Thomas grinning down at her.

He put a finger to her lips and beckoned her to follow him back into the safety of the woods.

"I thought you'd gone and left me," Eleanor murmured still with a frightened look on her face.

"Do you think I'd really do such a thing?"

Thomas thrust his hands into his trouser pockets and pulled out four eggs.

Handing two to Eleanor he cracked another and sucked out the contents. Shuddering, Eleanor gagged as the slimy egg-whites slid down her throat. Thomas picked a handful of grass and licked off the early morning dew wetting his cracked lips.

"We need some proper food and water or we won't survive much longer. If we could only find a stream," he complained observing the hard earth. "There's a farmhouse close by, but we can't risk being seen. If Kappler has already discovered our escape they'll search with the dogs until they find us. Our only hope is that they won't find out until they get to the camp. The train made dozens of stops so they would have to search a huge area. We've probably crossed into Poland heading for Auschwitz. One thing I know, they won't give up until they find us."

Temporarily refreshed they crawled again to the spot where Eleanor had seen the farm hand. The tractor was stationary now, its engine turned off. The boy was nowhere to be seen. Without warning he emerged from the trees, about twenty metres away, buttoning up his flies. Furtively, he looked around then sank to the ground and began whittling at a piece of wood. Eleanor shrank back as a loud shout came from a man striding over the slope from the direction of the farmhouse.

"Werner, shirking again, as usual!"

The lad scrambled to his feet blustering an excuse.

"But I was hungry papa," he complained.

"Hungry, after you scoffed all that ham and eggs for breakfast. Get to work, schnell!"

"They're German!" Thomas said in amazement. "How can that be? We've been on the train for days."

"We made a lot of stops," Eleanor offered.

"Not enough to warrant still being in Germany. We must have been going round and round. I've heard rumours about them doing this. They keep prisoners on the move until they have room in the camp after a mass extermination."

Eleanor didn't know whether to be terrified or relieved. At least they could speak the language which made it easier for them to move around, but they were filthy dirty. Their appearance would soon arouse suspicion.

"Still, at least now we have a small chance of survival. If we could only get back to the Brandenburg," she said. "There are people there who would hide us."

Thomas pulled her to her feet.

"First, we must find out where we are and cover our tracks as much as possible. Come on, let's go!"

They skirted the fields and came up to back of the farmhouse. A woman emerged from the back door. She scurried across to a shed, at the other side of a dirt yard, and shooed some chickens from inside. When she began throwing grain from a tin Thomas crept towards the open, kitchen window. He grinned when he saw the freshly-baked bread cooling on a ledge just inside the window. He reached in, grabbed one of the loaves and scurried back to Eleanor who was triumphantly clasping a rusty can filled with water.

"Over by the duck pond," she explained pointing to a small patch of green, cloudy water surrounded by mud. "There's some clean water in a trough under the pump."

After gorging on the fresh bread they drank greedily from the water can using what was left to wash their hands and faces. Eleanor tore off a piece of material from her ragged skirt and used it to wipe her neck.

For the rest of the day they rested in the wood planning their next move. When all the lights had been extinguished in the farmhouse they crept out and made their way across the fields, careful not to go near any farm buildings. As the first pink glow of dawn spread across the horizon they hid, this time in a haystack. On the third night they came upon a rutted, farm road. They trailed it for a couple of kilometres until they heard the noise of vehicles close by.

"We must be close to a main road," Thomas said. "I'll take a look. You wait there," he instructed as Eleanor started to follow.

"I don't believe it!" he exclaimed, "We're only fifty kilometres from Berlin!"

"Fifty kilometres! That's impossible!"

"There's a signpost over there," Thomas stated, inclining his head towards the road, "and that's what it says. That's why we were travelling so slowly, making endless stops, backing up the train, waiting hours in sidings. Bastards! They were just playing for time... children dying in the suffocating heat!" He slammed his fist into the ground with such force it left a shallow hole. "One day those bastards will pay!"

He glanced at Eleanor, but she wasn't listening. She was already thinking about how they could get to Friedrich without being arrested.

"We must get some clean clothes and try to change our appearance," she suggested. "We could go back to that farm." She pointed in the direction of a cluster of rough, stone buildings about five hundred metres away. "There's bound to be some clothes hanging about somewhere."

The following morning they watched and waited until a plump, flaxen-haired girl came out of an outhouse hauling a large basket full of wet washing. Swiftly, she pegged it on the clothes line and disappeared back inside. Within seconds they heard singing and the metallic clang of pots and pans being placed on the stove.

"Get down quickly!" Thomas ordered as the girl re-appeared carrying a bowl.

She sat down heavily on a wooden, milking stool and proceeded to peel a large quantity of potatoes. Impatiently, they waited. After half an hour the girl threw the peelings into a large vat and went back indoors. They could hear her singing again. Another few minutes passed.

"Now!"

They darted to the clothes line, yanked off some clothes and ran back out of sight.

"The trousers may be a bit short in the leg, but they'll do," Thomas grinned.

He disappeared behind some bales of hay to strip off his dirty clothes.

He reappeared in dark-brown trousers and a grey shirt. Wetting his fingers he slicked down his matted hair as best he could.

"Very pretty," he smiled.

Eleanor in dark-green, patterned skirt and white blouse, embroidered with colourful flowers, pushed her matted hair behind her ears. She blushed.

"I haven't felt this human for years. If only I could have a hot bath."

That night they straddled the road, about twenty metres from the edge, for hours. Eventually, they were bound to see a sign for a familiar village. No lights were visible anywhere just complete darkness. Eleanor cocked her head to one side and whispered,

"What's that noise?"

Thomas stopped in his tracks listening in the gloom.

"Water!" he exclaimed. "There must be a stream nearby."

They headed in the direction of the sound until they could hear the gurgling of water over stones.

"It is, it's a stream!"

Dropping onto all fours Eleanor thrust her face into the cool water and drank deeply.

"Not too much or you'll be sick; just a little at a time," Thomas warned sinking to his knees.

Eleanor thought she had never tasted anything so sweet, better than the best champagne in France.

"Now you can have your bath," he grinned wickedly. "You stay here and I'll go downstream a little way."

Muted splashes reached her as Thomas waded into the brook about ten metres away. Eleanor flopped into the water and lay in its shallow depths luxuriating in its coolness. Only her face remained visible like a glowing, white moon. She lay there until the skin on her fingers started to pucker. Reluctantly, she hauled herself up and sat on the bank for the water to drip off her body. That's how Thomas found her, motionless, like a marble statue; her arms resting on the grass behind her, head thrown back, water dripping from her face onto her breasts.

Mesmerised, he came up behind her and touched her shoulder. She turned to him as he lowered himself to the ground. Looking deep into his eyes, into his soul, she found a simple peace. He enclosed her in his arms, his lips brushing her milky-white breasts. He felt her nipples harden under his touch; felt the silky softness of her thighs. He wanted her, burned for her, like no other woman he had known. Raising her face to him she succumbed to the firmness of his lips as he pressed her to the ground.

Their love-making was urgent and brief, a release from their suffering, satisfying an emotional and physical hunger. To feel that closeness again, that exquisite communion of body and soul, was almost unbearable. Eleanor would keep the memory of this night in her heart hidden amongst the overpowering love she felt for Peter.

"Eleanor," Thomas whispered.

It would always be Eleanor.

The following night they continued to follow the road until they reached a dense wood. When the sun burst over the horizon they backed off from the highway. Traffic was increasing so they dared not go too close to the road for fear of being spotted.

"We'll hide in that copse." Thomas pointed to a clump of trees in the near distance. "We must get as much sleep as possible then move on again when it gets dark. It's too risky to move on during the day. We're sure to be spotted."

It took them three more nights to come to a road sign marking a familiar village.

"Friedrich's house is only about five kilometres from here," Eleanor said. "We can reach it easily before it gets light."

Eleanor pointed to wrought iron gates at the top of a rise that led down a long drive.

"There!" she exclaimed in an excited whisper.

The magnificent house was just visible from the road set like a jewel against the backdrop of an azure sky; its windows glittering in the early morning light.

The flower beds looked neglected, the grass longer than she remembered it, but it was the right place. As they approached a short, stocky figure emerged from the bushes wielding a rifle.

"Stop, who are you?"

Eleanor almost fainted with joy as she turned to face the little ruddy-faced man.

"Bruno!"

He pointed his gun menacingly.

"You're trespassing."

"Look closely Bruno."

Suspiciously, he stared at them, eyes narrowed. His gaze swept over the pitifully thin woman with dirty, unkempt blonde hair. Lowering his gun he gasped,

"Mein Gott Eleanor! Is it really you?"

Voice trembling with emotion he stepped towards them.

"We thought you were dead."

Quickly, he recovered his composure and urged them along a narrow path that ran through the trees to the rear of the house. Once inside the kitchen he motioned them to sit then disappeared into the passageway leading to the main living quarters.

A babble of excited voices reached them; hasty steps clattering on the decorative, tiled floor then the sound of another voice. Eleanor's breath caught in her throat when the door burst open and Friedrich rushed towards her.

"Eleanor, we thought you were dead!"

"I'm very much alive, as you can see," she grimaced looking at him with hollow eyes.

"You're the most beautiful thing I've seen in a long time," he murmured against her hair as he held her close.

Thomas stood up towering over Friedrich's tall, slim figure.

"This is Thomas," Eleanor stated simply. "If it weren't for him I'd probably be dead now."

He grasped Thomas' hand in both of his and squeezed hard.

"How can I ever thank you?"

Juliana was in the morning room looking out over the garden when they walked in. She turned at the sound of Friedrich's excited voice.

"My darling, whatever..." She stopped in mid sentence bringing her hands up to cover her mouth.

"Eleanor, is it you? I don't believe it!" she cried. "You're so thin."

Recovering her composure she pulled on a silk rope.

"You must eat and drink immediately then you can tell us everything."

They devoured the coffee and food, hardly stopping to chew the hot rolls. Juliana and Friedrich exchanged concerned glances, but did not comment until they had finished.

Thomas burped covering his mouth with embarrassment, remembering the manners he had not used for such a long time.

"Thank you. I haven't tasted anything so good in years," he smiled.

Eleanor told them how she had travelled to Switzerland in search of Peter and hidden in Mürren with Gisela.

"I had no word from our contacts in Switzerland otherwise I would not have allowed it!" Friedrich said angrily.

"They gave me money and clothes, but they warned me that I was on my own. They wouldn't risk any lives. When I tried to get into Germany I was captured by the Nazis. I didn't know the Japanese had bombed Pearl Harbour. Eventually, they sent me to Ravensbrück concentration camp. We were on our way to Auschwitz when the train crashed."

"The Russian Front!" Friedrich exclaimed when she told him what had happened to Peter. "We knew he'd been arrested and tortured, but after that he just disappeared. We tried everything to find out what had happened to him, but it was hopeless. Messages went out to Helga for a while, but we had to stop after Peter went missing. It was becoming too dangerous for our contacts. Peter had told us you were safe in America and that Helga was still in Sweden so we had no cause for alarm concerning you."

"I'll get the maid to prepare hot baths for you then you can choose something of mine to change into," Juliana smiled. "I'm sure we can find something for Thomas; something of Peter's. He's always kept spare clothes here."

Eleanor lay in the steaming bath, eyes closed, her mind empty of everything except the luxurious feeling of her body soaking in hot water. How long had it been since she had had a hot bath? Three years? She lay there until the water was barely tepid then dried herself with the fluffy towel laid out for her. Looking in the mirror she saw a semblance of the old Eleanor. Her cheeks were pink from the heat and her matted hair was clean, straggling in wet tendrils down her neck.

Feeling slightly dizzy she stepped out of the bath. The effect of hot water on her fragile body sent her reeling to the floor. For a few minutes she lay on the tiles struggling to control her breathing. Eventually, she hauled herself up and sat on the edge of the bath until she had regained her composure.

She towelled her hair vigorously and combed it neatly into place. Dressed in clean clothes, provided by Juliana, she went back downstairs. They were sitting on the terrace sipping cold drinks. She hardly recognised Thomas when he stood up. His blond hair had been washed and cut; his grizzled, matted beard had gone. In a crisp, white shirt and dark trousers for a fleeting moment she thought he was Peter until she looked into his gold-flecked, hazel eyes.

"He's very handsome?" Juliana cried.

"Yes, he is," Eleanor murmured, a catch in her voice.

Juliana saw the look that passed between them, the tenderness with which he drew her to the seat. She would see that look many times in the coming weeks.

For now they were safe, but plans had to be made to get them out of Germany into Switzerland.

"It won't be easy. We'll have to move you by night. Things are much tighter now than they were early on in the war. The train may have crossed into Poland before they discovered your escape so, with any luck, they'll still be searching there."

Eleanor shuddered when she thought of how she had been smuggled to Friedrich's in Walter Knecker's hearse, but it was nothing compared to what she had witnessed in the camp.

"Once you're in Switzerland the organisation will try to get you back to the United States via England. However, the Nazis have agents in Switzerland so we'll have to exercise great caution. We'll hide you in the east wing. It's been closed off for the past two years after my staff were conscripted into the Wehrmacht. You'll be safe there."

"After the camp it will be heaven," Eleanor smiled.

"Tomorrow, we're having house guests for the week... important members of Hitler's inner circle. Tomorrow night a few SS officers and Gestapo will be joining us for dinner."

Eleanor started angrily,

"Nazis, here in your home? How can you?"

"My dear," Friedrich explained, "how do you think I keep running this estate? I must pretend to be loyal to Hitler if the organisation is to do its work. Do you think I don't cringe whenever the beasts eat my food? I want to spit in their faces. Even Hitler himself has been a dinner guest here. Like always I'll smile, drink and toast the Führer into the early hours. You must hide in the attic until they've gone. The slightest suspicion and it is all over... you understand?"

"Yes... I understand."

The following day Bruno took them to the east wing.

"You can move freely here most of the time, but if you see anybody approaching the house you'll have to hide in the attic. It's up here."

They climbed up a narrow staircase to a small, dusty room. Bruno stood on a small stool, reached up and pulled down a ladder hanging horizontally across the ceiling on hooks. Underneath, there was a small, rectangular panel. He shoved it aside to reveal an opening just big enough to squeeze through.

Eleanor climbed up and looked inside the opening. It was filled with crates and cardboard boxes all neatly stacked against the walls. In the middle of the floor an old, threadbare armchair and sofa. A bare bulb dangled on a piece of flex from the rafters. A jug of water and some food covered a small table. Eleanor shuddered, remembering the naked bulb in the room where she had been tortured.

"The food is basic, but it's wholesome. Nothing hot to drink, I'm afraid, but there's plenty of water and a few bottles of wine," Bruno explained. "I'll try to smuggle up some coffee when the coast is clear."

"Dear Bruno, thank you."

Eleanor leaned over and kissed him turning his ruddy face even redder.

He mumbled something unintelligible and scrambled down the ladder. When he was back in the room below he called,

"Once you've pulled up the ladder draw in the rope and keep it inside. We don't want any sign of there being anyone or anything up there. Don't make any noise and don't open up for anyone except me."

The only light was from a chink in a shutter between the slats covering a small window set high on the wall. For a while they sat whispering in the darkness. Thomas came to her and drew her to him, holding her gently in his arms.

"Eleanor, you know how much I love you."

"I love you too Thomas, but as a dear friend."

"But Eleanor…"

"What happened by the stream was beautiful, but it was only a moment in time. Just two people hungry for human contact and a brief release from suffering. I love Peter. I'll always love him. Can you understand that?" she murmured gently.

Thomas' response was halted by the slamming of car doors punctuated by loud laughter. Feet clip-clopped on the stone steps that led into the magnificent hall. Eleanor pressed her face against the wooden shutter and strained to see what was going on. A group of high-ranking Nazi officers, accompanied by beautifully dressed women, were climbing the steps. They caught a glimpse of Friedrich standing in the hall dressed in white tie and tails. A sash sat diagonally across his chest held by some kind of insignia. Around his neck he wore an Iron Cross on a ribbon.

The reception hall was ablaze with lights. Crystal chandeliers glittered throwing sparks of light that reflected on the jewels decorating the necks of the women. Eleanor was overcome with anger and revulsion. All this opulence while people starved to death in the camps. She wanted to open the shutters and scream at them; scream the obscenities she had learned from the prisoners.

Men, women and children dying every day in appalling conditions. Shivering in ragged clothes that hung from their bones. They sat in their own vomit and excrement, waiting their turn to be herded to the gas chamber. She would never get those terrified faces out of her mind. Innocent children had gone without a whimper, clutching their parents' hands. Thousands of children who would never grow up to realise their dreams.

An image of a little girl floated in front of her eyes. Dark hair, liquid brown eyes and long lashes; such long eye-lashes. A small boy who had smiled at her as he was lifted into the box car clinging shyly to his mother's skirt. Rage filled her like a torrent of scalding water washing over her body. Feeding the revulsion, stirring it into an energy so powerful it nourished and sustained the hatred turning to bile in her throat.

Dimmed headlights crawled slowly up the drive appearing like a phantom out of the darkness. A large, black car pulled up alongside the steps. The driver jumped out, held open the rear passenger door and waited for a shadowy figure to step down. Clicking his heels he straightened up and extended his arm in the familiar salute.

"Heil Hitler!"

"Heil Hitler," the guest replied returning the salute.

His glasses glinted as he moved into the pool of light spilling from the hall.

"Fleischer!" Eleanor spat angrily.

"Who is he?" Thomas asked, startled by her venom.

"Fleischer's the man whose pigs tortured me. The same man who tortured Peter. If I could just get close enough I'd kill him!"

As Fleischer started through the open door he stopped, turned and looked back towards the east wing almost as though he had heard her words.

"Come away from the window," Thomas murmured guiding her back to the armchair in the darkness. "Remember what Bruno said, we must act with the utmost caution. It's not just our lives at risk."

Eleanor collapsed into a chair and covered her face with her hands. There were no tears in her eyes, only raw hatred. The sight of Fleischer had resurrected all the pain and suffering she had experienced at the hands of the Gestapo. It had been Fleischer who had sent her to the concentration camp. Fleischer who had sent Peter to the Russian Front. Fleischer who wanted her son to get to *Regis*.

She picked up the tattered boots she had refused to hand over to Juliana's maid. Lifting the insoles she felt for the folded scraps of paper she had concealed there. Notes she had compiled in the camp about Fleischer. The bestial treatment experienced by prisoners. Inhuman medical experiments; the dead children. It was all there. Feeling the creased paper gave her a perverse sense of satisfaction.

For months they stayed hidden away on the estate. Occasionally, they hid in the attic of the east wing while Nazi guests drank and partied into the small hours. The organisation had considered it too dangerous to move them. There was too much activity, too many convoys on the roads.

Christmas came bringing thick snow and winds that whipped it into drifts. Out there in the heart of the countryside the war seemed a long way away. On Christmas morning Eleanor and Juliana walked along the paths criss-crossing the gardens. Everything looked so pristine; the air pure and clean.

Overhead, a watery sun fought for control of the sky, piercing heavy, dark clouds that threatened a fresh fall of snow. Ice had formed overnight on the cleared paths creating intricate lace-like patterns. Tiny stones, embedded in the earth, sparkled like precious gems in the cold, white light. Icicles hung like silver swords from the sun dial. Frozen moisture dripped like strings of diamonds from branches heavy with snow.

"There'll be a big party at New Year. We'll have a lot of guests. As usual, I'll be a gracious host," Juliana said taking Eleanor's arm to steady herself on a slippery patch of ice.

"How do you do it?" Eleanor asked.

"I must otherwise all the work of the organisation will be in jeopardy. This life, the estate, is Friedrich's whole life, but it's also cover for his activities. Without it he couldn't have helped so many people. He was active before the war since Hitler first started his campaign to rid Germany of so-called 'undesirables'."

"How long has Peter been involved?"

"For years before the war, before you were married."

"He's still alive. I can feel it in my heart."

Juliana smiled and looked away.

The chill of winter disappeared bringing the first warm rays of spring. Everywhere trees were budding with fresh, green leaves. Flowers pushed their closed heads to the surface bursting into bloom with a mass of vibrant colour.

The months dragged on and on without any word from the organisation about moving Eleanor and Thomas. Friedrich had told them that things were looking bad for Germany on the war front. Tucked away in the heart of the country they seemed to be living in a bubble of tranquillity: a bubble that was about to burst.

Summer was almost upon them when Friedrich and Bruno rushed into the morning room.

"The war is over!" Friedrich exclaimed, his face flushed with excitement. "Hitler is dead!"

"Dead?" Juliana whispered in disbelief

"Yes, he and Eva Braun died together in his bunker in Berlin. He took a cyanide pill then shot himself in the head. The Soviets have captured the city. Hundreds of Berliners have left the city before the Russians can get at them."

"It can't be true!"

"It's true!" Bruno interjected.

"Hitler gave orders that his body should be burned. They poured petrol over him and Braun. Goebells, his wife and children... all dead... cyanide. Our contact says that his wife poisoned the children then went outside and played cards until they were all dead."

Eleanor pressed her hand to her mouth,

"It's horrific! How could she do that to her own children?"

Stunned, they went back into the house and called Thomas who was reading in the library. When they told him he crossed himself.

"Thank God, now the evil will cease."

For the rest of the day they talked about what they would do. It hadn't really sunk in that they were free to move around.

"But what will happen to you?" Eleanor looked at Friedrich. "Germans connected to high-ranking Nazis."

"The allies know of our activities throughout the war. How we despised Hitler and his henchmen. Only *Hitler*," he emphasised, "not my country or my people."

"Now I can go back to Berlin and start looking for Peter!"

"It's too dangerous. Berlin is in the hands of the Soviets."

"But...?"

"No, you'll wait until it is safe!" Friedrich said firmly.

Eleanor sank back in the chair. She had seen that look and tone of voice before. It was no use arguing, but she vowed that she wouldn't give up until she had found out what had happened to Peter.

"Our contact said it was a nightmare," Bruno added. "Even children were expected to defend the city. Hitler had frightened little boys, in baggy uniforms, throwing grenades at Russian tanks." He swallowed hard as he tried to keep control of his emotions. "A group of fanatical Nazis were stringing up civilians from lamp posts, because they tried to run away."

"I can't take it in," Eleanor murmured.

"He told me that General Wilding surrendered the city to the Russians yesterday. Trucks drove through the streets announcing it on loudspeakers. Swastikas and flags were torn down and trampled in the street. The Red army hoisted the hammer and sickle on the Reichstag. Most of the soldiers are so drunk they're just wandering the city looting houses and throwing furniture into the street," he told them. "He saw some soldiers with dozens of wrist watches up their arms, snatched from Berliners."

"What's being done to stop them?" Friedrich interjected angrily.

"Nothing! They're completely out of control. Women are so terrified of the Red Army they're hiding in underground cellars. Even some Russian women, who had been prisoners of war, have been raped and beaten."

"That settles it," Friedrich cut in. "You'll stay here until Berlin is safe again."

Finally, an ominous silence pervaded the city as though it had died leaving those alive to mourn its violent end. After the Americans moved in Thomas left the estate early one morning.

"I must go Juliana," he said mournfully. "I don't want to but I must. There is no hope for me here."

"I understand."

"I can't bear to say goodbye to Eleanor. Tell her I will always love her."

Thomas knew he had transgressed, but he could not regret his actions. Now he vowed to be obedient to the Church for the rest of his days.

Eleanor and Friedrich drove into Berlin, or what was left of it. The allies had pounded the city with thousands of tons of bombs. All that was left of her apartment block was a heap of rubble amongst a larger heap of rubble. Heads down, people scurried about their business afraid to meet the eyes of prying strangers. Thin, ragged children played amongst the debris. Occasionally, a figure appeared from behind a sheet of corrugated iron that served as a roof for makeshift shelters.

No food on the shelves of the shops that had survived the bombs. A black market economy flourished that few people could afford. Berliners were starving now like prisoners had starved in the concentration camps. Mothers traded sex for food and little luxuries for their children, but Eleanor could not pity them, only the innocent children. She had seen too much.

Windowless, roofless buildings stood stark against the sky, their sides open like a doll's house. It looked like the set of a Gothic horror film shrouded in a pall of dust that hung over the city. A surrealistic scene that left her feeling bereft and fearful. Huge craters dotted the roads. Abandoned military vehicles lay wheels up like overturned turtles. Frightened faces peering from windows covered with sacking. Occasionally, a little cloud of dust as someone foraged in the rubble for anything that might be of use. Women and children pushed wheelbarrows full of debris to build their makeshift homes. Some survived in bomb craters or had tunnelled into cellars.

They lived like nocturnal animals in dim, airless conditions surfacing only to search for scraps of food. The Unter den Linden and the Tiergarten had been stripped naked, their beautiful lime trees used for fuel. Eleanor's heart shrivelled in her chest as she surveyed the chaos. In every street and avenue thin, hollow-eyed children and blank-eyed women struggled to survive.

Eleanor looked up at the American military administrator towering over her.

"There must be records of where my husband was sent?"

Major Haines gave a harsh laugh,

"I'm sorry Mrs Brandt, but there's nothing I can do for you. I was told he'd been sent to the Russian Front in nineteen forty-one."

"That much I already know."

"Look, I know this is hard, but he's probably dead. Hundreds of German soldiers perished in Russia, particularly in forty-one. It was the harshest winter for years. Some have drifted back since the end of the war. Those that were captured probably ended up in labour camps in Siberia."

"If you can just tell me where I can start looking?"

"The Nazis destroyed thousands of records. They burned them before the allies could get hold of them. The fact is nobody is interested in German soldiers. They're too busy rounding up Nazis. Some are still hiding out in the ruins, but we'll get the bastards sooner or later... er... pardon me ma'am," he replied looking sheepish. "I just get so mad when I think about what they did in the concentration camps."

"I know," Eleanor replied quietly, "I was in Ravensbrück."

"I'm so sorry," Major Haines said apologetically. "Look, I'll see what I can do."

He picked up the telephone and spoke for a few minutes then turned to Eleanor.

"I've asked someone to make some enquiries, see what they can find out, but don't raise your hopes. He stood and opened the office door. "A lot of soldiers have disappeared without trace."

"Thank you Major," she replied.

"Good bye Mrs Brandt and good luck."

Two weeks later Major Haines telephoned.

"No luck, I'm afraid. We couldn't find a single scrap of information about your husband.

Eleanor knew it was time for her to go home to Johann.

PART THREE

CHAPTER TWENTY SIX

The Russian Front 1941 - 1944

Operation Barbarossa started well with the Wehrmacht advancing at a steady pace hard on the heels of the Red Army. Along the route, the retreating Russians abandoned trucks and equipment in their haste to escape the Germans. Throughout June of 1941, and the following months, Peter fought along the eastern front forging towards Moscow. He tried not to dwell on the unspeakable acts of brutality he witnessed. Much of the time he lived inside his head concentrating his thoughts on Eleanor and Johann. It was the only way he could survive the horror. By December they had captured large swathes of the country. Nothing could stop them. Nothing except the harsh, Russian winter that descended like a white, freezing pall over the land.

Their thin summer uniforms had been a blessing in the hot summer. Now they were lashed by heavy rain that soaked their clothes. Shivering in the Arctic winds they ploughed on, day after day. Soon after, the Russian winter set in bringing an intense cold so pervasive they could hardly breathe the rarefied air. Now the tables had turned. The Wehrmacht was in retreat.

Peter and his men dug into the snow to conceal themselves from Russian snipers.

"It's freezing! We'll die soon if we don't get thicker uniforms. Besides we're sitting targets in this gear," groaned his sergeant. Feebly, he slapped his arms to increase circulation. "It's all right for the Russians. They're used to it. They're wrapped up in thick overcoats and fur hats while we freeze to death."

Peter sighed, recognising the truth in the sergeant's words. In his blind belief of certain victory Hitler had sent his troops out badly equipped for a Russian winter. He glanced at a snow-covered mound over the top of the dug-out. The young man underneath had died just ten minutes ago. Already his body was covered by a thick layer of snow whipped up by the freezing wind. But he was just one amongst hundreds.

Sub-zero temperatures had taken their toll of his men. His thoughts were interrupted by a piercing scream.

"They're amputating Metzger's leg, poor sod."

"They may have to take the other one as well," said Captain Bercholtz."

"The men can't go on much longer. The generals have asked Hitler to withdraw the troops, but he's refused. He's convinced we'll beat the Soviets. Our men are dying of dysentery and typhoid while he sits in comfort on his backside in Berlin," Peter exploded angrily.

A sniper shot whined over their heads finding a fleshy target in an adjacent fox-hole. A muted scream then total silence.

"Bloody fools! Keep your heads down!" he roared over the howling wind. "There's probably more than one sniper!"

Bercholtz wriggled down into the snow pulling his cap tightly over the ragged muffler covering his ears.

"We'll move on tomorrow. If we don't keep going we'll all die in this blizzard."

Peter squinted through the tiny icicles clinging to his eyelashes. His body was stiff with cold. Slowly, he wriggled out of the shallow foxhole. It was barely deeper than a large indentation. The ground was too hard to dig in properly.

Gritting his teeth he stamped his leaden feet on the impacted snow in an attempt to warm them up. Untidy mounds of white indicated where men had frozen to death overnight.

His men had been fighting for over three years along the massive stretch of the Eastern Front, in the Battle for Moscow then Stalingrad. Their euphoric mood had soon been crushed by the ferocious Red Army. Disorientated, his troops had been separated from the main force during fierce blizzards. They found themselves wandering in a vast, white, endless wasteland unable to catch up with the retreating Wehrmacht. Some died quiet deaths. Just closed their eyes and drifted into a deep sleep with a mantle of snow for a blanket.

"On your feet! Move out!" Bercholtz ordered.

Slowly, men crawled out of the fox-holes stamping their feet to get the circulation moving.

"Move out," Bercholtz repeated angrily as he spotted a soldier still lying down.

He jumped into the dug-out and hauled the vacant-eyed man to his feet. Roughly, he pushed him forward towards the other men.

"Now, start walking!"

Wearily, they ploughed on, skirting snow-covered hillocks where men had fallen in battle. The sight no longer had any effect on them; they had seen too many. Their own misery and appalling conditions had de-sensitised them to the suffering of anonymous men.

Peter trudged through the deep drifts, his upper body bent into the wind. Flurries of snow filled his eyes and clung to the muffler covering his mouth. Needles of ice pricked his face whenever he raised his head. He was cold, so very cold he could hardly breathe. His whole body screamed for rest and warmth. He wanted to lie down and die, but he kept going; on and on and on in the glaring whiteout. Occasionally, a shout of encouragement from Bercholtz urging his men forward. A young soldier stumbled and fell head first into a drift. He lay completely still, his face in the snow.

"Get up!" Peter shouted.

"I can't," he whimpered. "I'm so tired... so cold. My feet hurt... can't walk... rest."

"Get up private or I'll drag you by the scruff. *That* is an order!"

Peter put his arms round the boy's shoulders and helped him struggle to his feet.

"Now march!" he barked.

Abandoned military vehicles littered the roads, their engines seized up from the intense cold. Muddy, rutted roads had frozen solid making them impossible to negotiate.

"Over here!" Bercholtz called.

He pointed to a cluster of soldiers huddled against an immobile tank sheltering from the biting winds.

"Dead, all dead," he murmured surveying the surreal scene.

Men sat clutching their guns aiming at something in the near distance. They had frozen to death as they slept.

Faces ghastly white; eyelashes frozen taut sticking out from their faces like silver spikes. Some in single isolation, others huddled in a macabre group. The soldiers stared at their dead comrades as they filed past acknowledging their own fate.

"We're all going to die like that!" a soldier cried shivering with fright.

"Not if we keep going!" Peter shouted. "We must keep marching!"

All day they ploughed through the blizzard. Night fell like a canopy of pitch over the frozen landscape. Bleak, white fields stretched out for miles in front of them lending the blackness a surreal, ghostly light. In the near distance tall trees, branches heavy with icicles, loomed like alien sentinels.

"We'll dig in here for the night," Peter said to his sergeant, "and move on at first light. Inform the men, and warn them to be on the look-out for snipers from those trees over there."

One by one soldiers dropped to their knees wearily shovelling into the snow drifts. The ground underfoot was frozen solid making it impossible to dig a conventional fox-hole. Their only hope was to create a shallow igloo in the drifts and pack it with snow. Soon the swirling blizzard would conceal them from the enemy.

Overnight, the blizzard increased whipped into a fury by cutting winds. By morning all traces of their presence had been wiped out. Underneath a layer of snow a ragged bunch of men huddled together for warmth. Feet bound in whatever they could forage to protect them from the cold, they lay dazed and half-starved in their makeshift shallow trenches.

Reluctantly, Peter pushed through the snow and gazed out onto an incredible sight. He had seen snow blizzards before, but nothing to compare with this. Everything was unbroken white as far as the eye could see. Some of the drifts were so high they almost obscured the trees. It was beautiful, awe inspiring. Frightening to behold like landing on a strange, alien planet.

A soldier staggered past wearing a tatty fur coat, the collar pulled up over his ears. Enviously, the other men watched shivering in their pitifully thin uniforms. Noticing their glances he hugged it tightly round him. During the night they would try to wrestle it from him and leave him to freeze to death. He had dragged the coat off the body of an old woman who had been shot as they retreated from Stalingrad. She was still alive, but would soon be dead like the others scattered in the fields.

Peter crouched down in the shallow, makeshift dug-out created from a grenade crater. He pulled his blanket tightly around his body. Howling winds sent flurries of dense snowflakes swirling around them obliterating everything in sight. When the wind subsided for a few minutes another sound; the wailing of dying men then a lone voice screaming,

"Shoot me! For pity's sake, shoot me!"

The sound of a single shot then silence except for the moaning of the wind.

Besides him there were three others in the crater. Captain Kurt Bercholtz and two privates. Bercholtz was comforting one of the young men who was groaning in agony.

"It's all right Hans, it's all right," he murmured.

"Mutti, mutti," whispered the boy whose blond hair was matted with dirt. "Mutti, I can't feel my feet Mutti."

Filthy pus oozed from a gangrenous wound in his leg above his blackened toes.

Grasping Bercholtz' hand with his frostbitten fingers he stared up at him with vacant eyes.

"Papa, is that you papa?"

"Yes Hans, you're with papa now. I'll take care of you."

"Papa…"

A faint smile hovered on the boy's lips before he sank back onto the snow, his last breath escaping almost like a sigh of contentment.

Bercholtz closed the boy's eyes and covered his face with his helmet. Then he stripped off his coat and handed it to the other young soldier. There was no room for sentiment anymore, only survival.

They couldn't bury him, the ground was too hard to dig so they heaved him up and carried him to the far side of the field. Piles of bodies lay in frozen, nightmarish poses. They lowered him gently to the ground. Bercholtz thought how peaceful he looked. He almost wished he could stay with him; just lie down in the snow and fall into a deep sleep. Pulling his collar up tightly he turned on his heel calling to Peter,

"There's nothing more we can do here Oberleutnant. Let's get out of this biting wind."

They ploughed back through the deep snow, occasionally stumbling forward into a deep drift.

"This is by far the worst blizzard we've had," Peter said looking at the heavy, black clouds overhead. "It's eased off but I don't think it's over yet."

"We'll have to stay here at least a couple of days until the men have rested."

Exposure meant certain death not just from the cold, but from the slashing sabres of the Russian horsemen.

"God help us if the Cossacks spot us," Peter continued.

Revenge foremost in their minds, the Cossacks had forced them back in a frenzied killing spree. Brutal revenge meted out after the wholesale slaughter of Russian soldiers and civilians. The SS storm troopers had razed villages to the ground. Women and children murdered in a bloodlust that made Peter shudder and despair at their inhumanity. Now they were hiding away too tired and dispirited to fight, desperately hoping they could survive the winter.

Peter and Kurt fell into the makeshift hole gasping from the sheer effort of walking and breathing the freezing air. Clouds of white vapour poured from their mouths and noses covering their faces. For a few minutes they sat panting like dogs until they were able to speak. The other young soldier lay curled up against the ice wall. Gurgling noises rasped in his throat in his struggle for breath. His eyes were glazed and uncomprehending. No longer aware of the intense cold and miserable conditions he stared without seeing.

"He won't last more than an hour at most," Kurt commented perfunctorily. Less than half an hour later Kurt and Peter dragged his body to the pile at the other side of the field. Gently, they laid him next to Hans. Kurt murmured a short prayer over the bodies. New snow had covered the soldiers before they even turned away.

Back in the fox-hole they huddled inside the jackets they had taken from the dead soldiers. The two men had become close friends during the fierce fighting. Fate had brought them together in this infernal place. Punishment doled out by the Gestapo and SS for daring to show a glimmer of compassion to the Jews.

Peter had recognised young Hans and Bercholtz. He had seen them in the street, below his apartment, when the Rosenbergs had been arrested. How terrified Eleanor had been as they watched them being bundled into a truck. Poor Hans; such a gentle boy. The son of a country pastor raised to value the sanctity of life. Kurt had followed his boyhood dream. The army was his life.

"I'm an officer of the Wehrmacht like my father and grandfather before me," he told Peter. "I am not a Nazi!"

Peter's thoughts were interrupted by a distant pounding. It ebbed and died on the wind gradually rising to a crescendo. Horses' hooves on ice! Cossacks!

Suddenly, they emerged from the white mist in a terrifying, frenzied gallop. Swords slashing the air they swept towards them. There was no escape. Nowhere for them to hide. Nowhere to run. Only vast, icy wastes stretching for miles and miles.

"Quick Kurt, get down! Pile some snow over us!" Peter urged.

Sweeping their arms over fresh snow they piled it over their bodies. Within seconds it started to freeze. Only their helmets were visible like dead bodies left to rot where they had died. They had nothing to fight with anymore. Their guns were jammed, frozen solid.

Blood-curdling screams filled the air as the Cossacks slashed and chopped their way through the camp. A loud thud as something landed in the fox-hole. Harsh shouts of command. Long, drawn-out screams. Stamping horses cracking the ice. Frenzied scuffling as a horse reared over their fox-hole. Laughing, jeering, pitiless voices. The thud of galloping hooves as the Cossacks rode away. Finally, deep, eerie silence.

It had been mere minutes, but it had seemed like an eternity. They must move quickly if they were to survive the cold. Kurt stirred near him. Clawing the snow from his face Peter tried to focus. He blinked as blinding white light pierced his eyeballs. Then he stared in horror.

Inches away from his face a man stared back at him. Eyes and mouth wide with horror under the helmet. Little strands of frozen saliva hung from the roof of his mouth like tiny stalactites. Peter recoiled, clamping his hand over his mouth to silence the scream rising in his throat. Blood had trickled from the empty eye socket of the decapitated head. Dripped over the face where it had frozen into icy rivulets. In a frenzy of horror he grabbed it. Mustering all his strength he flung the head as though it were a football. His stomach churned as he watched the gruesome object land with a dull thud.

He scrambled through the thin layer of ice covering the foxhole. Peering over the rim he surveyed the landscape. The

Cossacks had disappeared into the white wasteland. Nothing now except swirling snow and the thump of horses' hooves carried on the wind.

Freezing, white fog hung low in the sky touching trees that stood stark and grey on the horizon. Trunks black against the infinite whiteness like a monochrome painting. Spidery, leafless branches stretched towards a metallic-grey sky heavy with snow. Breathless with fear they strained their ears for the sound of horses' hooves. But there was only the howling of the wind.

Peter and Kurt scrambled out and started to search for survivors. The snow was red with spilled blood and entrails. Huge, irregular splodges as though a paint pot had been overturned. Mutilated bodies lay scattered haphazardly on the snow. Some lay half hanging into shallow trenches. Torsos lay in grotesque poses besides arms and legs that had been chopped off. Others lay with gaping wounds in their throats, congealed blood matted into their collars. One soldier had been sliced in two; his upper body separated at the waist. But it was their eyes that would haunt Peter for the rest of his life. Pleading eyes wide with horror and disbelief.

The smell of slaughter wafted on the wind filling his nostrils. The metallic stench of spilled blood mixed with rotten flesh and human filth. Incessant snow was already beginning to cover the butchered men. Clutching his stomach he retched violently then dropped to his knees and vomited onto the snow.

Suddenly, he heard a faint whimpering sound coming from somewhere hidden in the fog. Staggering against the wind he trudged towards the sound, Kurt close at his heels. Lying amongst a heap of bloody flesh a soldier lay writhing in pain. Both legs had been chopped off above the knees. One arm dangled from a piece of bloody sinew. Deep, oozing gashes ran from his throat to his waist criss-crossing his chest.

"We can't leave him like this," Peter cried in an anguished voice.

"He's as good as dead anyway," Kurt whispered. "I'm surprised he's still alive. He'll be gone soon."

The two men looked at each in silent acknowledgement of what they had to do. Simultaneously, they took out their pistols and fired at the same time. The man's eyes shot open for a brief moment. What was left of his body twitched spasmodically then he was still.

"We'll check for any other survivors," Kurt said.

They ploughed back to the carnage stopping briefly at each fox-hole. There were no survivors. The dead lay in their ready-made graves under a shroud of glistening white. In the raging wind and swirling snow they stood in the middle of the slaughter. The words of the Lord's Prayer hovered on their lips. Then they turned and walked away into the blizzard.

CHAPTER TWENTY SEVEN

Needles of snow lashed their faces as they trudged knee deep across the frozen wastes. Clothing stripped from dead soldiers helped to protect them from the elements. At night they put up a makeshift tent. A torn tarpaulin foraged from an abandoned, seized-up truck. Sometimes a copse of straggly trees helped to provide extra shelter to offset the wind. Each of them carried two rolled up blankets stripped from the dead. They took it in turns to wear the fur coat so jealously guarded by its owner. Only their eyes could be seen above their scarves and mufflers.

Day after endless day they trudged south not knowing where they were. Carefully, they measured out the few rations accumulated from the other soldiers' packs. There was no fear of them dying from thirst, not with all that snow around. When they were thirsty they picked up a handful and ate it.

Dark days turned into black nights without the light of moon or stars to guide them. The blizzard was relentless in its intensity. When it finally blew itself out soft snow still fell. Gently, it brushed their faces, settled on their eyelashes making them blink: fell like a lacy, white curtain drawn across a window.

They didn't know how long they had been walking since the Cossacks had left. Except for the harsh, white light at dawn and black, suffocating nights that followed there was no sense of time. They didn't know what day it was or what month. Whenever they came upon the bodies of soldiers they took their meagre rations. Stifling the hopelessness they kept going, hour after hour, day after day.

Eventually, the freezing fog lifted. In the gathering dusk Peter strained his eyes to see something outlined in the near distance.

"I think it's a house!" he exclaimed ploughing towards it.

A narrow beam of light shone yellow on the snow. Tentatively, they approached a murky window and tried to look inside. It was partially covered by wooden slats to protect the glass that was thick with condensation. Inside, blurred figures moved around the room. It was impossible to ascertain, at that distance, who or what they were. Suddenly, a figure opened the door and threw the contents of a tin mug into the snow staining it yellowish brown.

"Coffee," Kurt murmured longingly.

Whatever it was, it was hot. He had seen the brief cloud of steam before the liquid froze when it hit the ground. Panting, he was making his way to the door when Peter stopped him.

"No Kurt!"

Too late, they felt the cold metal of a rifle in their backs. Neither of the shadowy figures spoke. They nudged Peter and Kurt towards the hut and prodded them inside.

For a few seconds they stood blinking in the dim light from a flickering candle trying to take in the scene. Three German soldiers sat on wooden boxes around a roughly-fashioned table made from a split log. On the table a boiling Samovar and mugs of hot tea. Dazed, they still stood with their hands up unable to comprehend what they could see.

"Sit down sir. You look as though you could do with some food. Something hot to drink, ja?" offered one of the men.

Settled on a blanket on the floor they grasped the mugs of steaming tea. Gratefully, they slurped noisily, burning their mouths in the process.

"Eat sir," the soldier continued shoving some bread and meat at them.

"How did you get here?" Peter asked the German sergeant

"Like you we got separated from the army when we were driven back from the Front. We didn't know where we were. We just kept on marching for weeks… I don't really know how long. Then we stumbled across this little village. Not really a village, just a few farm buildings. There are three families living here. When they saw our uniforms they were terrified. We're deep in the countryside. It's extremely isolated here especially during the winter months. Still, I'm certain they've heard news about the fighting. About the SS storm troopers. They tried to kill us during the night, but they were no match for us."

"You didn't kill them?"

"What purpose would it serve Oberleutnant? They haven't got much themselves, but they were our only source of food and heat. If we killed them we would starve to death. We have a stock of wood for the stove, a little smoked meat and cheese. The old woman makes fresh bread from flour she stored up for the winter. Now you should sleep to regain your strength."

Peter didn't know how long they had been in the village. Each dawn brought silver-grey skies. Occasionally, a hard, white sun penetrated the sheet of cloud to give a fleeting warmth. Snow, every day more snow, added to the surreal landscape as they watched from the window. After weeks in harsh conditions they rarely ventured outside except for calls of nature. Peter sometimes tramped through the rutted farmyard and tried to engage the farmer in conversation. He grunted and turned away, hatred burning in his eyes.

At night, black skies hung over the countryside illuminated by gleaming fields of snow, silvering the trees with moonlight. No longer harsh and unforgiving, but a scene that caught at the heart like a breathtakingly beautiful painting.

"Such a wondrous night," he mused as he emptied his bladder onto the snow.

Hastily, he drew his coat around him and crunched over the ice towards the hut. A muffled noise stopped him in his tracks when he put his hand out to open the door. Suddenly, someone pushed him violently from behind. He fell flat on his face on the hard floor. When he looked up he was staring into the barrel of a gun.

The farmer pointed at the others indicating that they should get out of the hut. Once outside he backed them up against a large drift and took aim. Peter closed his eyes. An image of

Eleanor in her favourite summer dress, blue with tiny white flowers embroidered round the neck. Pushing Johann under the leafy trees in the Tiergarten. It seemed like an eternity ago. Now he would never see them again.

A sharp crack echoed across the endless waste. Bremner, the sergeant, dropped to his knees blood oozing from his chest. For a few seconds his eyes widened in disbelief then he fell forwards onto the snow. One of the soldiers lunged forward throwing himself at the farmer. He wasn't quick enough to stop the shot that killed him, but it threw the farmer off balance long enough for the others to wrestle him to the ground. The grizzly corporal took out his knife and slashed the man's throat. Blood poured through his fingers from the wound as he fell to the ground clutching at his neck.

They only had two choices. Murder three families or disappear into the night before the body was discovered.

"If we sneak up on them now we can kill them all before they know what's hit them," the corporal said picking up the farmer's gun.

"No," Peter snapped. "There's been enough killing. There are only women and innocent children left now."

"Well, it's them or us," the soldier said turning towards the dimly lit farmhouse.

"Give me the gun," Captain Bercholtz demanded.

The soldier stared at him defiantly, but didn't move.

"I'm still your commanding officer whatever the circumstances Corporal. Now give me the gun. That is an order!"

After a fleeting hesitation the soldier handed over the gun and started towards the hut. He stopped when Kurt shouted,

"You haven't been dismissed yet soldier."

Suddenly, a shot rang out. The corporal staggered a few paces then fell in a crumpled heap. He struggled to his knees and began to crawl toward the hut. The next volley of shots tore into his body. Blood and brains splattered the snow with gory, crimson patterns.

"Leave him," Bercholtz ordered. "We must gather as many provisions as we can and move on. It's not safe to stay here any longer."

For weeks they tramped through countryside unable to ascertain where they were. When their provisions ran out they stole whatever they could find from isolated farms. Sometimes they stoned birds from scraggy trees. They had no means of cooking so they ate the raw flesh. They gagged on every mouthful, but it gave them strength to plough on.

As they moved further south the severity of the weather decreased. Green patches of countryside emerged from the blanket of white. Little buds appeared on trees. Flowers poked their heads through the ground.

"It's been light much longer today," Peter observed. "It's warmer too; almost spring I'd say."

Twilight descended over the land like a curtain of midnight blue velvet. Peter squinted at something in the distance.

"Over there," he pointed, "looks like a fence."

About three hundred metres ahead a barbed wire fence sprawled horizontally across the fields. It stretched as far as the eye could see. Beyond it, another fence with coarse grass in between. At the extreme left, almost out of sight, what looked like an outpost of some kind.

"We must be at a border. It could be Poland!" Peter exclaimed.

"We've been travelling steadily southwest for weeks, but this infernal compass is useless." Bercholtz tapped the glass gently, but the needle didn't move. "It's completely kaput now."

"If we can get over as far as that outpost we may be able to get some idea of where we are," Peter suggested.

Under cover of darkness they crawled, on hands and knees, towards the building. Loud voices reached their ears, Russian voices. If they were seen now it would be all over for them.

"Quiet!" Peter spoke urgently.

Turning his head to one side he listened, a look of intense concentration on his face.

"My God," he whispered incredulously, "it's not the Polish border, it's Hungary."

"Hungary, but it can't be, it's too far south!"

"We must have been marching further south west than we thought. My Russian's very patchy, but I picked up enough to know what they're talking about. What they would do if they could get their hands on the Hungarians on the other side of the fence. We've got to get away from here as fast as possible!" Peter urged.

Making their way back they kept as low as possible expecting gunfire to break out at any moment. Their only hope was to cross 'no man's land' into Hungary somewhere between border lookout points.

"There's another look-out post," Kurt muttered pointing to another tower in the distance. "We can't attempt to cross here. It would be suicidal. We'll have to keep moving on until we're out of sight of the guards."

Keeping the fence in sight they manoeuvred their way past the next checkpoint.

"I can't see another tower," Peter said peering into the darkness ahead. "Let's go on a bit further just in case."

They crawled another two hundred metres; still nothing.

"This is the best chance we're going to get," Kurt speculated moving close to the fence. "Stay as low to the ground as possible. They don't seem to be using any searchlights. Most likely, it's an isolated part of the Ukrainian border."

"The wire is too close to the ground. We'll have to dig down a bit," Peter said.

Digging with short-handled spades they scraped out a shallow hole in the hard earth.

"That should be enough. Be careful!" Kurt warned.

Peter squirreled underneath and held the wire for Kurt to crawl under.

"Scheisen!" Kurt exclaimed freeing his trouser leg from a barb.

For a few seconds they lay quietly on their stomachs. No sounds, no movements, just the faint soughing of the wind.

"Move!" Bercholtz whispered urgently.

Slithering on their stomachs they moved across the grass as silent as snakes.

"Get down!" Peter pulled Bercholtz down beside him. "I'm sure I saw a light." Along the Soviet side of the border two faint lights bobbed up and down. "They're patrolling the area."

Cold sweat broke out on his forehead and ran down his face. His heart was beating so violently he thought it would rise up in his chest and choke him. As the lights came parallel with them they flattened themselves onto the grass. The bobbing lights passed them and suddenly went out.

"Now!"

Stumbling over the uneven surface they froze in the middle ground. A powerful flashlight swept over the coarse grass both sides of the fence.

"They're coming back! They're bound to see us!" Kurt exclaimed.

"Keep moving!" Peter urged.

Kurt scrambled towards the opposite fence. The wire wasn't as close to the ground on the Hungarian side. Turning his head sideways he slid underneath.

"Okay," Kurt said turning to haul up the barbed wire. What the hell....!" Peter was nowhere to be seen. Kurt peered into the gloom calling softly, "For God's sake move man!"

The bobbing lights had reappeared along the fence, their beams getting dangerously close. Suddenly, Peter stood up and haired diagonally in front of the guards. He burrowed back under the wire and crouched in the darkness well away from their line of vision. A guttural laugh as the taller of the guards stopped to urinate against the fence.

He crept up behind him and clamped his hand over the soldier's mouth. In a single movement he broke the man's neck. His limp body slid to the ground. Peter grabbed his gun and waited spread-eagled in the darkness.

Suddenly, the second guard loomed out of the night, his flashlight bobbing furiously. Peter stood up.

"What's wrong?" the guard shouted walking towards him.

Then he spotted the German uniform. Frantic shouts then the chatter of machine gun fire. He had almost reached the fence when the hail of bullets caught him. The force threw him against the barbed wire that clung to his clothes. Held there another blast of gunfire wracked his body. He jerked convulsively clawing at the wire, ripping his hands to shreds. His face caught on a barb tearing the flesh from his cheek. Blood dripped down into his gaping mouth.

"What the hell happened?" Kurt asked as Peter dropped down beside him. "Why did you stop, you fool?"

"Come on! Let's get away from here! "

Breathing hard they ran until they reached a small cluster of trees. All round them open countryside. Not a glimmer of light to indicate any sign of habitation. After constructing a makeshift shelter from broken branches they climbed inside and slept.

Bright light penetrated Peter's eyelids bouncing painfully on his eyeballs. A voice called to him from somewhere far away. Bercholtz shook him by the arm.

"Wake up Peter!"

Sun was filtering through the branches overhead mottling the grass with gold patches. Groaning, he struggled to sit upright. Every muscle in his body screamed in protest. Kurt was holding a scrawny dead rabbit by its hind legs.

"Breakfast," he said. "Raw, but we must eat."

Peter thrust his hand inside his jacket. Triumphantly, he produced two books of matches.

"Today we'll have cooked meat!"

"Where did you get them?"

"The guard was smoking remember?"

They placed strips of rags, torn from their shirt tails, under some twigs. Carefully, they touched a match to the rags blowing gently to create a flame. It sputtered briefly and died.

"We mustn't waste them all," Peter said striking another match.

This time it caught licking the twigs into a crackling fire. Peter fed it with broken branches until it glowed red. Taking an end each they held the skewered rabbit over the fire.

"I'd forgotten how good cooked meat smells," Kurt exclaimed salivating like a dog waiting to be fed.

They had no idea where they were except that they had crossed the border into Hungary from the Ukraine. Months of bloody fighting, in appalling conditions, had taken its toll on them, but they had kept moving. After they had been separated from the main thrust their only aim was to avoid the Soviets. Long lines of disoriented German prisoners of war trudged through the snow defeated, demoralised. They had no fight left in them. All they knew was excruciating cold and fatigue. They scattered across the countryside wandering aimlessly in arctic conditions. Bercholtz and Peter had marched their men over the white wasteland for weeks until the Cossacks found them. He shuddered, remembering the terrible slaughter.

Now, in the distance, they saw thick forests stretching away as far as the eye could see. Snow still covered large patches of the ground. It was cold, but a thaw was settling over the land.

"We must find more food soon if we are to survive," Peter observed rubbing his distended stomach. "That was the best meal I've had for a long time even though it was only half-cooked. But what I'd give for a brockfürst and a stein of beer..."

"There must be other wildlife around here," Bercholtz cut in, shutting out the thought of succulent, spicy sausages.

Peter rubbed snow on his face and ate what was left in the palms of his hands. The last of their meagre rations had been exhausted. Other than the rabbit they hadn't eaten anything solid for five days. Both men were weak and lethargic from lack of nourishment. Wobbling slightly, Peter stood up and surveyed the emptiness stretching out towards the trees.

"If there's any food around we'll probably find it in the forest," Peter observed. "There's no sign of any inhabitants or even a village."

"We'll head for that area of woods over there," Kurt instructed sweeping his arm towards the trees. It'll probably take us most of the day."

They marched slowly through the melting snow keeping their eyes and thoughts on the forest and what it might yield. Overhead, the sun intermittently pierced the metallic, grey sky edging the clouds with silver. Peter's head throbbed with nauseous pain. His eyes hurt from the glaring, white light. Light-headedness threatened to engulf him with every step. Suddenly, Kurt groaned, dropped to the ground and lay with his eyes closed.

"Kurt! Kurt! Get up!"

"You go. Just leave me here. I'm tired, so very tired."

"You think I'd leave you here? We've got to keep going otherwise we'll both die of exposure. Come on, get up," Peter demanded."

Kurt stirred, slowly opened his eyes, squinting against the strong light. Taking deep breaths he gradually forced himself into a sitting position.

"I'll be all right now; just a bit weak and light-headed," he grunted struggling to his feet.

Peter put his arm around Kurt's waist and supported him. The ground was softer now. Melting snow turning to yellow, coarse grass mottled with patches of earth.

Wearily they tramped southwards. It was late afternoon before they reached the perimeter of the woods. Tall trees loomed over them as they entered the gloom. A feeble sun emerged from the blanket of cloud spattering the ground with patches of weak, watery sunlight. It filtered through dense branches that had discarded most of the heavy, winter snow.

Tendrils of glistening liquid dripped to the ground like diamond necklaces, shimmering as they caught the light. The forest floor was wet and soggy in parts making walking difficult. Thick mud clung to their boots as they squelched ever deeper into the interior. Muffled rustling sounds; the sudden flapping of birds' wings aroused their attention. Suddenly, the woods seemed alive with multifarious wildlife. All they had to do was find it and kill it, but first they had to find shelter.

Coming upon a small clearing they dropped exhausted onto a flat, low-lying rock covered in soft moss. Covering themselves with their threadbare blankets they pulled their collars up tightly around them and slept.

Peter awoke to a cacophony of sound. The clamour of hundreds of birds chirping, singing and chattering. With a mighty effort he forced his eyes open. Through the web of branches high above chinks of blue parted the murky sky. Beams of sunlight poured through the lattice of branches warming his face. He brought his hand up to shield his eyes and smiled. It was years since he had heard the dawn chorus. Kurt's voice whispered urgently at his side,

"Look, over there between the trees," he pointed.

Peter's heart leapt as he spotted the deer standing motionless in a pool of light. Such a graceful, tranquil creature, so beautiful it made his heart ache.

"Dinner!" Kurt said perfunctorily. "Plenty of food to last us for a while if we can get close enough to kill it."

Peter recoiled at the thought of killing it, but his mouth watered just the same. There was no room for sensitivity. Before they could take aim the stag had disappeared into the trees.

"It was too big anyway. We should look for something else. Something easier to kill and easier to cook," Peter retorted.

He patted his pocket for the matches. They wouldn't last long.

Stumbling over fallen branches they chased small creatures into their holes. Kurt had been lucky with the rabbit. Now every living creature seemed to elude them. A wild boar pawed at the ground looking ready to charge. It was hopeless.

"Perhaps we'll come across a river. It'll be easier to catch fish," Kurt laughed.

They still had the farmer's gun and a pistol, but were reluctant to use the little ammunition they had saved. Besides, a shot would be heard for miles. Something rustled in the trees on the far side of the clearing. A stag ambled out, followed by a doe, and started nibbling at the grass. The two men looked at each and nodded.

Peter slowly unrolled his blanket and edged forwards whilst Kurt did the same. Startled, the stag ran towards the trees, but the pregnant doe was slower. Simultaneously, they threw themselves at the creature covering it with the blankets. Kurt grabbed a stone and brought it down on the wriggling bulge. For a few seconds they lay there panting until the doe stopped twitching and lay still. Kurt sat back on his haunches and pulled the blanket back to reveal the bloodied head of the animal.

Peter watched fascinated as Kurt took out his bayonet and expertly skinned the deer. He stripped the carcass away revealing the pink, glistening flesh underneath. Then he cut off the best cuts of meat, discarding the carcass.

"Where did you learn to do that?" Peter asked.

"Hunting with my father," Kurt laughed. "He took pride in preparing the meat himself. Don't forget he was a military surgeon!"

They took turns to hold huge venison steaks over the fire, occasionally turning it to cook its undersides. The smell of roasting meat sent their salivary glands into overdrive. Hardly able to wait until it had cooled down they each ripped off a piece and started to eat. Peter gasped, opening his mouth wide, moving the hot flesh around as it burned his tongue. Fat covered his lips, dripped down the sides of his face onto his muffler. Kurt had a look of sublime contentment on his face.

"Wunderbar," he mumbled cheeks bulging with meat. "If only we had some coffee it would be perfect."

"No such luck!" Peter observed grabbing a handful of snow. He wiped it over his face and pushed the rest into his mouth. "This restaurant only serves cold drinks."

They packed the rest of the meat in snow and ice.

"It could last a week to ten days in this weather. If it goes bad we'll have to throw it away."

That night they rested and planned their journey.

CHAPTER TWENTY EIGHT

Hungary 1944

They kept marching westwards leaving the woods behind. After a few days they came into a vast lowland of grass touched golden by the sun. Occasionally, they traversed swamps that sucked at their legs threatening to tear off their boots. Lower down, tributaries of rivers where wild duck floated on the surface of the water.

"If my geography serves me correctly I think I know where we are now," Peter remarked. "I've no idea how far it is, but these small rivers eventually flow into the Danube. If I'm right we could eventually get to Poland."

Boosted by the thought they walked with a renewed spring in their steps. It was warmer now. Little buds on the trees, grass turning green, a weak sun warming their backs beneath a sky mottled with blue. The air was still fresh, but the severe cold had gradually diminished as they traversed the Great Hungarian Plain.

Early one morning they came upon a small town, surprised to see German military vehicles parked in the street.

"That's odd," Peter remarked. "I know Hungary is part of the axis, but I wouldn't expect to see this."

People stopped and stared at the two bearded men in their filthy, ragged clothes. Cautiously, they approached a group of soldiers.

"Guten morgen!" Kurt ventured, but the soldiers ignored him.

Looking the other way a burly private said something to the others. Smirking, he sauntered towards Kurt and Peter. He spat on the uneven pavement.

"What is it you want filthy tramp?"

"What is it I want?" Kurt said dangerously quietly. "I want you to tell me what you are doing here in Hungary?"

Turning to the group he jeered,

"He doesn't seem to know what we're doing in Hungary. What do you think we're doing here? This is a uniform of the German army. The army that occupied this country you fool!"

"Stand up straight when you speak to me!" Kurt ordered.

"*Stand up straight when you speak to me,*" the soldier mimicked theatrically. Pushing Kurt backwards he snarled, "Who do you think you are scum?"

Kurt whipped off the muffler covering the upper half of his uniform.

"Captain Bercholtz of the Wehrmacht. *Now,* stand to attention before I have you court-martialled for insubordination!"

For a few seconds the soldier stood with his mouth hanging open then he clicked his heels and stood to attention.

"And this," he continued, "is Oberleutnant Brandt. Now take me to your commandant!"

"Ja!"

Peter and Kurt sipped their cups of hot, ersatz coffee luxuriating in the warmth of the hot fluid.

"We were separated from our battalion in a blizzard. The winters were hell at the Russian Front. Most of my men froze to death."

"Ja, I've heard about the terrible conditions especially in Stalingrad. You were there?"

"Moscow, Stalingrad. After that we didn't know where we were. All we know is that we crossed over from the Soviet Union somewhere along the Ukrainian border. We've been walking for weeks after our trucks seized up. But why are you here in Hungary?"

"Of course you wouldn't know. We occupied Hungary in March of this year – 1944. Our orders are the mass deportation of Jews to camps in Poland. Eichmann himself will administer it. In fact, it has already begun," the commandant said with a small shrug of his shoulders.

Peter's heart sank. Nothing had changed. The murder and atrocities still went on. It would go on until Hitler won the war he felt destined to win. The commandant spoke into the intercom,

"Corporal, take these men to the officers' quarters. Get them some decent clothes. A hot bath, food and some sleep then we'll discuss repatriation to your regiment."

"What was left of it," Peter replied bitterly.

Kurt cast him a warning glance as they saluted and walked from the office.

"Be careful what you say. I don't trust him," Kurt murmured getting into the staff car.

Shaved, dressed in clean uniforms, Kurt and Peter returned to the commandant's office. Hands in a praying position he swung from side to side in his chair.

"Tell me, how did you come to be detached from the main battalion? It seems a little strange considering you are both officers."

"As I told you yesterday," Kurt replied, "conditions were atrocious. We'd been fighting for days in terrible circumstances. We were freezing to death in the uniforms you saw us in yesterday. The blizzard was so vicious we could barely see the men in the next trench. I shouted at them to stick together, but they were running in all directions trying to get away from the Soviets. They didn't stand a chance. Most of them were shot on the spot. Others were hacked down by Cossacks who chased them for days. Myself, Oberleutnant Brandt and about thirty men managed to get away. The blizzard obliterated everything."

"Then what happened?"

"After a few hours we didn't know where we were. We had meagre provisions and no means of defence. Our rifles were frozen solid. Eventually, the Cossacks hunted us down. All of my men… hacked them to pieces… every single last soul."

He shuddered visualising the nightmarish scene, the screams of the men.

"All that blood," he murmured. "The snow was a sea of red."

"It was complete carnage," Peter added.

"How did you two survive?"

"We managed to dig into a snow-filled trench and cover ourselves. Fresh, falling snow helped to conceal us. I shouted to the men to do the same, but they weren't quick enough. There was little else we could do under the circumstances. It was every man for himself."

"I see. That will be all for now Captain," the commandant said dismissively. "Please, make yourself familiar with the town. We may have work for you to do here."

"What kind of work," Peter asked tentatively.

"As I told you we're rounding up the Jews. You'll be able to help us in assisting them on their journey to Poland."

The two men returned to their quarters and quickly closed the door behind them. Taking out a pack of cigarettes Kurt offered one to Peter, but he shook his head.

"They're probably sending them to Auschwitz. Well, I won't be party to Eichmann's plans!"

"Keep your voice down," Kurt warned. "Walls have ears. I saw a Gestapo officer when we left the commandant's office. If they're deporting the Jews they'll be everywhere."

"We must try to help them," Peter interjected fiercely.

"There's nothing we can do!"

"If I can get back to Germany…" Peter hesitated.

Kurt was his best friend. They had looked out for each other throughout the vicious fighting. Could he trust him with knowledge of the organisation?

"There's something you should know. The Gestapo may be looking for me if I return to Berlin. If you're with me you'll be in danger."

Kurt looked at Peter searchingly for a few seconds. He rose and paced the floor, a troubled look on his face.

"I despise Hitler," he whispered. "When I was a boy everybody thought he was Germany's salvation, but he has no respect for human life. My father..." he choked, "my father was tortured by the Gestapo, because he refused to participate in Himmler's sickening medical experiments."

"I'm sorry," Peter murmured.

"Oh, he's still alive. Mentally, he's as sharp as ever. Physically he's a wreck. He's been in a wheelchair ever since. He was a surgeon. All the bones in his hands were crushed. They left him like that until it was too late to rectify. Even holding a cup causes pain. The bastards! That's one of the reasons I was sent to the Eastern Front. That and hitting an SS corporal."

Peter hesitated for a few seconds.

"The reason they're after me is because I helped to get Jews out of Berlin. I also smuggled my wife and son out to Sweden.

"But how?" Kurt asked incredulously.

Peter looked searchingly at Kurt then took a deep breath before continuing in a quiet voice,

"I belonged to a secret organisation whose leader is known as *Regis*. We have contacts all over Germany. One, in particular, will hide us if we can get back to Germany."

"It's impossible!"

"Not if we can get into Poland. There's only one way. We must travel with a convoy of Jews. You're right of course. There's little we can do here to prevent their deportation."

Grasping Peter by the shoulders Kurt murmured,

"Yes, my friend."

CHAPTER TWENTY NINE

The deportations started in May. In June Kurt and Peter were detailed to escort a batch of Jews and political dissidents to the railway sidings. Hundreds of men, women and children were herded into stinking box cars like cattle. Packed tightly together they stood supporting each other unable to sit down.

Anger welled up in Peter when he watched the brutal guards prodding them with their guns. A little boy, about four years old, stumbled and fell. The guard laughed as blood oozed from the child's grazed knee. Peter started forward then stopped, spotting an SS officer watching him.

Their suspicions had been aroused when the commandant had questioned them further about their trek from the Front.

"He thinks we're deserters. I am sure of it," Peter said when they returned to the privacy of their quarters. "We must be extremely careful not to give them any reason to doubt us otherwise we'll ruin our chances of escape."

For two months they rode on the death trains. Aware they were being scrutinised they waited for a fortuitous moment to act. It came on a scorching late afternoon in July. The train stopped to replenish water for the boiler. All along the train hands and eyes appeared along the slats of the box cars.

"Water, please some water!"

Guards walked down the length of the train banging the wagons with their guns.

"Stay back!" screamed a guard, but they were mad with thirst.

The stench was unbearable. A mixture of human excrement, vomit and unwashed bodies. Bile rose in Peter's throat as he watched a guard drinking from a ladle. Carelessly, he threw the remainder onto the ground. Pitiful cries came from the wagons.

"Please, just a sip of water for my little girl!"

Grasping the ladle Peter filled it and ran to the woman. A hand grabbed the ladle and titled it inwards. Water spilled down into the box car. A dozen mouths craned their heads to catch the drips. Suddenly, a harsh voice shouted,

"No water for the prisoners! What do you think you're doing?"

An SS officer was stamping towards him.

"They must have water in this heat. Some are already dying; they're so weak."

"They'll be dead soon enough anyway. Why waste water?" he laughed harshly.

Peter turned on his heel. A red haze seemed to drop over his eyes. Something snapped in his head just as Kurt appeared at his side.

"Achtung!"

The command brought him back to his senses. Taking a deep breath he blinked. Kurt was standing in front of him.

"Oberleutnant Brandt! Check on the prisoners in the rear wagons, immediately!"

Stiffly, Peter turned and walked towards a group of guards who were banging on the wagons with their rifle butts."

Slowly, they rumbled through the night only stopping for signal changes. Once they stopped to connect another three box cars and load more prisoners. Loud wailing filled his ears as they pleaded for food and water. Only rarely had he seen an act of compassion when a guard quickly handed up some water. Most of them seemed impervious to their suffering.

"Jew pigs!" they laughed when the prisoners begged.

One pot-bellied soldier threw some water through the slats and guffawed. The prisoners scrabbled futilely, trying to catch some in their hands before it fell onto the filthy straw.

Propped in the corner by the window Peter leaned against the glass, hands clamped over his ears as though trying to sleep. He couldn't shut out the pitiful cries, especially the moaning of delirious children.

When Kurt joined him they sat silently until the lone officer sharing their compartment stood up and wandered down the corridor.

"I'm sorry," Peter apologised.

"You must be more careful. Look, I feel the same way as you, but we must keep our heads."

"You're right, of course. We can't help these people, but we can help others."

Two hours later, just after crossing the Polish border, they stopped again in a siding. The usual clamour of crying voices carried down the train. Suddenly, a new sound: breaking wood, guttural shouts, pistol shots, the chatter of machine gun fire.

"What the hell is happening?" Kurt queried springing to his feet. Hurrying towards the external door they jumped down and saw guards firing indiscriminately at fleeing prisoners.

"How did they get out?"

The door of the box car at the front end was wide open. Stragglers were still jumping out landing heavily on the gravel beside the rails.

Prisoners were scattering in all directions. Women running, half dragging, half carrying small children. One by one they fell to the ground as bullets hit them. Guards moved from body to body making sure they were dead. There was no mercy for the injured writhing in agony. A shot at point blank range solved the problem.

Horrified, they watched a woman struggle to her feet and stagger towards the grass bank. Her back arched as a hail of bullets ripped into her. For a brief moment her legs twitched then she was still. A soldier brutally kicked her lifeless body as though it were a piece of garbage. It was all over in minutes. The only survivors were those who had stayed on the train.

"Get those bodies off the track. There's another shipment coming through very soon," a voice ordered.

Guards dragged the dead away from the train and rolled them down the slope at the side of the track.

Pandemonium had broken loose at this unexpected, futile escape attempt. Soldiers were still running backwards and forwards reacting to orders. Eventually, they were ordered back onto the train.

"Corporal, take your men up front," Kurt ordered, "and keep a close watch on those wagons where the prisoners broke loose. Everything is under control here."

They climbed up onto the steps. Without speaking they knew what each of them was thinking. Peter held onto the door handle and leaned out. Satisfied that all had re-boarded he whispered,

"The engine had just started into a cutting when it stopped. Wait until the train is almost through."

With a steamy gasp the train lumbered forward. Peter opened the door a crack as the last few wagons entered the cutting.

"Now!"

Kurt jumped out and rolled down the bank into the undergrowth. Peter struggled onto the metal steps and fought to slam the door closed. He jumped clear landing about thirty metres away from Kurt.

"Why the hell didn't you jump with me?" he gasped.

"An open door would be spotted within minutes. With any luck they won't discover we've gone until the next stop. That's about seventy-five kilometres away."

For several minutes they lay there waiting to hear the metallic screech of brakes against wheels. Nothing happened. The train had gathered speed and rumbled out of sight.

After ten minutes Peter struggled up onto his elbows and peered around. There was nothing to be seen except fields stretching as far as the eye could see.

"We should be able to move with reasonable freedom in our uniforms. With any luck we won't be missed until they start unloading the prisoners. They won't waste any time coming back to search for us. They'll leave that to the Gestapo."

"Another few hours and it'll be dark then we can make a move," Kurt observed.

On hands and knees they crawled through the undergrowth casting nervous glances back at the track. Kurt stifled a yelp as his knee made contact with a sharp stone. A faint whimpering sound followed. Peter called,

"Are you all right Kurt?"

"I'm fine, just keep going."

Peter edged forward and stopped again as the crying continued. It was louder this time. Catching up with Kurt he found him on all fours, head down, listening intently.

"Did you here that? A kind of sobbing sound?"

"Yes, it's coming from over there," Peter whispered.

"It's one of the prisoners!"

The body of a young woman lay face down on top of a child.

"Mein Gott, it's a little girl!" Peter cried.

The child screamed with fear as they approached her. Peter put his hand over her mouth."

"It's all right liebling," he soothed dragging the body of the woman away.

Eyes wild with terror the child squirmed frantically as Peter rocked her gently in his arms. She looked up at him out of tear-filled, blue eyes; hair golden rather than blonde.

Swallowing hard Kurt stared down at the little girl, his eyes glistening with tears.

"She's about two years old I should think; about the same age as my little Renate."

"What's your name little one?" he said taking her hand.

She gripped his fingers tightly then started to cry again. Deep, convulsive sobs wracked her frail body.

"She can't understand what you're saying. Her language is Hungarian."

"There must be some form of identification on the mother, assuming it is her mother. She doesn't look Jewish."

"Only a strain of Jewish blood is needed to send them to the camps," Peter remarked thinking about Manfred.

Kurt rolled the body over and searched, but the skirt pockets were empty.

"Nothing. Wait, what's this?"

Kurt patted the skirt again near the hem, swiftly tearing the stitches. He pulled out a stiff, tattered piece of folded paper.

"It's a photograph; looks like a family group. The faces are a bit creased, but that's definitely the child," Kurt observed passing it to Peter, "and that's her mother."

The face of the dead woman smiled out at him. Standing next to her a slim, fair-haired man. Behind them an older man with darkish-blond hair. He had his arm around a petite, dark-eyed, dark-haired woman. Peter turned over the photograph and studied it.

"There's some writing on the back," he observed, squinting to make out the words. "It's in German! Josef, Anna and Erika with mutti and papa Fuchs. The grandmother looks Jewish, I think, but not the others. The grandfather must have been German. I can't imagine how they came to be in Hungary. They must have gone there before the war."

"She must be Anna or Erika," Peter said, smiling at the little girl who was sitting up staring at them. "Take her over there and face her away from me. Let's see what happens when I call out to her."

Kurt distracted the child, waiting until she was absorbed in the little game he played.

"Erika!" Peter called, but there was no response. He grinned and called again, "Anna!"

The child's head swung round in his direction. "Anna!" She stood up, wobbling slightly, and ran into his arms. "We'll keep you safe little one, I promise."

Food and milk for Anna was the first priority. They didn't have a great deal of money, but they had been issued some Zlotych before their trips to Poland. The special money minted by the Nazi administration for Wehrmacht troops to spend in occupied countries.

"If we follow the track we're bound to hit a station where we can get some provisions. At the same time we can ascertain how to get a train over the border into Germany. Once we're there I can get in touch with the organisation, assuming it hasn't been routed out by the Nazis," Peter said.

Taking it in turns to carry Anna they straddled the track throughout the night. Overhead, a white moon gleamed in a midnight-blue, velvet sky studded with dozens of brilliant stars. Stars so big Peter felt he could reach out and touch them. A cool breeze, little more than a soft movement of air, caressed their faces.

When the first pink rays of the sun crept across the sky they came across a small farm. Outside a gate leading into a lane sat four, large milk churns on a wooden platform. Peter took out the hip flask he always carried with him and dipped it into one of the churns.

"Drink this Anna."

She grasped the flask and noisily slurped the milk, gulping breathlessly in her haste to drink it.

After resting for a while they plodded onwards until they reached a small, neatly-kept station. It was little more than a single, stone-flagged platform. Wooden troughs, filled with brightly-coloured flowers, stood against the stone wall of a tiny waiting room. A hand cart loaded with newspapers, crates and a single suitcase was parked near the door.

"Look, there's a map on that board over there at the end of the platform," Kurt whispered out of the side of his mouth. "Let's take a look."

"I haven't got the vaguest idea where we are," Peter muttered, "except that we are somewhere in south Poland. We'll just have to buy a ticket to any north-westerly point and pick up another train." Nonplussed, he stared at the station name. "I can't even pronounce that!"

Kurt took out his handkerchief and spat on it. He wiped it over Anna's face and smoothed down her flimsy clothes. Both men brushed down their uniforms and wiped the dust from their boots.

Kurt clicked his heels adopting the arrogant stance of a Nazi officer.

Briskly, they marched into the ticket office and banged on the closed window. A bald-headed, plump man with a brush moustache darted from a side door. He muttered something in Polish they did not understand.

"Heil Hitler! Two tickets to the German border."

Blankly, the man stared back at him and shrugged his shoulders.

Peter drew a rough map in the dust on the counter. Drawing a diagonal line he pointed west.

"Germany, Dresden! Two tickets, dolt, at once!"

Peter banged his fist on the little counter beneath the glass partition, but the man shrugged again,

"Warsaw," he said shaking his head."

"We don't want to go to Warsaw!"

Tentatively, the man shook his head again,

"Warsaw."

Peter glared at him then stuck out his hand to receive the tickets. Hurriedly, the frightened man handed them over. Peter paid him and marched out with Kurt close on his heels. He shrugged his shoulders,

"He didn't understand a word, but at least we've got tickets to go somewhere. Perhaps we have to get to Warsaw to pick up a train for Berlin. There must be special military trains into Germany, but it would be too risky. We'll have to get over the border some other way, maybe by car."

For forty-five minutes they paced up and down the platform. The clerk was still in his office bent over a pile of papers. Finally, the rumbling of an engine caught their attention. Minutes later the train panted into the station and shuddered to a halt. An elderly man alighted from the carriage nearest to them.

Further along the platform a heavily-set woman struggled off the train. She had the deeply-lined face of someone who spent her life in the fields. Wearing a black peasant skirt and head scarf she carried a wicker basket covered with a red cloth. Keeping her eyes down she hurried towards the exit avoiding their eyes.

Peter noticed something protruding from the basket. He delved into his pocket and pulled out some money. Before she could pass he stepped out in front of her. Raw panic leapt into her eyes. Her whole body quivered with fear.

Peter pulled back the cloth to reveal two fresh loaves of bread, a hunk of cheese and some hard biscuits. Motioning towards the contents he waved some Zlotych. The woman breathed an audible sigh of relief and proffered the basket. Peter took one of the loaves of bread. He broke off a wedge of cheese, took some of the biscuits then pressed some money into her hand. Hastily, she scurried towards the exit looking furtively over her shoulder. She was still staring after them when the train chugged out of the station.

Kurt sank back against the seat in their empty compartment breathing a sigh of relief. They shared out some of the bread and cheese. Peter pulled off a piece of soft bread and gave it to Anna.

"Not really suitable food for a young child, but it's all we have."

He offered her a small piece of the strong-smelling cheese. She grabbed it and stuffed it into her mouth swallowing it without chewing.

"You must chew it Anna or you'll make yourself sick," Peter chided gently.

"She needs a proper meal," Kurt cut in, "and some clean clothes otherwise we'll arouse suspicion."

They travelled for hours over rolling countryside. Fields, isolated farm buildings, clusters of neglected cottages and dense woods. Occasionally, they stopped at some remote station to drop or pick up a passenger. Dusk fell as they reached the outskirts of a small town, little more than a large village. Slowly, they chugged into the dimly-lit, deserted station and screeched to a halt. Peter strained to look out of the grimy windows at a vague form at the end of the platform. Grasping the leather strap he lowered the window and stuck out his head.

"The gods are with us my friend," he grinned. He pointed. "Over there near that opening in the fence."

Hurriedly, Kurt picked up Anna, who was fast asleep, and followed Peter off the train.

"Stay in the shadows behind the fence. Be ready to move," Peter muttered.

Further along the platform a figure scurried towards them. When he saw the German uniform he started to make an about turn. Peter shouted,

"Fetch me a map!" sending the man running back towards the wooden building. He could see the dim outlines of people sitting in the waiting room.

Within seconds the man was back clutching a map. He proffered it to Peter who snatched it viciously from his grasp.

"Who does this motorcycle belong to?" Peter demanded.

"The station master," replied the squat, bald-headed porter in halting German.

"Well, I will need it to continue my journey!"

"But Oberleutnant!"

Peter swung round and glared at the man who cowered under his gaze.

"You dare to argue with *me*, an officer of the Wehrmacht! I am commandeering this vehicle for military purposes. I have urgent business to attend to in Berlin. A matter of great importance to the Führer. Heil Hitler!" he snapped marching towards the motorcycle and sidecar.

"Yes sir!"

"Now, get back to your duties!"

Kurt lowered Anna into the sidecar covering her with a sack that had been left on the seat.

"Let's get going!" he yelled jumping onto the pillion.

Peter gunned the engine and roared into the night.

South of Szczecin they travelled west from occupied Poland to the German border.

"Our papers are valid so we shouldn't have much trouble," Peter shouted. "Unless the Gestapo pigs are already on our trail!"

The border guard looked suspiciously at Anna who had stirred from under the blanket.

"You have papers for the child?" he queried looking at both men.

"No, she's Polish. A waif we picked up in the fields. Her mother was very obliging," Peter laughed harshly. "This one I'll nurture myself until she becomes a good German for the Fatherland."

"Ja Oberleutnant," the guard laughed knowingly, waving them through the checkpoint.

He watched the tail light of the motorcycle disappear then stepped into the hut and picked up the telephone.

"That could have been very nasty," Kurt remarked with a sigh of relief. "I can't believe you were so cool about it."

"Believe me it's not the first time I've had to get through a checkpoint when the Gestapo have been on the lookout for me."

"How much further?"

"It's about a hundred and thirty kilometres to Berlin from Szczecin, or thereabouts. Travelling south west we should be at my uncle's estate in the Brandenburg in a few hours."

Peter was familiar with the countryside they travelled during the night. Avoiding the main highway he drove along small, country roads that bypassed Berlin. They bumped along at an even speed. Occasionally, a stifled curse came from behind as the front wheel hit a pothole in the road.

"Berlin is over that way," he pointed towards the west. It shouldn't be much longer."

"Danke Gott! My backside is killing me!" Kurt laughed.

Suddenly, Peter slewed to a halt and stared ahead. Bulky shapes loomed out of the darkness ahead.

"What is it?" Kurt queried.

"Quiet! Trucks blocking the road. They must be on the lookout for someone. We can't risk trying to get through, not so close to Berlin."

Peter gunned the bike and drove back the way they had come. He turned onto a narrow track that led into a wood.

"We'll skirt the woods and come out the other side north of the blockade!" he shouted over his shoulder.

Hard, dry ground at the edge of the trees gave way to marshy patches that slowed their progress. More than once they jolted to a halt wheels spinning frantically; throwing up mud and grass. Eventually, they emerged from the woods and drove across a field back onto the same road.

Suddenly, a shout, running feet, revving engines, the grating of gears and gun shots in front of them. Peter screeched to a halt, slewed the bike around and headed back across the field. He drove like a maniac, machine gun fire peppering the air around them. Kurt lurched forward as the motorcycle skidded to a halt close to the woods.

"Keep going!" he yelled. "We're right out in the open!"

"No, take Anna with you!" Peter urged pushing a piece of paper into his hand. "Go to this address. They'll look after you. Memorise it then destroy the paper. Otherwise many people will be put in danger."

"But I can't leave you like this!"

Peter wasn't listening. He was already lifting Anna from the side car and pushing her into Kurt's arms.

"You must! Do you want the child to die? Until we meet again my friend," Peter said embracing Kurt. "Promise me you'll look after her."

"With my life."

"Go now and may God be with you!"

Peter hit the road at speed driving away from the trucks that were bearing down on him. He knew he was trapped even before he saw dimmed lights coming in the opposite direction. A car lurched to a halt behind the first truck. From the rear a figure emerged and leaned against the vehicle. Peter strained his eyes in the darkness as the man sauntered towards him.

"So Herr Brandt, we meet again."

"Fleischer!"

"Arrest him! He is a deserter from the Wehrmacht!" Fleischer snapped.

"No, I was separated from my men," Peter protested as they dragged him towards the truck.

He was playing for time until he knew Kurt had made some headway. Desperately, he pretended to lose his footing and fell to the ground.

"Filthy deserter!" growled a soldier giving him a vicious kick.

"My brother was killed on the Russian Front," the other man snarled.

He smashed down on Peter's skull with his rifle butt. Thrusting his face up close he spat in his face. Peter felt the slime trickling down his cheek.

"Enough!" Fleischer ordered. "I want him alive when I take him to Prinz Albrecht Strasse."

His eyes gleamed with anticipation. One way or another he would make Brandt talk.

CHAPTER THIRTY

Berlin 1944

For days Fleischer's thugs systematically tortured Peter. His whole body was covered with cigarette burns and bruises. Blood had congealed over his swollen lips and the gash on his cheek. He could hardly breathe through his broken nose. His eyes were slits in a mash of bluish-purple bruises.

Rough hands threw Peter into a small, cell-like room. He had been in this room before. The same stinking bucket full of human waste, bare flagstones, a naked light bulb. The same questions, over and over again, until he wanted to scream.

"Brandt, so nice to see you," a voice lisped from the open doorway.

Peter recognised the voice immediately.

"Brauer!" he sneered. "Still doing Fleischer's dirty work?"

"Not such a pretty boy now, eh Brandt?" Brauer smirked.

"The Führer doesn't like deserters, does he Brauer?" Fleischer hissed stepping into the cell.

"How were you separated from your men?" Brauer demanded. "How did you get into Hungary?"

"Some of us were separated from the main thrust in a blizzard. We were attacked by Cossacks. It was wholesale slaughter. Only two of us managed to escape. We tramped for weeks until we reached the Ukrainian-Hungarian border."

"You and your senior officer, Captain Bercholtz," Fleischer stated flatly.

"Yes, Bercholtz put all this in his report."

"He was with you on the train taking prisoners to Auschwitz?"

"Yes, he was on the train, but I don't know what happened to him. Some prisoners had got out of a wagon. They were running amok."

"Why did you run away?"

"I didn't! I got caught up in the chaos!"

"An officer of the Wehrmacht?" Brauer laughed incredulously.

"The guards were running around like fools shooting indiscriminately. Two Jews ran past me and the idiots fired. As I jumped out of the way I stumbled and fell against the metal steps of the carriage. I must have blacked out. The next thing I remembered was lying in the grass at the foot of the bank."

"Captain Bercholtz went to assist you?"

"No, as far as I know he was still checking the other box cars. I don't remember anything after that."

"You really expect me to believe such fantasy?" Fleischer laughed harshly.

"It's the truth," Peter lied.

"Then why has he disappeared? He's a deserter like you!"

"I'm not a deserter! I'm still ready to die for my country."

"But not for the Führer," Fleischer hissed, his black eyes gleaming with venom.

Peter stared at him defiantly,

"I repeat I am ready to die for my country."

"Oh, you're not going to die, not yet anyway. That would be too easy. I want you to suffer Brandt, suffer as much as possible. Tomorrow, you'll be on your way to Sachsenhausen concentration camp. This time you will *not* escape."

CHAPTER THIRTY ONE

Sachsenhausen 1944-1945

Peter lay sprawled on the floor of the vehicle barely able to lift his head. Other prisoners sat silently on the slat seats either side of the open truck. They were in Oranienburg about an hour north of Berlin. Peter thought how ironic it was that he was in the Brandenburg. The concentration camp was just a few kilometres from his uncle's estate.

They bumped along an uneven road towards the camp. Peter stared at the sign over the gates.

'*Arbeit Machfrei*', the words screamed at them: '*Work makes you free*'.

Peter grimaced as fresh pain shot through his skull. Freedom would only come with oblivion. Even before he had been sent to the Front his uncle had told him about the brutality in the camp. Prisoners were beaten or worked to death. That was the only freedom offered in Sachsenhausen.

Still slightly dazed he tried to focus on his surroundings. They seemed to be in a roll call area, close to the gate, covered by a machine gun post. Beyond, rows of wooden huts dominated the skyline.

After they had been processed they were taken to one of the barrack-style huts.

Peter looked down at the triangle on his sleeve; the mark of a political prisoner.

"Don't worry, we all have them. I'm Jewish so mine is yellow," said a man at his side patting his ragged sleeve.

"They're mostly Jewish here?" Peter queried.

"Not so many now. Most of them have been sent to Auschwitz. All the prisoners have patches. Violet for Jehovah's Witnesses, pink for homosexuals. Every category has a different colour."

Peter felt the red patch on his arm. There must be a way to escape!

On his return from his first day at the factory Peter made mental notes. It was impossible to climb over the perimeter wall. There were guards everywhere inside the camp. Dog handlers patrolled the path close to the electric fence. Even if he could clear the notorious *'Death Strip'* there were watchtowers along the perimeter of the camp. Angry shouts reached his ears as the detail approached the roll call area.

"Move pigs! Let's see you run!"

About twenty men were in the yard. Some were running, others could barely lift their feet from the ground. An SS sergeant laughed as they stumbled over the uneven surface.

"What's happening?" Peter whispered.

"Punishment… they're testing shoes," replied Alphonse, a tall, grey-haired aristocratic looking man wearing a black patch.

"They make them run in shoes too small for them. Sometimes they tie sand bags to their ankles. They're taking them to the cinder path to test military footwear. Sometimes they run them for days on end."

"Animals!" Peter spat.

"I'll never get used to it. The beatings, public hangings. Some prisoners are forced to stand in execution trenches."

Peter's shoulders slumped. Was this where he would end his days?

Winter set in bringing cold, lashing rain that turned to snow as the temperature dropped below zero. Prisoners huddled in the assembly area shivering in their flimsy clothes. They had been summoned to witness a flogging; punishment for some minor misdemeanour.

"Bastards!" Peter muttered clenching his fists.

The guards kicked the man to the ground and stamped on him. So vicious was the beating that flesh peeled back from his bones. Alphonse put a restraining hand on his arm.

"Don't do anything foolish," he warned.

A red haze floated over Peter's eyes as the man screamed again. The scream of an animal caught in a trap. In a knee-jerk reaction he stepped out of line and moved towards him. A guard lunged bringing his rifle butt down on his skull.

He dropped to his knees blood oozing down his face. His head felt too heavy to lift. Hot needles of pain stabbed his eyeballs when he tried to move them. A wave of intense pain coursed through him then he keeled over and blacked out.

When he regained consciousness he realised that his wrists had been tied above his head. His body was suspended from the ground. He tried to lift himself to take the strain from his arms, but it was impossible. He couldn't remember how he had come to be in this dark room bound up like a pig for slaughter. Shaking his head from side to side he tried to focus his mind, but it was a complete blank. Nothing, not even his name. A guard pushed open the door and stared inside.

"Where am I? Why am I here?" he shouted.

"Quiet!" the guard screamed, giving him a vicious stab in the stomach with his rifle butt.

Peter let out a low moan. His head slumped to one side before he sank back into oblivion.

Bright light pierced his eyelids forcing him to cover his face with his hands. He was still in the room, but now he was lying on the damp floor. Someone was sweeping a torch over him. Hands grabbed him roughly, pulled him to his feet and dragged him towards the door.

"Where are you taking me?" he asked in a thin voice.

"You'll be well looked after Brandt. We're taking you to the infirmary where you'll be treated by the doctors," laughed one of the men.

Peter struggled to free himself from the guard's grip, but he was too weak. Something buried in his memory flickered like a moving film. Before he could grasp the thought it faded into the recesses of his mind. When they dragged him towards the infirmary he felt a thrill of terror, but he didn't know why.

He lay on the hard examination table while two doctors prodded and examined every part of his body. Occasionally, they glanced at each other, nodded and jotted something onto a notepad.

"Some food and rest and you'll feel fine Brandt then we will talk, ja? Perhaps about your university days."

Confused, he tried to take in what he had heard, but he still couldn't remember who he was. Why had the doctor called him Brandt?

Black bruises covered his body where he had been beaten. Touching his swollen face he winced with pain as his fingers rested on a gash above his right eye. He wet the end of a ragged cloth and gingerly dabbed it. The effort of washing had exhausted him. When they had taken him back to his barrack hut the others had told him what had happened.

"They'll be watching you even more closely from now on. The slightest resistance and you'll be shot next time," warned Alphonse.

Little by little Peter pieced together images until he remembered the scene in the roll call area, but everything before that eluded him.

"I can't remember anything before the guard hit me Alphonse," Peter said looking up at the Count. "I've lost part of my life."

A few days later Peter realised why the doctors had been so keen to appear caring. For hours they questioned him about his activities before he had been sent to Sachsenhausen. A Gestapo officer entered the room and sat down facing him. Peter didn't recognise Fleischer even when he snarled,

"You're lying Brandt! This is a ploy to protect your organisation. I could shoot you now, but that would be too merciful for scum like you. Do what you will with him," he snapped turning to the doctor.

The doctor smiled malevolently, his eyes gleaming with anticipation.

"We'll start treatment tomorrow," he sneered.

Psychological experiments were important to understand the minds of criminals and dissidents like Brandt.

Time and again Peter was taken to the infirmary where he was subjected to intense psychological testing. In some ways the invasion of his mind was worse than the medical tests he endured. He had to muster all his emotional and mental strength not to drown in the brain-washing.

"I can't remember a thing," he told Alphonse. "Fleischer wants information from me, but I don't know what it is."

"Keep playing for time otherwise he'll kill you."

"Perhaps, but he seems desperate to find out about some resistance organisation."

Peter was safe for now. Fleischer wouldn't kill him until he got what he wanted.

CHAPTER THIRTY TWO

Germany 1945

In spring 1945 almost the entire camp was herded into the roll call area. A low buzz of frightened voices hung on the air.

"Something's going on Alphonse," Peter remarked. "Why are they rounding us up?"

"Quiet, the commandant has arrived."

"You are leaving here," he bellowed. "to move north to another camp. You'll be escorted by my guards. If there is any resistance along the way you'll be shot."

A whisper rippled through the lines of prisoners.

"They're going to kill us. I know it," whimpered a young lad.

Later that morning they were herded up country like a pack of starving animals. Every day they marched north in lashing rain and cold. An emaciated old man, so weak he could barely walk, dropped to his knees.

"You must keep going," Peter urged.

"Leave me. I can't go on any more."

"Yes, you can! You must!"

"No. I'm an old man. I haven't got the strength."

"Get up old man!" yelled a guard, prodding him with the muzzle of his rifle.

The guard kicked him viciously, but he didn't move. His eyes were glassy, waiting for death. Peter let out an anguished cry when the shot rang out. He dropped to his knees and cradled the old man in his arms.

"Get up or I'll shoot you too!"

"Come on Peter," a prisoner urged pulling him to his feet. "It's no use."

Day after day they trudged through mud dragging weaker prisoners along. When they dropped from exhaustion beside the road the SS shot them. At night they dug holes to sleep in, covering themselves with branches. In the woods they scavenged for anything they could find.

"This bark isn't bad. Better than the muck in Sachsenhausen," Peter laughed crunching on the brittle wood.

By the time the International Red Cross appeared bringing food many of the prisoners had died from starvation and exposure.

"It's a miracle," Alphonse murmured. "At last we have some food."

"I don't understand. What's happening?" Peter asked.

"The Russians are swarming towards Berlin. The SS have been ordered to release all German prisoners. The rest will be taken on to Schwerin. There's not a great deal, but we'll do our best to feed them. The guards are deserting in droves. Prisoners have been left to fend for themselves."

Peter couldn't believe it, not even when he was released with hundreds of other German nationals.

They trekked for days until they reached Oranienburg. Sachsenhausen had been liberated by the Red Army on the twenty-second of April. The day after they had been sent on the '*death march*'. Now terrified Germans were fleeing to the Brandenburg to hide.

"We have nowhere to go. If we wander the streets we'll be arrested," Alphonse said.

"We could go back to the camp. Speak to the Soviets."

The young Mongolian soldier prodded Peter towards the previous SS commandant's office.

"Who are you? Why have you come here?" the Russian officer asked languidly.

"My name is Peter Brandt. We were political prisoners here," he said nodding at Alphonse. "The SS were marching us north when we were suddenly released."

"You can give us information?"

"We'll tell the truth about what happened here."

When the Russians ordered the people of Oranienburg to the camp Peter stood at the entrance.

"Now do you believe?" he asked them quietly.

They hung their heads in shame at the sight. Emaciated bodies, piles of spectacles, teeth, suitcases, execution trenches. Bodies left hanging to rot, swaying backwards and forwards in the breeze. Sobbing silently a woman, her face covered with a handkerchief, clutched her husband's arm.

"We didn't know! We didn't know!" she cried.

"You turned a blind eye, that's the real truth!"

"Let's go Peter," Alphonse murmured.

"What will you do now?"

"Try to get to Leipzig any way I can. My sister lives there. If she's still alive. And you?"

"I can't remember anything about my life. If I go back to Berlin I may remember something. Fleischer, the Gestapo officer knew, but he's dead. The Russians strung him up. Pulled down the Swastika and hung him from the flagpole."

CHAPTER THIRTY THREE

Berlin 1945

For days Peter wandered the streets of Berlin shocked at the devastation. Everywhere mounds of rubble, craters in the roads and dust. Dust everywhere, swirling into the air clogging the lungs. In a side street an overturned truck upturned on its back like a disabled turtle. Hardly a building was left intact. Grey, surreal, like an alien planet. Skeletal, windowless buildings silhouetted against a brilliant blue sky. Dark apertures where doors had been blown off, concealing frightened Berliners from the victorious Red Army.

Drunken soldiers were still raping and pillaging their way through the city.

"There's nothing we can do," cried an elderly man running towards a bombed out apartment block.

A group of soldiers, out of their minds with drink, staggered down the street. Spotting the man they followed him into the building. Suddenly, a woman ran screaming into the street.

"My daughter! My daughter!"

Peter started forward then stopped. Two Soviet officers came out of an alleyway and ran into the building. Seconds later three of the soldiers stumbled out. An officer waved his pistol at them.

"Stay where you are and don't move," he ordered.

His fellow officer emerged prodding the fourth man with his gun.

"This is what happens to soldiers who disobey orders," he shouted.

Raising his pistol he shot the soldier in the head.

"Let that be a lesson to you. Anyone caught raping German women and girls will get the same treatment! Get back to your quarters!"

Peter slept wherever he could. In a hole in the ground, inside crumbling houses or cellars.

"There is no food to be had," a young woman told him. "Some women are so desperate they offer sex to the Russians in exchange for food. It's the only way they can feed their children."

"But you look well fed," Peter said.

"I'm lucky. I have a Russian friend. An officer…..he gives me food."

She stared at him defiantly.

"It keeps us alive. People are starving to death. There's no transport to get food into the city. Potsdammer Station was demolished in the bombings. Even the drinking water is contaminated by sewage."

Blank faced women and bare-footed children picked amongst the rubble looking for anything they could use to make their lives bearable. A woman emerged from her hideout below ground and struggled across the rubble. She joined a small group sorting bricks into piles.

"Take this one first," she ordered two young boys.

Struggling with the weight they pushed it down the street, occasionally stopping to pick up a fallen brick.

"What's going on," Peter asked.

"We've been ordered to clean up the streets and salvage any bricks that can be used for rebuilding. They've set up a central drop-off point in Tenfelsberg. That's where the boys are heading. They'll pick up help along the way."

Peter could barely comprehend the extent of the devastation as he walked towards the Unter den Linden. The avenue was bare, diminished by the absence of leafy greenery. It was the same in the Tiergarten. Everything looked grey, unreal, stripped of its beauty.

A brief image flickered in his memory. He was strolling through the park, sunlight glancing through the trees, a soft breeze fanning his face. Someone was holding his hand. Desperately, he struggled to hang on to the thought, but it faded like a shadow on the water.

Bleak and barren the park stretched out before him. Abandoned artillery cluttered the grass. Ominously, a big gun still pointed at ghost planes in the sky. The remains of a crashed fighter plane witness to the remnants of a lost battle

An old woman in a grimy, black skirt loaded a small handcart with wood. Pitifully thin and under-nourished she looked as though a breeze would blow her over. As she struggled to lift the handles it toppled over scattering pieces of firewood over the path.

"Let me do that," Peter said gently, righting the cart.

She stared at him, a mixture of fear and suspicion in her eyes.

"It's all right. I won't harm you. I used to live near here."

Together they stacked the wood in silence.

"Danke," the old woman murmured.

"Where do you live?"

She pointed towards Brandenburg Gate, a wistful smile playing on her lips.

"I had a fine house near the Tor. Quite grand, but there's nothing left of it except a pile of bricks. Now I live in the cellar underneath with my daughter and grandchildren. Compared to some we are very comfortable. At least we have somewhere safe to sleep."

"Let me help you push the cart home?"

"Home, I doubt we will ever have a proper home again. Danke, but my grandsons will help me."

She pointed to two distant figures busily gathering wood.

"Aufweidersein!" Peter called after her as she wheeled the cart unsteadily towards the two boys.

Feeling depressed he made his way towards the Mitte. Allied bombs had wreaked havoc on the university. A great sadness filled him at the sight, but he couldn't understand why this particular place accentuated his depression.

Slowly, he moved on staring aghast at the damaged buildings. The Pergamon Museum, the impressive Staatsoper Unter den Linden Opera House. All the great buildings destroyed. He stopped in the same spot where Eleanor had stared at the ruined remains of their apartment block. Again the strange sensation of déjà vu made his skin prickle. An image of a man clothed in black swam before his eyes. The same man standing in the shadows, his face illuminated by the glow of a cigarette.

"Fleisher!" he breathed heavily, sweat breaking out on his forehead.

He knew, without doubt, that there was a connection between this place and the Gestapo officer who had sent him to Sachsenhausen concentration camp. Pressing his fingers to his temples he struggled to remember, but it was no use.

He felt in his pocket for the lump of mouldy, hard cheese and dry bread he had been given when he left the camp. For days he had survived, nibbling a little each day. In his jacket he carried a large hip flask containing the last of his fresh water. He had been tempted to fill it from a dripping tap, but thought better of it. He couldn't risk drinking contaminated water. Every night he hid from the Soviets amongst the piles of rubble, but he needed more permanent shelter if he was to survive.

For no accountable reason he felt that this was where he wanted to make his home. Scrabbling around on his knees to clear a space he dislodged a small wall. Some of the stones disappeared into a large hole that had appeared. Peering into the gloom he saw that he had uncovered a cellar. Squeezing inside he dropped onto the flagstone floor with a dull thud landing painfully on his back.

Gradually, he dragged himself up to a standing position using the wall as leverage. His hand slipped on the green slime sending him crashing back onto the ground. Slipping and sliding on the wet stone he eventually managed to stand upright and look around the cellar.

Foul-smelling water dripped down one wall. It flowed onto the floor before disappearing into a crack in the flags. Mixed with the powerful stink of damp and mould another smell caught at his senses. He laughed out loud. Dozens of smashed wine bottles lay on mangled racks round the walls and floor. One or two still clung tenaciously to the solitary rack hanging dangerously away from the wall.

Pulling out the bayonet strapped to his leg he poked the cork out of one of the bottles. First he sniffed it then drank a small mouthful expecting it to be sour, but it tasted wonderful.

"A good vintage, full-bodied with just enough bite," he mocked. "Now all I want is a piece of juicy meat to go with it."

Two empty, rotten, beer barrels lay on their sides in a corner. Peter righted them and sat down contemplating his next move.

"This will do," he thought looking around the cell-like room. "With a little imagination and some kind of roof it will do very well. At least I won't die of thirst."

Placing one of the barrels underneath the gaping hole he hauled himself out and began searching for anything he could use. Half an hour later he returned dragging a piece of rusty corrugated iron, a splintered plank of wood and some sacking.

He positioned the metal sheet so that he could move it easily, leaving a small gap to let in light. Rummaging in his pocket he fished out one of the tallow candles and matches he had brought with him from the camp. Using the beer bottle as a candlestick he placed it on the table. He balanced the plank on one of the barrels and sat on the other. Looking at the makeshift table he grinned. Now all he needed was some decent food to put on it. Overcome with weariness he sank onto the sacking, closed his eyes and slept.

Bright shafts of sunlight, from the gap in the corrugated iron, pierced Peter's eyelids. Faint chinking sounds and low voices drifted into his consciousness. Stirring, he sat up on one elbow and listened intently. It was the women cleaning the bricks. A constant chip, chipping sound as they hacked away to fill their wheelbarrows.

He pushed the metal sheet away from the hole and stared out. It was a beautiful, hot summer's day. Overhead, a bright, yellow sun blazed in an azure sky. Tiny white clouds moved slowly across the sky blown by a gentle breeze. For a brief moment he felt uplifted; his spirits soared. When he stuck his head out reality hit him like a physical blow.

He ate the last of the cheese taking care to scrape off the mouldy bits. Carefully, he sipped a little water from his hip flask then took a large gulp of red wine to counteract the taste. Refreshed, he hauled himself above ground and relieved himself behind a pile of rubble. Stumbling through the ruins he made his way to where the women were working. Pitifully thin, their flesh hung loose from the bones.

"Guten morgen," he said cheerfully.

The women didn't respond. Silently, they chipped away at the bricks, occasionally stopping to throw them into a rusty wheelbarrow. As he drew closer one of them stared at him intently from eyes bleary with exhaustion. Her lined face was covered with a film of dust that clung to a weeping sore on her mouth. For a fleeting moment she appeared to recognise him.

"Have we met before?" Peter asked.

"Nein! Nein!" she muttered, looking suddenly fearful.

Unknown to Peter he was speaking to Frau Klocke who had lived in his apartment building.

"I have no food," Peter said simply, but there was no response.

As he turned to walk away an old woman straightened up and pointed to a forlorn line of people tramping down the rubble-strewn road.

"Follow them," she murmured. "It is my turn to help you."

It was the old woman whose cart he had loaded with wood in the Tiergarten.

Before he could thank her she followed the other women to the next pile of bricks and mortar.

"Thank you," he called after her.

He had heard there was a black market near the Reichstag, but he didn't have enough money for the exorbitant prices they charged. People were starving. Children were begging for food or rummaging through dustbins looking for scraps to eat. He let the column of bedraggled people pass and joined the rear.

"Where are you going?"

"They're taking us to a displaced persons' camp for processing. Processing," he muttered, "always processing."

In the camp a young woman was taking down details before waving them towards the food kitchen.

"Your name please?" queried the chisel-faced girl, pencil poised ready to write.

"Peter Brandt."

"Nationality?"

"German. I was born in Berlin."

The girl looked at him quizzically for a few a seconds then laid down her pen.

"This is for displaced persons not native Berliners."

"I have no food."

"None of the Berliners have sufficient food. We can't feed everybody. What are you doing here?"

"I was a political prisoner in Sachsenhausen. I have nowhere to go. My memory is gone after a beating from the guards in the camp. All I know is that I was living in Berlin until I was taken to the camp."

"Wait here."

She scurried off towards a makeshift office. Peter could see her talking animatedly through the open door. When she returned she motioned him towards a line queuing for food. Gratefully, he joined the queue for his bowl of soup and wedge of bread. Basic potato soup with vegetables and dumplings.

He dipped his wedge of bread into the soup and sucked at it. The man next to him burped noisily. Peter grinned at him.

"Good, ja?"

"Fit for a king," he sighed.

Later that evening they were allocated places to sleep and given another meal. More bread, a small piece of hard cheese and one potato. Peter pocketed his food and slipped out. He preferred to sleep in his cellar than surrounded by others listening to their sounds in the night. It reminded him too much of the concentration camp. Cautiously, he picked his way back to his hideaway, watchful of strangers who might follow him and commandeer his new home.

When he had almost reached the place he ducked behind a low wall that sat crazily where his apartment once stood. From the bombed out shell of a house opposite he heard low groaning sounds then quiet laughter. From behind a wall a soldier appeared and marched off down the road. A few minutes later a young woman emerged, glanced around furtively then hurried away.

Every day Peter turned up for his ration of food and returned to his cellar. Most days he spent wandering the Mitte, Pankow and other Soviet occupied areas. Bright-red hammer and sickle flags pierced the grey devastation enhancing the surreal atmosphere. He was drawn to the university and the pile of rubble that used to be his apartment. Something deep-seated in his memory told him that this was where he had lived.

Every day he questioned the women gleaning as much information as possible about the area, but it was a futile exercise. He thought again about the woman who had looked so fearful of him and determined to question her again.

Everywhere, the Soviets had been busy dismantling the transport system, closing off the city. Occasionally, he ventured into the British Sector to visit the Tiergarten, aware that the Russians were watching movements between the sectors.

In the middle of August Peter was convinced he was being watched. He was used to the surveillance tactics of the Gestapo. His suspicions were aroused when a man in a brown, light-weight jacket tailed him on his way back to the cellar. Peter bobbed in and out of buildings along the street, but the man stayed with him.

The next day he changed his route, but the tail stuck with him like glue. At night the faint, red glow of a cigarette in the darkness of the ruins opposite told him his stalker was still there.

On the fifth day Peter carefully pushed back his makeshift roof and hauled himself out. Crawling on his stomach, behind mounds of rubble, he skirted walls threatening to give way at any moment. Suddenly, he came up on the man from behind.

"Why are you following me?"

Startled, the man whirled round temporarily losing his balance on the uneven ground.

"I'll ask you again," Peter snapped. "Who are you and why are you following me?"

The man pulled out a Tokarev TT-33 7.62mm military issue pistol and pointed it at Peter.

"You are Peter Brandt?" he said in heavily-accented German.

"Why do you want to know?"

"I am an official of the Soviet Workforce Department. You are to come with me."

"You're arresting me?"

"No, Herr Brandt, not if you come quietly."

The official showed Peter into an ante room and nodded at the young soldier behind the desk. Quickly, he jumped up, knocked quietly on the door to his right and entered. A few moments later he reappeared and showed them in. Peter looked around warily as the uniformed officer came from behind his desk and motioned him to a chair.

"This is Major Levenko," the official said, retreating to the corner of the room.

"Good morning Herr Brandt. It is good to see you," Levenko smiled.

"What do you want with me?"

"I represent the Chief of the Workforce Department."

Peter didn't respond. He was waiting to see where the conversation was leading.

"I don't understand why I have been brought here."

"You were a political prisoner in Sachsenhausen, were you not? An enemy of the Third Reich?"

"An enemy of Hitler, not Germany," Peter said evenly.

"Ah, you are man of principle Herr Brandt."

Levenko rested his buttocks on the edge of the desk and leaned towards Peter.

"I have a proposition for you."

"What kind of proposition?"

"We would like you to work for us. We need your specialist skills. Your work in rocket research is important to us."

"I don't know what you're talking about!"

"You deny you were a professor of mathematics and physics at the university in Berlin?"

"I was a prisoner in Sachsenhausen. I know my name is Peter Brandt and that I lived in Berlin... that is all I know. How do you know this?"

"We know that you worked in close liaison with rocket engineers in Peenemünde. Everything in Peenemünde was destroyed when the Nazis knew the war was lost. Papers, equipment, designs, everything! Your particular research project was closed down by the Gestapo when you were sent to the Eastern Front. However, *some* research material was discovered at the university."

"You know this for a certainty?"

"We do. Of course you would be employed by the Soviet Union in one of the design offices here in Germany. Think Herr Brandt – a salary, food, new clothes, comfort. Hundreds of your scientists and engineers have already been recruited."

Peter thought back to the long nights in the concentration camp. Often he worked out equations for fun or problems thought up by the other prisoners. It was second nature to him.

Levenko opened the desk drawer and pulled out a thin sheaf of paper. Peter riffled through it, recognising familiar equations and designs.

"I understand the mathematics, but I can't remember anything else. You say this is my work?"

Levenko produced a pen and a blank sheet of paper.

"Write your name on this."

Peter did as he was told.

"Now, compare this with the signature at the bottom of the design."

"The signatures are identical!"

"Yes Brandt, these are your designs. You can be very helpful to us. What have you got to lose?"

Peter felt a stirring of interest, a sudden hunger to be involved with this work again. Besides, what choice did he have? If he didn't agree they would only force him to participate. He had no family, no friends he could remember. At least this way he could make a new life for himself.

"I don't seem to have much choice, but I'll need time to adjust to my new-found expertise."

Late August, Peter found himself working in one of the partially destroyed German design offices in the Russian Zone. For the first time in years he had a full stomach and somewhere comfortable to sleep. Gradually, he picked up the threads of his knowledge and immersed himself in his work. He resented working for the Soviets, but he enjoyed the intellectual challenge. The daily wrestling with intricate facts and figures afforded him a degree of satisfaction.

His colleagues were happy to be able to feed their families. Anything was better than the deprivations they had suffered when Berlin had fallen. He envied them the wives and children they went home to at night. Eventually, he made a few friends, but for the most part he suffered an indescribable loneliness. A loneliness he failed to understand; a constant feeling of something missing in his life.

Autumn had barely touched her paint brush to the trees when fate stepped in and swept away his comfortable but routine life. Tired, after a long day pouring over mathematical equations, he dragged back to his quarters long after others had left. As he entered the building a voice called softly,

"Peter!"

Startled, he spun round to see one of the other scientists beckoning to him from the open door of his room. Hurriedly, Bernhardt pulled him inside; a worried, excitable look on his face.

"What is it?" Peter asked.

"Haven't you heard?"

"Heard what? Spit it out man."

"We're being sent to Russia. Stalin's orders… the whole team."

"I don't believe it! Why?"

"I don't know except we'll still be doing the same work."

Some have already been ordered to pack and get their families ready to move out. I heard that hundreds are going."

There was an air of anxiety and apprehension amongst the men and their families. They didn't know what faced them except that they would be working on rocket design. That very night they found themselves en route to the Soviet Union.

"There doesn't seem to be much difference from what we were doing in Germany," Bernhardt commented when they were shown their work tasks.

"I have a feeling this is only the beginning," Peter replied. "They're still assigning scientists from Groetrupp's team to other areas. "

For three months they moved from one facility to another. Eventually, they were sent to a camp on Gorodomlya Island, on the Seliger Lake, three hundred kilometres northwest of Moscow in the Upper Volga.

CHAPTER THIRTY FOUR

The Soviet Union 1946 - 1957

Peter shared rooms with five other single men in a wooden building with no running water. They didn't starve, but food was scarce even for families. Stale bread was the norm most days and there were no luxuries. Conditions were harsh, but it was nothing compared to Sachsenhausen.

The scientists' wives did all they could to make the camp attractive. Grass was neatly cut, planters and window boxes filled with colourful blooms in an attempt to recreate gardens that made them feel at home. With a little imagination he could have been in the countryside in pre-war Germany. Even so he felt trapped; a prisoner with no means of escape.

Barbed wire enclosed the camp, heavily guarded by soldiers stationed at strategic points on the island. Peter survived by totally immersing himself in his work to the point of exhaustion. Sometimes he played chess with Bernhardt, or cards with the others, to while away a long winter's night. The Soviets were highly secretive about what they were working on. All they knew was that it was connected with missile research. What they planned to do with it was another matter.

Sometimes he joined one of the families for an evening, talking about their lives before the war. He had nothing to add to the conversation except his experiences in Sachsenhausen. Their frightened glances told him they did not want to be reminded of Hitler's brutality. He took to wandering the camp examining the gardens. Sometimes he sought the solitude of the forest wanting to be alone with his thoughts.

After supper one evening he slipped out of the hut and made his way into the woods. It was quiet and still, just the occasional sound of a small animal or a bird fluttering from the branch of a tree. Suddenly, he heard a different sound. The snapping of twigs underfoot and muffled crying. Straining his eyes to peer through the gloom he started as a young woman emerged from the trees. She stopped when she saw him looming in front of her and hurriedly dried her eyes.

"What is it? Has something frightened you?" Peter queried.

She didn't answer just stood staring at him uncomprehendingly.

"Ah, you are Russian," he pointed at her. "Do you understand German?"

"Da!"

Peter had managed to learn quite a bit of the language from one of the German engineers who was fluent in Russian and French.

Haltingly, he repeated his question. She looked up at him, eyes bright with tears, then turned and pointed. Peter walked slowly through the trees and stopped. A small dog lay whimpering on the damp ground. The poor creature had been pierced by a jagged piece of wood from a shattered branch. It lay on the damp leaves skewered to the ground.

He turned the girl towards him, looked at the dog, and shook his head. He motioned for her to go home. For a few seconds she hesitated then walked slowly in the direction of the village. Peter picked up a small rock and held it ready. The dog looked at him with liquid eyes, his little body trembling with pain and fear. He brought the stone down with as much force as possible. There was a sickening, cracking sound as the dog's head caved in. A final spasm and it was all over.

When he appeared from the trees the girl was still lingering, her eyes red and watery from crying. He nodded, which set her weeping again. She was not unattractive; well-built, but rather clumsy in her movements. Straw-coloured strands of coarse hair peeped from the sides of a threadbare headscarf tied under her chin. Her body was muscular rather than plump, well-toned from hard, physical work. Her black, peasant skirt reached to her ankles.

Peter laid a gentle arm around her shaking shoulders until she had composed herself sufficiently to return to her home. He watched from a distance as she skirted the village. When she came to a little house she turned, gave a half-hearted wave and disappeared inside.

Next day he saw her again and the next. It seemed that every time he walked towards the woods she was there giving her shy, tentative wave. The following week, when Peter strolled into the forest, the girl suddenly appeared from behind a tangle of undergrowth. She came up to him and pressed something into his hand. It was a small, highly-polished stone, almost like marble, hanging from a leather lace.

"Lucky," she reached up and put it over his head. "Lucky," she repeated.

Touched, Peter took her hand and pressed it gently,

"Thank you," he murmured. "My name is Peter. What is your name?"

He pointed at his chest then at the girl who laughed with delight.

"Martina," she replied. "I live in village with mother and brother."

"What abut your father?"

"He killed in war by Germans."

"I am German," Peter said simply.

For a few moments she hesitated looking down at the ground then said,

"I think you good German, da?"

"Da. I like to think so. Where did you learn to speak German?"

"I learn in camp when I do washing for wives," she explained.

In silence they meandered through the woods until they came to a huge conifer. Peter dropped onto the bed of brownish-green needles surrounding the tree and lay back against the trunk. The first snows had already arrived, but thick foliage had protected the forest floor leaving large patches devoid of snow.

The girl dropped down beside him laying her head on his chest. He watched as she took off her headscarf and shook out her hair. Washed and brushed it looked like molten gold, framing her head like a halo of light. He reached out and took one of her chapped, red hands that she had hidden in the folds of her skirt. Lightly, he brushed it with his lips. Sighing with contentment she rested her head on his chest, playing with the buttons on his thick jacket. Suddenly, she sprang up trying to drag him with her, but he was too heavy.

"Come," she said as he struggled to his feet.

They walked deeper and deeper into the gloom until they came to a small, wooden shack surrounded by sawn-up logs.

"My brother, he chop trees down for firewood. He shelter here in winter. We go inside, da?"

"Your brother has made himself very comfortable here," Peter smiled.

Near the wall stood a rough-hewn table and milking stool. A rusty storm lantern and two, dirty, tin mugs sat in a film of dust. In the centre of the room an old wood-burning stove threw out a blast of welcoming heat. Martina opened the door and fed it more logs. They sputtered and crackled as the flames took hold filling the shack with acrid smoke. Quickly, she closed the stove door and busied herself arranging things to her satisfaction.

A blanket had been neatly folded and placed on the rush matting covering the floor. She had been planning it for days to ensure they would be comfortable.

"He bring girls here. Now I bring you," she smiled coquettishly patting the blanket.

Peter's heart fluttered in his chest as he lay down beside her. He felt uncomfortable. It had been a long time since he had been with a woman, maybe before the war. He couldn't remember.

Clumsily, he fumbled with the buttons on her coat searching her warm flesh. Pulling him down to her she kissed him. A long-drawn out kiss as though she wanted to suck the life out of him. His breath rasped in his throat as he tried to control himself. In the back of his mind a flicker of memory made him hesitate when he stared into the girl's mischievous, blue eyes. The heat in his loins was unbearable. He couldn't think of anything except gratifying his lust. He took her without emotion, grasping and groping in the semi-darkness until he achieved the desired release.

Martina lay back and stretched her arms above her head. She smiled lasciviously at him and tried to pull him back down. Peter suddenly felt a peculiar emptiness in his soul; a nagging sensation he couldn't explain. Filled with contempt for himself and an unaccountable revulsion for the girl he pushed her away.

Hurriedly, he pulled his coat around him and staggered from the hut. As he crunched his way over the frosty ground back to his cabin he tried to analyse his reactions. He should have been feeling happy and content. His physical desires had been sated, but he still felt an acute loneliness that he couldn't explain.

The men looked up from their card game when he stumbled into the room looking flustered.

"What's wrong Peter? You look as though you've been chased by the Cossacks!" Bernhardt laughed heartily.

"Just walking quickly to keep warm," he replied trying to muster a grin.

Bernhardt shrugged his shoulders when Peter headed for the bedroom. He frequently retreated into his own world. Sometimes he sat with his eyes closed completely oblivious to the others. It was something he had to do; something to do with his time in Sachsenhausen.

Peter lay on his bed staring at the ceiling. He felt trapped. It was still a prison. A system of surveillance from which there was no escape. Just as he had in Sachsenhausen he lay awake at night planning his escape.

The camp was surrounded by thick forests of evergreen trees that afforded some concealment, but in his heart he knew it was just a game. He would have to contend with swamps and dangerous terrain. In winter deep snow covered the forest so thick it was impossible to walk. The island itself was a prison even without the presence of barbed wire fences and watchful guards. At times he felt a suffocating sense of claustrophobia that threatened to engulf him.

In his dreams at night he ploughed through the forest breaking out onto a sunny, lakeside beach. The sun glinted on the water as he ran towards it and jumped. He was swimming for his life, his arms threshing the water. Closer and closer he swam to the distant shore, but when he looked back he was still only metres from the beach. Laughing soldiers cast a net and scooped him up like a struggling fish. He started awake, his eyes wide with terror, his soul crying out for freedom.

Peter avoided the place where he had encountered Martina determined not to be drawn in again. Apart from his revulsion it was too dangerous. Only once he saw her from a distance near the little hut beyond the camp. When she waved to him a young, thick-set man came out of the hut door and looked in Peter's direction. Roughly, he grabbed the girl and pushed her inside.

The Russians still treated the Germans with suspicion. Hatred was never far below the surface; a simmering cauldron threatening to explode. They were the conquerors. Whatever carrots had been dangled in front of the engineers and scientists they were still prisoners of the Soviets. The girl would be treated harshly if they found out she was consorting with a German, especially a German working on top secret rocket design.

Peter kept away from the forest until winter set in, harsh and unforgiving. Battling deep snow was tiring so he took to skiing instead. Every moment of his free time he spent ploughing through the woods in an almost impenetrable gloom.

One morning in February he traversed the forest, going much further than he had on his previous excursions. Overhead, an unbroken canopy of slate-grey cloud threatened more snow. A low wind moaned through the trees obliterating every sound except the swish of his skis. Branches, heavy with snow, arched overhead. Icicles hung like crystal swords guarding a magical, ice-white palace. Beads of frozen moisture threaded the pine needles; dripped from branches like strings of diamonds. Clouds of vapour misted his snow visor as his breathing became more laboured in the biting, rarefied air.

Suddenly, he came out into a glade where a small pool of water had frozen solid. Little clumps of evergreen bushes, heavy with snow, dotted the perimeter. Overhead, a watery, white sun feebly penetrated the cloud glancing off patches of hoary ice clinging to a litter of rocks. A flurry of tiny prints ran across virgin snow from the water's edge into the undergrowth. The scene reflected in the mirror surface of the pool like the picture captured in a snow globe.

Peter caught his breath on the pure, icy air. It reminded him of Switzerland. He was a child on holiday. Boisterous laughter, clinking glasses; the smell of hot cheese and chocolate filled his senses. Laughing faces watched fat flakes of snow falling gently in front of an enormous window overlooking a lake.

Snowballs were flying past his ears. Laughing with excitement another boy pushed him face first onto the powdery snow. A tall blond man, blue eyes full of merriment, pulled him to his feet. The scene swam in and out of his mind's eye. He struggled to hold on to the thought, but it vanished into a wall of white.

When the snows started to melt Peter stayed within the confines of the camp eating his meals in the Stalovaya, the canteen designated for German workers. Occasionally, he went over to the clubhouse in the evenings to join the activities. But most nights he forced himself to join in the banter with the other men in the hut. It was only with Bernhardt that he felt comfortable.

A physicist and mathematician like Peter, he had become a close friend. They enjoyed the same things; chess, music, debate. Reading was a rare pleasure for there were few books in the camp of any real interest to either man. Some of the workers had brought a few books hurriedly stuffed into their suitcases. Most had been exchanged time and time again.

Bernhardt sometimes reminisced about his experiences in the Luftwaffe.

"To be in the air again with that sense of absolute freedom! That's what I want to do when I get out of here. Fly planes!"

"If we ever get out," Peter said dully. "One thing's for sure, we'll never get out of here in the winter. Besides we couldn't get across the water from here."

"I've never felt such cold," Bernhardt complained rubbing his stiff limbs.

"This is nothing compared to Operation Barbarossa. Frostbite, disease, guns and vehicles frozen solid. Conditions were horrific. All for that madman Hitler!" Peter spat vehemently. "Even when General Paulus wrote to him urging him to bring the troops home he refused. Every man must die for the Fatherland!"

It was useless, they would never leave, not with the knowledge they had accumulated.

The years passed in dull routine, discontent and a mounting sense of despair. Peter had resigned himself to spending the rest of his life in Russia. In 1951 rumours started to circulate that the German work force was to be sent home. No-one believed it until one of his roommates came crashing through the hut door. Stuttering with excitement, he yelled,

"They're sending people home!"

There was a stunned silence until one of the men laughed,

"Very funny Heinz. Another of your jokes?"

"No! No! They really are sending us home. Tell them Ferdie!" he said to the man who had followed him inside.

"It's true. I heard one of the engineers talking about it in the club. We're being sent home in batches."

"We've heard that before. It's always a rumour. It must be. How would he know that?"

"His superior, Christoff, has been told that they'll be selecting men soon."

"Well, I won't believe it until I hear it from Groetrupp himself," declared one of the men.

It seemed the Soviets no longer needed them. They had gleaned all the technical and design knowledge they needed from the Germans. They couldn't believe it when it was formally announced that they would be leaving the Soviet Union

Elated, Peter waited patiently for his orders, but they never came. When the last group left in 1953 he was devastated to find he had been relocated to work with a Soviet design team led by a German scientist.

You will be working here for a few more years yet," the Russian officer told him when he arrived.

"Years," Peter muttered. "I'll never see Germany again. At least this place isn't as claustrophobic as Gorodomlya Island."

Four years later, in 1957, Peter was finally allowed to go back to Berlin's Russian Zone. Attempts were made by American and British intelligence to glean information about the Soviet projects, but Peter was still being stalked by the Stasi. They had certain information about him and his activities before he was sent to the Russian Front that made them uncertain about his 'loyalties'. When other workers had been approached they had given patchy accounts and information that had been vetted by Soviet authorities. But they knew they couldn't trust Peter to toe the line.

Eventually, he secured a teaching post at his old university. He settled into a comfortable, small bed-sit in the Mitte. Refusing to join the Communist Party he knew his prospects for promotion were slim so he was surprised when he was offered the post of head of department in 1960. For the first time in many years he felt reasonably settled, but there was always a sense of something important missing in his life.

Alert blue eyes, a good physique, he still looked the typical Aryan that Hitler had so desired for Germany. He had lost his boyish features. Now, the slightly greying temples and fine lines etched into his face enhanced his looks. He had an aura of masculinity that women found irresistible. At forty-eight he was still a handsome man, a man who turned heads when he walked into a room. There was an air of confidence and authority about him that not even the Nazis had diminished in Sachsenhausen.

Occasionally, he escorted a female colleague to dinner or a concert, sometimes ending the evening in her bed. He rarely repeated the gesture preferring not to get too involved. For some inexplicable reason Peter always felt anguished when he faced the woman across the breakfast table, preferring to sneak out while she still slept.

This was the pattern of his life except for his excursions with Bernhardt. Ten years Peter's junior, he had re-trained as a commercial pilot flying on routes from Berlin to destinations in the Soviet Union and Poland. Once he smuggled Peter on board to sit in the jump seat when they flew to Warsaw for two days.

At other times they wandered the Unter den Linden towards the Brandenburg Tor or visited the museums in the Mitte. There was something about the Tiergarten that drew Peter like a magnet. He longed to walk through the park to see how it looked almost sixteen years after the war had ended, but it was in the British Sector. Some people moved between the British and Russian Sectors for their work, but they were carefully scrutinized.

"One day," he vowed, "one day I'll walk in the Tiergarten again."

CHAPTER THIRTY FIVE

East Germany 1961

On a hot, late July day, in the summer of 1961, Peter and Bernhardt took a trip to the town of Warnemünde on the Baltic coast. Leisurely, they strolled through the old town, admiring the church and the old lighthouse. Warm and sultry they soon tired of walking.

"I'm gasping for a drink," Bernhardt said. "Let's get a beer over there." Gratefully, they dropped into wicker padded chairs outside a little pavement café. "We might as well have something to eat now we're here," he continued edging under the parasol.

"Zwei bier bitte," Peter said when the white-aproned waiter appeared. "Und bringen sie mir die speisekarte!" he called as he scurried inside. "This sea air has made me ravenous."

Within seconds the waiter returned with two steins of beer. He placed the menu on the table and scurried away again.

"Mmmm, this is good," Peter remarked sipping the ice cold beer. He traced his finger down the glass leaving a trail through the condensation. "I haven't tasted beer as good as this in years."

They both ordered a fish cutlet and sautéed potatoes followed by a large slice of chocolate torte and ice-cream. Full and contented they sipped their second beer before heading for the promenade.

It was still very hot when they left the restaurant and strolled towards the lighthouse at the end of the promenade. The gentle slapping of waves against the rocks was soothing, almost soporific. Gulls keened, swooping and diving over the glinting waves. Landing on the pathway in front of them they pecked at the concrete looking for morsels of food. Overhead, the sun shone bright yellow suffusing everything in a golden glow.

A small motor boat bobbed through the water, bows dipping gently as it rose and fell on the undulating waves. Little white-sailed yachts, bright against an azure sea, tacked to catch the wind. Children were throwing a colourful beach ball, whooping with excitement in a jostling frenzy of fun.

The two men stopped to watch a large motor sailor with a red jib sail racing past the other boats. The man at the wheel threw his head back and laughed. He shouted something to his companion pointing to the stragglers bringing up the rear. When he had cleared the boats he tacked and turned his bows to the open sea. Another expert manoeuvre brought him up behind the last boat.

"I think he's going to try to pass them again," Bernhardt laughed.

Peter gazed across the glistening water, sunlight dancing on the waves. White foam followed in the yacht's wake as the rudder churned up the water. He turned away then looked again. There was something vaguely familiar about the man in the boat. Something about the way he threw his head back when he laughed, his right hand planted on his hip.

As the yacht sailed past close to shore it slowed down, a token gesture to the sailors behind. The red-haired, bearded skipper threw back his head and laughed again. Peter caught his breath; he knew this man. Suddenly, images fluttered before his eyes in a kaleidoscope of colour and movement. Pictures of Eleanor smiling into the camera on the stoop of her parents' house in Cape Cod. Johann gurgling up at him from his crib. Walking down the Unter den Linden, in the Tiergarten pushing Johann in his carriage. Burning the cabin in the forest with Manfred.

Rudi, the loud, florid-faced Bavarian who had bluffed his way into Hitler's inner circle. Good old larger than life Rudi who had risked his life for them.

Cupping his hands to his mouth he shouted,

"Rudi! Rudi!"

The wind caught his voice and carried it across the water. The man turned and stared uncertainly towards the shore.

"Rudi!"

Peter was screaming now, waving his arms frantically.

"What is it?" Bernhardt queried looking nervously at Peter.

"It's Rudi!" he yelled excitedly. "You don't understand. I remember. I remember everything!"

The man was edging the yacht as close to shore as the rocks would allow. He gave the wheel to his fellow sailor, leaned forward slightly and stared. Peter could see his face clearly now as recognition dawned on him.

"Peter!" he cried. "Mein Gott, it can't be!"

"It is Rudi, it's me!"

Tears of joy coursed down his cheeks. Rudi threw back his head and laughed with delight. He waved his arms towards the marina, grabbed the wheel and turned the boat to land.

"It's a miracle!" Rudi exclaimed later as they sat sipping large tankards of beer in a bar in the old town. "What are you doing here? I thought you were dead! Where are you living?"

Peter laughed, "One question at a time old friend! First, I want to know if you have heard anything about Eleanor and Johann."

Rudi sighed and shook his head.

"As you know they arrived safely in Sweden and eventually returned to the United States. Manfred… well you know what happened. Helga decided to stay in Sweden. She settled in a small village just outside Stockholm. She's still alive living in the same little village. In the nineteen fifties she married the local doctor, a widower with three sons she dotes on. Eleanor… nothing since she left for the United States. "

"And my Uncle Friedrich?"

"I'm sorry Peter. Prinz Friedrich is dead."

"Dead?"

"When the Red Army came they confiscated the house and the land. He barricaded himself inside until they smashed the

windows and dragged him out. It was a massive heart attack…
the shock killed him. You know how he loved the house."

"And Marie Juliana?"

"After Friedrich died she had no will to live. Bruno took
her to live in his cottage pretending that she was going to cook
and clean for him. Fortunately, the Soviets looked on him as a
down-trodden peasant exploited by the aristocracy. Little did
they know. She became very frail. There was no food.
Pneumonia took her in that dreadful winter of 1945. Bruno is
still living in the cottage."

An image of the elegant couple floated across his vision.
They had risked so much to help both Jews and Germans
escape from the Gestapo.

"What happened to the other *Regis* members?"

"Most of them are scattered across Germany. In
Magdeburg, Munich, West Berlin and here in the Russian Zone.
There are still contacts in Switzerland and France; all over
Europe in fact, but it has been dormant for a long time."

It started to fall apart when Friedrich died. Without him we
lacked a charismatic leader. We thought you were dead. Still, we
were lucky, unlike some such as the White Rose organization.
You wouldn't have known about them. They were a group of
university students opposed to Hitler. Hans Scholl, the leader
of the resistance group, all of them, were accused of treason
and executed by the Gestapo. Young, idealistic men like you."

"Like the 'The Swingers' before the war. Imprisoned or
shot just because they liked a certain kind of music"

Rudi shrugged his shoulders nodding in agreement.

"We're still not free Rudi." Peter clenched his fists angrily.
"We're still in prison under the Communists. This is not
freedom!"

"Peter!" Bernhardt laid a hand on his arm. "You must be
careful!"

"Still the same old Peter, eh?" Rudi chuckled. "Now tell me
about yourself."

362

Peter related everything that had happened to him. How he had been interrogated and tortured by the Gestapo and sent to the Eastern Front. Rudi and Bernhardt listened intently as he described the horrific conditions. How he and Kurt had been separated from their men, after the battle for Stalingrad, and eventually landed up in Hungary.

"I couldn't remember anything about my life before the vicious beating in Sachsenhausen. All I had was my name. When I was approached by the Russians to work on their rocket design I accepted. I didn't know I'd land up working in the Soviet Union for eleven years. But now…somehow I must get to the United States to find Eleanor and Johann."

"Are you crazy?" Rudi exploded. "With your background the secret police will still be watching you. Have no doubt about that! You can't leave without permission."

"I've written letters, but there's been no response – nothing! I have to get out!"

"If you're caught attempting to leave you'll be imprisoned!" Bernhardt interjected.

"It's almost twenty years since they escaped to America. They could be living anywhere. Johann is a full-grown man now. Perhaps… perhaps Eleanor has remarried," Rudi ventured quietly.

Peter stared hard at Rudi, an anguished look on his face. Leaning forward he spoke in a barely perceptible whisper,

Please Rudi, I can't rest until I find them."

"It's madness! The Stasi is no better than the Gestapo!"

"I just want Eleanor to know that I'm alive. If I can get a message to her I'll be a happy man whatever happens."

Rudi shrugged resignedly,

"Very well Peter, I'll do all I can, but it's probably hopeless after all these years. Give me a couple of weeks. I'll be coming to Berlin in mid August to visit my nephew. By then I may have some news… …or maybe not." He stood up and shrugged his shoulders. "It will be good to stroll together on the Unter den Linden like we used to in the old days."

Peter watched as Rudi walked away, turning to wave back at them as he rounded the corner and disappeared from sight.

Peter had arranged to meet Rudi and Bernhardt in a small café near the university in the Mitte.

"What have you found out?" Peter asked eagerly.

"Very little except that Eleanor no longer lives on Cape Cod. That explains why you didn't get a response from your letters."

"How do you know this?"

"Nils."

"Nils?"

"Sometimes his wife visits Helga when he's at sea. Apparently, she lost contact with Eleanor when she moved after the war. There's nothing more I can tell you."

Heaving a huge sigh Peter picked up his beer.

"One day we'll be free again Rudi then I'll find them. A toast!"

The three men raised their glasses,

"To freedom!"

Twenty-four hours later the East German government closed its borders. A barbed wire fence stretched between East and West Berlin dividing a city and its people.

CHAPTER THIRTY SIX

East Berlin 1961

Peter became more and more frustrated as he watched people go about their daily business watchful and wary of the East German police. The routine imposed on him, because of the restrictions on his freedom made him angry and rebellious. He knew he had to check his behaviour otherwise he could find himself back in the Soviet Union. Rumours had already circulated about outspoken critics of the so-called democratic republic who vanished without trace. Peter guarded his tongue, careful not to speak out in front of others. Not even when Bernhardt came to his bedsit. The only place they could talk freely was in a bar or café.

Peter strode towards the small restaurant in the Mitte near the Humboldt-Universität. He and Bernhardt had arranged to meet there for their usual weekend meal. Water dripped from the brim of his brown Homburg soaking the shoulders of his heavy overcoat. Pulling up his collar against the fine rain he dodged around people slapping home through the puddles. Every bobbing umbrella spoke seemed dangerously level with his eyes.

Overhead, a slate-grey sky loomed like a slab of polished metal. A weak, white sun had forced its way through the blanket of cloud illuminating glittering needles of rain that fell on pale patches of sunlit pavement.

He pushed into the restaurant behind a group of chattering women. Gratefully, he took off his soaking coat and hung it on the coat stand near the door. As he approached their usual table a figure turned and waved at him.

"Rudi, what on earth are you doing in Berlin?"

"I thought it was time to visit my nephew again," he replied. "I guessed you may be here so I took a chance and here you are," he laughed his contagious laugh.

"You don't know how pleased I am to see you Rudi," Peter remarked when the waiter had taken their order. "How long has it been? More than a year I think."

"Last year, the day before they closed the borders," Rudi spat the last words angrily.

Peter laid a hand on his arm to warn him as the waiter arrived with their beers then they huddled close together. The noise of clattering dishes and raised voices was a blessing at times. At least they could talk without fear of being overheard by the Stasi.

"I've been doing a great deal of thinking since I saw you last. I'm sick and tired of constantly being under surveillance," Peter said quietly.

Forlornly, they drank deeply from their steins. Rudi wiped foam from his mouth and looked at Peter who sat staring, a distant look in his eyes.

"What are you thinking Peter?"

"We go back a long way Rudi, don't we?"

"Ja, that is so."

"You remember how we used to outwit the Gestapo?"

"How could I forget? They were such dangerous times."

"We could outwit the Stasi too."

"What are you getting at?"

Rudi looked at him curiously.

"The *Regis* connection… our contacts… you can still reach them?"

"Most of the older members may be dead by now, but there'll be some like young Karl. He's here in Berlin, but he escaped to the West in 1957. He owns a small transport business. Sometimes he hires out his coaches to the army to bring visitors into the East to visit the Soviet War Memorial. On those occasions he likes to drive the coach himself to keep his hand in, or so he says. In reality, he does some work for British intelligence… unofficially, of course. "

"I was Friedrich's right-hand man in the organisation. He wouldn't have sat back without trying to resist the Communists. My mind is made up. We must reform, reactivate the organisation to help people escape to the West."

Rudi looked warily at Bernhardt then at Peter who nodded,

"I trust Bernhardt with my life. Are you with us?"

"Yes, I'm with you!" Bernhardt replied earnestly.

"Good, then I will lead *Regis*," Peter said firmly raising a quizzical eyebrow at his old friend.

For a few moments Rudi didn't respond then he clapped him on the shoulder.

"Tomorrow I'll contact one of our old agents here in the East. Between us we'll spread the word that we're back in business."

"Remember Rudi, we never reveal who we are to other members. We'll use our old code names. Only you and Bernhardt will know that I'm *Regis*. We'll work on a need to know basis only."

"Agreed," said the other two men in unison.

"We'll meet one month from today at my place. I've ransacked it searching for bugs. It's clean. The Stasi haven't been watching me as much since the Wall went up. My knowledge is stale so they're not concerned with me now."

"Tomorrow I'll return to Warnemünde," Rudi interjected, "to start putting the wheels in motion."

"Schnapps!" Bernhardt called to the waiter,

"And three more beers, large ones," Peter added. "Now, let's get drunk together one last time. After tonight we must have our wits about us at all times."

Four weeks later Peter opened the door to Rudi who stood shivering in his heavy coat. A week before Christmas it had turned very cold with the threat of a hard winter ahead.

"Come in! Come in!" Peter motioned Rudi inside. "Bernhardt is already here drinking my Schnapps, as usual."

Rudi rubbed his hands together eyeing the Schnapps.

"Just what I need to warm me up!" he laughed.

After taking his coat Peter poured him a large drink. They settled down in front of the little fire.

"Well Rudi, what news do you have for us?"

"Some good, some bad. I was able to contact Karl. He couldn't believe you had survived the war. Two of our agents here in Berlin were killed in the bombings. Max Strauss died of a heart attack two years ago. Johanna Christofferson, one of our Swedish contacts, died in a skiing accident in Switzerland five years ago. All the others are alive and ready to help in whatever way they can. Now it's up to us to get the wheels in motion."

The three men lifted their glasses of Schnapps.

"*Regis!*" they pledged.

Peter's eyes gleamed with anticipation. A tingle of excitement coursed through his blood. He had come full circle.

PART FOUR

CHAPTER THIRTY SEVEN

East & West Berlin 1962

The tall, athletic young man in the uniform of a British Army officer marched up and down the carriages of the military train. He had been serving in Berlin for over a year. After the first borders were erected the previous summer, movement in and out of West Berlin had become virtually impossible.

During the first days people had escaped into the West by climbing over fences. Others had run across from houses that bordered the Wall. In an attempt to stop the flow guards were ordered to fire at anyone attempting to cross over the border. East German police watched every movement, patrolling the fences with dogs and armed guards. People lived and worked without hindrance, but leaving the city was not so easy. Complete encirclement meant that all travel necessitated moving through Soviet occupied Germany. Likewise, East Berliners were confined on their side of the Wall; their activities constantly scrutinised by the secret police. Now West Berliners lived in the surreal world of freedom within a prison.

Jack remembered the night the first escapee had been shot about a week after the borders were closed. Within days they had started to build a concrete block wall preventing any movement between East and West. Over the ensuing months more barriers and watchtowers were assembled. Angry West Berliners ranted at the Volkspolitzei from the safety of the platforms in Potsdam. Others stared with a look of pure hatred at the Grepos near Brandenburg Gate; a gate that had become a symbol of their imprisonment.

Christmas Eve 1961 had been very cold. Jack had gone down to the Gate with the duty officer to boost morale. The soldiers on guard were miserable but efficient, their thoughts with their families back home. There was a feeling of snow in the air when Herr Willy Brandt and the general officer in command of Berlin troops did a press interview in front of the Gate. Just as the interview started it began to snow.

Plump flakes of snow falling gently to the ground lifted their spirits. Eyes sparkling like children they watched as it rapidly settled obliterating the ugliness of the Wall. A sense of peace and calm seemed to descend over the area cradling them in a soft, white blanket; suspending them in a fleeting moment of pure magic.

Out of the curtain of falling snow figures, wrapped in heavy coats and mufflers, shuffled towards the guards. Holding up bottles of Schnapps, whisky, gin and beer they called,

"Fröehliche Weihnachten!"

"Danke! Happy Christmas!"

Gifts for the soldiers from grateful Berliners: no longer their enemies but their protectors. To give the men something to do when the snow was down the army issued them with a few pairs of skis to slide down a slope near the guard hut.

It was during this time that Jack had been approached to work with the intelligence unit. He spent some time crazily careering down the slope with the men. A convenient front for watching the movements of the Grepos and the People's Police.

He spent a lot of his time driving round the perimeter of the British-Soviet Sector looking for weak points where he could attempt to cross. It was the notorious 'Death Strip' that posed the biggest problem. This bare patch of ground was lit by searchlights between the concrete Wall and a barbed wire fence. Grepos and dog patrols monitored the area night and day.

Jack's covert excursions into the Soviet Sector were becoming increasingly dangerous. But his athletics still served as good cover. His trips on the military train, as duty officer, were a front for gathering intelligence as they trundled through East Germany.

As officer in charge it was his job to ensure that the train was safe and secure when they reached the Alpha checkpoint at Helmstedt. He didn't want an international incident on his hands. The East Germans and Soviet troops guarded the border zealously, exploring any lapse in security to board the train. Lieutenant Jack Conrad had done the same trip at least a dozen times, but today was special. His new wife was travelling on the train.

They had met when he had taken a trip to Minden as part of the army's athletics team. She had been cheering on a young NCO who was running in the hurdles. When Jack won the 1,500 metres she came to congratulate him. Squinting up at the podium she flicked aside her long, chestnut hair. He looked down into her uplifted face, gazed into her green eyes and lost his soul. For a few moments he just stared at her before gathering his composure.

"Thank you," he mumbled incoherently, wondering why he felt so tongue-tied.

She shuffled uncomfortably under his intense gaze.

"I'd better be going," she remarked, acknowledging a wave from one of the group. "Well, goodbye and good luck!"

It was only when she started to walk away that he found his voice.

"What's your name?"

"Helen."

Jack struggled to phrase the invitation without making her think he was picking her up.

"Do you live here in Minden?"

"No, just visiting a friend on my way back to Berlin."

"Berlin, that's wonderful! Look Helen, I hope you won't think me too forward, but would you have dinner with me when I get back to Berlin?"

Helen hesitated slightly then smiled revealing even, white teeth; a smile that lit up her whole face. Jack thought it was the most beautiful smile he had ever seen.

"Okay, but on one condition. You pick me up at my parents' house. Dad is a bit old-fashioned about things like that."

"No problem, I'll pick you up at seven on Friday night."

At two minutes to seven Jack rang the door-bell of the elegant, stone-built house. Helen opened the door and ushered him inside. As he entered the sitting room a tall, well-built man, sporting a neat pencil moustache, rose to greet him. He brushed cigar ash from his grey, woollen cardigan.

"Dad, this is Lieutenant Jack Conrad," Helen said, a mischievous smile playing on her lips.

"Phillip Winters. Glad to meet you Jack. This is my wife," he continued as Charlotte Winters entered the room. She had the same chestnut hair and dazzling smile as her daughter.

"Put it on the coffee table please Greta," she instructed.

A stout woman in a black dress, partially covered with a white, lace apron, placed the tray on the table. Jack clicked his heels and gave a little bow.

"I'm delighted to meet you Mrs Winters.

"Such delightful manners!"

"Would the General like his aperitif now," Greta asked as she left the room.

"General!"

Jack automatically came to attention suddenly recognising the name now the rank had been applied to it. General Winters! How could he have been so stupid!

"My apologies sir, I didn't realise!"

"Relax, no apology needed my boy. We're both out of uniform."

"Why didn't you tell me your father was General Winters? I felt such a fool!" Jack remonstrated as they sipped aperitifs in a little bar on Kurfürstendamm later that evening.

"Sorry, but I thought with you being in the army you would have guessed."

"How long have you lived here?" Jack asked changing the subject.

"Not long. I took a languages degree at Oxford. My parents had moved to Germany so I decided to read for a post-graduate degree here in Berlin. I'm fluent in German, French, Italian and Spanish. My command of Russian is a bit ropy, but I'm working on that. I was lucky enough to get a two year teaching post at the university. Occasionally, I work as a translator for the British Embassy."

"Wow! I'm impressed. Brains as well as beauty."

From that evening on they spent as much time together as possible. A few months later they were married in the little church in Helen's home in Oxfordshire.

Jack smiled to himself as he remembered the sound of their feet crunching on leaves; church bells ringing clear in the crisp, autumn air. Trees lining the drive brilliant red and yellow, as though they had clothed themselves in their finery just for their special day. He had missed her during the two weeks she had been visiting her grandparents in Wales. Now she was coming back and he couldn't wait to see her.

The train steamed into the station, its wheels screeching metallically as it slowed to a stop. Doors opened spilling passengers onto the platform. Two British military guards walked smartly up the platform checking compartments, slamming doors closed. Jack spoke briefly with the men then hurried to the Rail Transport Office.

"Has Mrs Helen Conrad reported her arrival?" he asked the surly-looking civilian.

The clerk flicked through the papers on the counter. He studied the notepad on the small table behind him.

"Ja, she is in the café on the concourse," he said sourly.

Jack hurried off and immediately spotted Helen sitting forlornly at a little table. When she saw Jack her face lit up.

"We have a bit of time before the train returns to Berlin. Let's have a walk and a quick spot of lunch."

Two hours later they boarded the military train back to Berlin. It only ran once a day from Berlin to Brunswick, Hanover and back again. Once on board Helen settled in while Jack joined his men until it was time for dinner. It was the first time she had travelled on the military train through East Germany. She was startled by the elaborate precautions taken by the guards as they approached Helmstedt.

A soldier tapped on the door and handed her a mill board with a set of instructions.

"Read it carefully ma'am, but don't worry it's normal procedure," he smiled noting her anxious expression.

She could hear doors sliding open and closing again as he moved purposefully down the corridor. She felt even more unnerved when she read the instructions.

'*Do not show cameras, tape-recorders, binoculars or radios.*
Look straight ahead.
Do not smile, gesticulate or look at the guards on the platform.
Do not visit the lavatory while the train is in the platform.
Do not stand in the corridor.'

A short time before the train was due at the checkpoint Helen was alarmed at the sound of boots marching down the corridor. She held her breath, her heart pounding painfully in her chest. Suddenly, Jack slid the door open and stepped inside the compartment. Seeing her frightened look he soothed,

"Don't worry darling. Nobody will get on here once they've finished."

Two soldiers marched past and stopped at the external door at the end of the carriage. One placed a wooden stake into the metal handle while the other hammered it in firmly with a wooden mallet.

Half an hour later they arrived at Alpha Checkpoint in Helmstedt where watchful guards monitored every move. Afraid to turn her head Helen looked out of the corner of her eye. A group of Russian soldiers, dressed in khaki-coloured trousers and maroon jackets, sauntered up and down outside the train. Mere boys who didn't look much older than fourteen or fifteen years of age. All armed with pistols nestled in the folds of excess fabric at the small of their backs.

"Are you okay?" Jack queried sticking his head round the door.

"Well, I can't say the sight of those guns make me happy."

A couple of British soldiers leaned through the window as the border guards walked by inspecting the train. The Russians stopped and reached up to take something from them.

"What's happening?" Helen asked nervously.

"They're exchanging stuff. They're not supposed to, but it happens all the time. Our boys give them naughty magazines, the odd pack of cigarettes. In return they hand over cap badges, lapel insignia, sometimes a belt. Anything they can keep as souvenirs. Most of the officers turn a blind eye. It alleviates the strain."

Only when the train trundled away and the checkpoint faded into the distance did she relax and breathe freely. But she was worried. Now there was even more tension in Berlin because of the Cuban Crisis.

Army quarters were at a premium, even for officers, so they had rented a spacious house in Glienicke in a quiet cul-de-sac not far from the river. Even though it was so close to the Wall it was idyllic. The situation was slightly unreal as though they had stumbled into another dimension. Quiet and peaceful, except for the occasional mild explosion or gunfire from the East Sector, it was completely cocooned from reality. Every time she went into the city on a shopping expedition she experienced a thrill of fear at the proximity of the Wall. From the upper deck of the bus she seemed to be at eye level with the Grepos. Malevolently, they stared from the goon tower looming so close she felt they could reach out and snatch her.

Throwing his officer's coat over the sofa Jack scooped Helen up in his arms and hugged her tightly to him.

"I missed you so much when you were away," he breathed against her hair.

Helen pushed him away and looked up at him.

"What is it Jack? You've been so preoccupied lately."

"It's just the situation here has been pretty bad over the past year. A few East Berliners have tried to swim across the Spree. They've nearly all been shot or captured. Now it's virtually impossible to get out of East Berlin. It's a very tense situation especially since Peter Fechter was shot trying to escape."

"Yes, I heard about it on my transistor. The poor boy lay bleeding to death. Nobody tried to help him. It's such an unreal situation. All this happening while life in the West goes on, as usual."

"I'll be away for a few days now and again." Jack hesitated before continuing. "I'm fluent in German as you know. There's a scam going on luring young soldiers into the Russian Sector. The East Germans have women working for them here in West Berlin."

"Women? What kind of women?"

"She makes a play for a young soldier. Once he's hooked and in her bed she tells him she misses her family in East Berlin. Eventually, she lures him into the Russian Sector with the promise of a new life, a job and marriage to the girl of his dreams."

"But can't the British get them back out?"

"Not without absolute proof that they've gone over. Once the lad's on the other side he's interrogated and used as a source of information by the East German Secret Police. That's only one aspect. My job is to gather intelligence. I routinely take trips into East Berlin to monitor any military movement and get a general view of the situation."

Horrified, Helen brought her hand up to her mouth, her eyes wide with fear.

"This is what you've been doing all along? I can't believe it!"

"It's my job Helen," Jack replied quietly. "It was my job before I met you. I've booked a meal in that little inn on the river. It's close enough to walk there," he continued changing the subject. "I'll just change my shirt."

"I've put out your slacks and sports coat."

"Full uniform, I'm afraid. Orders from Brigade Headquarters. All servicemen are still on high alert and must be in uniform even when off duty."

Decorated for Christmas the little inn looked bright and festive. As they walked in a tall, thickset man with black hair and a large bristling moustache waved to them.

"Guten abend Jack!"

"It's good to see you Erich."

"Come, have a drink with us until your meal is ready." He motioned them to sit down next to his plump little wife. "Aberhardt, two more glasses bitte!"

After he had poured the wine Erich sat back looking thoughtfully at Jack. A look passed between them before they raised their glasses.

"To a Happy Christmas!"

The waiter appeared and announced their meal was ready. As Jack pushed back his chair Erich took a book from his overcoat pocket hanging on the coat stand near the table.

"This is the book you wanted to borrow."

Jack stuffed it unceremoniously into the inside pocket of his jacket then followed the waiter to their table.

"What was all that about?" Helen queried.

"Nothing, just a copy of Rilke's poetry he thought I might like to read."

CHAPTER THIRTY EIGHT

East Berlin 1962

Bernhardt sat motionless in the darkened apartment waiting for the signal to move. Outside a sudden commotion caught his attention. He opened the heavy drapes a crack and peered down into the street. Under the lamp, near the bus stop at the corner, two men were arguing loudly. Obviously drunk they half-heartedly pushed each other to emphasise a point. Workers on their way home after celebrating the start of the Christmas celebration.

Lights bounced up and down as a vehicle careered down the street and slewed to a halt. The stockier of the two men stepped aboard the bus. Unsteadily, he reached out a hand and hauled his companion up onto the platform. For a few seconds he hung onto the metal pole swaying backwards and forwards. Roughly, his companion pushed him towards the nearest seat and slumped down beside him. The conductor glared at the two men.

"Wash ish wrong?" slurred the stocky man.

"Drunken pigs!" he fumed under his breath.

That red-haired one looked like trouble. That's all he needed at the end of his shift. Studiously ignoring him the conductor moved down the aisle inspecting tickets.

Bernhardt thrust his arms into his overcoat, grabbed his hat, quietly let himself out and slipped down the stairs into the street.

On the bus the two drunks listed from right to left as it swerved round corners occasionally skidding on wet cobbles. The vehicle was crowded with tired, bleary-eyed workers. A foul, wet dog smell hung in the air mixed with sweat and dirty clothes. Seasonal greetings shouted by the drunken, stocky reveller drew glances of annoyance from those who just wanted to get home to a hot meal. Further along the bus a woman sat engrossed in a newspaper with a picture of Khrushchev on the front page.

"I think thish ish where we get off."

The taller of the two men nudged his companion as the bus trundled to a stop.

The drunks stumbled out onto the pavement looking dazed. One of them lurched towards a lamp post and hung on, swaying slightly. The other man caught him under the arm and led him unsteadily down the pavement.

Probably looking for somewhere to urinate after so much booze the conductor thought watching them stagger down the street. The woman on the bus watched as they slipped into the shadows of an alley dissecting the buildings.

"Come on!" Peter whispered to Rudi. "Let's get to the u-bahn station."

The streets were deserted except for a few stragglers huddled in heavy coats, mufflers wrapped around their heads concealing their faces. Alert for the Stasi they dodged in and out of doorways and passageways. Occasionally, they staggered into a bar demanding Schnapps to keep them warm.

The planned route was convoluted by necessity. They followed other passengers into the station and approached the ticket office.

"Freidrichstrasse – der einzelfahrschein!"Peter snapped.

"One single ticket," the clerk said, wearily pushing the ticket under the glass partition.

He grabbed the ticket and made his way to the platform. Behind him Rudi purchased a return fare and followed him.

Peter stood stamping his feet against the cold, breath steaming white from his nostrils like a smoking dragon. Further along the platform Rudi sat hunched over, his eyes closed as though he were asleep. A few passengers stood waiting in bored silence. One or two strode impatiently up and down the platform anxious to get home.

A plump little man jostled his way breathlessly through the bodies and stopped at Peter's elbow.

"It's cold, ja?" he gasped struggling with his briefcase.

"Ja, very cold."

"Still, we can look forward to the Christmas celebrations."

He gave a little sigh of contentment as he thought about his grandchildren.

Suddenly, the train appeared screeching to a stop with a grinding of metal. Peter boarded and found a seat facing Rudi lower down in the carriage. Within seconds doors slammed and they slid out of the station.

Peter stared straight ahead taking note of the burly man in the black, leather coat in the seat across the aisle from him. The coat reminded him of the Gestapo. A brief flutter of anxiety coursed through him. He studied the man's reflection in the window watching every movement and expression, but he stayed buried behind his newspaper. The train terminated at Freidrichstrasse for East and West Berliners so the journey would be short, just a few stops.

When he alighted Peter joined the throng exiting the station with Rudi close at his heels. Swiftly, he negotiated side streets and alleys until he came to a darkened, dilapidated building in a seedy, deserted street. All its windows had been smashed and boarded over with rotten planks.

Hurriedly, he looked behind him to see if he had been followed. Satisfied, he slipped inside the doorway and disappeared from sight. He waited in the blackness until Rudi joined him a few minutes later.

Together they pulled away a jumble of old metal: wheel hubs, a rusty filing cabinet and a mangled bicycle. Behind it criss-crossed planks closed off the entrance to an adjoining room containing more rubble and junk. The remnants of dismantled cars lay strewn over the floor. A dark shape loomed in the corner covered with a tarpaulin.

"Here it is," Peter whispered pulling the tarpaulin away to reveal an ancient motorcycle with panniers strapped to either side.

He felt inside for the contents.

"Everything's here," he grinned.

He wheeled the machine out of the building, gunned the engine and raced away into the night with Rudi clinging like a limpet on the pillion.

When they got within walking distance of Invalidenstrasse Peter stopped behind a cluster of buildings.

"Good luck," he whispered.

He handed Rudi a rucksack he had taken from one of the panniers. Rudi grabbed it and hurried in the direction of the border crossing. Behind the buildings opposite a black van waited shrouded in darkness. As soon as Rudi jumped into the passenger seat the driver nosed the vehicle out onto the road towards the checkpoint near the Spandauer Schiffahrtskanal.

When they were within fifty feet Rudi dropped the first petrol bomb, then another and another, until they were closing in on the checkpoint. He threw two more at the barrier as they hurtled towards it. For a few seconds nothing happened. Suddenly, frantic shouting followed by pounding feet. Through the black smoke he saw bodies running in all directions. Out of the mayhem two guards rushed forward firing a hail of bullets at the van. Rudi ducked instinctively as a bullet whistled past his head.

"Go! Go! Go!" he yelled at the driver.

Leaning out, he lobbed a home-made smoke bomb in their path. Taking the opportunity the driver suddenly slewed to a stop. With a grinding of gears he reversed the van back down Invalidenstrasse. He skidded into a side street and jolted to a halt. Both men tumbled out of the van and ran to a car waiting in the shadows.

"One down, one to go!" Rudi laughed as they raced back the way they had come.

At the Chausensee checkpoint the young woman, engrossed in her book when the two drunks boarded the bus, was creating another kind of commotion. Wringing her hands she called over the barrier to her 'husband' in the West. He shook his fist at the Grepos.

"Schweinhünds!"

Stretching out her arms the woman ran towards the barrier. Her 'husband' shouted for her to go back. The guards glared across at him, hands tightening on their weapons. They were jumpy tonight. Already there had been trouble at the Invalidenstrasse crossing and at Checkpoint Charlie. Berliners, on both sides, were angry that they were separated from their families at Christmas.

The young guard at Chausensee felt a surge of sympathy. Earlier that evening an old woman had collapsed and died at the checkpoint. Her distraught son in the West had watched helplessly as they carried her away.

Security had been stepped up all along the Wall, but it didn't stop crowds gathering to wave across at loved ones. Peter was satisfied that his distraction tactics were effective. It was vital to deflect attention away from sections of the Wall to the checkpoints. He pulled into an alley and watched for any signs of activity. Everything had been carefully planned, but this was East Berlin.

The only way in to St. Hedwig and Französische Domgemeinde cemeteries, since the erection of the Wall, was through a residential block on Wöhlerstrasse. He had to be very careful not to be seen. Few people would want to go into such a place after dark. Still, the Stasi would be on the alert.

He drove the motorcycle as far as he dared then cut the engine. Wheeling it within twenty metres of the entrance he concealed it under some dark, brooding trees. Bernhardt would already be inside near Otto's grave. They had found it after the war and laid flowers. He still couldn't get used to the idea of Otto being dead even after all these years. He wondered about Gisela and their baby. He'd be a grown man now. Steeling himself he pushed all thoughts out of his mind and clambered into the misty darkness of the cemetery.

Blurred outlines emerged out of a thin mist hanging like a pall over the graves. Single headstones and some larger family plots enclosed with chain fencing. White shapes with outstretched arms and wings loomed out of the darkness threatening to grasp him as he darted in and out of the gravestones. He cursed as he caught his foot on the edge of an elaborate grave topped with a tall, stone cross.

Cupping his hands to his mouth he imitated the call of an owl. Within seconds the sound echoed back across the cemetery. Slowly, he inched forward keeping low to the ground. Dim shapes moved on the goon tower at the Wall. He caught his breath as something moved in the wet grass near his feet then scurried away. Suddenly, a low, urgent whisper caught his attention,

"Over here!"

He crawled forward until he saw the vague outline of Bernhardt crouched behind a simple headstone. Screwing up his eyes he could just make out Otto's name. It had almost disappeared, eroded by the elements.

"One day he'll have a memorial befitting his courage," he vowed.

But now was not the time for debilitating sentiment.

"Be careful with these," Peter said rummaging in his rucksack.

He pulled out two dark-coloured sheets tightly rolled up. Carefully, he loosened the bundle and spread it flat over Otto's grave. A faint, greenish glimmer showed through a fold. Hastily, he covered it up. Wrapped inside the sheets two hooded shrouds glowed with luminous paint.

"Remember to cover up with the black sheet and drop to the ground if the guards start firing. At first they'll be frightened. Then they'll start shooting. We'll be easy targets, but we must distract them for as long as possible."

Crouching down behind an enormous tomb they pulled on the loose shrouds and hastily covered themselves with the black sheets. They didn't want any glimmer to be seen until they were ready.

Peter peered at his watch in the dim light. He waited a few seconds then nudged Bernhardt with his elbow. Silently, they crept forward until they were three rows in front of Otto's grave. He lay down on top of a large grave, overlooked by a glowing, white, marble angel. Bernhardt crawled on flattening himself on a grave a few metres away from Peter. What they had planned was akin to a childish prank, but it was highly dangerous.

Peter watched the searchlight sweeping along the Wall until it passed the spot where Rudi was waiting. Suddenly, he threw off the blanket and sat up on the grave. Nothing happened. The searchlights travelled back in the opposite direction. Still nothing happened. He sat rigidly on the grave while the lights swept back and started the sequence again. He knew he had to attract the attention of the guards.

Taking in a deep breath he howled as loudly as he could. Suddenly, he heard a muted shout from the direction of the watchtower. They had seen him. He rose up from the grave and extended his arms stiffly in front of him. Slowly, he stood up and walked forward a few steps. There was a commotion on the watchtower now. A babble of muted voices, the clatter of boots on concrete. Peter smiled. Now it would begin.

Further along the Wall Rudi lay in the darkness, whispering final instructions to a group huddled together against the inner fence.

"The searchlight sweeps the area every five minutes. The second it passes I'll give the signal for you to run across the strip to the wall there," he pointed.

"What if the guards see us?" whispered the woman, her voice trembling with fear.

"Whatever you do don't stop and don't look back. Every second counts. Wind the rope around your wrist. You'll be hauled up and over the Wall." He looked at the twelve year old girl. She could manage, but the boy was only eight years old. If he panicked it would be all over for them. "You first then the rest of you; every five minutes between the sweeps. Are you ready?"

The wide, white beam of a searchlight crept along illuminating the rough strip of ground between the Wall and barbed wire fence. Slowly, it passed leaving them in complete darkness.

"Now!" Rudi whispered urgently.

The girl squeezed under the barbed wire and ran across the '*Death Strip*'. Suddenly, a rope dropped over the Wall dangling about four feet from the ground. She grabbed it, wound it round her wrist once and tugged. The rope went taut as she was lifted off her feet and dragged upwards. Feet scrabbling against concrete she fought for purchase. Rudi sighed with relief when she reached the top and dropped over the other side followed by the snaking rope.

On the watchtower the guards were leaning forward looking at the ethereal figure glowing green in the cemetery.

"Mein Gott!" squealed a young Grepo. "It's a ghost!"

He turned to start down the steps when his superior yelled at him,

"Wait, you fool," he said uncertainly. "There's no such thing as ghosts. I can't see anything. It's a figment of your imagination."

He scanned the cemetery, but all he could see was a still, silent graveyard. As he turned away he caught sight of something in his peripheral vision. Straining his eyes he looked towards the spot.

"I can see it now! It's moving! There's another one over there to the left!"

Peter and Bernhardt ducked and dived behind headstones. Intermittently, they covered themselves with the blankets concealing their positions. Quickly, they darted to another grave a few rows in front and lay down again. Peter put his hands squarely on the earth and raised himself up. From a distance it looked as though he was hovering above the grave.

Suddenly, there was a clamour of voices followed by the crack of gunfire. Peter rolled off the grave and covered himself. Twenty yards away Bernhardt threw off his blanket and pranced amongst the graves. Shots swiftly changed direction pinging off the angel's wing over his head.

"That was close," he muttered diving onto the path. "We can't keep this up much longer."

He made his way towards Peter who was crawling on his stomach towards the entrance.

"Let's get out of here," he said urgently, "before they catch on!"

On the watchtower one of the Grepos was speaking into a wireless.

"Ja, they look like ghosts, all green and glowing in the dark!" he babbled. "Dozens of them moving all over the cemetery, coming out of graves!"

The voice at the other end was harsh and incredulous.

"Pull yourself together man! Are you a fool! There are no such things as ghosts!" the voice snapped. "Stay where you are and keep watching until my men arrive to search the cemetery!"

Crouching in the shadows Rudi watched the last of the group scale the Wall and drop from sight. Within seconds he had slipped into the night.

Peter and Bernhardt threw the shrouds behind a tombstone covering them with blankets and clodges of grass. Quickly, they examined each other for any signs of luminous paint then climbed back out the way they had come.

"Come on, the motorcycle's over here," Peter whispered.

He yanked the bike upright and pushed it along the dark perimeter of the cemetery wall.

"Get on!" he urged straddling the machine.

Bernhardt jumped onto the pillion as Peter quietly turned over the engine. Once they were a safe distance from the cemetery he gunned ahead. Twisting in and out of side streets and alleys they headed for the old, disused building. A surge of adrenaline coursed through him. Heart racing wildly he shouted over his shoulder,

"How do you feel Bernie?"

"Scared stiff, fantastic!" Bernhardt yelled back.

With a squeal of tyres they drove off into the night chuckling with glee.

In the cemetery reluctant guards searched tentatively amongst the black graves.

"Over here!"

An officer was prodding at something glowing green on the ground. He picked it up with the end of his pistol and thrust it at them.

"This is your ghost you idiots! Get a detail along the Wall. You can bet there's been an escape attempt. Incidents have been reported at three different checkpoints in the past few hours. Distraction tactics. Someone will pay for this," he spat.

Rubbing his chin thoughtfully he headed for the exit. This wasn't the work of a single individual. There must be some kind of organisation behind it. The Stasi would be interested, very interested indeed.

CHAPTER THIRTY NINE

West Berlin 1962

The DKW moved slowly down the British-controlled passageway in the Eiskellar. Jack looked around searching for any sign of movement. Either side of the road was East German territory. Beyond the fence a disused, dilapidated house loomed out of the darkness. This passageway was the only way in and out for people living on the two farms nearby. They were under British protection. Nervously, his driver looked to the left then the right watching for Grepos.

In the rear of the vehicle two soldiers, in khaki denims and balaclavas, waited tensely for the order. Guns were too cumbersome for this job. Their only weapon was a bayonet attached to their belts.

"Remember, this is just a recce," Jack instructed. "We'll have six minutes to take a look until the patrol returns. I don't want anyone taking any unnecessary chances with those gun happy guards. Is that clear?"

"Yes sir," the two NCOs whispered.

The house was believed to be used by East German guards to monitor movements in and out of the Eiskellar. Tonight they intended to find out the extent of their surveillance.

"Now!" Jack ordered as the DKW slowed down.

He jumped off and rolled into grass. Muffled thuds close by indicated his men had followed him. A muted curse came from the young corporal as he hit his head against a stone. They remained there while the vehicle disappeared as though on normal patrol.

"Okay, let's go!" Jack whispered urgently.

Slowly, they crawled on their stomachs over the damp grass towards the house. In the distance they could hear the guards talking and laughing. Reaching the door Jack prised it open and slipped inside. He switched on his pencil torch careful to keep the beam below the boarded-up windows. One of the NCOs went upstairs while the other stood guard just inside the door. Judging by the thickness of dust on the wooden floorboards the house had been unoccupied for some time. Then he saw the footprints.

"These are from boots," he whispered. "The others are smaller. Could be a child, maybe a woman."

Moving to the rickety table he spotted two, battered, tin tankards and an empty vodka bottle. Hand prints had disturbed the dust near an old, flat cap of the kind worn by East German workers. Satisfied there was nothing more he ascended the stairs. Harder to explain was the wardrobe containing a jacket and raincoat.

"Look at this sir!"

The corporal pointed to a football lying on top of the wardrobe.

"Looks like they've been having a rare old time in here," Jack said thoughtfully. "Perhaps they've been entertaining?"

In the distance the low-pitched whine of the DKW, making its way back along the passageway, caught their attention.

"Okay, let's go," Jack urged holding the door open.

The NCOs sidled out and dropped prone onto the grass.

Jack followed, forgetting that the door was on a strong spring. The door slammed shut behind him. In the quiet blackness of the night it reverberated like a clap of thunder. As soon as he hit the grass loud shots fired over their heads.

"Go!"

Haring towards the DKW they threw themselves inside. They were safe. The East Germans dare not shoot once they were on the road back in British territory.

"That was a close call sir," the young corporal said breathlessly as they trundled towards the guard post.

"Too close for comfort," Jack replied.

As they came to the narrowest strip of the Eiskellar Jack became aware of movement in the undergrowth.

"There's something going on down there sir!"

Jack brought up his night glasses.

"You're right corporal. Somebody's penetrating the border fence."

A shadowy figure crawled through the fence quickly followed by two more dark shapes. He couldn't make out their gender, whether they were civilians or guards. All he could see were dark shapes huddled on the British side of the fence.

As they came alongside one of the figures leapt out into the road.

"Stop!" a woman's voice shouted. "Help us, please!"

Cursing, the driver slammed on his brakes narrowly missing the young woman. The corporal drew his bayonet and held it out of sight.

"Knock off your lights!" Jack instructed shining his pencil torch on the girl's face, then on the other two who had cautiously emerged from the bushes.

The driver turned and looked at Jack before beckoning them into the vehicle.

"Move on, and make it fast!" Jack ordered.

On their arrival at the guard post the girls, whose ages seemed between eighteen and twenty-five, were ushered inside. Looking slightly bewildered they stood uncertainly in the middle of the room. Jack turned to the duty NCO.

"Corporal, see if you can get some Parka jackets and give them some hot coffee. They look frozen. Sergeant, once they've thawed out get them to the duty officer's room for debriefing and interrogation."

"Danke! Danke!" they cried in unison.

The sergeant marched off to prepare for the interviews. Within minutes he had returned clutching a mill board.

"Right, I'll take the first one down. Put the other two somewhere to get some rest. I have a feeling this is going to be a long night."

The corporal motioned for the women to follow him to the sleeping quarters at the opposite side of the guard room.

After an hour of painstaking questioning Jack had gleaned as much information as possible. The girl, whose name was Magda, told him they had been planning their escape for months.

"The guards usually met us in that old, empty house just inside the border. Sometimes we played cards or had some vodka. They liked to play football in the dark," she said scathingly. "It wasn't the only game they liked to play."

So they were using the house to meet girls Jack mused.

"That will be all for now," he said aloud. "Let's have the next one in."

"Yes sir!"

The sergeant marched smartly out with the girl in tow, crossed the floor and opened the door to the sleeping quarters. Two bodies lay huddled under a blanket in the bottom bunk.

"What the bloody hell is going on here?" he demanded.

A woman's head popped over the rough, army blanket. Angrily, the sergeant yanked it back.

"On your feet!"

Hurriedly, the soldier jumped out of the bunk and stood to attention. With a scurry of bedclothes a junior NCO jumped down from the top bunk. A mound of blankets revealed the presence of the other girl. They both snapped to attention.

"They were cold so they jumped in with us to keep warm," the private whined. "We weren't doing anything. It wasn't our fault."

"We are very grateful to the British Army," said the girl from the lower bunk.

The middle-aged sergeant was a solid family man with daughters of his own. Giving the soldiers a look of undisguised contempt he roared,

"You'll both be put on a charge for this! Get back to your post. And you, you'll probably be stripped of your rank," he fumed turning to the NCO. "Now get out!"

Jack had gleaned some useful information from the eldest of the girls. She was around twenty-five, dark-haired, stocky and rosy-cheeked. She looked like a farmer's daughter who had just stepped into the kitchen after milking the cows.

"Why were you in the old house?" Jack queried.

"We went there to meet the guards. We hoped to escape across the border, but the opportunity never came until tonight. We used to pretend to be drunk with them so we could stay in the house."

"How were you able to get over tonight?"

"The guards didn't show up after we saw the secret police there last night."

"The Stasi?"

"Ja, we saw them coming out of the house."

So, the Stasi had been using it after all. Apart from the guards taking girls there they also used it as a cover to spy on military activities in the Eiskellar.

"If we hadn't ducked down in the dark under the windows the Stasi would have caught us."

A look of naked fear sprang into her eyes.

"We were terrified they would see us. If we were caught by the secret police…" she shuddered. "We crept away and hid in the trees. We could hear muffled talking from inside the house. About fifteen minutes later the guards came out with a Stasi officer."

The girl stopped dabbing at her eyes. She sniffed loudly, her eyes liquid with tears.

"Go on," Jack said gently. "Perhaps you'd like a cup of coffee? Get some coffee please sergeant."

"Sir!"

Turning smartly on his heel the sergeant marched off into the adjoining room. He had been through this procedure many times before with the intelligence officer. Lieutenant Conrad didn't exercise aggression. He had a cajoling way with him, especially with the women. They usually spilled the beans before they had even realised it.

"I couldn't catch everything they were saying," the girl snivelled, "but they were definitely talking about escape routes. One of them mentioned some kind of organisation that had been getting people out of East Berlin."

"Can you describe him?"

"I couldn't see his face clearly."

"Did you hear anything else?"

"No, nothing except..." She hesitated. "It was rather odd; something about the university. The Stasi officer said he was going to the university to improve his education."

"His education?"

"That was all I heard."

"Are you sure?"

"Yes, I'm positive."

Jack rose from behind the desk just as the sergeant returned with the coffee.

"That will be all for now. Perhaps you would like to take your coffee with you?"

"Send the last one in," Jack sighed wearily.

His eyes were gritty and red-rimmed with tiredness. He flopped back into the chair. This was the second night in a row without proper sleep.

The car crunched up the gravel drive and lurched to a stop sending chippings flying in all directions. At the sound of the vehicle Helen jumped out of bed, drew back the curtain and waved.

"Sorry sir," the young soldier apologised.

"Forget it. It's been a long night." He smiled as he caught sight of Helen. She always worried herself sick whenever he was patrolling the Eiskellar. She suspected that he was going over on covert missions, but he was barred from telling her anything.

He thought about the information the girl had given about the university. There had been dozens of escape attempts. Most of them had been individuals like Peter Fechter or small groups trying to tunnel their way out. This was the fist time he had heard of an organisation helping people to escape into West Berlin. Yawning, he mounted the stairs wearily rubbing his stubbly chin.

So the Stasi agents were interested in the old the house. There's more to this than meets the eye he mused stretching out in the bed. It may be worth following it up. He had barely finished the thought before he fell into an exhausted sleep.

Drowsily, Helen ran her hand over the sheets alarmed to find a bare space. An engine droned on the road beyond the woods. A blaring, metallic voice penetrated her consciousness as she lay dosing. Startled, she shot up in the bed momentarily disoriented. Jack was standing at the window looking out.

"Rocking horse! Rocking horse! All out! All out! Rocking horse! Rocking horse!"

"What is it?" she asked querulously.

"Don't worry," Jack murmured as he hurriedly dressed in the dark. "It's just a drill; instant standby. If it were the real thing it would be a different call accompanied by a bugle blast. You remember I told you this happens periodically to keep military families alert. You still have your suitcase packed under the bed?"

Helen nodded and snuggled back under the bedclothes. She looked at the luminous clock on the bedside table.

"It's only four o' clock," she groaned.

"Families will be picked up and flown out from R.A.F. Gatow," Jack continued. "Whether I'm here or not you must go."

"I forget sometimes what a dangerous place Berlin is. Yesterday when I went into Charlottenburg on the bus I sat on the top deck. The Grepos seemed so close I could reach out and touch them."

Jack donned a woollen hat and wound an extra long scarf round his neck.

"Where are you going at this hour? Why aren't you in uniform?" Helen asked.

Jack bent over to peck her on the cheek.

"Just a little recce that's all."

"You're going over the Wall again, aren't you?"

"I'll be back in two days," he sighed zipping up his Parka.

He scooped up a small briefcase stuffed with papers and slipped out.

CHAPTER FORTY

East Berlin 1962

Jack lay prostrate on the hard, frost-covered ground in the Eiskeller. He waited a full two minutes before darting into the trees close to the dilapidated old house. Bright stars twinkled in a black sky; ominous snow clouds drifted across a watery, silver moon. Complete silence except for the thudding of his heart and the distant hoot of an owl. Under the trees the ground was soft and damp, clinging to his trousers and shoes. Guttural voices, accompanied by the crunch of footsteps, brought him to a dead stop.

From where he was hiding he could see the dim shapes of guards on their regular patrols. He had gleaned their movements from the girls who had escaped. Now he had to get across the strip of grass and through the fence as swiftly as possible. Luckily, there were no searchlights sweeping the area. Keeping low he edged forward towards the next fence. Carefully, he lifted the barbed wire, slid underneath and dived towards the bushes.

Crouched in the darkness he waited again for a few minutes. Suddenly, a man's voice whispered from behind him,

"Good evening."

Spinning on his heel Jack grabbed for his flick-knife, lunging at the stocky figure who danced to one side.

"Steady on old chap!"

"Markus!" Jack snarled, "How many times have I told you not to creep up on me like that. One of these days you'll get your throat cut!"

"Come on," the other man said ignoring the warning. "It's getting light. Let's get out of here. There's a safe house about a kilometre beyond the farm."

Markus stopped when the house came into sight.

"Give three taps then two. Repeat it three times. The woman will shelter you for a couple of hours. Her son attends the university. After breakfast, when he leaves for classes, you'll go with him. He often has fellow students to stay overnight. I can't help you more than that I'm afraid."

"Can we trust them?"

"One hundred per cent. Her brother was shot trying to escape into the West. She hates the communists."

Jack traversed the field coming up to the rear of the house. Yellow light poured through a chink in the curtains. Peering through the gap he saw it was the kitchen. Sitting round a large, scrubbed, wooden table the woman and her son were eating breakfast. His mouth watered as he watched the boy cut up a fat sausage and stuff it into his mouth. Silently, he moved towards the door giving the signal knock. After a few seconds the door opened a crack revealing one side of the woman's face.

"What do you want this time of the morning?" she demanded. "Who are you?" She sounded suspicious.

"Markus sent me to collect his book."

"I don't know any Markus."

He sent me to collect the copy of Rilke's poetry you borrowed."

"Come in," she instructed throwing the door open.

Light streamed onto the narrow path spreading over the grass like a pool of golden water.

"Close the door quickly!" she ordered. "Even fields have eyes and ears in the East."

A tall, blond, young man, around nineteen or twenty years old, got up from the table as she ushered Jack in.

"Franz," he introduced himself. "Please sit down and have some breakfast."

In her late forties, Wanda was still an attractive woman. Luminous brown eyes in an oval face framed by chestnut, shoulder length hair. Over breakfast Jack tentatively asked her about her involvement with Markus.

"He was a friend of my twin brother. Both of them tried to escape by swimming across the Spree last summer." A sob caught in her throat. "Martin was a journalist, but he felt stifled by the restrictions put on his work. He believed in freedom of speech for the press. She gave a little laugh. "Freedom! There is no such thing in East Germany. He wanted to get into the West… to write about living conditions under the communists. One of his colleagues informed on him. The Stazi started to follow him. You know the rest."

An hour later they bundled into an ancient Skoda. Wanda drove them to the university and dropped them off. Franz motioned to Jack to follow him inside.

"You must be careful," he whispered.

He cracked a joke, laughing loudly as a group of students passed them in the corridor.

"If you wander about too much someone might start asking questions."

Jack started to say something, but Franz silenced him.

"One of the professors might talk to you, but I can't promise anything."

Franz ushered Jack into a small laboratory filled with equipment used for experiments. A flask bubbled away over a Bunsen burner with a long tube attached to another flask a few feet away. Test tubes, Petri dishes and sample slides littered the work bench in what appeared to be organised chaos. Suddenly, a short, dumpy, grey-haired man appeared from a room at the back of the laboratory. Momentarily startled, he stopped and looked over the top of his half glasses.

"Franz," he beamed. "I forgot you were coming to use the lab today. My memory is not what it was."

Absent-mindedly, he turned to the work bench and started to fiddle with the heated flask.

"You're not fooling me old man," Jack murmered watching the man's gaze sweep appraisingly over him.

"Who is your friend?"

"Jochem Schultz, this is Professor Reinhold Jung. Jochem needs your help with his research," he said heading for the door. "I must rush. My first lecture is starting shortly."

Jung motioned for Jack to follow him into the storeroom and waved him to a chair.

"Perhaps you would like some coffee, ja?"

He set about filling a battered old kettle from a brass tap set over a butler's sink leaving the water to run.

"Sometimes I run the water, because it tastes brackish after the weekend," he said loudly. "Walls have ears and I suspect your 'research' is delicate," he continued quietly. "Now, how may I help you Herr Schultz?"

"Franz has told you the nature of my 'research' activities and the organisation that funds it?"

"Ja, ja, it is very interesting."

"I understand that you've helped others with their 'research'." Jack lowered his voice and leaned towards Jung. "Some girls were caught crossing into West Berlin under the noses of the Stasi. Apparently, the crossing point had been under surveillance for some time. They were very angry, because they hadn't managed to foil the escape attempt. One of the girls overheard the Stasi officer say he was going to the university to improve his education; presumably for information."

The old man's eyes widened with fear.

"Mein Gott! How could they know anything? I usually just pass on information. There is an organisation, but it's highly secret. I know very little about it. All I know is that the leader is known as *Regis*. There are two other people at the top, but nobody knows who they are either. Everything is carried out on a need to know basis. It's considered paramount for individual safety. What they don't know cannot be revealed to the secret police if they are arrested."

"Do you know of anybody else in the university connected to the organisation? Students like Franz who may be part of it?"

"No, Franz knows nothing except that I helped his uncle with his 'research'. Unfortunately, he ignored my advice to wait for a signal to move and lost his life for it. All I do is pass on requests for help. Coded information is left in a secret location to be picked up. I haven't had a request for months."

Jack left the old man tinkering with his experiments and wandered along the corridor. As he started towards the exit a big car raced into view through the main gate. With a screech of tyres it lurched to a stop outside the entrance.

Hurriedly, he darted back inside the building and mingled with the milling students changing classes. Seeing a tall, well-built man, blond hair turning to grey at the temples, he froze. In seconds, he had recovered his composure and marched towards the man who was carrying a sheaf of papers. The older man looked directly at him and smiled; a smile that lit up his whole face.

"Guten morgen," he nodded at Jack as he passed.

Jack returned the gesture, looking back over his shoulder as he turned a corner. Suddenly, he heard the man's footsteps stop. He was standing stock still staring back up the corridor with a curious look on his face. Shaking his head, as though slightly bewildered, he disappeared into one of the laboratories. Puzzled, Jack cautiously made his way down the corridor again.

As he rounded another corner he saw two Stasi agents marching towards him. The flustered woman with them pointed towards the laboratories. Alarmed, he tried to dart into a nearby doorway, but he was jostled aside by frightened students scuttling out of their way. Jack pressed himself against the wall making sure he didn't have eye contact. Breathing heavily, he watched them until they disappeared from sight. Jack feared for the elderly Professor Jung who was too old and frail to withstand interrogation by the Stasi. But it was not Jung they were after.

Peter, donned in a white laboratory coat, sat poring over the intricate designs on his desk. He walked to the blackboard and scribbled some equations. Suddenly, the door crashed open behind him shaking the glass. Turning swiftly on his heel he saw the Stasi agent looming in the doorway.

"Guten morgen Herr Schrader," Peter said casually. "What brings you to the university?"

"You Brandt!" Schrader was still smarting from his fruitless surveillance of the past weeks. "We are investigating an escape carried out two weeks ago. Two students from this university escaped into West Berlin near the Kreuseberg district. Recently, three young women also escaped in the Eiskellar."

Peter raised a quizzical eyebrow and looked directly into Schrader's hooded, venomous eyes.

"I don't know how I can help you Herr Schrader. Why have you come to me?"

"We know all about you Brandt," Schrader sneered, "You've been under surveillance ever since you returned from the Soviet Union in 1957. The Gestapo didn't manage to destroy all the files. Fleischer handed what was left over to us before the Russians strung him up. Your file made interesting reading. Now, what can you tell me about these escapes?"

Peter sighed,

"I know nothing about any escapes. Why would I? My work takes up all my time."

"You're lying Brandt, just as you lied to the Gestapo about getting the Jews out of Berlin."

"You disagreed with helping those people?"

"No, no it was admirable, of course," he added hastily looking over his shoulder. "But, you have experience of subversive operations. Now, answer me Brandt….who is helping you? Is it someone here at the university?"

"I repeat, I know nothing!"

Peter glared defiantly at Schrader.

Red patches of anger mottled the Stasi agent's neck. His eyes bulged like marbles; pieces of glittering steel. He moved menacingly forward until his face was just inches away. Peter could see black hairs in his nostrils, smell his hot, rotten breath.

"We'll be back Brandt. Next time you won't get off so easily," he hissed.

Peter's shoulders sagged as Schrader pushed past the trembling woman and clumped down the passageway.

Bernhardt glanced up as Peter came into the bar and shuffled past the tables to a dark corner at the back. He signalled to the waiter,

"Zwei bier bitte!"

When the waiter had delivered their drinks Peter turned to Bernhardt and whispered,

"The Stasi paid me a little visit today."

"Why? What about?"

"Three young girls escaped into West Berlin from the Eiskellar."

"The Eiskellar, but that had nothing to do with the organisation," Bernhardt cut in."

"Schrader also questioned me about the crossing in Kreuseburg."

"What about the cemetery crossing last night?"

"Nothing. They must know about it by now so they must be keeping quiet for some reason."

"Well, I suppose it must have made them look pretty stupid," Bernhardt chuckled.

Peter rubbed his chin thoughtfully, a worried look on his face.

"We had better pass the word down the line. They're definitely on to something. Jung doesn't know who I am, but it's paramount that the organisation ensures his safety. It must be arranged as soon as possible."

"I'll pass the word along before I fly to Moscow."

Two weeks later Professor Jung, who was due to retire, announced he would be leaving to live with his sister and her husband in Leipzig.

CHAPTER FORTY ONE

West Berlin 1962

Jack had been very thoughtful since his last excursion into East Berlin. Franz had passed on the information about Professor Jung's sudden departure from the university. More intriguing was that the Stasi hadn't been after him. So who were they after? His thoughts were interrupted by Major Bryant impatiently tapping his desk with a ruler.

"Intelligence knows about all escape attempts into the British Sector. The Americans keep us pretty much up to date with what's going on as well. But I've been informed that a family escaped into the French Sector near St. Hedwig's cemetery right under the noses of the Grepos. The Stasi believe it was the work of an organised group with contacts in West Berlin."

"From what you've told me that makes sense," Jack responded.

"I want you to meet with our contact in Glienicke and see what you can find out Jack. If there is an underground movement it would be useful to know who's running it?"

"Okay, I'll do what I can, but I'm sure we would have heard from our contacts in East Berlin if there is an organisation. Personally I'm rather sceptical."

Jack was nursing a beer in a darkened corner of the inn when Erich walked in.

"Guten abend Jack."

"Good evening Erich. Beer?" Jack queried signalling to the waiter.

"Schnapps bitte. My bones are frozen! It's been so cold and so much snow!" Erich exclaimed.

Settled with their drinks he leaned towards Jack conspiratorially. Occasionally, they laughed loudly as though they were sharing a salacious joke.

"Did you hear about the escape into the French Sector a couple of weeks ago?" Jack whispered.

"Ja, breathtakingly dangerous, but so brilliant!" Erich chuckled. "I would have given anything to see Schrader's face."

"Schrader? He was the one I saw marching down the corridor in the university. I assumed he was going to see Jung."

"Jung has left the university, as you know. No, there has to be someone else there the Stasi is interested in. I don't know who, but I'll find out what I can."

"I must admit I'm intrigued. It must be someone very daring, or very foolhardy, to try to outwit the Stasi."

"Have you finished with Rilke's poetry yet?" Erich said loudly enough for fellow drinkers to hear him.

"Yes, it was wonderful," Jack replied handing it over. "Perhaps I could borrow another? You have such an interesting collection."

"Ah, I've brought you something by Heinrich Böll. It was a gift specially bound for me."

Handing him the book Erich whispered,

"Tonight... the Blue Swan near the river... nine o' clock."

Jack and Helen walked quickly towards the restaurant near the river. A laughing group pushed their way inside already intoxicated with the atmosphere. Bright light spilled from the open doorway, pooling into frosty, golden puddles.

"It's freezing!" Helen exclaimed. "I think I'd rather have stayed in and curled up with a good book."

Little clouds of white vapour floated in front of her face. She slapped her gloved hands together blowing out through her nostrils to emphasise her point.

"Look, I'm smoking like a dragon," she laughed.

Jack pushed the door behind him as they entered a small foyer where an attendant was handing out cloakroom tickets.

"This way sir," beamed a short, rotund man with wobbly jowls.

He seated them at a table near a window, fussed with the tablecloth; adjusted the candle flickering in a glass holder in the centre of the table. With a flourish he gave each of them a red, leather-bound menu.

"You would like some drinks?"

"Yes, something to warm us up. Whisky bitte."

Jack looked enquiringly at Helen.

"I'll have a dry sherry."

"Steak, pomme frites and coleslaw. Helen?"

"Veal with sautéed potatoes."

Sipping their drinks they surveyed the room. Tables set with white cloths, covered with squares of bright red, edged a highly-polished, postage-stamp dance floor. Candlelight flickered on the gleaming cutlery and glass bud vases holding a single, white flower.

A man on one of the tables was speaking into a telephone. Moments later he stood and crossed the room to where a young woman was getting up from her table. Her companions smirked surreptitiously behind their hands. Bowing slightly he whisked her onto the dance floor. Suppressing a giggle Helen remarked,

"Did you see that? There are telephones on all the tables. You've brought me to a pick-up joint."

"Not at all, this is a perfectly respectable place. Major Bryant often comes here with his wife."

He didn't mention that British intelligence often used the restaurant for unofficial 'business'.

It was secluded, dark and discreet. The lights had been dimmed even further for the benefit of the dancers swaying in the middle of the floor. Suddenly, his eyes rested on a couple sitting against the back wall. He sat up and peered through the haze of smoke hovering above the tables. Occasionally, a cigarette glowed red in the darkness. Nodding barely perceptibly the man looked directly at him.

"That must be them."

"What did you say darling?" Helen looked at him quizzically.

"Nothing, I just hit my knee on the underside of the table."

By ten-thirty they had finished their meal. Jack sipped his glass of wine wondering if the contact would approach him. The band leader picked up his baton to announce the next dance.

"The next special request is for *Danke schön*"

That was the signal.

As the band started their rendition the telephone on their table rang, the tone muted for the comfort of diners.

"Mr. Conrad?" a voice queried in heavily-accented English. "Willy Schmidt. When I wave return the gesture as though you have seen a friend then come and join us."

The man waved at him from across the room. Jack waved back.

"Who are you waving at?" Helen asked.

"It's Willy Schmidt!" he laughed. "I haven't seen him for ages."

Helen shrugged her shoulders while Jack continued the conversation, laughing animatedly into the telephone while he looked across at the couple.

"Willy Schmidt? You've never mentioned a…"

"They want us to join them. Come on, it'll be fun! Willy is a real character!"

Jack edged his way around the dancing couples, squeezing through the narrow gaps between the tables.

"Jack, so good to see you again," Willy laughed, standing up to help Helen with her chair. "Marta, my wife," he introduced the dark-haired woman with him.

"It's a pleasure to meet you Frau Schmidt."

"Please call me Marta."

For the next half an hour they talked and laughed like old friends. Willy reminisced about times they had spent with mutual friends before the Wall went up. Nonplussed, Helen listened to the banter. This was the first she had heard of Willy Schmidt.

"Would you like to dance Helen?" Willy asked.

She hesitated, looking at Jack and Marta who nodded their approval.

Willy took her hand and escorted her to the floor. He was an excellent dancer and soon she was lost in the rhythm of the tango.

Turning to Jack, Marta lowered her voice so that he had to lean in closely to hear what she was saying.

"I've found out that Schrader has been keeping a close eye on certain people. What I've discovered, from a reliable source, is that there is an organisation getting people out of East Berlin. Nobody knows who they are. Information is handed down the line on a need to know basis only. It's shrouded in secrecy. The rumour is that it's fronted by someone known only as *Regis*. A mysterious character like the Scarlet Pimpernel. It could be a man or a woman, nobody knows."

"Are there ways of contacting *Regis*?"

"Not *Regis*, but there are ways of forwarding 'requests' for help. Messages are left in specific places. The message is picked up, processed and sent along the line in the same way until it reaches one of *Regis*' deputies."

"Are the deputies known within the organisation?"

"No, they are also shrouded in mystery."

Jack rubbed his chin thoughtfully, pretending to watch Helen dancing as she dipped and swayed to the music.

"Is it possible to request a meeting with *Regis*?"

"No, there's never any physical contact. There are a few trusted members who know each other from the old days, but not even they know the identity of the big three."

"The old days?"

"Apparently, they are the ones who worked for a German underground movement during the war. Most of them were tortured and killed by the Gestapo, but a few survived undetected."

"Find out if I can send a message to *Regis* myself; where I can make the drop?"

"Very well, but it could take some time."

He opened his mouth to speak, but Marta cast him a warning look as Helen returned to the table.

Jack waited impatiently for word from Marta. Days had passed with no sign of contact. At the end of the week he met up with Erich for a drink in the inn on the river.

"Our friend tells me that your message has been sent. Now you must wait a while longer. They will check you out before responding."

"Check me out?"

"Yes, they will want to be sure you are who you say you are. They won't take Marta's word for it or mine. They'll cover their tracks every inch of the way to ensure there are no leaks, no informants. Not even Willy and Marta are who you think they are," Erich chuckled.

CHAPTER FORTY TWO

West Berlin 1963

The sky was a bright sheet of gleaming white, interspersed with heavy, slate-grey snow clouds. Weak beams of light from a colourless sun slanted off icicles hanging like frosted pendants on the pine trees. Slush slapped against the mud flaps as Jack negotiated the rutted side road amongst the large, detached houses near the river in Glienicke. Affluent West Germans had summer retreats here closed up now for the winter.

He glanced quickly at one of the houses. He had spent some pleasant evenings there last summer sitting by the pool, illuminated by toadstool lights. Rolf, the big, bluff banker, who had fought under Rommel in the Second World War, entertained them with old Bavarian folk songs while they sipped steins of cold beer

The harsh brightness bounced painfully off his eyeballs. Snow cleared from paths lay piled in front of houses. Dirty now from slush and mud thrown up by passing vehicles. A man came out and threw sand on his drive. He glanced briefly across at the uniformed man in the Ford Tournus then turned away. It was not an unusual sight. A number of servicemen lived in rented accommodation in the area.

Jack continued down towards the river, slewed the car around and back-tracked the way he had come. Quickly, he unwound the window and pushed a buff-coloured envelope into a mailbox set into the wall of a grey, stone-built house. As he drove away a man came into sight carrying a briefcase. Swiftly, he opened the mailbox, reached in, grabbed the letter and hurried away. It had taken less than a minute for the drop off and pick up.

The response was swift and clear. There would be no meetings, but *Regis* was prepared to cooperate with British

Intelligence to aid escapes to the West. Jack would be contacted when the organisation was ready to move. There was no other information.

Jack knew there had been a number of escape attempts organised by *Regis* mainly at the border crossings on the outer ring. One near the Bornholmer border point and another at Heinrich-Heine Strasse, one of the largest border crossings

Their first collaboration took place in the spring of 1963 at the Sonnenallee border crossing. An area that attracted less attention than the more notorious crossings such as Checkpoint Charlie. *Regis* had planned it meticulously, but the risks were enormous.

It couldn't have been a more perfect night for an escape. The moon, shrouded by dark, unbroken clouds; a sky so black it felt suffocating. Sheets of water beat into the ground already soaked from days of unrelenting, driving rain. Concealed under some trees Jack waited with a small detachment of soldiers ready to haul the escapees into the West.

Overhanging branches, burdened with an excess of moisture, dripped onto his shoulders soaking the collar of his camouflage jacket. A man rustled in the undergrowth at his side. Jack held up a hand to silence him.

"Quiet!" he whispered.

Muffled shouts, amidst the clatter of boots, sounded on the canal bank.

Jack shuddered when he saw the young boy running towards him clothes soaking wet, hair plastered to his head. Eyes wide with terror he stumbled and fell as shots cracked all round him. For a few heart-stopping seconds he lay prone on the damp ground.

In that instant the heavens parted as though a sluice gate had been opened. It obliterated everything. The boy raised his head slightly and began to crawl towards them.

"Come on! Come on!" Jack urged. "He's almost there! Now!"

Two soldiers rushed towards the boy. They stretched out as far as they dared, grasped his hand and hauled him to safety.

"We've got you son; you're okay,"

"Danke! Danke!"

By the time the downfall had abated the boy was wrapped in an army blanket, bundled into the back of a DKW and whisked away.

Now summer had arrived the city bustled with the usual tourists and families of service personnel. Glienicke was a haven of tranquillity. Jack lay in bed listening to the dawn chorus coming from the woods opposite the house. Hundreds of them singing their individual songs in a cacophony of music.

Helen lay next to him breathing quietly. Her long lashes fluttered as she dreamed her dreams. He felt for the flatness of her stomach, placed his hand over where their unborn child had been. The doctor had smiled benignly; told them it was just one of those things when she had miscarried six weeks into her pregnancy. But he knew that his intelligence operations caused her continued stress. He was away from home too much during the night. So far she had refused every suggestion to go and stay with her parents for a while. Now he was preparing for another escape attempt.

The sun shone hard and bright in a cloudless blue sky as Jack drove from Glienicke towards Spandau. A gentle breeze ruffled the leaves on the street trees. Everything seemed so peaceful and calm. If it were not for the Wall on his left it would be difficult to believe that Berlin was in crisis. As usual the Grepos followed his progress from their position high on the looming goon tower. Seeing it never failed to depress him. It was a constant reminder that this beautiful city was divided.

In the summer months soldiers' families took the opportunity to visit West Berlin during their tour of duty.

Today he was escorting a party around the city. Visits into East Berlin were restricted, but they were allowed a sightseeing tour to the Soviet War Memorial at Treptow. Intelligence had ensured that he had been assigned as the accompanying officer.

"This is going to be a dangerous operation Jack," Major Bryant warned him earlier that morning. "The bus will be full of civilian passengers. Not even the sergeant assigned to the tour knows what's been planned. The less anyone knows the better."

"Understood sir."

"Well, good luck Conrad."

Jack left Major Bryant's office knowing that this time he was on his own.

His stomach gave a slight lurch when he pulled up outside the hotel in Charlottenberg and saw the crowd of sight-seers getting on the coach. Whatever happened he couldn't put their lives at risk. Apart from their safety it would be all too easy to spark an international incident.

Regis had contacted him via the usual channels. Jack had passed the information on to intelligence. They would be standing by in case it all went pear-shaped. But if the Stasi caught him intelligence would have to deny all knowledge of the escape attempt.

As they drove towards the checkpoint Major Jamieson, the official guide for the day, painted a vivid description of Hitler's last days.

"Over there is the bunker where Hitler and Eva Braun committed suicide. Their bodies were doused with petrol and burned."

One of the male tourists piped,

"Some say he didn't die, that he was smuggled out to South America."

Jamieson nodded,

"There were dozens of 'sightings' of Hitler. He was supposedly spotted in Argentina, Brazil and a lot of other places. None of them were proved. However, I did hear a very strange story when I was in Rome last year."

"I'm sure we'd all like to hear about it, wouldn't we?" the man urged.

"Well, it was in June last year. I was having a mid morning coffee on the terrace of the hotel where I was staying. A man on the table next to me remarked on the glorious weather. We struck up a conversation and it turned out he was German. He had been one of the Führer's dentists and swore that the remains of the teeth found weren't Hitler's. I queried this account, because another dentist had verified that they *had* been Hitler's teeth. But he was adamant that *his* story was true. I leave it to you to make up your own minds."

Excited chatter filled the coach as they approached Checkpoint Charlie. Armed East German guards watched warily as the coach eased its way towards the barrier. A guard motioned to Jack to get off the bus. He turned to the group who had suddenly fallen silent at the sight of guns pointed at them. Jack showed the authorisation papers and jumped back on.

"You must all open your passports and hold them flat against the window so that the guards can see them clearly."

Muted voices as they pulled them out and put them on view. A deathly hush fell over the group. A guard walked along the side of the coach examining the documents. He stopped in front of a plump, dark-haired woman and scrutinised her passport. Her hand trembled as she struggled to keep it against the window. Two British soldiers stood on the steps of the bus preventing the guards boarding. After what seemed an eternity they waved them on.

The woman slumped in her seat. Turning to her husband she said in a voice querulous with anxiety,

"I thought we'd had our chips then!"

CHAPTER FORTY THREE

East Berlin 1963

Grey and dilapidated the contrast between East and West Berlin was stark and unreal. Bombed out buildings still lined the deserted streets almost twenty years after the war. Some had sacking covering the windows. As they passed an old woman plucked the coarse material aside and gazed forlornly at the coach. One of the tourists waved at her. In a spontaneous gesture she lifted her hand then let it drop. She was too afraid to wave back in case she was seen by the ever-present Stasi. Quickly, she dropped the sacking and disappeared from sight.

Everything seemed so silent and deserted. At intervals the coach swerved to avoid small craters in the road. What had struck Jack the first time he had gone into the Russian Sector was the absence of traffic. Unlike West Berlin there were very few vehicles around. The whole area portrayed a sense of despair and desolation.

His thoughts were interrupted by an excited voice.

"Look, there it is!"

Looking around uneasily the driver, planted by *Regis*, eased to a stop outside Treptow Park.

"This is the only place you're allowed to get off the coach," Jack warned the group. "You can go inside and wander about, but don't approach any of the soldiers. You'll be under surveillance all the time you're here. You may not see anybody, but you can be certain they'll be watching so don't take any chances."

"Can we take photographs?"

"Yes, but only inside the memorial park. No binoculars," he instructed an elderly, dapper man wearing a natty bow tie.

Passengers fussed with their belongings, grabbing cameras and sunhats. Uncertainly, they stood alongside the coach eyeing the Russian soldiers with trepidation.

"They're just young boys," whispered a woman to her companion. "I'm sure that one can't be more than fifteen years old at the most."

The young soldiers swaggered with their hands behind their backs. Peaked caps, maroon coloured tunics gathered at the back, and black jackboots. In the small of the back a pistol sat ominously visible to all.

Hesitantly, the group shuffled towards the entrance. In the avenue leading to the entrance an enormous, imposing figure of Mother Russia wept for her dead heroes. They walked up the avenue lined with trees that seemed to be weeping with her. A corporate gasp of admiration emanated from the group.

"Look at that!" one of the men muttered. "It's enormous. I've never seen anything like it!"

Awed, they walked between the huge, red, Soviet flags carved from marble recovered from the demolished Reich Chancellery. At the base of each flag a statue of a kneeling Soviet soldier faced another on the opposite side.

In the central area sat huge wreaths cast in bronze. Flanking the main concourse sixteen stone sarcophagi representing each of the Soviet republics. Relief carvings of battle scenes adorned the sides with quotes from Stalin in German and Russian.

"Over five thousand Red Army soldiers are buried here," Jack commented.

"It's incredible, just magnificent!" the man with the bow tie exclaimed.

"It makes me feel so sad," one of the women murmured, "so many sons, so many mothers who mourn."

"Look at the size of that statue!" exclaimed another. "It's fantastic!"

Walking towards the main monument, set on a small hill, they found themselves over-shadowed by the size of it. They stared up at the impressive twelve-metre structure. On top of the enormous plinth a soldier stood on a crushed Swastika carrying a child on one arm. In his other hand he wielded a sword.

They mounted the steps leading up to the base and stepped inside. People were laying wreaths under the huge, colourful mosaics of figures leaning over mourning their dead. This was where Jack was to make contact.

He watched as a woman came out from the base and walked slowly along the concourse. Occasionally, she stopped to gaze at the inscriptions on the sarcophagi then made her way back towards the monument. Again she paused, standing back to admire it before stepping back inside. Jack followed her stopping a few feet away to scrutinise the mosaic.

"Wonderful workmanship!" she exclaimed.

"I wonder who the artist is? Russian, I suppose?" Jack queried.

"Yes, Gorpenko, I believe," the woman replied.

"The Soviets certainly know how to impress."

"The hearts of Russian mothers lie here."

Jack breathed a sigh of relief. It was the signal he had been waiting for. He tailed the woman when she left the monument. Taking care to stop and admire the reliefs on the sarcophagi he wandered back towards the entrance. As he passed her he whispered,

"Follow me to the coach and mingle with the crowd."

Jack had made contact with two others by the time he had rounded up the group. Getting them on the coach was the tricky part. They had been counted when they arrived. Another count would be made when they got back on. The man in the bow tie was still lingering at the entrance taking a photograph.

"Start getting them on," he urged the driver, "I'll go and round up our roving photographer."

As the passengers were checked onto the vehicle, bow tie man approached a small group of Russian soldiers wielding his camera. He had been thoroughly briefed. Jack had gone over the plan, time after time, to ensure there were no loopholes. A large bribe of American cigarettes and a couple of cheap souvenirs had persuaded the young Russian soldiers to pose.

"Look at that idiot! He's asking them to have a photograph taken with him!" cried a woman nervously.

Jack rushed over to intervene, but one of the soldiers snapped to attention and grinned at the camera. The others followed suit.

"What a fool! He'll get us all into trouble!"

Everyone turned to look including the driver who was busily checking numbers. As Jack stepped forward to shout at the man three figures sidled out of the group and disappeared into the coach.

"Wonderful! Wonderful! Wait till I show this to the folks back home!" piped bow tie man.

"Get on the coach," Jack said sharply.

Their eyes met for a brief instant before he was counted and bundled aboard.

Jack was perspiring heavily by the time they got back to Checkpoint Charlie. He had three extra passengers on the coach hidden under the back seat. An engineer had lifted the seat off the box, hinged it and raised it slightly. Air holes had been drilled concealed by the lip of the upholstery. There was barely enough room for them to move. In this hot weather conditions would be unbearable, especially with the weight of passengers sitting on top of them. Jack couldn't believe the brazen scheme had actually worked, but they weren't out of trouble yet. They still had to get through the heavily-guarded border post.

The checkpoint seemed more secure and threatening than when they had first come through it that morning. Sullen guards strolled leisurely round and round the coach tapping the bodywork and peering under the chassis. A few months before a young student had tried to escape by hanging onto the chassis of a lorry. When the guards started to search underneath he dropped to the ground, crawled away from under the lorry and ran. Gunfire cracked in the air as he dodged and weaved under the barrier. A hail of bullets brought him crashing to the ground with his upper body in the East and his feet in the West.

For ten minutes he lay writhing in agony. Guards both sides stood poised to shoot, but they didn't move to help him; afraid to shoot at the Grepos, because it was outside their jurisdiction. Finally, a G.I. tried to pull him to safety. As soon as he grabbed the boy's feet the guards trained their guns on him. The Grepos left him to bleed to death. Only when they were sure he was dead did they drag his body from beneath the barrier.

A guard stepped onto the coach and looked down the aisle. Heart hammering Jack stood on the top step. If the Grepo insisted he would have to let him walk the length of the vehicle to take a head count. The guard started forward, hesitated, then stepped off the coach complaining loudly about the heat.

Jack breathed a huge sigh of relief when they were waved through. They passed through the checkpoint and headed towards the busy, colourful, cosmopolitan streets of West Berlin. The buzz of shoppers and workers returning from lunch was somehow comforting. Tourists laughed and talked in the pavement cafés. Impatient drivers dodged and weaved through traffic snarling the roads. Trams lurched their way down the main thoroughfares. This could be a city anywhere in Europe he thought, out of sight of the Wall.

After dropping off passengers at the hotel they drove swiftly to the coach depot and parked up behind the buildings. Jack and the driver rushed to the back and prised up the seat. The two men struggled out taking huge gasps of air into their lungs.

Between them they reached in and pulled the woman out. She flopped like a rag doll, eyes closed in her pale face. Jack lay her down on the seat and gently shook her.

"Water!" he yelled.

The driver thrust a bottle at him. Jack held it to the woman's lips, but she didn't respond. He grabbed it and slowly let the water trickle into her mouth. Pouring some onto his handkerchief he dabbed her forehead and neck while gently tapping her face with the palm of his hand. Her eyelids flickered then opened wide. A pair of misty grey eyes stared up at him.

"You're safe now, you're in the West," Jack murmured.

Slowly, she sat up, tears spilling down her cheeks. She grasped Jack's hand and kissed it. He looked at the driver and grinned.

"Another one like today and I'll be sprouting grey hairs!"

The situation was getting more and more dangerous. Sooner or later, everything was going to blow up in his face.

CHAPTER FORTY FOUR

West Berlin 1963

Crowds lined the streets as they waited expectantly for the cavalcade to appear. There was an unusual excitement and tension in the air. It pulsed and vibrated through the mass of people jostling for a good view. A shout went up when a black police car came into sight followed by an open-topped limousine.

"There he is!" Helen yelled above the roar and cheers of the crowd.

President John F. Kennedy stood in the rear of the vehicle. Hair glowing auburn, white teeth flashing, he smiled and waved at the crowds. Behind the car a contingent of *'white mice'* on their motorcycles; West Berlin police dressed in white jackets.

An excited woman sprang from the pavement to get a better view. From nowhere a figure appeared and ushered her back into the crowd. Jack gave a brief nod to a familiar face near the barrier. There were plain clothes police and intelligence agents everywhere.

Outside the Schöneberg Rathaus thousands of Berliners, wild with excitement, clapped and cheered as though they would never stop.

"Isn't he handsome?" Helen squeaked with delight.

"Yes, I suppose he is," Jack responded in a perfunctory tone.

"You're just jealous!"

Jack wasn't listening. He was scanning the area for any sign of unusual activity.

Total silence fell over the crowd. All eyes were on the President as he began to speak. But Jack's eyes were still searching the mass of people. An assassination attempt could turn the Cold War into a third world war conflagration.

Jack turned his gaze back to the podium. JFK was coming to the end of his speech. Mesmerised, the crowd was gazing up at him still hanging on to every word. Flashing his charismatic smile he announced,

"Ich bin ein Berliner!"

A deafening roar split the air like the rush of wind through a tunnel. The crowd went wild, cheering, shouting, clapping, waving their arms with excitement. Sombrely, Willy Brandt reminded them about those still imprisoned behind the Wall. As he finished speaking a haunting sound filled the air. A hush descended on the crowd.

"What's that?" Helen whispered.

"It's the Freedom Bell in the Rathaus. A gift from the Americans after the war. It's tolled every day at noon."

With a final wave the President was whisked away surrounded by his bodyguards. Reluctantly, people were beginning to push their way through the mass of bodies.

"Come on, let's start moving or we'll never get out of the crowd."

Jack drove home through the gloom of a late autumn evening. Patches of gold, red and brown littered the roadside where leaves had fallen, leaving the trees bare and stark against the failing light. Clouds scudded across a pale moon like ghostly ships in full sail. A slight mist blurred the outline of trees in the woods to his left as he skirted the Wall on his way to Glienicke. Except for the vibrant colours, he had always hated the sense of decay in November. A restlessness and melancholy filled him. He didn't want to leave Berlin, but in another few months he would be going back home before re-assignment.

"We have to cool it for the time being," Major Bryant had said, "and no protests Jack. It's come directly from the top."

"Yes sir, but…"

"No more escape attempts."

"But sir!"

"That will be all Mr. Conrad."

Tensions had increased between East and West German guards at checkpoints and border crossings. This had meant a stop to his activities with *Regis*. They couldn't afford to risk sparking an international incident. Especially after the Bay of Pigs and the Cuban Missile Crisis which had exacerbated the Cold War. Nothing had happened for months until two days ago.

Regis was planning another escape attempt. If only he knew more about him, but there was nothing. Drops for information and requests were the only connection he had to him. He had made exhaustive enquiries via Erich, but his identity remained a complete mystery. Nonetheless, Jack was determined to cooperate with *Regis* this last time before he was posted.

The house was in darkness when he arrived home. Helen had gone to a late lunch with friends, but she should have been home by now. Still, Walter, the German civilian driver employed by the army, would bring her home safely.

Jack piled some logs on the smouldering fire from the basket in the hearth. He poured himself a large whisky and settled into the big armchair. The logs caught a flame spitting and crackling in the grate. Firelight danced off the walls in the semi-darkened room giving it a mellow, golden glow. The heat lulled him into a gentle torpor. Yawning loudly, he drifted into a light doze.

He sat up, immediately alert, at the sound of wheels crunching on gravel. Doors slammed, feet clattered on the stone flags of the porch.

"Goodnight Walter," Helen called as she closed the front door. "Jack! Jack!"

"In here. What's wrong?" Jack queried noting her flushed, excited face.

"Haven't you heard?"

"Heard what?"

"President Kennedy! He's been assassinated!

"Assassinated?"

"He was shot in Dallas, Texas! It was about 12.30 p.m. in the States - central standard time." Her eyes filled with tears. "Oh Jack, to think he looked so full of life... so handsome when we saw him in June. I just can't take it in."

"Sit down and drink this," Jack ordered pushing a whisky into her hand. "This is bound to have international repercussions. Accusations will be flying right, left and centre. Just relax while I ring headquarters."

A few minutes later he re-appeared rubbing his chin thoughtfully.

"As I suspected, all sorts of rumours are flying around. Conspiracy theories involving the CIA, KGB, all sorts. All intelligence personnel are being briefed at nine o' clock tomorrow morning."

"I'll prepare dinner," Helen said without enthusiasm.

"Tell you what, let's go out for dinner. You can bet Erich will be down at the inn tonight. It'll cheer us up."

The restaurant was a buzz of excited, incredulous conversation. Everyone was talking about JFK, creating their own version of the assassination. Helen dropped into a chair beside Erich's petite wife.

"This could be very tricky if the Russians are involved," Erich stated. "Some are saying Kennedy's been murdered as payback for the Cuban Missile Crisis; that the KGB is to blame."

"Well, it's possible, I suppose," Jack pondered, "but I don't think the Soviets would be stupid enough to order the assassination of the President of the United States. Still, security will be tightened even more until the government issues a definite statement."

"Have you thought about the latest request?" Erich asked abruptly changing the subject.

"I'm having problems with Major Bryant. He's put a hold on my activities. Won't budge an inch. Now with this business…."

Jack left the sentence hanging in the air.

"I'll pass it down the grape vine."

"No, somehow or other I'm going to help this last time."

"Ah, I almost forgot to give your book back," Erich laughed, handing over a copy of '*Wuthering Heights*'.

Jack stuffed it in his pocket as the waiter approached to take them to their table.

Later that evening he riffled through the pages and found the coded message he was looking for. Tomorrow morning he would go to Toc H in Spandau before the intelligence briefing.

At 0900 hours Jack joined his colleagues in Major Bryant's office. He had very little to tell them except that security had been tightened.

"Conspiracy theories are rife. The border guards are as jumpy as hell," he warned. "Obviously, the KGB is denying all knowledge. The same goes for the CIA and Castro's lot. We'll just have to sit tight and see what develops."

Jack approached him as the others filed out.

"Sir, can you spare me a few moments."

"What is it Conrad?"

"I know you've put a hold on helping *Regis* but this 'activity' is vital. The group concerned must get out of East Berlin. Lives are at stake."

"I'm sorry Jack. I can't sanction something that could create more tension."

"Hear me out sir. This morning I was briefed by a member of *Regis* here in West Berlin. I don't know much, but it seems the men they want to get out are key people in the organisation. Apparently, they worked for the Russians after the war in their rocket research centres in the Soviet Union. They must have incredible amounts of intelligence that would be invaluable to us. We shouldn't pass up a chance like this to glean first-hand information."

"Do you know who they are?"

"No, but as soon as I give the nod I'll be contacted again."

Major Bryant crossed his long legs and ran a hand over his balding head. Finally, he said,

"Wait outside a moment."

A few minutes later he opened the door and motioned Jack inside.

"All right Mr. Conrad, but this is the last time. And another thing; you'd better not be seen in uniform anywhere near the contact. That will be all."

Jack saluted smartly and headed for the door before Bryant could change his mind.

"And make sure you hand pick the best men. We can't afford to be caught out on this one, not in the present climate."

Jack breathed a sigh of relief. All he had to do now was go to the cinema.

Helen and Jack lounged in the back of the Volkswagon as Walter manoeuvred the traffic in the Heerstrasse.

"This is such a surprise. I thought you didn't care for the 'flicks'?" Helen teased.

"I don't usually, but this picture is supposed to be very good," Jack enthused.

Ten minutes later they pulled up outside the main entrance of the military cinema.

Settled into comfortable seats they sat back to enjoy the film. The lights dimmed as the projector light whirred into action above their heads.

"Thank goodness nobody is allowed to smoke, not like back home. Sometimes in the Odeon the smoke is so thick you can hardly see the film."

Jack watched patiently as colourful advertisements filled the screen followed by a Pathé news reel. Just as the main feature was about to start a message flashed up on the screen. The audience groaned and stamped their feet.

'*There will be a slight delay while the relief projectionist takes over.*'

He started in his seat as the words loomed in front of his eyes.

"What is it darling? You're getting twitchy, as usual?"

"Nothing, it's just I need to spend a penny before the film starts, I'll pop out now. Won't be long."

He picked his way along the row of seats and hurried to the exit. Quickly, he went into the lavatory and emptied his bladder. While he was washing his hands a man came out of the cubicle behind him. He flicked a brief glance at Jack, rinsed his hands and walked quickly out.

Jack kept washing his hands, staring into the mirror playing for time. Another man came and went. A cleaner idled in with a mop and bucket. Kicking open a cubicle door he mopped the floor, moved to the next one then the next. Slowly, Jack pulled out the roller towel and dried his hands. He took out a comb and slicked back his hair examining the result in the mirror. The attendant crossed to the basins and wiped around the taps without looking at him. Looking at the floor he muttered,

"The golden autumn leaves fell fast this year."

"The woods are alive with colour; first gold and red then brown," Jack replied.

His heart started to thump in his chest anticipating the signal message.

"They will make a pretty bonfire."

"There'll be a great deal of smoke with the fire."

"Listen carefully," the attendant spoke urgently. "Saturday night at Club Bartok. When they parade with the lanterns into the garden wait there."

Suddenly, the lavatory door opened and slammed behind a scrawny, fair-haired youth with acne-scarred skin. He loped to the urinals and stood with his back to them looking nervously over his shoulder. The attendant briefly met Jack's eyes in the mirror before scuttling off with his mop and pail.

CHAPTER FORTY FIVE

West Berlin 1963

For four days Jack had been on tenterhooks trying to find a plausible reason to drag Helen out on the Saturday night.

"I want a quiet weekend in, just the two of us pottering about," she insisted.

"Wouldn't you like to go out for dinner or something?"

"No, we don't get much time alone together these days so let's make the most of it and stay in tonight."

"There's a great cabaret act on at Club Bartok. Come on, let's go. We've had all day today and we'll have all day Sunday to mooch about."

"All right, but only if you shower me with champagne," she laughed teasingly.

"Champagne it is!"

"I'll get dressed."

"Wow!"

Jack let out a low wolf whistle when Helen minced down the stairs, complete with high-heeled winkle pickers and Audrey Hepburn little black dress. The diamond encrusted comb in her hair complemented the glittering drop ear rings that flashed as they caught the light.

"You don't brush up too badly yourself," she beamed.

Jack liked Club Bartok. It was bright and cheerful. They had been there three hours, eaten a wonderful meal and watched the cabaret. Slowly, he sipped from a large brandy balloon surveying the room over the top of the glass. Late diners leaned inwards chatting and laughing animatedly to friends. Waiters scurried amongst the tables with white napkins over their arms. In the middle of the floor dancers swayed to the sound of '*Moon River*'.

Abruptly, the music stopped. A wave of anticipation rippled across the room. Waiters appeared with coloured, paper lanterns hanging from sticks and handed them to the women. Suddenly, the lights dimmed the room to twilight darkness. The band struck up a jolly rendering of some German folk song.

As a body, the diners rose and wandered in and out of tables in a long crocodile swaying their decorated lanterns from side to side.

"Let's join in," Jack enthused.

"It's one surprise after another tonight," Helen retorted. "I've never known you to be so eager."

Jack and Helen tagged on to the crocodile and filed out through the huge glass doors into the garden. He could see the vanguard of the procession, their lanterns like brilliantly-coloured glow worms illuminating the darkness. The cold air hit him like a sledge-hammer, even though he hadn't drunk as much as Helen suspected. He had to keep a clear head.

The conga-like procession weaved unsteadily around the paths and trees. Finally, it headed back to the warmth of the dining room. The procession had been broken at intervals by guests pushing in to join in the fun. Helen was fifteen bodies in front of him. He slowed down and fell back onto a seat letting the rest of the line pass by.

A man, obviously worse for wear, staggered across the grass and leered at him. He stood swaying from side to side then fell onto the seat next to Jack. A woman broke out of the passing line and tried to pull him up, but he shook her off with a jovial smile,

"My head is muzzy fraulein; too much Schnapps, ja?"

Taking out a cigarette he put it between his lips with great deliberation. He offered the pack to Jack.

"You would like a cigarette?"

"No, thanks."

"But I will give you a whole packet of German cigarettes for one British."

"I'm sorry I don't smoke."

"Not even one Senior Service?"

"No, not even for ten packs of German cigarettes."

The man pushed a fountain pen into Jack's cummerbund.

"Conceal it when we stand up. Now, my friend," he laughed loudly, "let's go back inside."

A waiter held open the door for stragglers who gratefully stumbled out of the cold. Both men wobbled and staggered their way back. When the maitre d' opened the door Jack's companion tumbled inside to hoots of laughter from a nearby table. He bowed theatrically before staggering off to join his friends, jolting against tables as he passed.

"Where on earth have you been?" Helen hissed as Jack slumped down beside her.

"Talking to him over there." He pointed at the man holding court to a group of giggling women. "He's jush a lil tipshy thash all," he grinned inanely.

"He's not the only one!"

Frostily, Helen picked up her handbag and marched in the direction of the ladies' powder room.

"I think I'll finish that drink now," Jack grinned to himself.

Bending under the table he retrieved two half full glasses of rather flat champagne. He felt for the pen concealed in his inside pocket. Tomorrow, when Helen was cooking lunch, he would be able to examine its contents. He wondered what daring plan *Regis* had devised this time.

CHAPTER FORTY SIX

East Berlin 1963

In East Berlin Peter, Rudi and Bernhardt huddled in a corner of the dark, dank bar. Wet beer rings on the table glistened dully in the muted light. Peter absent-mindedly jabbed his finger into the liquid and drew it across to meet the others until they were all interlinked.

"While the Wall remains standing free-thinking spirits will always try to escape," he told Rudi.

"But it's more dangerous now. Schrader has suspected you for months. He knows you're involved with the escapes. It's just a matter of time before he puts two and two together," Rudi stated impatiently. "You must get out Peter before it's too late."

"How many lives have been lost already? Young lives like Peter Fechter. Is my life more valuable than theirs? Besides you're also under surveillance. I'm convinced Schrader knows there's a connection between us other than pure friendship."

"All I'm saying is that you must back off for a while," Rudi continued. "Let things cool down. It might put Schrader off the scent."

"Rudi's right Peter," Bernhardt interjected. "You have to be more cautious now."

"Very well, but I must finish what I've started. I got you into this now I'll help you get out."

"But…?"

"You're as much at risk as I am. You'll go first or I will stay here," Peter said emphatically. "I've set up a meeting with someone who can help us; someone loyal to the organisation. He'll be known only as Uncle Max. He works a boat taking river trips on the Spree from Treptower Park. More importantly, his son is in West Berlin. He also runs chartered

432

river trips on the Havel for military families. Pleasure craft are not allowed to traverse the waterways border crossings as you know."

"They have to be thoroughly searched and loaded on to ships to cross over so that's out of the question," Rudi intervened.

"Both men served in the German Navy during the war. They have many contacts on commercial freight carriers navigating the border crossings on the rivers. Some of the ships go out of Hamburg and the Baltic ports. That could be useful to us if we have to leave Germany in a hurry."

"I don't see your point."

"The point, my friend, is that the Spree goes through the centre of Berlin in the Soviet sector and joins the Havel in the western quarters of the city at Spandau. Somehow, Uncle Max contacts his son via a crewman who ships into Berlin regularly, just to let him know how things are with his mother in the East. Young Max is going to reconnoitre the banks of the Havel for the best crossing place and get the information back to his father who'll pass it on."

"You make it sound easy Peter, but the risks are enormous. We'd be shot before we could swim across. It's already been tried."

"Lothar Lehmann tried swimming across the Spree in '61; and what about Erna Kelm who died trying to swim across the Havel last year," piped in Bernhardt. "I agree with Rudi, it's too dangerous."

"Besides it's impossible to cross anywhere especially near Glienicke Bridge. It's too heavily guarded," Rudi continued. "And what about the temperature of the water. You haven't taken that into account."

"The worse the weather the better it will be for us. We must study the forecasts and hope for heavy rain, or better still, snow. I'll need a wetsuit, of course, but you'll be ferried across."

Rudi let out a roar of laughter,

"You are either delusional or a complete madman! There are searchlights everywhere and dogs!"

"I'll be your decoy," Peter murmured.

Rudi and Benhardt looked at each other in stunned silence.

"I'll distract the guards on the Potsdam side, somewhere between the bridge and Pfaueninsel Island, while you cross over above the bridge near Wannsee. The Soviets are allowing West Berliners to apply for permits to visit relatives in the East. Between eighteenth of December and January fifth. This gives us a small window of opportunity to make our move. With any luck it may draw attention away from possible escape attempts."

Peter fell silent waiting for a response from the two men. Rudi rubbed his chin thoughtfully.

"What day will it be?"

"Christmas Eve. That's when the Grepos are most likely to be off their guard, especially with West Berliners going over to visit for the first time. Even some of the guards will want to see family from the West. We strike when their defences are at their weakest."

"What happens if you're seen?"

"That's the whole point. I want to be seen. That way they'll be concentrating on me, not you. Are you with me?"

"Very well," Rudi sighed.

Bernhard gave a slight nod, his face set like cold marble.

"Once the wheels are set in motion there's no going back," Peter stated emphatically. He stood up to leave. "Agreed?"

"Ja, agreed," muttered Rudi and Bernhard heading for the exit.

A blast of icy air slapped across their faces as the door opened. Two hefty men in heavy coats, collars pulled up to their ears, pushed into the bar.

"Stasi," whispered Peter. "I can smell the pigs!"

They crossed the road towards the darkness of the buildings opposite. "They're watching us constantly now. Meet here for a drink on the night of the twenty-first."

Separately, the three men hurried home aware that other agents would be staring after them with watchful, brooding eyes.

CHAPTER FORTY SEVEN

West Berlin 1963

Jack prised the small piece of paper out of the hollow shank of the fountain pen with a paper knife and unrolled it. He grabbed a magnifying glass from the desk and studied the tiny writing. So small it looked like lines of gibberish. He jotted down the second letter of the first and every alternate word then the third letter of those in between. His mouth dropped open as he read the coded contents. He knew that *Regis* had pulled some dangerous stunts, but this latest plan was nothing short of suicide.

"Bryant won't go for this," he muttered. He looked at it again. "I swim on Christmas Eve. I prefer to run. Enjoy your run tomorrow at the peak."

Jack knew that was a reference to the Charlottenburg Athletics Club. The 'peak' meant there would be a drop near Summit House where he would pick up the final instructions.

"Madness! Sheer madness!" he growled.

"What was that darling?" Helen asked as she came into the room.

"Nothing, just thinking out loud."

He had to get down to Charlottenburg as fast as possible.

"I've got to go down to headquarters," he told her bolting through the door before she could question him further.

Jack's brain was in overdrive as he sped along the perimeter of the Wall. In the weak sunlight the goon tower stood out like a watchful, vengeful beast. Two Grepos, immobile against a gun-metal grey sky, followed his progress until he was out of sight.

Charlottenburg was alive with tourists even at this time of year. The clouds had parted revealing a watery, silver sun that glanced off the fountains transforming shooting spray into cascading, liquid diamonds.

Hurriedly, he parked and made his way to the main entrance of Summit House. A British soldier and his family spilled out onto the pavement. He came to attention saluting smartly.

"Sir!"

"At ease corporal," Jack responded.

Unsure of what to do next he entered the building and waited behind the small queue that had formed in front of reception. Realising he would be next in line for information he wandered back outside. A man called,

"Hot chestnuts! Hot chestnuts!"

He shovelled a pile into a bag and offered them to Jack who was about to refuse. The man looked at him, his hand still extended.

"It is very cold mein herr, but I will still swim on Christmas Eve."

Jack straightened up, immediately alert.

"I prefer to run."

"Enjoy your run tomorrow at the peak."

Jack grabbed the bag of chestnuts, slapped some Deutschmarks into the man's hand and hurried away. Impatiently, he drove back to Glienicke dodging lunchtime traffic. Once he was on the open road he put his foot down.

With a screech of brakes he pulled into the drive and darted inside. Breathlessly, he dived into his study, closed the door and delved into the bag. Nothing! He emptied the nuts onto his desk and felt around in the bag exploring the joins. Carefully, he pulled back the layer of paper covering the bottom. Still nothing. Exasperated, he tore the layer off and threw it on the desk.

He slumped heavily into his chair. It has to be here somewhere he thought. Prodding the chestnuts into a heap he swept them into his hand. Then he spotted it. One half-cracked chestnut. Sticking his thumb into the crack he forced it open to reveal a tiny piece of paper screwed into a ball. He unravelled it and stared at the contents.

"This is madness!" he muttered for the umpteenth time that day.

Jack entered Major Bryant's office the next morning with more than a little trepidation. He watched his face as he read the coded message. A flush of red rose up his neck to meet his collar then he threw the paper onto his desk.

"They want to *swim* across the Havel near Glienicke Bridge?" he asked incredulously. "But the bridge is impassable. It's very heavily guarded. No! Absolutely not! There's no way I can sanction this!"

"Sir, these three men are important as I told you before. Think about the intelligence they'll have. You did say you would back *Regis*."

"Not in this kind of foolhardy stupidity!"

"All we'll be doing is covering them as they swim across."

"There'll be an exchange of gunfire. That's inevitable if the Grepos start shooting at them," Bryant snorted. "You know they've agreed to allow West Berliners into the Russian sector to visit families. Something like this could sour the whole process."

"I agree, but we'll be acting solely as British military surveillance personnel protecting the Havel which is in the British Sector. Once they're under the wire and in the water they're on their own until they get close enough for us to assist them in whatever way we can."

Major Bryant dropped into his chair, leaned forward, his chin in his hands. He picked up the paper again and carefully studied the details as he swung from side to side.

"All right, but this had better be done by the book. I have serious reservations about this lunatic plan. Whatever happens you don't put a foot wrong. Is that clear? They'll probably be shot or dead of exposure within minutes," he muttered.

"Yes sir!"

"Fine, now pick your men. Usual arms, SLR 7.62 rifles and light machine guns. God help us all if this goes wrong. Do you know all the details yet?"

"No sir. *Regis* only gives out information on a need to know basis. That way only a small handful have information that could incriminate the organisation and endanger lives."

"Thank God you're being posted in the New Year," Bryant muttered.

CHAPTER FORTY EIGHT

West Berlin 1963

Word had been passed to *Regis* that the British would be waiting for them on the bank of the West side close to Wannsee. Jack shuddered, remembering what plans had been executed in this beautiful suburb. What goes around comes around he thought.

It was here that Obergrüppenfürer Reinhard Heydrich had led the Wannsee Protocol: the Nazis' Final Solution for the deaths of millions of Jews. Now the German people were incarcerated in their own city. In summer they sailed and swam in the blue waters of Lake Wannsee constantly aware of spying eyes.

On Glienicke Bridge and beyond, Grepos silently monitored the waterway with their field glasses. Night after night, day after day, fingers ready on the trigger at the slightest sign of unusual movement along the banks of the river. Why the hell has *Regis* chosen such a dangerous area for this escape attempt? It's suicidal Jack thought. Something's bound to go wrong.

He lay flat on his stomach scanning the opposite bank with his night glasses. His sergeant and four of his men had been positioned at Kleine Wannsee. Another four soldiers lay straggled twenty feet apart from each other as close to the water as they dared.

"Keep down. I don't want to alert the Grepos to anything suspicious," Jack warned as they fanned out. "Just be ready to move as soon as you see anything in the water."

He glanced at the illuminated dial on his watch. Dead on 01.30 hours. Thirty minutes to wait. Sounds of loud music reached their ears from the brightly-lit restaurants along the bank. Christmas revellers would be partying well into the early hours of the morning.

A searchlight slowly panned over the water illuminating deserted pleasure craft bobbing on the surface. Freezing needles of rain sparkled and danced on the surface of the water. Shallow waves rippled across the river as the wind caught the rain slapping it against the shore. Thankfully, thick cloud had obscured the moon camouflaging their presence. He shivered as rain dripped off his beret and trickled down his neck saturating the net camouflage scarf. Once again the beam swept over the water and along the bridge then complete blackness.

East Berlin 1963

Near the river bank in the Soviet sector two men huddled in the undergrowth. On the other side of the Wall a third man waited until the searchlight had panned the *'Death Strip'*. Throwing a grappling hook up over the concrete barrier he hurled a rope over. Satisfied it was secure he waited until he heard the scuffle of feet clambering up the concrete. Clutching a pair of wire cutters he ran towards the barbed wire fence watchful of the probing searchlight.

He cursed as a barb stabbed through his gloves and grazed his skin. He had to work quickly now. In a few minutes the searchlight would be sweeping its way back along the *'strip'*. Every lost second could find him caught like a rabbit in car headlights. Quickly, he sliced through the wire and bent it back giving him just enough room to squeeze underneath. Hurriedly, he closed the gap in the wire before the beam hit the spot and ran for cover.

Rudi pushed from behind as Bernhardt scrambled up the rope using the Wall as leverage. Warily, he watched the searchlight sweeping back towards them. Rudi was only half way up, his feet slipping and sliding on the wet concrete. He was panting from the exertion, his breath coming in short, painful gasps.

"Go on, I can't make it!"

"Yes you can, just a couple more feet."

Bernhardt hauled on the rope, his hands burning with pain. With a last mighty heave Rudi fell on his stomach on top of the Wall. Bernhardt dropped down the other side and ran towards the barbed wire fence. Pressing himself flat he wriggled between the cut wires. The barbs tugged at his clothing, scratched arms and legs until they bled, but still he kept going. Free of the fence he lunged across the open space towards the river and dropped to the ground beside Peter.

Peering through the gloom they waited, but there was no sign of Rudi.

"Something's wrong!" Peter muttered. "Wait here. If I'm not back when the searchlight returns make a run for it!"

Before Bernhardt had time to protest he had gone.

Rudi was caught up in the wire tugging frantically to free his clothes. Peter emerged from the shadows and darted towards him. He held the wire up for him to squeeze underneath just as the harsh light licked the grass a few feet away. Adrenaline flooding his chest he ran towards the bushes and threw himself flat on the ground. Rudi fell down beside him, his breath wheezing in his throat. Suddenly, loud shouts, the sound of muffled feet squelching through damp grass.

"Run for it!" Peter shouted, sprinting towards the river bank.

Now they were scrambling into the water gunfire exploding all round them. Peter shouted something at the two men, but they kept splashing deeper into the cold water. Suddenly, Bernhardt screamed as submerged barbed wire ripped through his leg.

The vague shadow of a boat loomed in the middle distance. Frantically, he swam around straining his eyes for a glimpse of Rudi. He reached out and touched something floating against him in the inky black river. Recoiling in horror he saw it was

Rudi pinned face down in the water by a coil of barbed wire. Struggling against his own fatigue he turned him face up. He grabbed at the wire frantically trying to free him, but it was too late. His mouth was wide open in a silent scream; his eyes bulbous in death.

Something slapped on the water near him.

"Grab the rope and hold on!" a voice ordered.

Guttural shouts echoed across the river. A beam of light searched the water landing on the figure clinging to the rope. Shots cracked all round the boat as it weaved in snake-like fashion towards the British Sector. They hit the bank with a slushy thump.

West Berlin 1963

Bernhardt wanted to sleep; to sink into the water and oblivion. A kind of icy calm suffused his whole being as though he had been wrapped in cold cotton wool. Rudi's face swam before his eyes. Rudi, head thrown back laughing at his own jokes. Rudi, red hair blowing in the wind as he tacked and manoeuvred his yacht over the waves. Rudi, in his death throes; little, black, slimy fish oozing out of his mouth.

He was so tired. His hands slipped off the wet rope and he slid into the water face down. It seemed oddly comforting like drifting into a welcome sleep. He felt himself float away then a cold hand grabbed him and hauled him back to the boat. Voices, different this time; hands grasping to pull him out of the icy river.

A face loomed over him. Strong hands wrapped him in a blanket.

"You're free now," said the face smiling down at him.

"Rudi," he murmured.

"I'm sorry," Jack muttered. "He didn't make it. You were lucky. *Regis* planned this well, sending a decoy in. We're standing by to get him ashore as soon as he crosses into the western reaches of the river."

Suddenly, a shout went up from the Grepos. An arc of harsh, white light drenched the channel separating Pfaueninsel from the bank. Rifle shots cracked, machine-gunfire strafed the water sending plumes of spray into the air. Everything seemed to focus around Pfaueninsel Island. Jack trained his night glasses on the land mass, sweeping over the fairytale castle with its twin towers. Then he saw a dark figure swimming close to the island. It was their man!

"Look at him go! He's a strong swimmer. I think he's going to make it. Just another few metres and he'll be with us. Come on! Come on!"

Jack willed him to keep going, but the figure suddenly disappeared. Jack waited, keeping his glasses trained on the area until he surfaced again. Machine gun fire stuttered all round. Suddenly, a dark shape reared up then fell back into the water.

"He's caught a bullet!" Jack exclaimed.

Peter knew he'd been hit before he felt the pain in his legs and arm. Waves of nausea washed over him. His eyes clouded as though a mist had risen over the river. Still, he thrashed in the black waters. He must focus, keep going. Eleanor's smiling face swam before his eyes, her blue eyes sparkling with merriment as she bounced little Johann on her knee. Keep thinking of the happy times. Keep swimming to Eleanor. Don't black out now or you're a dead man.

Breath rasping in his throat he struggled to keep control. Disorientated, lungs bursting, he swam with his good arm slapping towards the dark outline of Pfaueninsel. Suddenly, something loomed beside him; caught him a glancing blow on the head. Rough hands dragged him out of the water and threw him into the bottom of a boat. Viciously, a boot kicked out at him landing a crippling blow to his stomach. He winced as hands ripped off the rubber headpiece of his wet suit. Someone shone a powerful torch onto his face momentarily blinding him.

"Got you at last *Regis*," a voice sneered.

Peter knew it was all over for him when he heard Schrader's excited, accusing voice.

Across the river Jack stared incredulously at the scene through his night glasses.

"My god, I don't believe it!"

"Sir?" his sergeant spoke enquiringly.

"The decoy they've captured. It's the man I saw in the university. So he was the one the Stasi was after, not Professor Jung," Jack murmured thoughtfully.

Stunned, he watched the boat as it headed for the Soviet Sector shore and bumped against the bank. A flurry of activity echoed across the water; slamming doors, the metallic grinding of gears. In a squeal of tyres they were gone.

Early the following morning Bernhardt was ushered into Major Bryant's office. He gestured for him to sit down.

"Well, you were very lucky. You certainly had a very narrow escape," Bryant observed. "I'm sorry your friend didn't make it."

Bernhardt looked down at his trembling hands, clenching them together to stop them shaking.

"He almost made it," he whispered, but he wasn't as fit as I am, and older. What happened to the decoy?"

"He was captured by the Stasi," Jack said quietly. "He'd been shot, but he was still alive when they dragged him on board the boat."

"He didn't have a chance. He knew the Stasi suspected him; have done for a long time. That's why he acted as a decoy. Schrader's had him watched night and day for months."

"But why was he so interested in the decoy. Surely, Schrader would go after *Regis*, the leader of the organisation."

Bernhardt smiled ruefully.

"The organisation is finished now. I've been involved with *Regis* since the Wall went up, getting people out of the Soviet Sector. But Rudi was a member of the organisation during the war working with the first *Regis*."

"The first *Regis*?"

"Yes, the decoy's uncle. He died of a heart attack trying to protect his estate from the Red Army. A very brave man. He helped hundreds of Jews escape from the Nazis. Peter was his deputy."

"Peter?"

Jack waited for him to continue, but Bernhardt hesitated realising he had said too much. Finally, he muttered,

"Peter Brandt."

Stunned, Jack's mouth fell open. His heart began to bang in his chest like a piston; his mouth felt like dry cork.

"Peter Brandt?" he asked incredulously.

"Yes, but what does it matter now? He'll be a dead man by the time the Stasi finish with him."

CHAPTER FORTY NINE

East Berlin 1964

In Leistikowstrasse KGB prison in Postdam Peter lay on the hard, damp floor. His gunshot wounds had received only perfunctory attention. A squalid medic had extracted the bullet from his left leg. Hot, excruciating pain suffused his body as iodine was poured into the wound. Peter had almost passed out with pain. Miraculously, his arm and right leg had only been grazed.

A glimmer of grey light seeped into the isolation cell from a tiny window high on the wall. The room was barely big enough to hold a man. Peter sat up and gingerly stretched out his good arm. He could touch the walls on either side without moving. Now his eyes were accustomed to the dim light he could see black paint flaking and peeling from the walls. No water to wash or drink. A dirty, thin mattress covered three quarters of the cell. An uncovered bucket, still containing human waste from the previous occupant, stood in a corner. Peter retched as the fetid smell enveloped him. He lay down and forced himself to breathe evenly until the nausea subsided.

Suddenly, a harsh electric light snapped on. Peter shut his eyes and held his arm up to shield himself against the glare. He knew all about this place and the torture techniques employed to get prisoners to talk. This was just one of them. Bright, intrusive light that never dimmed. Constant light that could drive a man mad. He started as he heard the jangle of keys against metal outside. The door swung open silhouetting a stocky figure that almost filled the doorway.

"Good morning *Regis*," Schrader smirked.

Instead of going inside the cell he stayed in the doorway with a handkerchief over his nose and mouth. A delicate, effeminate motion that looked almost comical for the heavy-jowled, hard-faced Stasi agent.

"Take him!" he ordered.

Two Stasi police grabbed his arms and dragged him out of the cell. He was taken to an adjacent building that Peter knew was used for executions as well as interrogation. They threw him into a cell and slammed the door.

He lay on the hard, damp ground with a bright, electric light searing his eyes. On two occasions the door creaked open. Food and water were placed just inside and the door slammed shut again. Eventually, he drifted into a fitful sleep. Dark, evil faces leered at him: Fleischer, Schrader, Brauer. In sleep they came back to haunt him as they always did.

A guard tramped along the corridor. He stopped outside the cell and banged on the metal door with his rifle. When Peter started awake he didn't know whether it was night or day. This was the start of the psychological breaking down of his defences. Every time he drifted into sleep a soldier repeatedly banged on the door until he felt like screaming. You must focus he cautioned himself, otherwise you're lost.

Listening intently he realised that the guards patrolled regularly. He counted the number of seconds between the patrols, scratching a tiny line into the paint on the damp wall with his finger nail. Then he counted the minutes until they returned.

They patrolled every half an hour. Laboriously, he counted off the half hours until the duty team was relieved. He could hear them laughing and joking. One complained about his feet after six hours of marching up and down. One of the new contingent moaned about catching the midnight slot again when he could have been tucked up in bed with his girl. The other guards sniggered.

"Guten nacht," they chorused as they stomped down the corridor.

So it was midnight. The previous guard had come on duty at 18.00 hours.

Peter forced himself to stay awake until the guard changed again, recording every second of every minute. He sang songs in his head, composed silly jingles or conducted an imaginary orchestra. Pacing the few footsteps in the tiny cell he delivered lectures to his university students: anything to keep awake and functioning.

Every time he started to drop off the guards unwittingly helped him by banging on the door. Just as fatigue threatened to engulf him he heard heavy footsteps echoing in the corridor. The guard was changing! It was 0.600 hours! The next change-over would be at midday then again at 18.00 hours. A full circle!

His eyelids drooped involuntarily as he drifted into blessed sleep. It didn't matter now. He knew he could keep track of the days by the changing of the guards. Besides they wouldn't let him sleep for long. Thirty minutes at most.

Over the coming days the Stasi employed its new tactics for interrogation. Physical torture had been repeatedly condemned by the media. Now they resorted to psychological torture. Torture that left men weeping, bereft and confused. No bruises, no cigarette burns, no broken arms. They employed more sophisticated tactics now. Instead they broke a man's mind and spirit.

Peter had lost the first two days, but knew that another two days had passed since he had been thrown into the cell. On the fifth day he heard the screech of metal against metal as bolts were drawn back. Schrader and another Stasi agent stood in the open doorway.

"You must be feeling confused Herr Brandt," Schrader laughed as he dangled Peter's watch in front of him.

"Yes," Peter lied. "What time is it?"

"Time for you to tell me what I want to know *Regis!*" he snarled.

"I have nothing to tell you. I don't know this *Regis*. I don't know what you're talking about."

"You, *Regis*, have been organising escapes into the West for a number of years. That is a crime against the State."

"It's true I was trying to escape along with my friends, but that's all. I have no connection with anyone known as *Regis*."

Schrader's eyes bulged in his heavy face. His hand flashed towards Peter then stopped. He let it drop and hang limply at his side. Spittle oozed from the corners of his mouth, but he managed to control his anger. He had read Brandt's Gestapo files: how they had beaten and tortured him. This man would not break easily. Casually, he leaned against the cell wall, took out a cigarette and offered the pack to Peter who shook his head.

"Your friend Rudi Schiller is dead," he said quietly. "The other one was shot as he tried to swim to the West."

Dropping his head into his hands Peter let out an anguished cry.

"You bastard!" he screamed lunging for Schrader.

"Ah, so I have touched a nerve *Regis*."

Peter felt angry with himself for allowing Schrader to rattle him. This was just the beginning. He must remain calm and unruffled. With a mighty effort he managed to compose himself.

"Well Brandt, how do you feel now?"

"I have nothing more to say."

"All we want is for you to confess that you are *Regis*."

"'I've told you, I am not *Regis*. *Regis* is dead. He died during the war."

"Very well Brandt. We will talk again when you are feeling more cooperative."

Schrader marched out. The door slammed shut. The lights stayed on. The only relief from the glare was when he lay on his stomach and buried his face in his arms. He thought of smashing the bulb, but they would only replace it; keep on replacing it.

Peter slept in snatches relying on the survival instincts he had nurtured in Sachsenhausen. The rattling of keys and banging on cell doors woke him every half hour reminding him of the time. Every roster registering the parts of the day. By the following morning he felt refreshed, resilient and determined. When Schrader arrived he was surprised to see Peter sitting cheerfully on the floor, his legs drawn up to his chin.

"Now Brandt, let's get down to business. You are *Regis*. You have regularly organised escapes into West Berlin. We know you were involved in getting Jews out of Berlin during the war. Very admirable. We approve of your stance against the madman Hitler, but now you are working against the State. We cannot allow that to happen."

"I repeat, I have nothing to say except that I am not *Regis*."

"Peter, I may call you Peter?" Schrader asked politely.

"Call me whatever you like."

"Peter, think about your wife Eleanor and your son, Johann."

Peter froze, mouth dry, heart beating violently against his ribcage. How could he know about them?

"Your files were salvaged from Fleischer's office before he could finish destroying all the incriminating evidence against you. She is very pretty."

Schrader leaned forward and held out a photograph. It was a picture of him with Eleanor and Johann sitting on a bench in the Tiergarten. A rush of love filled his chest mixed with such pain he could hardly bear it.

"Where did you get it?"

"It was with a number of photographs in the files. We know your wife was smuggled out of Germany with your son. We know where they are now."

"You're lying!" Peter snarled.

"Why don't you be reasonable? Tell us what we want to know about the organisation. In return you will be given safe passage to join your family in the United States."

Peter sat stock still staring at the opposite wall, his face impassive.

"Think about it Brandt. This is your last chance!" Schrader hissed.

Peter wasn't listening. He was in another place in another time. Birds sang amongst the ruffling branches in the Tiergarten. Eleanor smiled at him as happy families strolled by enjoying a sunny afternoon.

During the following weeks the Stasi tried every psychological method to break his spirit. Promises of freedom, imprisonment or execution had no effect. All he gave them was lies. Worse than the threat of death was the incessant, loud, grating music that filled the cell. The single light overhead switching on and off, on and off, on and off. The sound of water dripping, dripping, dripping until he wanted to scream.

But he never screamed, just bit his lip until it bled. Sometimes they showed him his reflection in a mirror. He didn't recognise the haggard man staring back at him. His hair matted with filth, bloodshot eyes, weeping sores seeping through the unkempt beard. Every day the constant questioning: the same questions over and over again. He struggled to focus on anything that took his mind away from Schrader's grating, insistent voice.

By the time he was tried and sentenced he had become an automaton. Waking, sleeping, eating meagre rations, savouring the rancid supply of water. But he didn't break. After six months of interrogation he was sentenced to twenty years hard labour in the Siberian Gulag.

"That will be the end of you *Regis*," Schrader gloated as he was bundled away. "Not even you will last that long in the Gulag."

But the Party had other ideas. Peter's expertise and knowledge of rocket design and astro-physics were again invaluable to the Communists. He had been working on new design data for one of the projects in the Soviet space programme when he was arrested.

Siberia 1964 - 1984

After three months of unspeakable deprivation and savage beatings in the Gulag he was dragged from his bed in the middle of the night.

"Where are you taking me?" he asked.

The surly, broad-faced soldier ignored him. Roughly, he prodded him with the muzzle of his rifle into the back of a truck.

This was it. His time had come. He had persistently denied having anything to do with *Regis*. It was the only thing he could do to protect members of the organisation from certain death. Now, he was to be shot like a dog in this bleak wasteland.

For days they bumped and jerked along the rutted roads. The isolation in the truck was a blessed release from the over-crowded conditions in the camp. He lay on the cold, metal floor curled into a ball. Every jolt to his bruised, emaciated body made him wince with pain. Too exhausted and weak from hunger he didn't even think of trying to escape. Lulled by the darkness in the vehicle he closed his eyes and drifted into a dreamless sleep.

He was awakened by a harsh voice issuing orders.

"Get out!"

A rifle butt poked him in the stomach nudging him down from the truck. A soldier prodded him inside a building and pushed him into a small ante room leading to a larger office. A man in Soviet army uniform emerged quietly and parked himself on the edge of the small desk.

"Where am I?"

Still in Siberia. You are to work for us again here at our research centre."

Peter's heart sank. He knew why he was here. It was Peenemünde all over again.

453

"Use some common sense Brandt. The Gulag is no place for you. We can utilise your talents much more effectively here at the Centre. You will be treated well, but you are still a prisoner. You will live under close house arrest. With others of your kind you will serve the Motherland until we no longer have any use for you."

East Berlin 1984

It was late 1984 before Peter was released and allowed back to East Berlin. There was a new, different kind of tension in the air. People were restless, resentful, dissatisfied. It was more evident now than it had been in the first years after the Wall had been erected. He was almost seventy-five years old. Too old to be a problem for the Soviets. He had nothing more to do, nothing left to live for except his work and that was finished. He lived alone in his little bedsit spending his days reading, listening to music or walking near the Humboldt. Occasionally, he strolled close to Brandenburg Gate watching West Berliners shouting obscenities over the Wall from the safety of the wooden platforms.

"One day I will be free!" he shouted. "One day we will all be free!"

EPILOGUE

West Berlin 1989

Umbrellas mushroomed against a light veil of grey drizzle filling the air. Crowds of West Berliners stood in tight-knit groups hugging each other, crying, shouting with jubilation. Initially, an announcement had been made that the Soviets were allowing East Berliners to visit the West. But now people were beginning to surge through the barrier. Startled, the Grepos just stood around uncertainly, afraid to stop them.

Two East German guards jumped the barbed wire, landing in the West with a triumphant whoop. Sobbing men and women fell into the arms of complete strangers. Others held bunches of flowers, food and bottles of champagne. Mothers clung to sons they hadn't embraced for years. An old man wept as he held his grandson for the first time.

Along the Wall people chipped away with ice picks. A burly man, wielding an enormous sledgehammer, pounded at the concrete grabbing huge chunks as they fell away at his feet. A woman, stabbed at it with the point of her umbrella. Following her cue the young boy at her side excitedly jabbed at the concrete with a pen knife.

Television cameras, mounted on vans, zoomed in to film the ecstatic scenes for posterity. Journalists spoke rapidly reporting every aspect of the event: wandering through the crowds, shoving microphones under their noses.

"How do you feel now that you're free?" asked a reporter.

"Wunderbar! Wunderbar!" cried the woman dancing a jig in front of the cameras.

As evening approached the crowds grew. People came from all parts of the city and suburbs to witness the miraculous falling of the Wall. When night fell crowds danced in the street. People climbed on top of the Wall gorging out chunks to keep as souvenirs. A few were selling pieces to the surging crowd as mementoes. The atmosphere was electric; charged with emotion, passion and the euphoria of sudden freedom.

Jack witnessed it all at first hand. Without warning his orders had come unexpectedly from the top brass a week ago. He had been sent to Berlin from the United Kingdom on a military intelligence assignment – his last one before leaving the army.

Helen had been tetchy with him, because he was going without her.

"Why can't I go with you Jack?" she begged.

"There's no time to arrange anything. Besides this is my last assignment then we can retire to Wales just like you've always wanted."

"But it would give me a chance to see Jack."

Jack junior had been attached to intelligence in Berlin the year before. He loved every minute of it.

"He'll be too busy to run around Berlin with you."

"Like father, like son," she remarked petulantly.

When Jack had asked his son to make some enquiries about *Regis* he had agreed immediately. He wanted to find out as much about him as his father did.

Three months later young Jack discovered that *Regis* had been sent to Siberia where he had been working for the Soviets.

"He came back to East Berlin in 1984 where he's still living."

Jack's heart skipped a beat.

"He's still alive?"

"Apparently, he lives not far from Humboldt University."

"One way or another I have to contact him," Jack determined.

This surveillance and infiltration assignment was his opportunity to do a bit of digging himself.

Helen couldn't wait to have him home for good after what she called *'traipsing round after spies'*. They had bought a roomy house, overlooking Cardigan Bay, close to her parents. He wondered how he would cope with living in rural Wales after the high adrenaline activities he had been used to for over twenty five years.

They were parked close to Brandenburg Gate. People had been wandering in and out of the Soviet Sector for days. The crowds were thinner now. Most were waiting for relatives to appear. An elderly woman rushed forward and threw herself into the arms of a middle-aged man. They were still clinging to each other as they walked away, their faces wreathed in smiles.

For two hours he had watched and waited for any sign of *Regis*, but he hadn't appeared. Jack had sent word to him that he would be waiting, but no reply had come back.

The elderly woman sitting in the rear of the Mercedes fingered the white scar that ran from her hairline down to her chin. Her heart fluttered like the wings of a bird. Apprehension and excitement gleamed in her pale, blue eyes. Every sense was sharpened by the events going on around her. Sensing her heightened anxiety Jack turned and smiled at her reassuringly.

Impatiently, he got out of the car. He wondered if something had happened to *Regis*. Had the Soviets finished him off before he had a chance to come out? After all he had worked with very sensitive information that could be useful to the allies in the West. Still, if he had suddenly disappeared intelligence would have ferreted it out by now.

"Don't worry dad," Jack Junior said at his elbow. "I'm sure he'll come out fairly soon. Intelligence has been watching him for weeks. Bryant, I mean General Bryant, is out here too. You were the last two intelligence officers to have any contact with *Regis*."

"Bryant is out here. Well, I'll be damned. I haven't seen him since I left Berlin in the sixties…"

Suddenly, young Jack nudged his elbow and pointed towards a loose crowd of people on the other side of the Wall, about a hundred metres away. Such a casual group, almost like strolling tourists enjoying the sights. They approached hesitantly as though they were uncertain of what to do when they reached the gap where the barrier had been. Jack strained his eyes, searching the crowd. Now they were only fifty metres away walking slowly in a peculiar, hesitant gait. Eventually, they separated fanning out in a wall of bodies.

Suddenly, an elderly man appeared from somewhere at the corner of Jack's eye. A tall, erect man with a shock of snow-white hair. He strode purposefully with just the hint of a limp. Jack would have recognised that proud, defiant look anywhere. A choked cry emanated from the woman in the rear seat of the Mercedes. She struggled out of the car and stood next to Jack. Swaying slightly she clung to him, her fingers digging into his arm.

As the man drew closer Jack noticed the deep lines etched into his face; the thin white scar on his right cheek. Then *Regis* was standing in front of him, his eyes a blaze of blue fire. The two men stared at each other. *Regis* looked in amazement at the woman then let out an anguished cry. He held out his arms to her.

"Eleanor! Is it really you?"

"Peter, Peter," she sobbed, melting into his arms.

Jack's throat constricted. His heart felt as though it would burst. Tears rolled down the old man's face as a great, shuddering sob racked his thin frame. Taking Jack's hands in his he pulled him close, holding him as though he would never let go. Through his tears he whispered,

"Johann, Johann, my son."

POST SCRIPT

The author actually lived in Glienicke close to the Wall. She visited many of the places such as Treptow Park in East Berlin, the site of the Russian War Memorial, and travelled on the military train. Two of the night clubs mentioned did exist in the 1960s, but they have been given different names.

The experiences of the author, living in the British Sector in Berlin, have been used merely to add a sense of authenticity to what is a complete work of fiction. Where necessary some geographical details, such as escape routes along the Berlin Wall, have been tweaked slightly to fit the action. A select bibliography has been used purely for background reading and is not intended to alter the entirely fictitious character of the book.

SELECT BIBLIOGRAPHY

Anonymous. (2005) *A Woman in Berlin*. Introduction by Beevor, A. Afterword by Enzensberger, H.M. Virago Press.

Beevor, A. (2007 edition) Berlin: The *Downfall 1945*. Penguin Books, London.

Beevor, A. (2007 edition) *Stalingrad*. Penguin Books, London.

Bonincontro, A. G. (2002-2008) *An Overview of the Harsh Weather Conditions on the Eastern Front of World War Two*. Helium Inc. Internet Article. www.helium.com

Brooks, M. (2002-2008) *An Overview of the Harsh Weather Conditions on the Eastern Front of World War Two*. Helium Inc. Internet Article. www.helium.com

Clark, A. *Barbarossa*. 2005, Cassell Military Paperbacks Edition, London.

Curtis, J. (2002-2008) *An Overview of the Harsh Weather Conditions on the Eastern Front of World War Two*. Helium Inc. Internet Article. www.helium.com

Duncan, G. *Lesser Known Facts About World War Two*. Internet Article, ww.ii.au~gduncan/ index.html.

Hopkins, M. (2002-2008) *An Overview of the Harsh Weather Conditions on the Eastern Front of World War Two*. Helium Inc. Internet Article. www.helium.com

Laurie, W. (2002-2008) *An Overview of the Harsh Weather Conditions on the Eastern Front of World War Two*. Helium Inc. Internet Article. www.helium.com

Lovenheim, B. 2002, *Survival in the Shadows*. Peter Owen Publishers.

Mockridge, J. (2002-2008) *An Overview of the Harsh Weather Conditions on the Eastern Front of World War Two*. Helium Inc. Internet Article. www.helium.com

Pruit, C.A. (2002-2008) *An Overview of the Harsh Weather Conditions on the Eastern Front of World War Two*. Helium Inc. Internet Article. www.helium.com

Smothers, C. J. (2002-2008) *An Overview of the Harsh Weather Conditions on the Eastern Front of World War Two*. Helium Inc. Internet Article. www.helium.com

Vassiltchikov, M. (1999 Pimlico edition) *The Berlin Diaries 1940-1945*. Pimlico, London.

Wiseman, G. (2002-2008) *An Overview of the Harsh Weather Conditions on the Eastern Front of World War Two*. Helium Inc. Internet Article. www.helium.com